THE LOEB C

FOUN

PROPERTIUS

ELEGIES

LCL 18

PROPERTIUS

ELEGIES

EDITED AND TRANSLATED BY

G. P. GOOLD

HARVARD UNIVERSITY PRESS
CAMBRIDGE, MASSACHUSETTS
LONDON, ENGLAND
1990

Library of Congress Cataloging-in-Publication Data

Propertius, Sextus.
[Elegiae. English]
Elegies / Propertius; edited and translated by G. P. Goold.
p.   cm. — (Loeb classical library; 18)
Half title: The elegies of Sextus Propertius.
Includes bibliographical references.
ISBN 0–674–99020–X
1. Elegiac poetry, Latin — Translation into English.
2. English prose literature — Translations from Latin.
3. Elegiac poetry, Latin.
I. Goold, G. P.   II. Title.
III. Title: Elegies of Sextus Propertius.   IV. Series.
PA6645.E5G6   1990   90–30547
874′.01—dc20   CIP

Typeset by Chiron, Inc.
Printed in Great Britain by St. Edmundsbury Press Ltd,
Bury St. Edmunds, Suffolk, on acid-free paper.
Bound by Hunter & Foulis Ltd, Edinburgh, Scotland.

CONTENTS

CONTENTS

PREFACE

BUTLER'S edition of Propertius was one of the first volumes to appear in the Loeb Classical Library, and in its time it was the best. But what was an elegant translation in 1912 now wears a very old-fashioned look, and if after the research of the last seventy-seven years there still remain a number of uncertainties, many have been definitively laid to rest, while the literary scholarship of this period furnishes today's editor with a much juster perception of the poet's art. The present edition, then, is an entirely new volume and not a refurbished version of the old one.

In it I have sought above all to present Propertius to the largest possible audience both in a reliable Latin text and in a graceful and accurate English translation: to classical scholars and students, of course, but no less to lovers of literature generally. For the benefit of the latter I have expanded the index to give a good deal of explanatory material that must otherwise have been sought in reference books or given in overloaded footnotes.

Just as in establishing the text of Propertius I owe an enormous debt to the great scholars whose work is listed in the bibliography, from Lachmann

PREFACE

in the 19th century to Shackleton Bailey in our own, so too I gratefully acknowledge my indebtedness to former translators, especially Phillimore and Butler, from whom I have taken many an apt word or phrase when the alternative was to settle for something inferior; and on several occasions I have taken over renderings given by Camps and other commentators. But the basis of the translation was a complete version of my own made directly from the Latin.

In an endeavour to eliminate not merely slips and oversights but also aberrations of my own to which I was blind, I submitted parts of my work at various stages to a number of scholars for criticism and discussed sundry problems with others. If I have not accepted all their suggestions (Propertians, alas, do not yet speak with a single voice), I gladly thank them for freeing me from much damaging error and for effecting much improvement. I hope they will excuse me if I do not name them all. I must, however, thank by name Professor Otto Skutsch, who to my vast profit worked through the first draft of this book, and Professors Barrie Hall, John Morgan, Charles Murgia, Michael Reeve, and James Willis for significant assistance.

But my greatest debt is to Dr. Stephen Heyworth, editor of the forthcoming Oxford Classical Text of Propertius. In the hope that each of our editions would gain thereby we met in Oxford for long

PREFACE

discussions in the summers of 1988 and 1989, and in correspondence have shared our views without reservation. He has unselfishly allowed me to make use of his dissertation and unpublished papers, and has studied drafts of my work. If his positive contributions are—as I trust—properly acknowledged, I must also record that he has in many places persuaded me out of deeply held convictions, apprised me of palmary conjectures of others that I had missed, and tightened the accuracy of the translation; on the fundamental question of book division and the nature of Book Two, I follow him as a guide.

The genesis of this edition, which goes back to my undergraduate days, has been sketched in my 1987 article. In it, as in a later article (1989), I comment on the failure of scholars to admit and retract their mistakes publicly; I feel certain that it was a reluctance to do so which was chiefly responsible for Housman's abandoning his Propertian aspirations. Let me not embark on self-criticism here, but simply emphasize that the judgements expressed in this edition supersede any contrary views which I may have published earlier.

Yale University   G. P. GOOLD
June 1990

THE ELEGIES OF
SEXTUS PROPERTIUS

INTRODUCTION

About the Poet

From Propertius himself we learn that he was a native of Assisi in Umbria, of a well-to-do (but not aristocratic or equestrian) family, and it would seem that the confiscation of its estates after the Perusine War (in which a kinsman was killed, and possibly also his father, who died about the same time) did not reduce him to poverty. His mother intended him for a legal career, but his moving to Rome (like Ovid's) served rather to bring him into contact with a coterie of poets, and it was to the Muses that he devoted his life. We learn little about him from others. Donatus tells us his praenomen, Sextus, and Ovid, that Propertius was older than he (so that he will have been born about 50 B.C.).

His first book is, to judge from the first and the last poems, dedicated to Tullus, the nephew of Lucius Volcacius Tullus (consul with Octavian in 33 and proconsul of Asia in 30); young Tullus went off on an official mission to the east about 29, and to 30 or 29 we are probably justified in assigning its publication. It at once established Propertius' reputation and brought him a call from Maecenas, the influential patron of the Augustan poets.

On admission to the privileged circle he produced over the next few years what we know as Book Two. It is now reasonably certain that this, in a defective and disordered form, is what survives of his second and third books. Datable events fall between 28 and 25.

Book Three cannot be earlier than the death of Marcellus and the publication of Horace, *Odes* 1–3, both in 23; but it can hardly be later than 22. A number of echoes of Horace (see Index), none showing the unreserved admiration he had expressed for Virgil in 2.34, may indicate some personal antipathy between the two poets, who never overtly refer to each other (still, neither do Propertius and Tibullus).

The death of Virgil in 19 left Augustus without his most effective encomiast in literature and prompted him to assume the role of a more demanding patron than Maecenas had been: Book Four shows that Propertius no less than Horace felt obliged to respond to the increased pressure. The final poem securely dates it to 16 or a little later.

It is likely enough that Propertius died soon after, for his last book breaks new ground and it is not in an artist's nature to abandon a promising mine of material barely opened up. A reference in Ovid (*Rem. Am.* 764) shows that he was dead by

A.D. 1. But before he died he seems to have married and become a father, if we can believe Passennus Paullus (*ap.* Pliny, *Ep.* 6.15.1; 9.22.1), who claimed Propertius as an ancestor.

Propertius and Roman Elegy

Elegia quoque Graecos provocamus, cuius mihi tersus atque elegans maxime videtur auctor Tibullus. sunt qui Propertium malint. Ovidius utroque lascivior, sicut durior Gallus: 'In elegy also [i.e. as well as in hexameter poetry] we rival the Greeks. Among poets of this genre I think that Tibullus achieves the greatest polish and elegance, though some give the palm to Propertius. Ovid is more flippant than either, as Gallus is harsher.' Quintilian's pithy account of Roman elegy (*Inst. Or.* 10.1.93) is valuable for confirming Ovid's statement (*Trist.* 4.10.53f) of the canon of the elegists and also for implying that Propertius disputed primacy among them with Tibullus. Gallus is lost and cannot be profitably discussed, and Ovid would seem only to be considered for his *Amores*. Interestingly Ovid (*Trist.* 2.465; 5.1.17) terms Propertius *blandus* 'attractive' and Martial (14.189), *facundus* 'eloquent'; Pliny (*Ep.* 9.22.2) commends the elegies of Passennus Paullus as *opus tersum, molle, iucundum, et plane in Properti modo* [*domo* mss] *scriptum* 'a polished, delicate, and charming work, quite in

3

the manner of Propertius.' Since the ancients regarded Propertius' poetry as elegant and attractive, it would seem to follow that clumsiness and ugliness in manuscript readings are probably the result of textual corruption and not to be imputed to the poet's incompetence.

In one respect Quintilian's summary is misleading, for he implies that Augustan elegy was merely the Roman counterpart of a Greek genre. It is true that Propertius confessedly regards Callimachus and Philitas as his models, and that the former particularly exercised a great influence on Roman poetry; but the employment of the elegiac metre in long and elaborate poems wherein the poet bared his heart was a peculiarly Roman development. The genesis of this may be seen in Catullus: his 66th poem, a straight translation of Callimachus, is typical of the narrative elegy we find in the *Aetia,* completely lacking any involvement of the poet himself; but poem 68 is quite different in its use of the same style to communicate the fluctuating emotions of his love affair. Even in the epigrammatic section of Catullus' oeuvre, in poems 76 and 99, we can see that the lapidary nature of the epigram is giving way to a less restrained expression of his feelings.

Though it may at first cause surprise, the choice of the elegiac metre for emotional outpourings was really inevitable. Catullus' lyrics are perfect gems, but in spite of their appearance of immediacy

INTRODUCTION

sustained effort and artifice have gone to produce them; and, no less pertinently, they are subject to a limit in size. The very thought of a large-scale hendecasyllabic or choliambic or sapphic or other lyric poem must have seemed utterly inappropriate. Nor was the hexameter suitable. True, it was the prescribed form for detached love-poetry like Catullus' *Peleus and Thetis,* but its epic resonance rendered it ill-suited to personal confessions, which demand uncontrived and spontaneous language. The elegiac metre, then, which had long been used for an epigrammatic expression of erotic motifs, was ideal. The separateness of a couplet enables thought and feeling to be reflected in a series of discrete pulsations, which permits, as the continuum of the hexameter does not, abrupt and frequent changes of mood and shifts of direction.

No doubt Gallus (who published before 39) paved the way, but we can see clearly in Propertius' oeuvre the complete development of the genre. One might infer from Ovid that Propertius followed Tibullus and started with an inheritance of the latter's contribution. That is a quite false notion. The first book of Tibullus appeared in 27, at least a year after Book One of Propertius. The latter shows the earliest stage of the genre: the poems are of moderate compass, almost wholly confined to a lover's emotions and still betraying by the large proportion of polysyllabic pentameter endings something of the grand style, well adorning the pretentious poetry of Callimachus but not fully appropriate to the intimate tone of the passionate lover. Still, the sharp change in form which confronts us at the opening of Propertius' Book Two must be attributed to the influence of Tibullus I: the proportion of polysyllabic endings found in Book One is significantly reduced; the size of many of the compositions has been significantly increased; and we should recognize Tibullan influence in the way in which our poet glides from one subject to another without a perceptible break and markedly reduces the detectible basis of book structure and stanza composition.

As I show below (under "Stanza Composition"), some poems of Book One exhibit a discernible structure, and Skutsch has convincingly demonstrated that the book itself was arranged in an elaborate way. I reproduce here the pertinent details of his schematic tabulation. Moreover, it is difficult to withhold assent when he says (page 239): 'A symmetry such as that shown here arises neither by accident nor even by careful arrangement of matter created previously: a certain amount of writing must have been done to meet the demands of the symmetry intended.' Indeed, the symmetry would seem to be even greater, for if we allow Courtney's claim (*Phoenix* 22 [1968] 250) that

INTRODUCTION

Otto Skutsch's analysis of Book One
(simplified from *CP* 58 [1963] 238)

A^1	1	Tortured by love
	2	Advice to Cynthia
	3	Cynthia asleep
	4	Leave me to Cynthia
	5	Leave Cynthia to me
B^1	6	Tullus and Propertius
	7	Warning to Ponticus
	8A	Fear
	8B	Fear dispelled
	9	Warning to Ponticus come true
B^2	10	Gallus' love
	11	Fear
	12	Fear confirmed
	13	Gallus' love
	14	Tullus and Propertius
A^2	15	You do not care
	16	The locked-out lover
	17	Solitude (stormy shore)
	18	Solitude (quiet grove)
	19	Will you forget me?
Coda	20	Hylas epyllion
	21	Perusine episode
	22	*Envoi*

1.7.23f (transposed by several) are intrusive verses having their origin outside Book 1, we are confronted with the remarkable equation $A = B + C$, in which $A = A^1 + A^2$ (each of 176 verses = 352), $B = B^1 + B^2$ (each of 140 verses = 280), and $C = 72$. Woolley's observation (*Bulletin of the Institute of Classical Studies* 14 [1967] 81) that in Book Four poems 2–5 and 7–10 each approximate to the same number of verses (in my text they possess exactly the same, namely 306), if significant, may be connected with the column length of the papyrus the poet used and suggest that the abnormally brief compass of poem 10 was a result of working with a limited space.

If the reader is tempted to dismiss with impatience the very idea that an ancient artist resorted to such formal and numerical schemes, let him reflect that poets have indeed often indulged in such ornamentation, from Homer (whose symmetries in A and Ω were pointed out by J. L. Myres, *Journal of Hellenic Studies* 52 [1932] 264ff) to Dylan Thomas (in whose four-page poem introducing his collected works the first line rhymes with the last, the second with the penultimate, and so on up to the middle). Even Virgil seems to have employed Golden Mean sections and certainly attempted a symmetry of rhyming quatrains in the paragraph Georgics 1.393–423 (see Owen Ewald, *Harvard Studies in Classical Philology* 93 [1990]). These are literary curiosities, but no less real for all that. And it is bound to happen that excessive constraints will occasionally inspire the artist to heights he would otherwise not reach, as Proust's grandfather realized in his felicitous reference to good poets whom the tyranny of rhyme forces into the discovery of their finest lines.

Cynthia prima fuit, Cynthia finis erit wrote the poet with perfect truth. Who was she? Was she married, was she a courtesan, was she indeed one Hostia, as Apuleius (*Apology* 16) will have it? Surely none of these, and in fact no person who ever lived at all—save in the poet's imagination. No doubt his imagination was fuelled by some model or models who had a historical existence, but his relationship to her or them we cannot know. What we may assert is that Cynthia is Propertius' dream-girl, with an endowment of all that his mind can contrive: she is beautiful, high-born, intelligent, educated, artistic, a poetess even; and of course passionate (and unresponsive), loyal (and treacherous) and audacious (for both good and bad); and since the poet has to cap what has gone before, we receive ever more colourful and extravagant accounts of her. By Book 3 the poet is, embarrassingly, running out of love material. A new character is introduced, Lygdamus, Cynthia's slave, who acts as a go-between; and with her new household Cynthia, too, is given a new look. At 3.16 she is given a residence at Tibur and is imperiously commanding her lover's presence; finally, at the very end of the book, somewhat abruptly, one might think, we come upon Propertius' savage renunciation of her.

Hostia, if that is her real name, for the poem gives none, makes her appearance in 3.20: she has been jilted by her lover, who has gone off to Africa; and captivated by her beauty and her intellectual and artistic skills, and evidently meeting with encouragement, Propertius is looking forward to the first night of love. The crucial reference comes in line 8: her grandfather's fame is reflected in her. The particularity has convinced many scholars that she came of a good family and, following Apuleius, that her grandfather was the poet Hostius, who wrote an epic on the Bellum Histricum of 129. However, the *puella* of 3.20, who is a recent acquaintance, cannot possibly be the Cynthia to whom we were introduced in 1.1. How Apuleius came by the name Hostia can only be surmised: perhaps he knew it to be the name of Propertius' wife and perhaps Hostia actually was the name of the woman who inspired this poem. But that Cynthia was Hostia and even more that Hostia was Cynthia we may confidently deny.

Furthermore, we should be careful not to misunderstand the Cynthia of Propertius' fantasies: she is not conceived in realistic terms, as a lost, degraded woman, but rather as an ideal heroine, who by her insouciant disregard of convention turns Roman morality inside out and upside down; she is in fact a *meretrix* counterpart of the servus Tranio in the *Mostellaria,* whom we are to applaud for his successful flouting of legality and not to identify as a potential Sertorius. The structure and traditions of Roman society did not make it easy for highborn Roman youths to meet, fall in love with, and marry highborn Roman girls in a natural sequence; what *was* natural, therefore, was that the dream liaisons depicted in the Roman elegiac poets should be invested with a universal appeal. Escapist literature, yes! But then, how much of literature, how much of mankind's nobility, springs from the heart's irrepressible yearning to transcend the reality by which we unhappy mortals are fettered!

The evidence compels us to recognize that in Book Two we have the remains of two books, a conclusion supported by the chaos visible at various points in the middle. But Lachmann's identification of 2.9 as the last poem of one book and 2.10 as the first of the next is not acceptable inasmuch as 2.1–9 amount to an inadequate 356 lines, 2.10–34 to the excessive 1036. What complicates the search for the point of division between the poet's second and third books is the probability that some dislocation of poems has occurred. Still, it is significant that whereas the average length of a poem in Book One came to 32 lines (longest 52), in Book Two the author is now venturing compositions on a larger scale (the first poem being of 78, or rather 80, lines).

Book Three marks the poet's formal entry into the groves of Callimachus and Philitas: he is no longer the abject slave of Cynthia but a national poet with a priestly status; personal elegy is not abandoned, but his most memorable compositions deal with other themes. This shift of focus is even more noticeable in his last book, which presents us with some of his finest poems and proves that neither his creativity nor his development as an artist had abated. One would never guess that it was Augustus who had pressured him to write on national and public subjects. Here Propertius fully justifies his boast of being the Roman Callimachus. Let it be observed that this book anticipates the final stages of Augustan elegy, with Arethusa's letter foreshadowing the *Heroides,* Acanthis' precepts the *Ars Amatoria,* and Vertumnus and other aetiological pieces the *Fasti;* and it includes two Cynthia poems which are simply non-pareil.

INTRODUCTION

The Manuscripts

[Butrica; Hanslik (v–xxii); Heyworth (diss.);
Richardson (16–22); Tarrant]

The total number of Propertian manuscripts known
to exist is 146: they are duly registered and dis-
cussed in a *catalogue raisonné* by Butrica, but few of
these are unanimously agreed to be independent
carriers of the tradition. Indeed, orthodox opinion
holds that, where the chief two codices are extant,
the rest are totally dispensable as witnesses to the
words of the poet.

(1) N = Wolfenbüttel, Gud. lat. 224 (*olim* Neapoli-
tanus), written in northern France about
1200; complete except for the loss of
4.11.17–76 (which was contained on a leaf
now cut out), a loss editors repair from two
mss (which may here be derived from N's
missing leaf):

> M = Paris, BN lat. 8233 (olim Memmi-
> anus), ann. 1465 (usually μ: I con-
> form to the sigla which Heyworth
> has adopted for the forthcoming
> OCT)

and U = Vatican, Urb. lat. 641, c. 1465–70
(usually v).

(2) A = Leiden, Voss. lat. O. 38, written near Orleans
about 1240; though once complete it contains

13

no text after 2.1.63, the end of the second quire.

N and A certainly derive from a medieval archetype (Ω), as is demonstrated by their close agreement in significant error. Here may be mentioned two 13th-century florilegia, Vatican, Reg. lat. 2120 (possibly culled from the archetype) and Paris, BN lat. 16708 (taken from A), but since no unique reading is involved, they concern us no further here.

Now, even after A breaks off, we can usually infer its readings, which I indicate in my textual notes by A*, from the text of its nearest descendants. These three descendants, however, are not immediate copies, but were transcribed (L and P at one remove) from a copy made for and perhaps by Petrarch, a manuscript unhappily no longer extant.

(3) F = Florence, Laur. plut. 38.49, copied from Petrarch's ms for Coluccio Salutati about 1380 and containing many corrections by four hands.

(4) L = Oxford, Bodl. Holkham misc. 36, written at Genoa in 1421 (now containing 2.21.3 *ad fin.*).

(5) P = Paris, BN lat. 7989 (which, in addition to Propertius, also contains Catullus, Tibullus, and—its chief claim to fame—the only copy of the *Cena Trimalchionis*), written in 1423.

Both L and P carry readings given also by N, and

from N they may have derived them. Certainly the
appearance in 15th-century manuscripts of readings
alien to their pedigree occurs so frequently that we
shall be wise not to jump to conclusions when FLP
are at variance. Of course, most of these alien
readings are conjectures of the Italian humanists,
attempts to restore the poet's original hand in pas-
sages which are difficult and perhaps corrupt. As
the century proceeds and correction of error swells,
more and more manuscripts are found to exhibit
readings agreeing with N. The orthodox view is
that N had crossed the Alps by the early 1420s,
and that these N-readings stem from humanistic
activity. Butrica, however, proposes a quite dif-
ferent explanation, namely that in addition to N and
A there was once a third tradition-carrier, X, which
'Poggio perhaps acquired around Paris during his
journey to England in 1418': X is now lost, but is
perpetuated in some six manuscripts (all disconcert-
ingly late), which thus claim our attention no less
than N or A. However, the movements of N from
1418 to 1647, when Heinsius consulted it in Naples,
are quite unknown, which makes Butrica's theory
hard to uphold against a more likely explanation,
namely that the reconstructed X is sometimes none
other than N itself and sometimes a much edited
copy of N. Where, as at 4.3.11, the testimony of N
and A each diverge in error, and one might have
expected an independent witness to the archetype

to provide an independent reading, it never does. Whether or no we accept X (Heyworth's Λ) as independent, it does not seem to make any practical contribution to the textual criticism of our author.

The Division into Books

[Skutsch; Heyworth (diss.)]

The manuscripts of Propertius, followed by the great majority of editors, divide the poems into four books; and this division has established the standard system of references to his work. Nothing but confusion could result from any attempt to alter this numeration.

But the fact is that Propertius composed *five* books of elegies, our Book Two being the extant remains of *two* books (i.e. the 2nd and the 3rd) which, through circumstances beyond our power to determine, became mutilated and then treated as one.

(1) The length of Book Two exceeds by over 300 lines any other Augustan book of poetry; and the fragmentary nature of much of its contents obliges us to postulate a considerable amount lost in lacunas, so that in its original form this section of the poet's work must have filled on a conservative estimate over 1500 lines.

(2) A crucial verse, now numbered 2.13.25, *sat mea, sat magnast, si tres sint pompa libelli,* implies

that when the verse was composed, Propertius believed himself to have been writing his third book.

Obviously there would be no room for argument if we could definitely identify within our Book Two the end of the poet's second book and the beginning of his third. The matter is not easy, but I myself am persuaded that Heyworth (diss. pp. 126ff.) has arrived at a correct hypothesis, which I summarize without argument: poem 2.10 (lacunose at the beginning: so Lachmann) ends Propertius' second book (so Giardina) with a promise to embark— sometime—upon an epic theme; but when he gets the chance, he resorts to another *recusatio,* for poem 2.13 (as Richmond suggested) is the beginning of the third book. Poems 11 (patently a fragment) and 12 are simply disordered.

There is no reason to doubt, indeed there is much to support, the natural assumption that Books One, Three, and Four are the autonomous and designed units the poet intended. What did the poet call them? Richmond and Skutsch hold that 1 was called *Monobiblos,* the other books of elegies being numbered 1 to 4. Two considerations raised by Heyworth tell against this:

(a) The word *monobiblos* seems to have originated from the heading of Martial 14.189 *Monobiblos Properti* (an *apophoreton* or 'take-away' gift), which ought to mean 'Propertius in a single volume' (i.e. a collection of the poet's work, and most obvi-

ously an anthology): a priori it is unlikely that a
young poet should so describe his first book.

(b) The word *tres* in 2.13.25 must come from what
the poet thought of as *Liber Tertius* and meant the
booksellers to advertize as such; similarly at 2.3.4 *et
turpis de te iam liber alter erit* the author is specify-
ing *Liber Secundus*. True, he may have nicknamed
his first book *Cynthia* (cf 2.24.2: perhaps misplaced
from an original position before 2.10), as Tibullus
may have nicknamed his books *Delia* and *Nemesis*
(but even Tibullus' books circulated with numbered
titles).

One single citation from antiquity specifying
Book 3 or Book 4 would clinch the matter, and it is
regrettable that the only such reference we have is
attended by a doubt about the reading. Nonius, in
quoting 3.21.14, gives the reference as *Propertius
Elegiarum lib. IIII*—so the first hand of the best
manuscript (which would accord with the view
given above), but the second hand has erased the
last stroke to give *III* (which would support the posi-
tion of Birt, Richmond, and Skutsch, who see Pro-
pertius' oeuvre as a monobiblos followed by a tetra-
biblos).

Nevertheless, all these scholars agree that Pro-
pertius published five books.

INTRODUCTION

Problems of the Text

[Richardson (20–2); Goold (1987, 1989)]

The transmission of Propertius from late antiquity took place in a single manuscript, and the journey of its text to the archetype was affected by various vicissitudes which collectively have left it in a deplorable condition.

To begin with, the poet himself is given to novel and recondite ways of expressing himself; likewise his chain of thought is often unexpected; and his mythological allusions are often abstruse to the point of being unintelligible except to initiates. Secondly, it is highly improbable that the division between poems (which never bore any titles) was indicated in any but a perfunctory manner, and at times no division was marked at all. Then we are obliged to infer, from the absence of evidence to the contrary, that Propertius aroused no special attention from the late empire until the age of John of Salisbury. Not only were there no scholia, there was hardly a reader, and certainly none schooled in the appreciation of the poet's art.

If we should consider what was involved in copying Propertius in the Middle Ages, and copying with a view to reading the text with enjoyment, it will seem only natural—given that Propertius was ever copied at all—that some effort was made to smooth

19

INTRODUCTION

the path of understanding by attempting to clarify
much which was obscure and also to correct the
manifold errors with which the text abounded. It is
unlikely that many engaged in these attempts, but
we can dimly discern at least one energetic figure
whose bold dedication and endeavours have proved
not a salvation but a disaster for Propertius. A sim-
ple example is furnished by 3.11.5, where the poet
wrote *ventorum ... morem:* at an earlier stage of
the tradition a slight error produced *mortem.* Our
medieval corrector realized that this was absurd,
but altered the wrong word; so we find in the arche-
type *venturam ... mortem.* One of Propertius' finest
poems will serve to illustrate another kind of
mishap: exasperated at the perversity of Love, he
had at 2.12.18 written *si pudor est, alio traice tela,
puer;* in the aetas Ovidiana someone quoted in the
margin a similar expostulation, *Ars Amatoria* 3.735f
... supprime tela, ... puella tuo. Our medieval
corrector, sensing a superior critic, crossed out *tela*
and substituted *puella tuo;* but what about *puer*?
Well, he wasn't too sure about *pudor* earlier in the
line, so he replaced it with *puer.* It verges on the
miraculous that Housman, unaware of what actu-
ally happened, was able, by sheer intuition of the
poet's words, to restore them. But the greatest dam-
age to the poet's text concerns verses which the
medieval corrector transposed.

20

INTRODUCTION

Transposition

Since the couplet is the unit of elegiac verse, it is only to be expected that problems of verse-order should mostly involve couplets. Some of these are mechanical, as for example 1.15.15f: it appears that when the scribe reached 14 *laeTITIAE* his eye was distracted by 22 *pudiCITIAE* and he mistakenly copied the couplet he found after that word; possibly he noted his error at once and entered dots to signify the correction; but if so, they have been lost: to ·restore the hand of Propertius we are obliged to transpose 15f after 22. A similar phenomenon is the anticipation of one couplet ahead of what the scribe should have written, as at 4.4.83–86, and the shuffling of consecutive pentameters (likewise owing to anticipation), which has happened at 2.3.30, 32 and elsewhere.

But if these dislocations were caused by unintentional aberrations, the same cannot be argued of others. At 4.8 the couplet 19f is now recognized as causing an impossible interruption of its context and needing to be restored to its proper place after 2. But the mistake was hardly a mechanical one. It seems that the corrector was misled by the words *sine me:* surely Propertius *was* present on the Esquiline and surely he did *not* participate in Cynthia's escapade, to which the couplet must therefore refer. Accordingly the corrector boldly transferred 19f to its manuscript position. Another example crops up at 2.3.11f which illustrate line 15, white Cynthia wearing red silk, proving that the couplet must follow 16. How then did it arrive at its present position? Clearly, because someone could not believe that it followed the (parenthetical) remark in 16, and thoughtlessly jumped to the conclusion that it amplified *alba* in 10; and so moved the couplet after that verse.

The chaos of 3.7 exceeds that of all other poems in Propertius. But the underlying reason is both simple and clear: from some pre-archetypal manuscript a leaf became detached and was replaced back to front, thus moving 43–66 twenty-four lines away from their original position: consequential transpositions by the corrector only made matters worse.

So far mention has been made only of transpositions within a poem. But proof that more drastic changes have occurred is given by 4.5.55f, which are a senseless repetition of 1.2.1f. It is clear that someone, led thereto by *Coae* in 4.5.56, copied them into the margin and from there they made their way into the text. Possibly this kind of quotation has happened elsewhere and the original couplet erroneously deleted: at all events several couplets like 3.18.29f cannot belong to the poems in which they are found.

INTRODUCTION

Book Two

That the damage perpetrated by minor dislocations of sundry couplets can be largely repaired may perhaps be conceded. But the restoration of Book Two to its original form is impossible without more evidence that we can hope to obtain. It has been shown above that we have here the remains of two books, the earlier probably ending with Poem 10, the later beginning with Poem 13. Poems 11 and 12 probably belong to the earlier book, but then so does Poem 24 (well, 24A, at any rate). Not infrequently in this book one encounters verses seemingly alien to their context, perhaps even to the author; not infrequently the suspicion arises that we are faced with pastiche, explicable, if only we knew, by the loss of many verses and even poems: but the facts preclude any deep conviction. An editor is helpless in these circumstances and can only endorse the opinion of Richardson when he writes (22): 'the chaos of the text beyond the middle of Book 2 points to a violent physical damage to the archetype and must preclude any notion that minor surgery is all that is required.'

Stanza composition

A conviction has been steadily gaining ground among editors of Propertius that in composing some of his work the poet had set before himself a definite structure, a structure which determined the dimensions of a poem and did not occur as an unforeseen result. In Book 1, for example, some poems fall fairly obviously into regular blocks of verses:

1. $6 = 6 : 6 : 6 : 6 : 6 : 6$
1.10 $= 10 : 10 : 10$
1.14 $= 8 : 8 : 8$

No less obviously, Propertius sometimes closes with a sign-off couplet:

1. $9 = 8 : 8 : 8 : 8 : 2$

Occasionally a transposition made on independent grounds seems to gain support from the resultant symmetry. Thus, moving 25f after 36 produces

1.16 $= 8 : 8 : 8 : 8 : 8 : 8$

Naturally, the danger of persuading oneself into reshuffling verses to fit a preconceived scheme is great, and was frighteningly illustrated by Richmond's edition; and even without manipulation different editors are likely to analyze a poem in different ways. Still, the possibility that Propertius was at least to some extent composing with a definite scheme in mind confronts the critic with yet another stern challenge.

INTRODUCTION

Editorial Principles

Establishment of the text

In the effort to determine exactly what Propertius wrote and what he meant his editor is frequently faced with a choice between the certainly false (and often unintelligible) reading of the tradition and an essentially true restoration of the original that, in verbal fidelity, may vary from being highly probable to merely possible. Clarity and common sense recommend the second of these two options, and I have preferred it every time.

In orthography I have continued the principles adopted in my other editions. Certainly we cannot expect our defective tradition to have preserved the words of the poet exactly as he wrote them; and it is by no means certain that he was consistent in assimilating or dissimilating words, in transliterating Greek names, and even in spelling the same word. The most sensible thing is to publish the poems of Propertius with the best imperial forms (*cycnis*, not *cygnis*) and standardized spellings (*Baiis, Maiis,* not *Bais, Mais*). I continue to give accusative plurals of *i*-stems as *-es* for substantives and *-is* for adjectives and participles sooner than perpetuate the utter unreliability of the manuscripts in this regard (as may be illustrated from 4.5.47, where the theoretically correct spelling

25

derives confirmation from what was once scribbled on a wall in Pompeii [see Index]). Prodelision is everywhere written (*famast, gavisa's,* not *fama est, gavisa es*): this will at least ensure the correct pronunciation.

Critical notes

The notes beneath the Latin text are not designed to be an apparatus criticus: in a controversial author like Propertius that would consume a huge amount of space and still not serve the most useful purpose. What I have done is to limit myself to essential notes, taking for granted those corrections of the manuscript tradition (Ω) which have won general acceptance. Thus I give no note at such places as 1.20.12 Adryasin (adriacis Ω); 2.7.20 nomine (sanguine Ω); 3.9.16 vendit ab (vindicat Ω); 4.11.84 iace (tace Ω), for my text reproduces the textus receptus. I have made it a point to record all discrepancies from Barber's *OCT,* as well as those conjectures which, though endorsed by Barber, do not appear in other recent editions: for example, 4.7.69 sancimus *Rossberg* (*OCT, Loeb*): sanamus Ω (*most editors*). On the other hand, where Barber incorrectly (in my judgement) resorts to conjecture, I give the ms reading without a note: for example, 1.11.21 non Ω, *Loeb* (nunc *Beck, OCT*); 2.7.13 patriis Ω, *Loeb* (Parthis *Ruhnken, OCT*); 3.8.26 tua Ω, *Loeb* (mea *Barber, OCT*); 4.6.22 apta

Ω, Loeb (acta ς, *OCT*). The standard numeration is naturally preserved. I have tried to indicate with special clarity the transpositions adopted by giving the line-numbers of transposed verses in the left-hand margin: Richardson very properly accepts Housman's proposal to transpose 2.16.17f, but the irregular sequence of numerals in his margin, besides being confusing to the eye, somehow suggests that he has shuffled the verses to a greater extent than merely moving a single couplet which was dislocated through homoearchon (*semper ... semper*).

In the critical notes signs and abbreviations are used as follows. Ω denotes the archetype as reconstructed from the available witnesses, thus:

1.1.1–2.1.63: Ω = N + A
2.1.64–2.21.2: Ω = N + A* (= FP)
2.21.3–4.11.16: Ω = N + A* (= FLP)
4.11.17–76 *om. N*: Ω* = N* [= MU] + A* (= FLP)
4.11.77–4.11.102: Ω = N + A* (= FLP)

The sign ς marks conjectures of the Italian humanists. For the most part I have used, purely for reasons of economy, the conventional Latin abbreviations, but in recording verses alien to their ms position (signalled in the text by square brackets) I distinguish between *del(evit)* and *secl(usit)*, the former branding verses as non-Propertian, the latter denoting verses out of place rather than unauthentic. Where it could be done compendiously, I have

27

occasionally ventured to suggest a possible stage in the corruption of the text: thus at 1.18.27 *continui,* first written as c̄tinui, may have been misread as *dinui,* leading to the impossible diuini of Ω: hence—divini (<dinui). Angle brackets indicate letters accidentally omitted, square brackets indicate letters wrongly added: thus at 1.13.13 (*quā*)*do* was by haplography omitted before *do*(*rmit*), and a scribe repaired the metre, but falsely, by adding a preposition: hence—quan<do> *Alton* : [cum] qua Ω. The date and work in which a conjecture is first recorded may be found in Smyth's *Thesaurus Criticus;* those conjectures made later or not there listed have an asterisk affixed to the author's name.

Presentation of poems

'More than once in this epistle a reader who wants to grasp the trend of thought could blame the editors for not using indentation to guide him. Why do they not mark the break after l.4, which is as sharp as can be?' Thus Eduard Fraenkel, *Horace,* page 384. This was a point well raised, and decidedly needing to be raised again, for the paragraphing of hexameters is possible, and in the case of Virgil is today more or less canonical. But elegiac couplets cannot be paragraphed: they must be presented with breaks, as in Kenney's edition of the *Ars Amatoria.* The desirability of indicating the structural scheme of, say, Catullus 68 can hardly be gainsaid; and the same applies to the sections of Propertius' poems. Richardson's edition is distinguished for its many-sided and detailed and independent and unpretentious commentary: but his printing of the poet's text is unlovely, and whoever wants to appreciate 1.3 or 4.4, for example (two of the poet's finest compositions), will not be assisted by his (or most others') presentation of them. Therefore, following the lead of Luck in his edition and Camps in his of Book 2, I have converted my considered paragraphing into separate sections. The previous Loeb editor automatically paragraphed his translation, but without any implication that Propertius would have done the same.

I must be careful to acknowledge that this method of paragraphing the Latin text is (like punctuation) subjective, and is not intended to brand any alternative system as definitely wrong. Nevertheless, it is not arbitrary, and will, I hope, always be discovered to agree with the analysis of others (or some other) or at least communicate some insight into the poet's conception of his work. We may be sure that a simple and uniform system of stanza-composition does not exist in Propertius: my own opinion is that simple and detectible stanza-patterns exist in Book 1 (as I have stated above), but taper off in his later writing to less rigid structures as he emancipated himself from principles that proved too constricting.

INTRODUCTION

The translation and index

In an allusive and even cryptic author like Propertius the translator is constantly faced with the temptation to paraphrase as also to fill the page high with footnotes. I have tried to hold fast to a faithful rendering of the Latin, and since users of the Loeb Classical Library are entitled to a full elucidation of such a rendering, I have used the index as a means of reducing the amount of annotation that must otherwise have been given in footnotes. Thus, for all explanation of proper names the index should be consulted; and to encourage the reader to do so constantly I have given many cross-references, so that even entries like *Dream of Callimachus* 2.34.32 and *domus ista* 4.1.9 may be quickly found. Other entries, like *adynata, Cassandra, dogs, Horace,* and *Lycophron,* all clued to the text of Propertius, if not indicated in a footnote reference, will be readily located by the interested and the inquisitive.

Select Bibliography

[Pauly-Wissowa *RE* XXIII (1957) 758–796 s.v. Propertius, Sextus (Rudolf Helm); Schanz-Hosius, *GrL* 2 (1935[4]) 193–206; and see Harrauer and Fedeli-Pinotti, last two items below]

Editions

(*p* = preface; *i* = introduction; *t* = text; *r* = translation; *a* = apparatus criticus; *c* = commentary or annotations; *e* = essays or excursuses; *n* = index of names)

Editio princeps, Venice 1472.
[For incunabula see Butrica, chapter 9; for editions before 1780 see Enk (ed. Book I 1 pp. 80f), but here may be briefly noted Scaliger, Paris 1577]
Petri Burmanni Secundi (*tc*): *Sex. Aur. Propertii elegiarum libri IV* (completed by L. Santen), Utrecht 1780.
Karl Lachmann (*ptc*): *Sex. Aur. Propertii Carmina,* Leipzig 1816. Contains concordance to Burman's numeration. 'The first scientific recension of Propertius' (Housman).
G. A. B. Hertzberg (*itce*): *Sex. Aurelii Propertii elegiarum libri IV* (*i–iii*), Halle 1843–1845.
Emil Baehrens (*pta*): *Sex. Propertii elegiarum libri IV,* Leipzig 1880. This edition provided the first apparatus

criticus, and inaugurated the modern era in the textual criticism of Propertius.

A. Palmer (*it*): *Sex. Propertii elegiarum libri IV,* London-Dublin 1880.

J. P. Postgate (*it*[some *r*]*c*): *Select Elegies of Propertius,* London, Macmillan 1881.

J. P. Postgate (*pta*): *Sexti Properti Carmina,* London and Cambridge 1894 (the editor's own contribution to his *Corpus Poetarum Latinorum*).

Max Rothstein (*itc*[copious]): *Die Elegien des Sex. Propertius,* 2 vols (I = Books 1,2; II = Books 3,4), Berlin 1898 (I: 1920[2]; II: 1924[2]; reprinted with addenda by R. Stark 1966[3]).

Jesse Benedict Carter (*itc*): *The Roman Elegiac Poets,* Boston 1900. Selections from Tibullus, Propertius (51 poems), and Ovid's *Amores*. Regrettably out of print.

J. S. Phillimore (*ptan*): *Sexti Properti Carmina* (OCT), Oxford 1901 (1907[2]). Very conservative.

H. E. Butler (*itacn*): *Sexti Properti Opera Omnia,* London 1905.

J. S. Phillimore (*t*): *Sexti Properti Elegiarum Libri IV* (Bibliotheca Riccardiana [with Ellis's Catullus and Postgate's Tibullus]), London 1911. Apart from transpositions (eschewed) an enterprising text.

H. E. Butler (*itrn*): *Propertius* (Loeb Classical Library edition), London 1912.

O. L. Richmond (*itae*): *Sexti Properti quae supersunt opera,* Cambridge 1928. Contains much that is splendid, but the edition is seriously flawed by being tied to a reconstruction of the archetype and a theory of stanza composition which are both untenable.

SELECT BIBLIOGRAPHY

D. Paganelli (*itar*[French]*n*): *Properce, Elégies* (Budé edition), Paris 1929.

H. E. Butler and E. A. Barber (*itacn*): *The Elegies of Propertius,* Oxford 1933.

P. J. Enk (*itace*): *Sex. Propertii Elegiarum Liber I* (*Monobiblos*), 2 vols (I: prolegomena, text; II: commentary), Leiden 1946.

E. A. Barber (*ptan*): *Properti Carmina* (OCT), Oxford 1953, 1960².

W. A. Camps (*itac*): *Propertius, Elegies,* 4 vols, Cambridge (I: 1961; IV: 1965; III: 1966; II: 1967).

P. J. Enk (*itace*): *Sex. Propertii Elegiarum Liber Secundus,* 2 vols (I: prolegomena, text—and contains a page facsimile of *N, F, L, P, D, V,* and *Vo;* II: commentary), Leiden 1962.

Georg Luck (*itr*[German] some *c*): *Properz und Tibull, Liebeselegien* (Artemis edition), Zürich 1964.

Paolo Fedeli (*ptacn*): *Properzio: Elegie, Libro IV,* Bari 1965.

L. Richardson, Jr. (*itc*): *Propertius, Elegies I–IV* (APA series of classical texts), Norman, Oklahoma 1976. Besides full commentary gives an introductory appreciation of each poem.

R. I. V. Hodge and R. A. Buttimore (*itre*): *The 'Monobiblos' of Propertius,* Cambridge, Brewer 1977. Contains literary-critical essay on each poem.

G. C. Giardina (*ptac*): *Sex. Properti Elegiarum Liber II* (Paravia edition), Turin 1977.

Rudolf Hanslik (*ptan*): *Sex. Propertii Elegiarum Libri IV* (Teubner edition), Leipzig 1979.

Paolo Fedeli (*ptacn*): *Sesto Properzio: Il primo libro delle Elegie* (555 pp.), Florence 1980.

33

SELECT BIBLIOGRAPHY

Paolo Fedeli (*ptaen*): *Sexti Properti Elegiarum Libri IV* (Teubner edition), Stuttgart 1984.

Paolo Fedeli (*itrc*): *Properzio: Il Libro Terzo delle Elegie* (787 pp.), Bari 1985. The translation (Italian) is incorporated in the commentary.

English Translations (* = verse)

J. S. Phillimore (Oxford Library of Translations), Oxford 1906.

H. E. Butler: see Editions (Butler 1912).

Seymour G. Tremenheere, London, Marshall 1931.*

E. H. W. Meyerstein, London, OUP 1935.*

Constance Carrier, Bloomington, Indiana 1963.*

A. E. Watts (Penguin Classics), Harmondsworth 1966².*

W. G. Shepherd (Penguin Classics), Harmondsworth 1985.*

[Here may be mentioned Ezra Pound's *Homage to Sextus Propertius* 1917, a free and controversial interpretation of portions of Books 2 and 3, best accessible in J. P. Sullivan, *Ezra Pound and Sextus Propertius,* Austin 1964: valid though Pound's work is in its own right, it should not be regarded as a trustworthy rendering of the Latin poet]

Text and Transmission

A. E. Housman: 'The Manuscripts of Propertius,' *Journal of Philology* 21 (1892) 101–197; 22 (1893) 84–128.

B. L. Ullman: 'The Manuscripts of Propertius,' *Classical Philology* 6 (1911) 282–301.

D. R. Shackleton Bailey: *Propertiana,* Cambridge 1956.

G. P. Goold: 'Noctes Propertianae,' *Harvard Studies in Classical Philology* 71 (1966) 59–106.

34

SELECT BIBLIOGRAPHY

R. J. Tarrant: 'Propertius' in *Texts and Transmission* (ed. L. D. Reynolds), Oxford 1983, 324–326.

James L. Butrica: *The Manuscript Tradition of Propertius,* Toronto 1984. Contains critical edition of 1.20; 2.8; 3.6; and 4.11.

S. J. Heyworth: "The Elegies of Sextus Propertius: Towards a critical edition," diss. Cambridge 1986 (unpubl.).

G. P. Goold: 'On Editing Propertius,' *Papers in Honour of Otto Skutsch,* University of London Institute of Classical Studies (Bulletin Supplement Number 51, 1987) 27–38.

G. P. Goold: 'Problems in Editing Propertius' in *Editing Greek and Latin Texts* (ed. John N. Grant), New York 1989, 97–119.

Charles E. Murgia: 'Propertius 4.1.87–88 and the Division of 4.1,' *Harvard Studies in Classical Philology* 92 (1989) 257–272.

Facsimiles

Theodor Birt: *Codex Guelferbytanus Gudianus 224 olim Neapolitanus* (= N) *phototypice editus,* Leiden 1911.

Propertius Codex Guelferbytanus Gudianus 224 olim Neapolitanus, preface by Paolo Fedeli (Accademia Properziana del Subasio-Assisi), Assisi 1985.

Echoes of Propertius in the Classical Latin Poets

D. R. Shackleton Bailey: *Mnemosyne* 5 (1952) 307–333; *Propertiana* (see above), especially 269–316.

P. J. Enk: ed. Book I, vol. I (see above), pp. 54–77.

G. B. A. Fletcher: *Mnemosyne* 1 (1933–34) 192f; *Latomus*

SELECT BIBLIOGRAPHY

19 (1960) 736–738; *Latomus* 20 (1961) 85–92; *Latomus* 48 (1989) 354–359.

General

Theodor Birt: *Das antike Buchwesen,* Berlin 1882.

J.-P. Boucher: *Etudes sur Properce,* Paris 1965.

Francis Cairns: *Generic Composition in Greek and Latin Poetry,* Edinburgh 1972.

Frank O. Copley: *Exclusus Amator: A Study in Latin Love Poetry,* A.P.A., Madison, Wisconsin 1956.

Theodore H. Feder: *Great Treasures of Pompeii and Herculaneum,* New York 1978 (my refs to pages).

Pierre Grimal: *Les intentions de Properce et la composition du livre IV des Elégies,* Brussels 1953.

Margaret Hubbard: *Propertius,* London, Duckworth 1974. An excellent introduction to Propertius.

Georg Luck: *The Latin Love Elegy,* London, Methuen 1959, 1969[2].

R. O. A. M. Lyne: *The Latin Love Poets,* Oxford 1980.

Theodore D. Papanghelis: *Propertius: A Hellenistic Poet on Love and Death,* Cambridge 1987.

Gilbert Picard: *Roman Painting,* Greenwich, Conn. 1968 (my refs to illustration numbers).

G. E. Rizzo: *La pittura ellenistico-romana,* Milan 1929.

W. Y. Sellar: *The Roman Poets of the Augustan Age: Horace and the Elegiac Poets,* Oxford 1899.

O. Skutsch: 'The Structure of the Propertian Monobiblos,' *Classical Philology* 58 (1963) 238f.

O. Skutsch: 'The Second Book of Propertius,' *Harvard Studies in Classical Philology* 79 (1975) 229ff.

J. P. Sullivan: *Propertius: A Critical Introduction,* Cambridge 1976.

SELECT BIBLIOGRAPHY

Hermann Tränkle: *Die Sprachkunst des Properz und die Tradition der lateinischen Dichtersprache,* Wiesbaden 1960.

Paul Veyne: *L'élégie érotique romaine: L'amour, la poésie et l'Occident,* Paris 1983 (translated by David Pellauer as *Roman Erotic Elegy,* Chicago 1988).

Gordon Williams: *Tradition and Originality in Roman Poetry,* Oxford 1968.

Metre

Maurice Platnauer: *Latin Elegiac Verse,* Cambridge 1951 (rev. R. J. Getty, *Classical Philology* 48 [1953] 189–192).

Reference

J. S. Phillimore: *Index Verborum Propertianus,* Oxford 1905.

B. Schmeisser: *A Concordance to Propertius,* Hildesheim 1972.

W. R. Smyth: *Thesaurus criticus ad Sexti Propertii textum,* Leiden 1970. Lists by poem and line-number almost every conjecture made in Propertius up to 1970.

Bibliography

Hermann Harrauer: *A Bibliography to Propertius,* Hildesheim 1973. Over 1800 items from 1472 to 1973, arranged in sections chronologically, with an *index locorum* listing the references to each poem and to each line, and an *index rerum et nominum.*

P. Fedeli and P. Pinotti: *Bibliografia Properziana* (1946–1983), Assisi 1985.

SEXTI PROPERTI ELEGIAE

BOOK ONE

The first book of Propertius consists of 20 poems, in each of which his sweetheart, though she is not always named, plays some part; but the poet has added a coda of three poems (possibly earlier work) having nothing to do with Cynthia, consisting of an epyllion and two epigrams. That this book stands quite apart from any other of the poet's is shown most strikingly by its distance from them in metrical technique: nearly 40 percent of its pentameters end in polysyllabic words (as against 14 percent in Book Two, 5 percent in Book Three, and 2 percent in Book Four). This is one reason for confidence that the coda is an integral part of Book One, another being that the last poem, like the first, is addressed to Tullus. Lacking the Elegies of Gallus we do not know how far our poet was dependent on him; but for the rest, Book One is remarkably fresh and original and varied, Cynthia asleep (3), Cynthia threatening to leave Propertius (8), the song of the excluded lover (16), and the Hylas epyllion (20) being some of its memorable pieces. From the absence of Maecenas' name we may fairly infer that the poet had not yet been admitted to his circle.

LIBER PRIMUS

I

Cynthia prima suis miserum me cepit ocellis,
    contactum nullis ante cupidinibus.
tum mihi constantis deiecit lumina fastus
    et caput impositis pressit Amor pedibus,
donec me docuit castas odisse puellas   5
    improbus, et nullo vivere consilio.
ei mihi, iam toto furor hic non deficit anno,
    cum tamen adversos cogor habere deos.

Milanion nullos fugiendo, Tulle, labores
    saevitiam durae contudit Iasidos.   10
nam modo Partheniis amens errabat in antris,
    rursus in hirsutas ibat et ille feras;
ille etiam Hylaei percussus vulnere rami
    saucius Arcadiis rupibus ingemuit.

---

[7] ei *Rossberg*: et Ω
[12] rursu<s in hirsu>tas *Courtney*: ibat et hirsutas Ω |
ibat et ille *Courtney*: ille [videre] Ω

---

[a] The opening four lines of Propertius derive their
inspiration from Meleager, A(*nthologia*) P(*alatina*)
12.101.1–4.

[b] It is especially characteristic of Propertius that he

42

THE FIRST BOOK

Cynthia

CYNTHIA first with her eyes ensnared me, poor
wretch, that had previously been untouched by
desire. It was then that Love made me lower my
looks of stubborn pride and trod my head beneath
his feet,[a] until the villain taught me to shun decent
girls and to lead the life of a ne'er-do-well. Poor me,
for a whole year now this frenzy has not abated,
while I am compelled to endure the frown of heaven.

[9] It was, friend Tullus, by shrinking from no
hardship that Milanion broke down the cruelty of
harsh Atalanta.[b] For now he wandered distraught
in the glens of Parthenius, and now he would go to
confront shaggy wild beasts. He was also dealt a
wound from the club Hylaeus bore, and on the
rocks of Arcady he moaned in pain. Thus he was

---

dignifies his love by relating it to mythology, thus endow-
ing it with a timeless splendour. Gilbert Highet (*Poets in a
Landscape* 80) well adduces as an example of the device
'the moonlight scene in the last act of *The Merchant of Ven-
ice,* where the young lovers remind each other of similar
nights, also filled with intense love, in the past.'

43

ergo velocem potuit domuisse puellam: 15
    tantum in amore fides et benefacta valent.

in me tardus Amor non ullas cogitat artes,
    nec meminit notas, ut prius, ire vias.
at vos, deductae quibus est pellacia lunae
    et labor in magicis sacra piare focis,   20
en agedum dominae mentem convertite nostrae,
    et facite illa meo palleat ore magis!
tunc ego crediderim Manes et sidera vobis
    posse Cytinaeis ducere carminibus.

aut vos, qui sero lapsum revocatis, amici,   25
    quaerite non sani pectoris auxilia.
fortiter et ferrum saevos patiemur et ignes,
    sit modo libertas quae velit ira loqui.
ferte per extremas gentes et ferte per undas,
    qua non ulla meum femina norit iter.   30

vos remanete, quibus facili deus annuit aure,
    sitis et in tuto semper amore pares.
nam me nostra Venus noctes exercet amaras,
    et nullo vacuus tempore defit Amor.
hoc, moneo, vitate malum: sua quemque moretur 35
    cura, neque assueto mutet amore torum.

---

[16] fides *Fontein* : preces Ω
[19] pellacia *Fruter* : fallacia Ω
[23] manes *Morgan** (et m. *Housman*): vobis Ω | vobis
Housman : et amnes Ω

able to subdue the swift-footed girl: such power in love have devotion and service.

[17] In my case dull-witted Love thinks up no stratagems, and remembers not to tread, as formerly, his well-known paths. But you, whose practice it is to lure the Moon down from the sky and to propitiate spirits over the magic fire, come, alter the heart of my mistress and see that she turn paler than this cheek of mine. Then should I credit you with the power of summoning ghosts and stars with Thessalian spells.

[25] Else you, my friends, who too late call back the fallen, seek medicines for a heart that is sick. I shall bravely submit to the knife and cautery, if only I were free to utter the promptings of anger. Carry me through distant lands and over distant seas, where no woman may know my path.

[31] Stay you at home, to whose prayer the god has nodded with easy ear, and be ever paired in a safe love. For I am harassed by our goddess Venus through nights of torment, and Cupid is never idle, never absent. Shun this plague, I counsel you: let everyone cling to his own sweetheart, nor switch his affections when love has grown familiar. But if

---

quod si quis monitis tardas adverterit aures,
 heu referet quanto verba dolore mea!

II

QUID iuvat ornato procedere, vita, capillo
 et tenuis Coa veste movere sinus,
aut quid Orontea crines perfundere murra,
 teque peregrinis vendere muneribus,
naturaeque decus mercato perdere cultu,   5
 nec sinere in propriis membra nitere bonis?
crede mihi, non ulla tuaest medicina figurae:
 nudus Amor formam non amat artificem.

aspice quos summittat humus non fossa colores,
 ut veniant hederae sponte sua melius,   10
surgat et in solis formosior arbutus antris,
 et sciat indocilis currere lympha vias.
litora nativis praefulgent picta lapillis,
 et volucres nulla dulcius arte canunt.

non sic Leucippis succendit Castora Phoebe,   15
 Pollucem cultu non Helaïra soror;

[8] formam *Heinsius*: formae Ω
[9] <non> fossa *Skutsch**: formosa Ω
[11] formosior ς: formosius Ω
[13] praefulgent *Baehrens*: persuadent Ω
[16] Helaïra *Schulze*: tel- Ω*: Hil- *vulgo*

anyone turn a deaf ear to my warning, ah, with
what pain shall he recall my words!

Beauty unadorned

WHAT avails it, my love, to step out with the latest
hair-style and to swing a sheer skirt of Coan silk?
What avails it to drench your locks with Syrian per-
fume and to vaunt yourself in foreign finery, to des-
troy your natural charm with purchased ornament,
preventing your figure from displaying its own true
merits? Believe me, there is no improving your
appearance: Love is naked,[a] and loves not beauty
gained by artifice.

[9] See what coloured flowers the earth untilled
sends forth[b]; see how ivy grows better wild, the
arbute arises lovelier in lonely glens and water has
wit to flow in untaught channels. Shores shine
brightest when painted with natural pebbles, and
birds sing more sweetly from their lack of art.[c]

[15] Not thus did Phoebe, daughter of Leucippus,
set Castor afire, or Hilaïra, her sister, Pollux with

[a] Propertius' pleasure in the sight of the naked body is
frequently attested: see Index, *nudity*.

[b] Cf. St. Matthew 6:28f.

[c] In this paragraph the poet seems to be suggesting that
his sweetheart's natural endowment of complexion, hair,
height, carriage, and nightingale voice is perfect, which
artifice could only spoil.

PROPERTIUS

non, Idae et cupido quondam discordia Phoebo,
  Eueni patriis filia litoribus;
nec Phrygium falso traxit candore maritum
  avecta externis Hippodamia rotis: 20
sed facies aderat nullis obnoxia gemmis,
  qualis Apelleis est color in tabulis.
non illis studium fuco conquirere amantes:
  illis ampla satis forma pudicitia.

non ego nunc vereor ne sis tibi vilior istis: 25
  uni si qua placet, culta puella sat est;
cum tibi praesertim Phoebus sua carmina donet
  Aoniamque libens Calliopea lyram,
unica nec desit iucundis gratia verbis,
  omnia quaeque Venus, quaeque Minerva probat.
his tu semper eris nostrae gratissima vitae,   31
  taedia dum miserae sint tibi luxuriae.

III

QUALIS Thesea iacuit cedente carina
  languida desertis Cnosia litoribus;

---

²³ fuco *Eldik* : vulgo Ω   ²⁵ sis ς: sim Ω

---

a The rape of the Leucippides is told by Theocritus
22.137–211 and was a popular theme of vase-painters (e.g.
Meidias, Brit.Mus. hydria E224).

b Propertius, who possessed an unusual sensitivity for
visual art, is apt in his mythological examples to depict

her ornaments[a]; not thus on her father's banks did
the daughter of Evenus once set Idas and ardent
Phoebus at strife; nor by false glamour did Hippo-
damia win a Phrygian husband, she who was borne
away on a stranger's wheels: these had beauty
which owed nothing to jewellery, pure as the hues in
paintings by Apelles. These had no eagerness to
gain lovers with cosmetics: for these chastity was
beauty fair enough.

[25] In fact I am sure that you do not count yourself
inferior to those women: if a girl finds favour with
one man, she is adorned enough; all the more since
Phoebus endows you with his songs, and Calliope,
nothing loth, with Aonia's lyre; and a charm all your
own graces your happy talk, and you have all that
Venus, all that Minerva approve. These assets will
ever make you the great love of my life, if only you
tire of this wretched gaudiness.

Cynthia surprised in sleep

LIKE the maid of Cnossus as in a swoon she lay on
the deserted shore when Theseus' ship sailed away[b];

paintings or sculptures that had attracted him. Here com-
mentators mention the sleeping Ariadne in the Vatican
Museum, but this was a popular theme for painters (at
Pompeii anyway), and that a painting was in the poet's
mind is suggested by the reference to Theseus' ship disap-
pearing over the horizon.

qualis et accubuit primo Cepheia somno
   libera iam duris cotibus Andromede;
nec minus assiduis Edonis fessa choreis   5
   qualis in herboso concidit Apidano:
talis visa mihi mollem spirare quietem
   Cynthia consertis nixa caput manibus,
ebria cum multo traherem vestigia Baccho,
   et quaterent sera nocte facem pueri.   10

hanc ego, nondum etiam sensus deperditus omnis,
   molliter impresso conor adire toro;
et quamvis duplici correptum ardore iuberent
   hac Amor hac Liber, durus uterque deus,
subiecto leviter positam temptare lacerto   15
   osculaque admota sumere tarda manu,
non tamen ausus eram dominae turbare quietem,
   expertae metuens iurgia saevitiae;
sed sic intentis haerebam fixus ocellis,
   Argus ut ignotis cornibus Inachidos.   20

et modo solvebam nostra de fronte corollas
   ponebamque tuis, Cynthia, temporibus;

---

[8] consertis *Guyet*: non certis Ω
[16] tarda *Scaliger*: [e]t arma Ω

---

a Cf. Pompeian wall-painting (House of the Citharist) of
a sleeping Maenad (Rizzo, pl.112).

b The Hellenistic prototype of this poem is lost, but a
derivative Byzantine version (Paulus Silentiarius, *A.P.*
5.275) enables us to see how by dramatization and the

like Cepheus' daughter Andromeda as she rested in her first slumber on her release from the rugged cliff; no less like the Thracian bacchant, exhausted after incessant dances, when she collapses on the grassy bank of the Apidanus[a]: even so did Cynthia seem to me to breathe a gentle repose, her head pillowed on a cushion of her hands, when home I came[b] dragging footsteps unsteadied by much wine and the slaves were shaking their dying torches in the far-gone night.

[11] Not yet were all my senses gone, and I tried by leaning gently on the couch to reach her; and, although seized with a double passion, for the two inexorable gods, on this side Love, on that Bacchus, were urging me to edge my arm deftly beneath her and try her as she lay, and, bringing up my hand, to steal belated kisses, yet I did not venture to disturb my lady's peace, fearing the chidings of a cruelty I had tasted before; but I remained rooted with eyes intent upon her, like those of Argus upon the strange horns of Inachus' child.[c]

[21] And now I was taking off the garlands from my brow and arranging them about your temples,

---

addition of apt detail Propertius has transformed an epigram into an elegy (cf. E. Fraenkel, *Kleine Beiträge* [Rome 1964] II 215).

[c] The House of Livia on the Palatine has a painting of Io watched by Argus, a copy of the celebrated work by Nicias (cf. Pliny, *NH* 35.130).

et modo gaudebam lapsos formare capillos;
  nunc furtiva cavis poma dabam manibus:
omnia quae ingrato largibar munera somno,   25
  munera de prono saepe voluta sinu;
et quotiens raro duxti suspiria motu,
  obstupui vano credulus auspicio,
ne qua tibi insolitos portarent visa timores,
  neve quis invitam cogeret esse suam: 30

donec diversas praecurrens luna fenestras,
  luna moraturis sedula luminibus,
compositos levibus radiis patefecit ocellos.
  sic ait in molli fixa toro cubitum:
'tandem te nostro referens iniuria lecto   35
  alterius clausis expulit e foribus?
namque ubi longa meae consumpsti tempora noctis,
  languidus exactis, ei mihi, sideribus?
o utinam talis perducas, improbe, noctes,
  me miseram qualis semper habere iubes!   40

'nam modo purpureo fallebam stamine somnum,
  rursus et Orpheae carmine, fessa, lyrae;
interdum leviter mecum deserta querebar
  externo longas saepe in amore moras:

---

[25] quae *Dousa sen.* : -que Ω

Cynthia; and now I took pleasure in building up your fallen locks, then with hollowed palms I stealthily gave you apples. But all these gifts I was bestowing on ungrateful sleep, gifts which repeatedly rolled down from your lap; and when from time to time you stirred and heaved a sigh, I held my breath, believing in a vain divination, for I feared lest some nightmare be bringing you fantastic terrors, and a phantom lover forcing you to yield to him against your will.

[31] At length the moon hurrying by the parted shutters, the officious moon with light that would fain have stayed,[a] opened with its gentle beams Cynthia's fast-closed eyes. Then, with elbow propped on the soft couch, she cried: 'Has another's scorn then at last brought you to my bed, expelling you from doors closed in your face? For where have you spent the long hours of the night which was due me, you who come, ah me, exhausted, when the stars are driven from the sky? Oh, may you spend nights like these, you villain, such as you are always compelling poor me to endure!

[41] 'For now I was beguiling sleep by spinning crimson thread, and now in my weariness by music of Orpheus' lyre; and sometimes, all forlorn, I softly complained to myself of the long time spent by you in another's embrace: till Sleep with soothing wings

---

[a] Cf. Philodemus, *A.P.* 7.122.1f.

53

dum me iucundis lassam Sopor impulit alis.   45
    illa fuit lacrimis ultima cura meis.'

IV

QUID mihi tam multas laudando, Basse, puellas
    mutatum domina cogis abire mea?
quid me non pateris vitae quodcumque sequetur
    hoc magis assueto ducere servitio?

tu licet Antiopae formam Nycteidos, et tu   5
    Spartanae referas laudibus Hermionae,
et quascumque tulit formosi temporis aetas;
    Cynthia non illas nomen habere sinat:
nedum, si levibus fuerit collata figuris,
    inferior duro iudice turpis eat.   10

haec sed forma mei pars est extrema furoris;
    sunt maiora, quibus, Basse, perire iuvat:
ingenuus color et motis decor artubus et quae
    gaudia sub tacita discere veste libet.
quo magis et nostros contendis solvere amores,   15
    hoc magis accepta fallit uterque fide.

---

[45] lassam *P*: lapsam Ω
[13] motis *Goold**: multis Ω | decor ç: decus Ω | artubus *Marcilius*: artibus Ω   [14] discere *Heinsius*: dicere Ω

---

[a] 'Theirs would seem to be a very domestic arrangement, if he can come to her late at night after a party and expect to be admitted' (Richardson).

overcame my exhausted body. That was my weeping's last concern.'[a]

To Bassus: a rebuke

WHY, Bassus,[b] by praising so many other girls do you press me to change and forsake my mistress? Why do you not rather let me spend whatever time I have left to live in bondage I have grown used to?

5 Though your praises recall the loveliness of Antiope, Nycteus' child, and of Spartan Hermione, and all the women the years of the age of beauty produced: Cynthia would make their glory pale. Much less, if compared with trivial beauties, need she fear the disgrace of being pronounced inferior even by a fastidious judge.

11 Yet this beauty is the least part of my frenzy; she has greater charms, Bassus, which I am glad to lose my head over: her well-bred complexion, her grace when she moves her limbs, and thrills I love to experience beneath the secrecy of the coverlet. And the more you endeavour to undo our love, the more each of us foils you through the pledge which is cherished.

[b] Although Bassus is named only in this poem, he was a real person, who with Ponticus and Ovid formed part of Propertius' literary circle. The poem makes it fairly clear that he had not met Cynthia, as was natural if she were a fiction.

non impune feres: sciet haec insana puella
  et tibi non tacitis vocibus hostis erit;
nec tibi me post haec committet Cynthia nec te
  quaeret; erit tanti criminis illa memor,   20
et te circum omnis alias irata puellas
  differet: heu nullo limine carus eris.

nullas illa suis contemnet fletibus aras,
  et quicumque sacer, qualis ubique, lapis.
non ullo gravius temptatur Cynthia damno   25
  quam sibi cum rapto cessat amore decus,
praecipue nostro. maneat sic semper, adoro,
  nec quicquam ex illa quod querar inveniam!

invide, tu tandem voces compesce molestas   5.1
  et sine nos cursu, quo sumus, ire pares!   2

V

QUID tibi vis, insane? meae sentire furores?   3
  infelix, properas ultima nosse mala,
et miser ignotos vestigia ferre per ignes,   5
  et bibere e tota toxica Thessalia.

---

[26] decus *Kraffert*: deus Ω
[5.1,2] *huc Enk*   [3] meae *Hemsterhuys*: meos Ω

---

[a] A suitable adjective for an iambographer.
[b] Here, unlike the preceding poem, the addressee is not
named until the last couplet. He, though the recipient

[17] You will not get away with it: my furious sweetheart will hear of this and be your foe with no unspoken words; nor hereafter will Cynthia entrust me to you or seek you out (she will not forget such a dire offence), and in her anger she will discredit you with all other girls: woe to you: no doorstep will welcome you then.

[23] No altar will be too mean to receive her tears, or whatever sacred stone there is, no matter of what kind and where. No loss more keenly provokes Cynthia than when love has been stolen from her and her charms lie idle, especially when that love is mine. May she ever thus remain, I pray, and may I find nothing in her of which to complain!

[5:1] Envious man, curb now at last your tiresome[a] tongue and leave the pair of us to proceed on our way together!

To Gallus: a rebuff

WHAT are you after, lunatic?[b] To feel my sweetheart's fury? Wretch, you are hastening to experience the ultimate in woe, to make your luckless way through unimagined fires, and drink all Thessaly's supply of poison.

of other poems of Book One, viz. 10 and 20, and no doubt a real person, has no very deep acquaintance with Cynthia, and has to be told about her.

non est illa vagis similis collata puellis:
    molliter irasci non sciet illa tibi.
quod si forte tuis non est contraria votis,
    at tibi curarum milia quanta dabit!   10
non tibi iam somnos, non illa relinquet ocellos:
    illa ferox animis alligat una viros.

a, mea contemptus quotiens ad limina curres,
    cum tibi singultu fortia verba cadent,
et tremulus maestis orietur fletibus horror,   15
    et timor informem ducet in ore notam,
et quaecumque voles fugient tibi verba querenti,
    nec poteris, qui sis aut ubi, nosse miser!

tum grave servitium nostrae cogere puellae
    discere et exclusum quid sit abire domum;   20
nec iam pallorem totiens mirabere nostrum,
    aut cur sim toto corpore nullus ego.
nec tibi nobilitas poterit succurrere amanti:
    nescit Amor priscis cedere imaginibus.

quod si parva tuae dederis vestigia culpae,   25
    quam cito de tanto nomine rumor eris!
non ego tum potero solacia ferre roganti,
    cum mihi nulla mei sit medicina mali;
sed pariter miseri socio cogemur amore
    alter in alterius mutua flere sinu.   30

---

[8] sciet ς: solet Ω
[12] ferox *Luck**: feros Ω

⁷ She is not like flighty girls and is not to be compared with them: she will not be able to restrain her anger with you. And if by chance she does not turn a deaf ear to your prayers, yet what countless sorrows will she cause you! Soon she will not allow you to sleep or close your eyes: she is fierce and just the one to curb men with her will.

¹³ Ah, how often will you run to my door after a rejection, when your brave words will break down in sobs; trembling and shuddering will come over you with unhappy tears, and fear will trace unsightly lines upon your face, and any words you are groping for will die on your lips as you complain, nor in your distress will you succeed in knowing who or where you are!

¹⁹ Then you will be forced to experience the harsh bondage of my sweetheart and what it means to go home when the door is shut in your face; and by that time you will not so often be surprised by my wan colour, or why my whole body is shrunk to nothing. And your high birth will not help you in love either: Love scorns to defer to ancestral portraits.

²⁵ But if you leave the least trace of infidelity, how quickly will your noble name become a subject of scandal! Then when you ask me, I will be unable to bring you any comfort, since I have no medicine for my own malady; but, comrades in love and woe, we shall be equally compelled to weep each in turn on the other's bosom.

quare, quid possit mea Cynthia, desine, Galle,
    quaerere: non impune illa rogata venit.

VI

Non ego nunc Hadriae vereor mare noscere tecum,
    Tulle, neque Aegaeo ducere vela salo,
cum quo Rhipaeos possim conscendere montes
    ulteriusque domos vadere Memnonias;
sed me complexae remorantur verba puellae,   5
    mutatoque graves saepe colore preces.

illa mihi totis argutat noctibus ignes,
    et queritur nullos esse relicta deos;
illa meam mihi iam se denegat, illa minatur
    quae solet ingrato tristis amica viro.   10
his ego non horam possum durare querelis:
    ah pereat, si quis lentus amare potest!

an mihi sit tanti doctas cognoscere Athenas
    atque Asiae veteres cernere divitias,
ut mihi deducta faciat convicia puppi   15
    Cynthia et insanis ora notet manibus,
osculaque opposito dicat sibi debita vento,
    et nihil infido durius esse viro?

---

[a] This poem is a variation on a type known as the *propempticon,* in which a friend is bidden a fond farewell (for these types see Cairns).

³¹ Wherefore, Gallus, cease asking what my Cynthia is capable of: heavy the toll they pay whose invitation she accepts.

An invitation declined

I fear not now to brave the Adriatic with you, Tullus,ᵃ or spread sail upon the Aegean sea; I could scale with you the mountains of the extreme north and travel farther south than Memnon's halls ᵇ; but the words of a clinging sweetheart hold me back and her urgent pleas, given weight by frequent changes of colour.

⁷ All night long she shrills her passion at me, complaining that, if I desert her, there are no gods; she tells me she is no longer mine and utters those threats that an upset mistress is wont to cast at an ungrateful lover. Amid these complaints I cannot last for an hour: perish the man who can be indifferent in love!

¹³ Is it worth so much to me to visit learned Athens and set eyes on the ancient riches of Asia only for Cynthia to abuse me when my ship is launched and scratch her face with frantic fingers, crying that she owes my kisses only to the wind that forbade me sail and that no one is crueller than a faithless man?

ᵇ In this address to Tullus the poet contrasts the lover with the man of action.

tu patrui meritas conare anteire secures,
 et vetera oblitis iura refer sociis.   20
nam tua non aetas umquam cessavit amori,
 semper at armatae cura fuit patriae;
et tibi non umquam nostros puer iste labores
 afferat et lacrimis omnia nota meis!

me sine, quem semper voluit fortuna iacere,   25
 huic animam extremam reddere nequitiae.
multi longinquo periere in amore libenter,
 in quorum numero me quoque terra tegat.
non ego sum laudi, non natus idoneus armis:
 hanc me militiam fata subire volunt.   30

at tu, seu mollis qua tendit Ionia, seu qua
 Lydia Pactoli tingit arata liquor,
seu pedibus terras seu pontum remige carpes,
 ibis et accepti pars eris imperii:
tum tibi si qua mei veniet non immemor hora,   35
 vivere me duro sidere certus eris.

VII

Dum tibi Cadmeae dicuntur, Pontice, Thebae
 armaque fraternae tristia militiae,
atque, ita sim felix, primo contendis Homero
 (sint modo fata tuis mollia carminibus),

---

26 huic . . . extremam *Housman* : hanc . . . -ae Ω
33 remige carpes *Skutsch** : carpere remis Ω

¹⁹ You must attempt to surpass your uncle's merited axes and to restore the old laws to forgetful allies. For your youth has never had time for love, but you always thought of your warring fatherland; and may Cupid never bring you torments such as mine and all the sorrows known to my tears!

²⁵ Allow me, whom Fortune willed to lie ever prostrate, to give up my final breath to this worthlessness. Many have contentedly perished in a long love-affair; in their number may the earth cover me too. I was born unfit for glory, unfit for arms: love is the warfare fate wishes me to undergo.

³¹ But whether you are to be found where stretches luxurious Ionia or where the water of the Pactolus steeps the ploughlands of Lydia, whether you speed on foot over land or by ship over sea, go you will and become a part of popular government: then, should there come a moment when you remember me, never doubt that I live under an unkind star.

A warning to Ponticus

WHILE you are singing, Ponticus, of Cadmean Thebes and the sombre warfare of fraternal strife, and, upon my oath, are vying with Homer himself (if Fate but deal tenderly with your verse[a]), I, as is my

---

[a] Alas, it didn't, and he enjoys only the vicarious immortality bestowed on him by Propertius and Ovid (*Trist.* 4.10.47).

nos, ut consuêmus, nostros agitamus amores,   5
    atque aliquid duram quaerimus in dominam;
nec tantum ingenio quantum servire dolori
    cogor et aetatis tempora dura queri.

hic mihi conteritur vitae modus, haec mea famast,
    hinc cupio nomen carminis ire mei.   10
me laudent doctae solum placuisse puellae,
    Pontice, et iniustas saepe tulisse minas;
me legat assidue post haec neglectus amator,
    et prosint illi cognita nostra mala.

te quoque si certo puer hic concusserit arcu —   15
    quo nollem nostros me violasse deos! —
longe castra tibi, longe miser agmina septem
    flebis in aeterno surda iacere situ;
et frustra cupies mollem componere versum,
    nec tibi subiciet carmina serus Amor.   20
tum me non humilem mirabere saepe poetam,
    tunc ego Romanis praeferar ingeniis.
[nec poterunt iuvenes nostro reticere sepulcro
    'ardoris nostri magne poeta iaces.']

tu cave nostra tuo contemnas carmina fastu: 25
    saepe venit magno faenore tardus Amor.

---

[16] quo ς: quod Ω | nollem *Tappe*: nol(l)im Ω | me
violasse *Otto*: eviolasse Ω
[23,24] *secl. Courtney*

wont, am still busied with my love poetry, seeking something to use against a hard-hearted mistress; and I am obliged to serve less my talent than my feelings, and bewail the hard season of my youth.

9 This is how my life is spent, this is my fame, from this I wish the renown of my verse to arise. Let my praise be that I alone found favour with a scholar maid, Ponticus, and often endured her unjust threats; hereafter let the disdained lover read me avidly, and let it profit him to learn of my torments.

15 You, too, if the Boy stuns you with his unerring bow—with which I wish the gods I serve had not so outraged me!—, it will be away with your camps, poor wretch, away with your seven hosts, and you will weep that they lie unresponsive beneath dust ne'er to be disturbed; and in vain will you desire to put together tender couplets, for Love come late will not supply you with song. Then will you oft admire me as no mean poet, then shall I be ranked above Rome's men of genius. [And youths will be unable to refrain from saying over my grave: 'You who lie here are the great poet of our passion!']

25 But do you beware of scorning my verse in your pride: when Love is slow in coming, he often exacts a heavy interest.

VIIIA

Tune igitur demens, nec te mea cura moratur?
    an tibi sum gelida vilior Illyria?
et tibi iam tanti, quicumquest, iste videtur,
    ut sine me vento quolibet ire velis?
tune audire potes vesani murmura ponti   5
    fortis, et in dura nave iacere potes?
tu pedibus teneris positas fulcire pruinas,
    tu potes insolitas, Cynthia, ferre nives?

o utinam hibernae duplicentur tempora brumae,
    et sit iners tardis navita Vergiliis,   10
nec tibi Tyrrhena solvatur funis harena,
    neve inimica meas elevet aura preces
et me defixum vacua patiatur in ora   15
    crudelem infesta saepe vocare manu!

sed quocumque modo de me, periura, mereris,
    sit Galatea tuae non aliena viae;
  13 atque ego non videam talis subsidere ventos,
  14   cum tibi provectas auferet unda rates,
ut te felici post victa Ceraunia remo
    accipiat placidis Oricos aequoribus.   20

nam me non ullae poterunt corrumpere, de te
    quin ego, vita, tuo limine verba querar;

<hr />

13,14 *post* 18 *Carutti*
19 *post victa Heinsius :* praevecta Ω

BOOK I.8A

The voyage proposed

ARE you then out of your mind, and does not my love cause you second thoughts? Do I matter to you less than frosty Illyria? And is that fellow, whoever he is, so highly prized by you that you are ready to go without me by any wind that blows? Can you listen unmoved to the roar of the stormy seas and make your bed on a ship's hard deck? Can you tread with your dainty feet the hoar-frost on the ground? Can you endure, Cynthia, the unfamiliar snows?

9 Ah, would that the season of winter's storms might be doubled and the sailor delayed in port through the tardy rising of the Pleiads,[a] and your cable not loosed from Tuscan strand or the cruel wind make light of my prayers and leave me rooted to the empty shore oft with clenched fists crying out upon your cruelty!

17 But however you have deserved of me, faithless one, may Galatea be not unfriendly to your voyage; and when the wave carries your ship out to sea, may I not see any dropping of such winds as bring you, after safely rounding Cape Thunder with your oars, to Oricum's calm haven.

21 For no woman will be able to lure me away from uttering at your door, my dearest, words of

---

[a] The rising of the Pleiads in April marked a change (*vergere*) in the year's seasons, permitting navigation, and so acquired the name *Vergiliae*.

PROPERTIUS

nec me deficiet nautas rogitare citatos
    'dicite, quo portu clausa puella meast?',
et dicam 'licet Artaciis considat in oris,   25
    et licet Hylaeis, illa futura meast.'

VIIIB

Hɪᴄ erit! hic iurata manet! rumpantur iniqui!
    vicimus: assiduas non tulit illa preces.
falsa licet cupidus deponat gaudia livor:
    destitit ire novas Cynthia nostra vias.   30

illi carus ego et per me carissima Roma
    dicitur, et sine me dulcia regna negat.
illa vel angusto mecum requiescere lecto
    et quocumque modo maluit esse mea,
quam sibi dotatae regnum vetus Hippodamiae,   35
    et quas Elis opes apta pararat equis.

quamvis magna daret, quamvis maiora daturus,
    non tamen illa meos fugit avara sinus.
hanc ego non auro, non Indis flectere conchis,
    sed potui blandi carminis obsequio.   40

[25] Artaciis *Palmer*: atraciis Ω
[27] *sep. Lipsius*
[36] apta *Phillimore*: ante Ω

grievance about you; nor will I cease to accost and ask of sailors: 'Tell me, what harbour shelters my sweetheart?' And I shall aver 'Though she settle on Propontic shores or shores beyond Scythia, yet shall she be mine.'

The voyage abandoned

HERE she will stay! Here she is pledged to remain! Let envy burst! I have won: she could not resist my ceaseless prayers. Let lustful jealousy renounce its illusions of joy: my Cynthia has ceased to travel on an unknown course.

[31] She loves me and because of me loves Rome of cities best, and says that without me even a kingdom would not please her. She has preferred to lie with me, though narrow is my bed, and to be mine, whatever our style of life,[a] than to possess the ancient kingdom that was Hippodamia's dowry and all the wealth horse-pasturing Elis[b] had amassed.

[37] Although he offered much and was prepared to offer more, still she has not been tempted by greed to flee my embrace. I was able to move her, not with gold, not with pearls from India, but with the homage of endearing verse.

---

[a] Cf. Marriage service 'For better, for worse, for richer, for poorer.'

[b] Cf. Homer, *Od.* 22.347, πρὸς Ἤλιδος ἱπποβότοιο.

PROPERTIUS

sunt igitur Musae, neque amanti tardus Apollo,
    quîs ego fretus amo: Cynthia rara meast!
nunc mihi summa licet contingere sidera plantis:
    sive dies seu nox venerit, illa meast!
nec mihi rivalis certos subducet amores: 45
    ista meam norit gloria canitiem.

IX

DICEBAM tibi venturos, irrisor, amores,
    nec tibi perpetuo libera verba fore:
ecce iaces supplexque venis ad iura puellae,
    et tibi nunc quaevis imperat empta modo.
non me Chaoniae vincant in amore columbae   5
    dicere, quos iuvenes quaeque puella domet.
me dolor et lacrimae merito fecere peritum:
    atque utinam posito dicar amore rudis!

quid tibi nunc misero prodest grave dicere carmen
    aut Amphioniae moenia flere lyrae?   10
plus in amore valet Mimnermi versus Homero:
    carmina mansuetus lenia quaerit Amor.
i quaeso et tristis istos sepone libellos,
    et cane quod quaevis nosse puella velit!

---

⁴⁵ subducet ς: -it Ω
¹³ sepone *Heinsius*: compone Ω

70

70

⁴¹ So the Muses do exist, and Apollo is not slow to help a lover: in these as a lover I put my faith: the peerless Cynthia is mine! Now for very joy I can set my feet upon the stars in heaven: come day or night, she is mine! Nor will a rival steal my true love from me: that boast shall prevail when my hair is grey.

The warning come true

WHEN[a] you mocked me I used to say that love would get you and that you would not always be able to talk like a free man: see, you are down, and abjectly make submission to your mistress, and a mere nobody, lately bought, now gives you orders. In the field of love Dodona's doves cannot surpass me in prophesying what youths each girl is to subdue. Suffering and tears have deservedly gained me the title of expert: would I could lay love aside and be called a novice!

⁹ What does it now avail you, wretch, to declaim grand epic or lament the walls built by Amphion's lyre? In love Mimnermus' verse is worth more than Homer's: peaceful Love calls for gentle strains. Go and discard those gloomy volumes of yours and sing songs a girl wants to hear! It would be different

---

[a] The poem is a pendant to 1.7.

quid si non esset facilis tibi copia! nunc tu   15
    insanus medio flumine quaeris aquam.

necdum etiam palles, vero nec tangeris igni:
    haec est venturi prima favilla mali.
tum magis Armenias cupies accedere tigres
    et magis infernae vincula nosse rotae,   20
quam pueri totiens arcum sentire medullis
    et nihil iratae posse negare tuae.
nullus Amor cuiquam facilis ita praebuit alas,
    ut non alterna presserit ille manu.

nec te decipiat, quod sit satis illa parata: 25
    acrius illa subit, Pontice, si qua tuast,
quippe ubi non liceat vacuos seducere ocellos,
    nec vigilare alio limine cedat Amor.
qui non ante patet, donec manus attigit ossa:
    quisquis es, assiduas tu fuge blanditias!   30
illis et silices et possint cedere quercus,
    nedum tu possis, spiritus iste levis.

quare, si pudor est, quam primum errata fatere:
    dicere quo pereas saepe in amore levat.

---

[15] quid si non *interpret. Pope**
[28] limine *Heinsius*: nomine Ω
[30] tu fuge *Tappe*: aufuge Ω

---

[a] Like Tantalus: W. R. Smyth (*Classical Quarterly* 43
[1949] 122ff) lists a number of places where Propertius'
language suggests well-known mythological situations.

if you had no ready material for your pen! As it is, you are insane, standing in midstream and looking for water. [a]

¹⁷ Moreover, you are not yet even pale or touched by real fire: this is but the first spark of the evil to come. Then you will rather tackle Armenian tigresses and rather experience the chains on Ixion's wheel, than feel Cupid's bow strike to your very heart again and again, and be unable to deny a thing to the tantrums of your mistress. Never has Love provided anyone with easy wings without pulling him down with alternate hand. [b]

²⁵ Nor be deceived by her total compliance: once a woman is yours, Ponticus, she steals more deeply into your soul, especially as you will not be able to withdraw your eyes from the spell, nor Love allow you to keep watch at any other's door, that Love who does not reveal himself until his hand has pierced you to the bone [c]: do you, whoever you are, flee his perpetual allurements! If stone and oak might yield to them, [d] then how much more might you, poor vain spirit that you are!

³³ So, for very shame, admit your error at once: it oft lightens the pangs of love to reveal the source of one's undoing.

[b] Cf. Shakespeare, *Romeo and Juliet* 2.2.178ff.
[c] Cf. Theocritus, *Id.* 3.17; 7.102 ὀστίον.
[d] As to Orpheus.

PROPERTIUS

X

O iucunda quies, primo cum testis amori
    affueram vestris conscius in lacrimis!
o noctem meminisse mihi iucunda voluptas,
    o quotiens votis illa vocanda meis,
cum te complexa morientem, Galle, puella   5
    vidimus et longa ducere verba mora!
quamvis labentis premeret mihi somnus ocellos
    et mediis caelo Luna ruberet equis,
non tamen a vestro potui secedere lusu:
    tantus in alternis vocibus ardor erat.   10

sed quoniam non es veritus concredere nobis,
    accipe commissae munera laetitiae:
non solum vestros didici reticere dolores,
    est quiddam in nobis maius, amice, fide.
possum ego diversos iterum coniungere amantes,   15
    et dominae tardas possum aperire fores;
et possum alterius curas sanare recentis,
    nec levis in verbis est medicina meis.
Cynthia me docuit, semper quae cuique petenda
    quaeque cavenda forent: non nihil egit Amor.   20

tu cave ne tristi cupias pugnare puellae,
    neve superba loqui, neve tacere diu;

---

[19] cuique *Mueller*: -cumque Ω

74

BOOK I.10

Gallus in love

O delightful night, when I was there to witness your
first hour of love and was a spectator as you both
wept![a] What delightful pleasure for me to
remember that night, a night how often to be
invoked in my prayers, when I saw you, Gallus,
swooning in your girl's embrace and uttering each
word in drawn-out delay! Although sleep weighed
heavily on my drooping eyes and the blushing moon
was driving her team across mid-heaven, yet I could
not turn away from your dalliance: such passion
animated the words that passed between you.

[11] But since you did not hesitate to confide in me,
accept the reward for the joy you let me share. Not
only have I learned to keep quiet about your love-
pangs: I have something greater to offer than loyal
discretion. I can join estranged lovers again, and I
can open a mistress's reluctant door; I can cure the
fresh love-wounds of another, and the healing power
of my words is not slight. Cynthia has taught me
what everyone must always seek and what avoid:
Love has done something for me.

[21] Beware lest you seek to quarrel with a girl in
ill-temper, or speak haughtily or keep silence for

---

[a] 'The story Propertius tells in I,10,1–12 is more
shameless than anything to be found in Ovid's works'
(Hermann Fränkel, *Ovid: A Poet between Two Worlds*,
Berkeley and Los Angeles 1945, p. 190). Cf. 1.13.13–8.

neu, si quid petiit, ingrata fronte negaris,
    neu tibi pro vano verba benigna cadant.
irritata venit, quando contemnitur illa,   25
    nec meminit iustas ponere laesa minas:
at quo sis humilis magis et subiectus amori,
    hoc magis effectu saepe fruare bono.
is poterit felix una remanere puella,
    qui numquam vacuo pectore liber erit.   30

XI

Ecquid te mediis cessantem, Cynthia, Baiis,
    qua iacet Herculeis semita litoribus,
et modo Thesproti mirantem subdita regno
    proxima Misenis aequora nobilibus,
nostri cura subit memores adducere noctes?   5
    ecquis in extremo restat amore locus?
an te nescio quis simulatis ignibus hostis
    sustulit e nostris, Cynthia, carminibus,
15 ut solet amoto labi custode puella,
16   perfida communis nec meminisse deos?

atque utinam mage te remis confisa minutis
    parvula Lucrina cumba moretur aqua,   10
aut teneat clausam tenui Teuthrantis in unda
    alternae facilis cedere lympha manu,
quam vacet alterius blandos audire susurros
    molliter in tacito litore compositam!

long; if she asks for something, do not refuse her
with a graceless expression, nor let her spend kind
words in vain upon you. When she is slighted, she
shows annoyance, and, when hurt, has no mind to
discard her justified threats: but the meeker you are
and the more subservient to love, the more often
will you enjoy success. The man to find lasting bliss
in one girl is he whose heart is never empty and
fancy-free.

Cynthia at Baiae

WHILE you dally in the heart of Baiae, Cynthia,
where lies a causeway on shores made by Hercules,
and marvel that the waters but recently below
Thesprotus' kingdom are now close to renowned
Misenum, does any concern arise to bring on nights
when you remember me? Is any room left for me in
a far corner of your heart? Or has some rival by his
pretended rapture stolen you, Cynthia, from your
place in my songs, since, when there is none to
watch her, a girl will stray and, betraying her lover,
will forget the gods that sealed their troth?

[9] I would rather that some toy boat, propelled by
tiny paddles, be amusing you upon the Lucrine lake,
or that waters yielding easily to the swimmer's
alternating strokes be keeping you cloistered in the
shallow waves of Teuthras, than you be free to hear
the seductive whispers of another, comfortably
couched on a beach that tells no tales: not that you

77

non quia perspecta non es mihi cognita fama,   17
   sed quod in hac omnis parte timetur amor.
ignosces igitur, si quid tibi triste libelli
   attulerint nostri: culpa timoris erit.   20

ah mihi non maior carae custodia matris
   aut sine te vitae cura sit ulla meae!
tu mihi sola domus, tu, Cynthia, sola parentes,
   omnia tu nostrae tempora laetitiae.
seu tristis veniam seu contra laetus amicis,   25
   quicquid ero, dicam 'Cynthia causa fuit.'
tu modo quam primum corruptas desere Baias:
   multis ista dabunt litora discidium,
litora quae fuerunt castis inimica puellis:
   ah pereant Baiae, crimen amoris, aquae!   30

XII

QUID mihi desidiae non cessas fingere crimen,
   quod faciat nobis Cynthia, Roma, moram?
tam multa illa meo divisast milia lecto,
   quantum Hypanis Veneto dissidet Eridano;
nec mihi consuetos amplexu nutrit amores   5
   Cynthia, nec nostra dulcis in aure sonat.

15,16 *post* 8 *Housman*
21 ah *Lachmann* : an Ω
29 fuerunt *Scaliger* : fuerant Ω
2 Cynthia ς : conscia Ω

78

are not known to me as of tested repute, but because in this regard fear is felt for every love. So forgive me if my letters cause you any offence: my fear must take the blame.[a]

[21] Ah, I could not show a more watchful care for my dear mother[b] or have any thought for life without you. You alone are my home, Cynthia, you alone my parents, you are my every moment of happiness.[c] Whether I am downcast or joyful when I meet my friends, I shall tell them, whatever my mood, 'Cynthia was the cause.' Only, depart with all speed from corrupt Baiae: those shores will cause many to part, shores which have ever been harmful to virtuous girls: a curse on the waters of Baiae, that bring reproach on love!

Cynthia absent

WHY, Rome, do you constantly charge me with sloth, saying that it is Cynthia who causes my procrastination? She is as many miles sundered from my bed as the Hypanis is distant from the Venetian Po. Cynthia neither feeds my wonted passion with her embraces nor whispers sweetly in my ear.

[a] Cf. Shakespeare, *Venus and Adonis* 1021, 'Fie, fie, fond love, thou art so full of fear.'

[b] I.e. if she were still alive (as in the pentameter *sine te* means 'if you were to die').

[c] Cf. Homer, *Iliad* 6.429. We may surmise that Propertius had only recently lost his mother.

olim gratus eram: non ullo tempore cuiquam
    contigit ut simili posset amare fide.
invidiae fuimus: num me deus obruit? an quae
    lecta Prometheis dividit herba iugis?   10

non sum ego qui fueram: mutat via longa puellas.
    quantus in exiguo tempore fugit amor!
nunc primum longas solus cognoscere noctes
    cogor et ipse meis auribus esse gravis.

felix, qui potuit praesenti flere puellae   15
    (non nihil aspersus gaudet Amor lacrimis),
aut, si despectus, potuit mutare calores
    (sunt quoque translato gaudia servitio).
mi neque amare aliam neque ab hac desistere fas est:
    Cynthia prima fuit, Cynthia finis erit.   20

XIII

Tu, quod saepe soles, nostro laetabere casu,
    Galle, quod abrepto solus amore vacem.
at non ipse tuas imitabor, perfide, voces:
    fallere te numquam, Galle, puella velit.

dum tibi deceptis augetur fama puellis,   5
    certus et in nullo quaeris amore moram,

^{7} ullo ς: illo Ω
^{9} num ς: non Ω
^{16} aspersus *Palmer*: aspersis Ω

[7] Once I found favour with her: never was any so fortunate as to love with such return of devotion. We challenged Envy. Can a god have crushed me? Or was it a magic herb picked on Caucasian hills[a] to divide lovers?

[11] I am not what I was: a distant journey changes a woman's heart. How great a love has vanished in such a little while! Now for the first time I am forced to face long nights alone and to become a nuisance to my own ears.

[15] Happy the man who can weep in his sweetheart's presence (Love takes great joy in being sprinkled with tears) or, if spurned, has been able to change his passion (there is joy, too, in transferring one's bondage). For me it is not ordained to love another or to break with her: Cynthia was the first, Cynthia shall be the last.

Gallus going downhill

As is your way, Gallus, you will exult in my misfortune, for my love has been stolen from me and I am left alone. But I shall not copy your language, traitor: may no girl, Gallus, ever wish to play you false.

[5] While your renown for deceiving girls grows and you resolutely avoid a lasting attachment in

---

[a] Referred to as the land of Medea and witchcraft generally.

perditus in quadam tardis pallescere curis
   incipis, et primo lapsus abire gradu.
haec erit illarum contempti poena doloris:
   multarum miseras exiget una vices.   10
haec tibi vulgaris istos compescet amores,
   nec nova quaerendo semper amicus eris.

haec non sum rumore malo, non augure doctus;
   vidi ego: me quaeso teste negare potes?
vidi ego te toto vinctum languescere collo   15
   et flere iniectis, Galle, diu manibus,
et cupere optatis animam deponere labris,
   et quae deinde meus celat, amice, pudor.

non ego complexus potui diducere vestros:
   tantus erat demens inter utrosque furor.   20
non sic Haemonio Salmonida mixtus Enipeo
   Taenarius facili pressit amore deus,
nec sic caelestem flagrans amor Herculis Heben
   sensit ab Oetaeis gaudia prima rogis.

una dies omnis potuit praecurrere amantes: 25
   nam tibi non tepidas subdidit illa faces,

---

[13] non \<sum\> *Rossberg*: non *N*: [ego] non A
[17] labris ç: verbis Ω
[24] ab *Scaliger*: in Ω | rogis *Schrader*: iugis Ω

any affair, you have fallen for someone and begin to pale with a belated heartache, and, having slipped for the first time, to go astray. This girl will be the penalty for scorning those others' woes: one will exact the piteous requital for many. This girl will put a stop to your promiscuous affairs, nor, when you are for ever seeking new attachments, will you be her friend.

13 It was not from spiteful rumour or from soothsaying that I learned this; I saw it[a] with my own eyes: dare you deny it, when I was a witness? I saw you languish, Gallus, your neck tightly fastened in her embrace, and with your arms about her weep a long while; I saw you desperate to breathe out your last on those longed-for lips, and then what happened, friend, my modesty conceals.

19 No strength of mine would have availed to part your embraces: such a mad frenzy raged between you both. Not thus did the god of Taenarum, in the disguise of Haemonian Enipeus, embrace Salmoneus' child,[b] the willing victim of his love, nor thus did the passion of Hercules, all afire for divine Hebe, taste its first raptures after he had burned on an Oetean pyre.

25 A single day has achieved the outstripping of all lovers: it is no tepid torch she has kindled in your

[a] Cf. Paulus Silentiarius, A.P.5.255.
[b] Neptune and Tyro.

nec tibi praeteritos passast succedere fastus,
　　nec sinet: addictum te tuus ardor aget.
nec mirum, cum sit Iove dignae proxima Ledae
　　et Ledae partu gratior, una tribus;　　　　　　　30
illa sit Inachiis et blandior heroinis,
　　illa suis verbis cogat amare Iovem.

tu vero quoniam semel es periturus amore,
　　utere: non alio limine dignus eras.
qui tibi sit felix, quoniam novus incidit, error;　　35
　　et quotcumque voles, una sit ista tibi.

XIV

Tu licet abiectus Tiberina molliter unda
　　Lesbia Mentoreo vina bibas opere,
et modo tam celeris mireris currere lintres
　　et modo tam tardas funibus ire rates;
et nemus omne satas intendat vertice silvas,　　　5
　　urgetur quantis Caucasus arboribus;
non tamen ista meo valeant contendere amori:
　　nescit Amor magnis cedere divitiis.

---

[28] addictum *Skutsch* : adduci Ω
[29] dignae *Heinsius* : digna et Ω
[35] qui *Palmer* : quae Ω
[36] quotcumque *Fruter* : quocumque Ω

---

[a] This poem to Tullus (not named till line 20) contrasts the lover with the man of wealth.

veins, nor has she allowed your former haughtiness to come over you again, nor will she let it: your own passion will drive you into bondage. No wonder, since she is the near-equal of Leda, who was worthy of Jove, and fairer herself alone than all three of Leda's daughters; she could be even more seductive than the heroines of Argos, and with her talk force Jove to love her.

[33] But since you are about to die once and for all from love, make the most of it: your worth deserves to enter no lesser door. Since this is a new experience of love which has befallen you, may it prove propitious: and all the women that you desire, may she in her single self be to you.

Love and wealth

THOUGH you lie in luxurious[a] ease by the waters of the Tiber, drinking Lesbian wine from silverware of Mentor, and watch with enjoyment now the skiffs that speed on so fast and now the towed barges that move so slow[b]; and though your whole grove lift up its planted trunks with tops as high as the trees that press upon Caucasus: yet all those pleasures could not match my love; Love knows no yielding to enormous wealth.

[b] Cf. Tennyson, *The Lady of Shalott,* '. . . Slide the heavy barges trail'd / By slow horses; and unhail'd / The shallop flitteth silken-sail'd / Skimming down to Camelot.'

nam sive optatam mecum trahit illa quietem,
    seu facili totum ducit amore diem,   10
tum mihi Pactoli veniunt sub tecta liquores,
    et legitur Rubris gemma sub aequoribus;
tum mihi cessuros spondent mea gaudia reges:
    quae maneant, dum me fata perire volent!
nam quis divitiis adverso gaudat Amore?   15
    nulla mihi tristi praemia sint Venere!

illa potest magnas heroum infringere vires,
    illa etiam duris mentibus esse dolor:
illa neque Arabium metuit transcendere limen
    nec timet ostrino, Tulle, subire toro,   20
et miserum toto iuvenem versare cubili:
    quid relevant variis serica textilibus?
quae mihi dum placata aderit, non ulla verebor
    regna vel Alcinoi munera despicere.

XV

SAEPE ego multa tuae levitatis dura timebam,
    hac tamen excepta, Cynthia, perfidia.
aspice me quanto rapiat fortuna periclo!
    tu tamen in nostro lenta timore venis;
et potes hesternos manibus componere crines   5
    et longa faciem quaerere desidia,

---

[a] A stunned Propertius has just been informed by a
carefree and smartly groomed Cynthia that she is leaving

⁹ For whether Cynthia spends a longed-for night with me, or passes a whole day in unruffled love, then the waters of Pactolus flow under my roof, and gems are brought me from the bed of the Indian Ocean; then my joys give proof that kings will yield before me: may these endure till fate decrees my death! For who rejoices in wealth if Love smiles not on him? Let there be no riches for me if Venus frowns.

¹⁷ She can break the mighty strength of heroes, she can cause pain even to the hardest heart: for she has no dread of crossing a threshold of Arabian onyx nor fears, Tullus, to steal into a couch of purple, and to keep a poor lad twisting and turning all over his bed: what then avail his silks of varied texture? So, as long as she comes to me in good humour, I shall not hesitate to scorn the realms of any monarch, nor gifts such as Alcinous might give.

Never such treachery as this

I dreaded oft much hardship from your fickleness, Cynthia, but never such treachery as this.ᵃ See into what peril fortune plunges me! But you are slow to visit me in my hour of dread. And you have the nerve to finger and reset your hair disordered since last night, and spend idle hours trying to improve

him, her attitude recalling that of Helen in Aeschylus, *Agam.* 404ff.

nec minus Eois pectus variare lapillis,
    ut formosa novo quae parat ire viro.

at non sic Ithaci digressu mota Calypso
    desertis olim fleverat aequoribus: 10
multos illa dies incomptis maesta capillis
    sederat, iniusto multa locuta salo,
et quamvis numquam post haec visura, dolebat
    illa tamen, longae conscia laetitiae.

nec sic Aesoniden rapientibus anxia ventis   17
    Hypsipyle vacuo constitit in thalamo:
Hypsipyle nullos post illos sensit amores,
    ut semel Haemonio tabuit hospitio.   20
coniugis Euadne miseros elata per ignes
    occidit, Argivae fama pudicitiae.
15 Alphesiboea suos ultast pro coniuge fratres,
16   sanguinis et cari vincula rupit amor.

quarum nulla tuos potuit convertere mores,
    tu quoque uti fieres nobilis historia.
desine iam revocare tuis periuria verbis,   25
    Cynthia, et oblitos parce movere deos;
audax ah nimium, nostro dolitura periclo,
    si quid forte tibi durius inciderit!
alta prius retro labentur flumina ponto,
    annus et inversas duxerit ante vices,   30

[15,16] *post* 22 *Lachmann*   [29] alta . . . retro *Burman* :
multa . . . vasto Ω (cf. Ovid, *Tr.* 1.8.1)

your looks, and as eagerly adorn your breast with oriental gems as a girl determined to meet a new lover looking her best.

9 Not thus was Calypso affected by the Ithacan's departure, when in ages past she wept to the lonely waves: for many days she sat disconsolately with unkempt tresses uttering many a complaint to the unjust sea, and although she was never to see him again, yet she still felt pain when she recalled their long happiness together.

17 Not thus, as the winds hurried the son of Aeson away, stood Hypsipyle full of foreboding in the empty bedchamber: Hypsipyle never knew another love after that, once she had melted in welcome to her Haemonian guest. Finding her funeral on the sad pyre of her husband, Evadne died the glory of Argive chastity. In vengeance for her husband Alphesiboea slew her brothers, and her love broke the ties of kindred blood.

23 But none of these could mend your ways by her example, so that you too might become a noble legend. Cease now, Cynthia, to remind me of your infidelity by your words, and do not provoke the gods now that they have forgotten. Ah, woman all too rash, it is at my cost that you will suffer, should any harm befall you! Sooner shall deep rivers flow backward from the sea and sooner the year bring on

quam tua sub nostro mutetur pectore cura:
  sis quodcumque voles, non aliena tamen.

tam tibi ne viles isti videantur ocelli,
  per quos saepe mihi credita perfidiast!
hos tu iurabas, si quid mentita fuisses,   35
  ut tibi suppositis exciderent manibus:
et contra magnum potes hos attollere Solem,
  nec tremis admissae conscia nequitiae?
quis te cogebat multos pallere colores
  et fletum invitis ducere luminibus?   40
quîs ego nunc pereo, similis moniturus amantes
  non ullis tutum credere blanditiis.

XVI

QUAE fueram magnis olim patefacta triumphis,
  ianua Patriciae vota Pudicitiae,
cuius inaurati celebrarunt limina currus,
  captorum lacrimis umida supplicibus,
nunc ego, nocturnis potorum saucia rixis,   5
  pulsata indignis saepe queror manibus,

its seasons in inverted order, than the love for you in my heart shall change: be whatever you like, but be not another's.

33 Let not your eyes seem of so little worth to you, thanks to which I oft put faith in your treachery! By them you swore that, if in aught you had spoken false, they would fall out for your hands to catch! And can you lift them up to the mighty sun and not tremble to think of the wantonness you are guilty of? Who forced you to blench and turn all colours and to draw tears from your reluctant eyes? These wiles are my undoing and prompt me to warn lovers like me that there are no woman's allurements it is safe to trust.

The door's complaint

I[a] who of old stood open to welcome splendid triumphs, a door vowed to Patrician Chastity, whose threshold was thronged with gilded chariots and moistened with captives' suppliant tears, today, scarred by the nightly brawls of drunken youths, I oft complain at being battered by ill-bred hands,

---

[a] This poem is a variation of the *paraclausithyron,* the song of the excluded lover. The genre and the imagery derived from it (which pervades all Latin love poetry) are excellently treated by Copley. Distinctively, Propertius represents the door as the speaker, and the lover's song as being quoted by it.

et mihi non desunt turpes pendere corollae
  semper et exclusi signa iacere faces.

nec possum infamis dominae defendere voces,
  nobilis obscenis tradita carminibus;   10
nec tamen illa suae revocatur parcere famae,
  turpior et saecli vivere luxuria.
has inter gravius cogor deflere querelas,
  supplicis a longis tristior excubiis.
ille meos numquam patitur requiescere postes,   15
  arguta referens carmina blanditia:

'ianua vel domina penitus crudelior ipsa,
  quid mihi tam duris clausa taces foribus?
cur numquam reserata meos admittis amores,
  nescia furtivas reddere mota preces?   20
nullane finis erit nostro concessa dolori,
  turpis et in tepido limine somnus erit?
me mediae noctes, me sidera prona iacentem,
  frigidaque Eoo me dolet aura gelu.

'o utinam traiecta cava mea vocula rima   27
  percussas dominae vertat in auriculas!
sit licet et saxo patientior illa Sicano,
  sit licet et ferro durior et chalybe,   30

---

[8] exclusi *Lipsius* : -is Ω
[9] voces *Housman* : noctes Ω
[13] gravius ... querelas *Scaliger* : gravibus ... querelis Ω
[23] prona ς : plena Ω
[25,26] *post* 36 *Richmond*

and shameful garlands fail not to hang from me or torches ever cease to lie before me, signs of the excluded lover.

9 Nor am I able to protect my mistress from scandalous allegations, now given over, though once so noble, to indecent lampoons; nor is she called back to have regard for her good name and from a life more shameful than the licence of the times. While I thus complain, I am forced to more bitter lament, distressed by the long vigil of a certain suppliant. He never allows my portals any respite, as with artful blandishment he repeats his serenade.

17 'O door, far crueller even than your mistress herself, why are you silent with your rigid panels shut tight against me? Why are you never unbolted to admit my love, incapable of being stirred and passing on my stealthy prayers? Shall no end be granted to my sufferings, and mine be a shameful sleep on a doorstep scarcely warm? For me, as I lie prostrate, grieve the midnight hours, for me the stars as they set, and for me the chill breeze that comes with the frosty dawn.

27 'O that a word of mine might pass through an open crack, and reach and strike upon my sweetheart's ears! Though she be more impassive even than Sicilian lava, though she be harder even than iron or steel, yet she will not be able to control

non tamen illa suos poterit compescere ocellos,
    surget et invitis spiritus in lacrimis.
nunc iacet alterius felici nixa lacerto,
    at mea nocturno verba cadunt Zephyro.

'sed tu sola mei, tu maxima causa doloris,   35
    victa meis numquam, ianua, muneribus,
25 tu sola humanos numquam miserata dolores
26   respondes tacitis mutua cardinibus.
te non ulla meae laesit petulantia linguae;
    quae solet irato dicere tanta ioco,
ut me tam longa raucum patiare querela
    sollicitas trivio pervigilare moras?   40

'at tibi saepe novo deduxi carmina versu,
    osculaque innixus pressa dedi gradibus.
ante tuos quotiens verti me, perfida, postes,
    debitaque occultis vota tuli manibus!'
haec ille et si quae miseri novistis amantes,   45
    et matutinis obstrepit alitibus.
sic ego nunc dominae vitiis et semper amantis
    fletibus alterna differor invidia.

---

[38] tanta ioco ς: tota loco Ω
[40] moras? *N*: moras. *A**
[42] innixus pressa *Alton*: impressis nixa Ω
[48] alterna *Markland*: aeterna Ω

her eyes, and sobs will arise amid involuntary tears. Now she lies cradled in the happy arms of another, while my words fall unheeded on the night wind.

35 'But you, the only, you the supreme cause of my sorrow, O door, never won over by my gifts, you only never take pity on human sorrows and, your hinges silent, never make sympathetic answer. No outburst of my tongue has injured you. What awful remarks is it wont to utter in bitter jest that you should suffer me, hoarse with lengthy complaints, to spend long vigils in torment at the street corner.

41 'Often have I rather spun you new strains of song and, upon my knees, passionately kissed your steps. How often, deceitful door, have I turned round before your portals and with stealthy hands paid the due vow!' Thus cries he, with all the pleas known to you wretched lovers, and his voice is raised against the dawn chorus. So now through my mistress's vices and her lover's incessant laments I suffer defamation amid ill-will on either count.

XVII

ET merito, quoniam potui fugisse puellam,
    nunc ego desertas alloquor alcyonas.
nec mihi Cassiope salvo visura carinam,
    omniaque ingrato litore vota cadunt.

quin etiam absenti prosunt tibi, Cynthia, venti: 5
    aspice, quam saevas increpat aura minas.
nullane placatae veniet fortuna procellae?
    haecine parva meum funus harena teget?

tu tamen in melius saevas converte querelas:
    sat tibi sit poenae nox et iniqua vada.   10
an poteris siccis mea fata reposcere ocellis,
    ossaque nulla tuo nostra tenere sinu?

ah pereat, quicumque rates et vela paravit
    primus et invito gurgite fecit iter!
nonne fuit levius dominae pervincere mores   15
    (quamvis dura, tamen rara puella fuit),
quam sic ignotis circumdata litora silvis
    cernere et optatos quaerere Tyndaridas?

illic si qua meum sepelissent fata dolorem,
    ultimus et posito staret amore lapis,   20

[3] salvo *Richmond*: solito Ω
[11] reposcere *Baehrens*: reponere Ω

BOOK I.17

The poet shipwrecked

YES, and deservedly, for I had the gall to run away from my sweetheart, do I now address my lament to the solitary sea-gulls. Nor is Cassiope's haven[a] destined to behold my ship arrive with me safe and sound, but all my vows are wasted on a heartless coast.

5 Even though you are not here, Cynthia, the winds are taking your side: see what fierce threats the gale is muttering! Shall the blessing of the storm's abatement never come? Is this small strip of sand to cover my corpse?

9 But give your fierce complaints a kindlier turn: consider the darkness and treacherous shoals as penalty enough. Will you be able to ask about my death dry-eyed and never hold my bones to your breast?

13 Death to whoever first produced ships and sails and journeyed over the reluctant sea! Was it not easier to conquer my mistress's temper (cruel though she was, she was still beyond compare) than thus to look upon a strand hemmed in by strange forests, and vainly seek Castor and Pollux, whom I need so much?

19 Were it at home that some fate had put an end to my sorrow, and a gravestone stood upon my buried love, she would at my funeral have made

[a] It lay on the route between Brundisium and Greece (but it would be rash to assume that Propertius was ever shipwrecked on the way there).

97

illa meo caros donasset funere crines,
  molliter et tenera poneret ossa rosa;
illa meum extremo clamasset pulvere nomen,
  ut mihi non ullo pondere terra foret.

at vos, aequoreae formosa Doride natae,   25
  candida felici solvite uela choro:
si quando vestras labens Amor attigit undas,
  mansuetis socio parcite litoribus.

XVIII

HAEC certe deserta loca et taciturna querenti,
  et vacuum Zephyri possidet aura nemus.
hic licet occultos proferre impune dolores,
  si modo sola queant saxa tenere fidem.
unde tuos primum repetam, mea Cynthia, fastus?   5
  quod mihi das flendi, Cynthia, principium?
qui modo felicis inter numerabar amantes,
  nunc in amore tuo cogor habere notam.

quid tantum merui? quae te mihi crimina mutant?
  an nova tristitiae causa puella tuae?   10
sic mihi te referas, levis, ut non altera nostro
  limine formosos intulit ulla pedes.

⁹ crimina ς : carmina Ω

ᵃ Locks of hair were offered to the dead from Homeric
times onward, cf. Homer, *Il.* 23.141; Ovid, *Her.* 11.116.
  ᵇ For flowers in the urn, cf. Juvenal, 7.207f.

offering of her precious hair[a] and gently laid my bones in a soft bed of roses[b]; she would have cried out my name[c] over my ashes, praying that earth lie lightly on me.

25 But you, mermaid daughters of lovely Doris, come in prospering dance and unfurl our white sails: if ever Cupid swooping down has touched your waves, be merciful to a fellow victim and grant him quieter shores than these.

The poet in solitude

THIS at least is a lonely spot that will keep silent about my grievances, and the zephyr's breath holds sway over the empty grove. Here I can freely pour forth my secret anguish, unless the lonely rocks fail to keep faith. At what point, my Cynthia, shall I begin the story of your proud disdain? What, Cynthia, was the initial cause of my tears? I, who lately was reckoned among happy lovers, must now wear a mark of shame in the register of your love.

9 What is my great offence? What allegations have made you change towards me? Is another girl the cause of your coldness? As surely as I wish your return, capricious one, no other girl has ever set her dainty feet on my threshold. Although my distress

---

[c] A reference to the conclamatio, the custom of calling on the dead repeatedly by name, cf. 2.13.28.

quamvis multa tibi dolor hic meus aspera debet,
    non ita saeva tamen venerit ira mea,
ut tibi sim merito semper furor, et tua flendo   15
    lumina deiectis turpia sint lacrimis.

an quia parva damus mutato signa colore,
    et non ulla meo clamat in ore fides?
vos eritis testes, si quos habet arbor amores,
    fagus et Arcadio pinus amica deo.   20
ah quotiens vestras resonant mea verba sub umbras,
    scribitur et teneris Cynthia corticibus!
ah tua quot peperit nobis iniuria curas,
    quae solum tacitis cognita sunt foribus!

omnia consuevi timidus perferre superbae   25
    iussa neque arguto facta dolore queri.
pro quo continui montes et frigida rupes
    et datur inculto tramite dura quies;
et quodcumque meae possunt narrare querelae,
    cogor ad argutas dicere solus aves.   30
sed qualiscumque's, resonent mihi 'Cynthia' silvae,
    nec deserta tuo nomine saxa vacent.

[21] vestras *Koppiers*: teneras Ω
[22] teneris *Guyet*: vestris Ω
[23] ah . . . quot ς: an . . . quod Ω
[27] continui (>c̆t-) montes *Heinsius*: divini (<dinui) fontes Ω

owes you much ill-treatment, yet my anger shall not vent itself in such ferocity that I should give you just cause for everlasting fury or that in weeping your eyes should lose their beauty by shedding floods of tears.

¹⁷ Or is it that I give scant token of my feelings by change of complexion and there is no loyalty that cries aloud on my lips? You trees will be my witnesses, if trees know any love, Beech and Pine[a] beloved of the god of Arcady. Ah, how often my words echo beneath your shade, and Cynthia's name is written on your delicate[b] bark! Ah, how much anguish has your cruelty caused me, anguish known only to your silent door!

²⁵ Faint-hearted, I have accustomed myself to put up with a woman's every tyrannical command and not complain in shrill cries of what she has done. My reward for this is endless hills, cold rock, and comfortless repose in the trails of the wilderness. And all that my dissatisfaction can express I am forced to utter in solitude to the twittering birds. Yet, whatever you are, let the woods echo to my song of 'Cynthia,' let the lonely rocks reverberate with your name!

---

[a] Pitys (πίτυς = pinus), a wood-nymph changed into a pine tree to escape Pan's attentions.
[b] Cf. Virgil, *Ecl.* 10.54f *teneris . . . arboribus.*

XIX

NON ego nunc tristis vereor, mea Cynthia, Manes,
    nec moror extremo debita fata rogo;
sed ne forte tuo careat mihi funus amore,
    hic timor est ipsis durior exsequiis.
non adeo leviter nostris puer haesit ocellis,   5
    ut meus oblito pulvis amore vacet.

illic Phylacides iucundae coniugis heros
    non potuit caecis immemor esse locis,
sed cupidus falsis attingere gaudia palmis
    Thessalis antiquam venerat umbra domum.   10
illic quidquid ero, semper tua dicar imago:
    traicit et fati litora magnus amor.

illic formosae veniant chorus heroinae,
    quas dedit Argivis Dardana praeda viris:
quarum nulla tua fuerit mihi, Cynthia, forma   15
    gratior et (Tellus hoc ita iusta sinat)
quamvis te longae remorentur fata senectae,
    cara tamen lacrimis ossa futura meis.

quae tu viva mea possis sentire favilla!
    tum mihi non ullo mors sit amara loco.   20

---

[10] Thessalis ς : -us Ω

---

[a] 'In Propertius there is more frequently a culminating

BOOK I.19

The poet faces death

I fear not now, my Cynthia, the grim world of the
dead, nor grudge I the fate owed to the final pyre;
but that my funeral may lack your love is a fear I
dread more than death itself. Cupid has not so
lightly settled on my eyes that my dust could forget
and lose my love for you.

[7] There, in the regions of darkness, the scion of
Phylacus could not forget his lovely wife, but yearn-
ing to touch with unreal hands his heart's delight,
came, a ghost of Thessaly, to his ancient home.
There, whatever I shall be, I shall always be called
the shade that belongs to you: the might of love
crosses even the shores of death.[a]

[13] There, even if in a troupe to greet me come all
the lovely heroines whom the sack of Troy gave to
the heroes of Greece, there is none of them, Cynthia,
whose beauty would please me more than yours;
and (so may the righteous Earth permit) though the
destiny of a long old age detain you, still will your
body be dear to my tears.

[19] If only you could feel this, you alive and I then
ashes! Then, wherever I was, death would hold no

than a subsiding effect in the second line of the couplet.
The pentameter instead of being a weaker echo of the hex-
ameter is the stronger line of the two, and has a weightier
movement' (Sellar, p. 307).

quam vereor, ne te contempto, Cynthia, busto
    abstrahat a nostro pulvere iniquus Amor,
cogat et invitam lacrimas siccare cadentis!
    flectitur assiduis certa puella minis.

quare, dum licet, inter nos laetemur amantes: 25
    non satis est ullo tempore longus amor.

XX

Hoc pro continuo te, Galle, monemus amore,
    quod tibi ne vacuo defluat ex animo:
saepe imprudenti fortuna occurrit amanti:
    crudelis Minyis sic erat Ascanius.

est tibi non infra specie, non nomine dispar,   5
    Theiodamanteo proximus ardor Hylae:
huic tu, sive leges Umbrae rate flumina silvae,
    sive Aniena tuos tinxerit unda pedes,
sive Gigantei spatiabere litoris ora,
    sive ubicumque vago fluminis hospitio,   10
Nympharum semper cupidas defende rapinas
    (non minor Ausoniis est amor Adryasin);
ne tibi sit duros montes et frigida saxa,
    Galle, neque expertos semper adire lacus.

---

^{22} a ç: e Ω ^{2} quod *Heyworth**: id Ω
^{4} sic erat *Baehrens*: dixerat *A*: dixerit *N*
^{5} specie *Baehrens*: speciem Ω
^{7} huic *Auratus*: hunc Ω | Umbrae <rate> *Richmond*: umbrosae Ω ^{9} Gigantei ç: -ea Ω

sting for me. How I fear, Cynthia, that you would spurn my grave, that cruel Love may tear you away from my dust and force you against your will to dry the falling tears! Eventually the truest girl yields to incessant importunity.

25 So, while we may, let us love and be happy together: never, however long, does love last long enough.

The story of Hylas

IN[a] return for your unwavering love, Gallus, I give you this warning, and let it not drain away from your unthinking mind: chance often confronts the lover when he least expects. Just so did the Ascanius prove cruel to the Argonauts.

5 Your flame resembles Hylas, son of Theodamas, not inferior to his beauty, not unlike in name. Whether you sail on the river that flows through Umbria's woods, or bathe your feet in Anio's waters, or pace the shores of the Giants' strand, or anywhere a river's wandering waters welcome you, ward off from him the ever lustful hands of the Nymphs (the western Dryads are no less amorous than their sisters), lest it be your fate, Gallus, in endless quest to visit bleak hills and icy crags and pools not tried before.

[a] A cautionary tale for Gallus, who risks losing his boy-friend (= Hylas) to one of the pretty girls (= Hamadryads) attracted by him.

quae miser ignotis error perpessus in oris   15
    Herculis indomito fleverat Ascanio.
namque ferunt olim Pagasae navalibus Argo
    egressam longe Phasidos isse viam,
et iam praeteritis labentem Athamantidos undis
    Mysorum scopulis applicuisse ratem.   20
hic manus heroum, placidis ut constitit oris,
    mollia composita litora fronde tegit.
at comes invicti iuvenis processerat ultra
    raram sepositi quaerere fontis aquam.

hunc duo sectati fratres, Aquilonia proles   25
    (nunc superat Zetes, nunc superat Calais),
oscula suspensis instabant carpere plantis,
    oscula et alterna ferre supina fuga.
ille sed extrema pendentes ludit in ala
    et volucris ramo summovet insidias.   30
iam Pandioniae cessit genus Orithyiae:
    ah dolor! ibat Hylas, ibat Hamadryasin.

hic erat Arganthi Pege sub vertice montis,
    grata domus Nymphis umida Thyniasin,

---

[17] Argo *Volscus* : argon Ω
[26] nunc superat (*bis*) *Rossberg* : hunc super et Ω
[27] plantis ς : palmis Ω
[29] sub extrema pendens secluditur Ω, *corr. Heinsius*

---

[a] 'Propertius is not so much telling a story as describing a picture' (Rothstein).

106

[15] Such woes the ill-starred wanderer Hercules endured in a foreign land when he wept by the unrelenting Ascanius. For once on a time, they say, the Argo left the dockyards of Pagasa and went on its long voyage to Phasis, and having now glided past the waves of the Hellespont brought its hull alongside the cliffs of Mysia. Here the band of heroes set foot upon the peaceful shore and covered the ground with a soft carpet of leaves. But the squire of the invincible prince ranged farther afield to seek the choice water of a sequestered spring.

[25] Pursuing him, two brothers, sons of the North Wind (now Zetes overtakes him, now Calais overtakes), pressed with airborne feet to snatch kisses, retreating each in turn to plant kisses from below. But he at wing's length mocks them as they hover and wards off with a bough their winged assault.[a] At last they of Pandion's line, the sons of Orithyia, gave up, and Hylas went on, alas, went on[b] to the Hamadryads.

[33] Here beneath the crest of Arganthus' mount lay the well of Pege, a watery haunt[c] dear to Bithynia's nymphs; overhead from deserted trees

---

[b] Jumping from the frying-pan into the fire.

[c] Regrettably only a few lines of James Elroy Flecker's versions of Propertius have been preserved, among them:

> Wherein Bithynian Naiads take their ease,
> By leafage overarched, where apples hide
> Whilst the dew kisses them on the unknown trees.

quam supra nulli pendebant debita curae   35
   roscida desertis poma sub arboribus,
et circum irriguo surgebant lilia prato
   candida purpureis mixta papaveribus.
quae modo decerpens tenero pueriliter ungui
   proposito florem praetulit officio,   40
et modo formosis incumbens nescius undis
   errorem blandis tardat imaginibus.

tandem haurire parat demissis flumina palmis
   innixus dextro plena trahens umero.
cuius ut accensae Dryades candore puellae   45
   miratae solitos destituere choros
prolapsum et leviter facili traxere liquore,
   tum sonitum rapto corpore fecit Hylas.
cui procul Alcides ter 'Hyla!' respondet: at illi
   nomen ab extremis montibus aura refert.   50

his, o Galle, tuos monitus servabis amores,
   formosum ni vis perdere rursus Hylan.

---

[35] nulli ς: nullae Ω
[47] et *add. Heinsius: om.* Ω
[49] ter Hyla respondet at *Fontein* : iterat responsa sed Ω
[50] montibus *Heinsius* : fontibus Ω
[52] nymphis credere visus Ω, *corr. Palmer*

hung dewy apples, owing naught to the hand of man, and round about in the water-meadow grew white lilies mingled with crimson poppies. Now in boyish delight plucking these with delicate nail, putting flowers before his appointed task, and now unwarily bending over the beauteous pool, he prolongs his truancy because of its charming reflections.

[43] At length, with lowered hands he prepares to cup the water, leaning on his right shoulder to draw a full measure. When the tree-nymphs, fired by his beauty, abandoned in wonder their accustomed dance and on his slipping pulled him nimbly through the yielding water, then by the snatching of his body did Hylas cause a loud sound.[a] In answer Hercules from afar thrice called out 'Hylas!,' but to him from distant hills the breeze echoes naught save the name.

[51] Be warned by this tale, Gallus, and guard your love, unless you wish to repeat the loss of beautiful Hylas.

***

[a] For he had no time to utter a word.

PROPERTIUS

XXI

Tu, qui consortem properas evadere casum,
    miles ab Etruscis saucius aggeribus,
quid nostro gemitu turgentia lumina torques?
    pars ego sum vestrae proxima militiae.
sic te servato possint gaudere parentes,   5
    haec soror acta tuis sentiat e lacrimis:
Gallum per medios ereptum Caesaris enses
    effugere ignotas non potuisse manus;
et quaecumque super dispersa invenerit ossa
    montibus Etruscis, haec sciat esse mea.   10

XXII

Qualis et unde genus, qui sint mihi, Tulle, Penates,
    quaeris pro nostra semper amicitia.
si Perusina tibi patriae sunt nota sepulcra,
    Italiae duris funera temporibus,
cum Romana suos egit discordia cives —   5
    sic mihi praecipue, pulvis Etrusca, dolor,

---

[5] [ut] possint Ω, *corr. Passerat*
[6] haec *Beroaldus* : ne Ω
[6] sic ς : sit Ω

Epitaph: on Gallus

SOLDIER,[a] wounded on the Tuscan ramparts, who hasten to avoid your comrade's doom, why at my groan do you not turn bulging eyes upon me? I am the closest person to you among your comrades-in-arms. On this condition may your parents rejoice at your safe return: from your tears let your sister learn the news that Gallus, though he passed unscathed through Caesar's lines, yet could not escape an unknown killer; and, whatever bones she finds scattered on the Tuscan hillside, tell her that these are mine.

Epilogue: the poet's birthplace

WHAT[b] is my rank, whence my lineage, and where my home, Tullus, you ask in our eternal friendship's name. If you know Perusia, grave of our countrymen who fell in the days of Italy's agony, when discord at Rome took hold of her citizens—soil of Etruria, especially to me do you

---

[a] The poet imaginatively dramatizes the epitaph so as to represent the dead Gallus as uttering it to the brother of his betrothed; the poem which follows reveals that both were kinsmen of Propertius.

[b] The poem, addressed to the dedicatee of Book 1, serves as a *sphragis* or signature, much as the last lines of the *Georgics*.

PROPERTIUS

tu proiecta mei perpessa's membra propinqui,
   tu nullo miseri contegis ossa solo —
proxima suppositos contingens Umbria campos
   me genuit terris fertilis uberibus.   10

[9] suppositos . . . campos *Postgate* : -o . . . -o Ω

bring grief, for you have borne the abandoned limbs of my kinsman[a] with not a handful of earth to cover his poor bones—there neighbouring Umbria, bordering on the plains below, a country rich in fertile fields, gave me birth.

[a] We are meant to identify him with the dead Gallus of the preceding poem.

BOOK TWO

As Lachmann first realized, Book 2 is a conflation of two books: its bulk is far too large for an Augustan poetry book; and at 2.13.25 the poet implies that he is writing his third book. But this section of Propertius' oeuvre is badly mutilated. We often meet with sequences which are fragmentary or dislocated or even interpolated, a baffling situation only emphasized by the unflawed beauty of 2.12, the poet's finest lyric. The themes of this section are still centred on a lover's emotions, and Cynthia still dominates them. Although Maecenas would like Propertius to sing of loftier themes, the poet in 2.1 protests his lack of ability to do so, but in 2.10 (perhaps the conclusion of the second book) brashly promises to celebrate Augustus in the future. However, in 2.13 (possibly the opening of his third book) he confesses his helplessness. Still, as he proceeds, Propertius begins to spread his wings in varying and dramatizing his material, in embarking on extensive compositions, and in confidently assuming his poetic greatness.

LIBER SECUNDUS

I

Quaeritis, unde mihi totiens scribantur amores,
    unde meus veniat mollis in ora liber.
non haec Calliope, non haec mihi cantat Apollo:
    ingenium nobis ipsa puella facit.
sive illam Cois fulgentem incedere vidi,   5
    totum de Coa veste volumen erit;
seu vidi ad frontem sparsos errare capillos,
    gaudet laudatis ire superba comis;
sive lyrae carmen digitis percussit eburnis,
    miramur, facilis ut premat arte manus;   10
seu compescentis somnum declinat ocellos,
    invenio causas mille poeta novas;
seu nuda erepto mecum luctatur amictu,
    tum vero longas condimus Iliadas:
seu quidquid fecit sivest quodcumque locuta,   15
    maxima de nihilo nascitur historia.

---

[5] vidi ς: cogis Ω (*dittography of* cois)
[6] totum de ς: hac totum e Ω
[11] compescentes *Leo*: cum poscentes Ω

---

[a] 'You ask, why thus my Loves I still rehearse?
    Whence the soft Strain & ever-melting Verse?'

THE SECOND BOOK

The task

You ask how it is that I compose love poems so often, how it is that my book sounds so soft upon the lips.[a] It is not Calliope, not Apollo that puts these songs in my mind: my sweetheart herself creates the inspiration. If I have seen her step forth dazzling in Coan silks, a whole book will emerge from the Coan garment; if I have seen the locks straying scattered on her brow, I praise her locks and for joy she walks with head held high; if with ivory fingers she strikes the melody of the lyre, I marvel how skilfully she applies her easy touch; or if she lowers eyelids that fight against sleep, the poet in me finds a thousand new conceits; or if, her dress torn off, she struggles naked with me, then, be sure of it, I compose long Iliads: whatever she has said, whatever she has said, from absolutely nothing is born a grand legend.

Thomas Gray, whose translation of the whole poem (1742), sent to Richard West, is to be found (with the latter's criticisms) in the *Correspondence* (ed. Toynbee and Whibley) I 197ff.

quod mihi si tantum, Maecenas, fata dedissent,
    ut possem heroas ducere in arma manus,
non ego Titanas canerem, non Ossan Olympo
    impositam, ut caeli Pelion esset iter,   20
nec veteres Thebas, nec Pergama nomen Homeri,
    Xerxis et imperio bina coisse vada,
regnave prima Remi aut animos Carthaginis altae,
    Cimbrorumque minas et benefacta Mari:
bellaque resque tui memorarem Caesaris, et tu   25
    Caesare sub magno cura secunda fores.

nam quotiens Mutinam aut civilia busta Philippos
    aut canerem Siculae classica bella fugae,
eversosque focos antiquae gentis Etruscae,
    et Ptolemaeei litora capta Phari,   30
aut canerem Aegyptum et Nilum, cum attractus in
    septem captivis debilis ibat aquis,   [urbem
aut regum auratis circumdata colla catenis,
    Actiaque in Sacra currere rostra Via;
te mea Musa illis semper contexeret armis,   35
    et sumpta et posita pace fidele caput.
Theseus infernis, superis testatur Achilles,
    hic Ixioniden, ille Menoetiaden;

---

[a] Embarking on a *recusatio* (see Index), a refusal to comply with a request (usually to write an epic) as did Callimachus in the prologue to the *Aitia*.
[b] Both battles were victories of Octavian.

^{17} But^a if only fate had so endowed me, Mae-
cenas, that my Muse could lead a hero's hands
to arms, I should not sing of Titans, or Ossa piled
on Olympus that Pelion might become the path
to heaven; or of ancient Thebes, or Pergamum,
Homer's glory, and the union of two seas at Xerxes'
command, or the early reign of Remus or the fury of
lofty Carthage, the Cimbrian menace and the splen-
did feats of Marius: I should tell of your Caesar's
wars and policies, and after mighty Caesar you
would be my second theme.

^{27} For as often as I sang of Mutina or Philippi,^{b}
where Roman brought Roman to the grave, or the
naval war and the rout off Sicily,^{c} or the ruined
hearths of Etruria's ancient race,^{d} and the coasts of
Ptolemaic Pharos captured; or I should sing of
Egypt and the Nile,^{e} when, haled into Rome, it
flowed flagging with its seven streams captive; or
the necks of kings encircled with chains of gold and
Actian prows speeding along the Sacred Way: my
Muse would always be weaving you into these
exploits, you the soul of loyalty in commending as in
rejecting peace. Theseus to the shades below,
Achilles to the gods above proclaim a comrade's love,
the one of Ixion's, the other of Menoetius' son;

^{c} The defeat of Sextus Pompeius at Naulochus in 36.
^{d} The operations against Perusia in 41–40.
^{e} The Alexandrian War following the battle of Actium;
and the subsequent triumph in Rome in 29.

3.9.33   Caesaris et famae vestigia iuncta tenebis:
3.9.34   Maecenatis erunt vera tropaea fides.

    sed neque Phlegraeos Iovis Enceladique tumultus
       intonet angusto pectore Callimachus,   40
    nec mea conveniunt duro praecordia versu
       Caesaris in Phrygios condere nomen avos.
    navita de ventis, de tauris narrat arator,
       enumerat miles vulnera, pastor oves;
    nos contra angusto versamus proelia lecto: 45
       qua pote quisque, in ea conterat arte diem.

    laus in amore mori: laus altera, si datur uno
       posse frui: fruar o solus amore meo,
    [si memini, solet illa levis culpare puellas,
       et totam ex Helena non probat Iliada.]   50
    seu mihi sunt tangenda novercae pocula Phaedrae,
       pocula privigno non nocitura suo,
    seu mihi Circaeo pereundumst gramine, sive
       Colchis Iolciacis urat aena focis.
    una meos quoniam praedatast femina sensus,   55
       ex hac ducentur funera nostra domo.

    omnis humanos sanat medicina dolores:
       solus amor morbi non amat artificem.
    tarda Philoctetae sanavit crura Machaon,
       Phoenicis Chiron lumina Phillyrides,   60

3.9.33,34 *post* 38 *Housman*
[45] versamus *Volscus* : -antes Ω   [49,50] *secl. Carutti*

your footsteps will march along with Caesar's renown: Maecenas' loyalty shall prove his true trophies.

³⁹ But neither would the slender utterance of Callimachus suffice to thunder forth the battle waged on Phlegra's plain between Jove and Enceladus, nor are my powers fitted to enshrine in martial strains the name of Caesar among his Phrygian ancestors. The sailor tells of winds, the ploughman of oxen; the soldier counts his wounds, the shepherd his sheep; I for my part wage wars within the narrow confines of a bed: let everyone spend his life in the trade he practises best.

⁴⁷ To die in love is glory: and glory yet again to enjoy a single love: O may I alone enjoy the love that is mine, [As I recall, she likes to blame fickle girls and on Helen's account censures the whole Iliad] though I be doomed to taste the potion of stepmother Phaedra, a potion not destined to corrupt her stepson, though I have to die of Circe's herbs, or the Colchian witch heat for me her cauldron upon the hearths of Iolcos. Since one woman has stolen away my feelings, from her house only will my funeral train set forth.

⁵⁷ Medicine can cure all human pains: only love loves not a doctor of its disease. Machaon healed the lame legs of Philoctetes, and Chiron, son of Phillyra, the blindness of Phoenix; and the god of Epidaurus

et deus exstinctum Cressis Epidaurius herbis
    restituit patriis Androgeona focis,
Mysus et Haemonia iuvenis qua cuspide vulnus
    senserat, hac ipsa cuspide sensit opem.
hoc si quis vitium poterit mihi demere, solus   65
    Tantaleae poterit tradere poma manu;
dolia virgineis idem ille repleverit urnis,
    ne tenera assidua colla graventur aqua;
idem Caucasia solvet de rupe Promethei
    bracchia et a medio pectore pellet avem.   70

quandocumque igitur vitam me fata reposcent,
    et breve in exiguo marmore nomen ero,
Maecenas, nostrae spes invidiosa iuventae,
    et vitae et morti gloria iusta meae,
si te forte meo ducet via proxima busto,   75
    esseda caelatis siste Britanna iugis,
taliaque illacrimans mutae iace verba favillae:
    'huic misero fatum dura puella fuit.'

II

LIBER eram et vacuo meditabar vivere lecto;
    at me composita pace fefellit Amor.
cur haec in terris facies humana moratur?
    Iuppiter, ignosco pristina furta tua.

---

[71] me ς: mea Ω (cf. 24.35; 4.2.5)

by his Cretan herbs restored the lifeless Androgeon
to his father's hearth; and the Mysian prince who
received his wound from the Thessalian's spear,
from the selfsame spear received its cure. Only a
man who can rid me of this failing will be able to put
fruit in Tantalus's hand; he too will fill the casks
from the maidens'[a] pitchers, lest their delicate
necks be bowed by the eternal burden of water; and
he too will release Prometheus' arms from his crag
on the Caucasus and drive the vulture away from
the middle of his breast.

[71] When, therefore, fate claims back from me my
life, and I become a brief name on a tiny marble
slab, then, Maecenas, hope and envy of Roman
youth, my rightful pride in life and in death, should
your travels chance to bring you close to my tomb,
halt your British chariot with its figured harness,
and, shedding a tear, pay this tribute to my silent
embers: 'An unrelenting girl was the death of this
poor man!'[b]

Cynthia the nonpareil

FREE I was, intending to live with an unshared bed;
but in making peace Love tricked me. Why does
such beauty linger on earth among mortals? Ah,
Jove, I pardon your amours in days of old.

---

[a] The Danaids.   [b] 'He lived, while She was kind,. &
when she frown'd, he died' (Gray).

fulva comast longaeque manus, et maxima toto   5
   corpore, et incedit vel Iove digna soror,
aut ceu Munychias Pallas spatiatur ad aras,
   Gorgonis anguiferae pectus operta comis;
aut patrio qualis ponit vestigia ponto   *8a*
   mille Venus teneris cincta Cupidinibus.   *8b*

cedite iam, divae, quas pastor viderat olim   13
   Idaeis tunicas ponere verticibus!
hanc utinam faciem nolit mutare senectus,   15
   etsi Cumaeae saecula vatis aget!

III

'Qui nullam tibi dicebas iam posse nocere,
   haesisti, cecidit spiritus ille tuus!
vix unum potes, infelix, requiescere mensem,
   et turpis de te iam liber alter erit.'
quaerebam, sicca si posset piscis harena   5
   nec solitus ponto vivere torvus aper;
aut ego si possem studiis vigilare severis:
   differtur, numquam tollitur ullus amor.

---

[7] ceu *Baehrens*: cum Ω | Munychias *Heinsius*: dulichias Ω
[8a8b] *lac. coni. et suppl. ex grat. Housman*
[9–12] *post* 2.29.28 *Richardson**

---

[a] 'Propertius stands alone among the poets of his day in his praise of the *fulva coma* and his opposition to the

124

BOOK II.3

[5] She has auburn[a] hair and taper hands; her tall figure is regal, and she walks worthy even of Jove, as his sister; or like Pallas as she steps up to Athenian altars, her bosom covered with the Gorgon's chevelure of snakes; *or like Venus attended by a thousand tender Cupids, setting foot upon the sea that gave her birth.*

[13] Make way at last, ye goddesses whom the shepherd saw disrobe on the peaks of Ida long ago. Oh, may old age refuse to change these looks, although she lives the centuries of Cumae's Sibyl!

Enslaved again

'You were saying that no girl could hurt you now, and here you are caught! Your proud spirit has succumbed! You can scarcely keep quiet for a single month, poor wretch, and now a second book[b] will prove a source of scandal about you.' I tried to learn whether a fish could live on dry sand or a wild boar, against his habit, in the sea; to learn, that is, whether I could spend my nights in serious study: love may be put off, but is never got rid of.

---

flava coma [cf. 2.18D.26] or artificially colored "golden" hair, which was the fashion of the time ... possessed by Catullus's Berenice, Vergil's Dido, Tibullus's Delia; and in Horace, Pyrrha, Phyllis, Chloe, and Ganymedes' (Carter, *ad loc.*).

[b] A clear indication that Propertius regarded this poem as occurring in his *Elegiarum Liber Secundus.*

PROPERTIUS

nec me tam facies, quamvis sit candida, cepit
    (lilia non domina sunt magis alba mea),   10
nec de more comae per levia colla fluentes,
    non oculi, geminae, sidera nostra, faces,
nec si quando Arabo lucet bombyce puella   15
    (non sum de nihilo blandus amator ego)
11 ut Maeotica nix minio si certet Hibero,
12   utque rosae puro lacte natant folia,
quantum quod posito formose saltat Iaccho,   17
    egit ut euhantis dux Ariadna choros,
et quantum, Aeolio cum temptat carmina plectro,
    par Aganippaeae ludere docta lyrae,   20
et sua cum antiquae committit scripta Corinnae
    carminaque Erinnae non putat aequa suis.

non tibi nascenti primis, mea vita, diebus
    candidus argutum sternuit omen Amor?
haec tibi contulerunt caelestia munera divi,   25
    haec tibi ne matrem forte dedisse putes.
non, non humani partus sunt talia dona:
    ista decem menses non peperere bona.
gloria Romanis una's tu nata puellis:
32   post Helenam haec terris forma secunda redit.
nec semper nobiscum humana cubilia vises;   31
30   Romana accumbes prima puella Iovi.

[10] sunt ç: sint Ω   [11,12] *post* 16 *Housman*
[15] quando *Pucci* Arabo *Garrod* : qua arabio Ω
[22] Erinnae (-es *Beroaldus*) *Butrica** : quivis Ω
[23] non *N* : num *A**   [30] *cum* 32 *comm. Sterke*

BOOK II.3

⁹ Nor is it so much her face that has ensnared me, fair though it be (and lilies are not whiter than my mistress), nor her hair falling attractively over her smooth neck, nor the twin torches of her eyes, my lodestars, nor when my girl shimmers in silks of Araby (I am no lover who flatters for no reason)—as if snows of Scythia were to vie with Spanish vermillion, and like rose-petals floating in pure milk—as much as the fact that, after the wine is put out, she dances as beautifully as ever Ariadne leading her frolic maenads, and when she attempts songs on the Aeolian lyre, gifted to compose something fit for Aganippe's harp, and when she pits her writings against those of ancient Corinna and deems Erinna's poems no match for her own.

²³ Did not a propitious Love, my darling, in your first days sneeze a clear-sounding omen[a] on your birth? These celestial gifts were surely bestowed by the gods; do not imagine that your mother gave you them. No, no, such endowments are no part of human parentage: ten months never produced those gifts of yours. You were born to be the unique glory of Roman maidens: Helen had this beauty once, and now it comes to earth again. Nor will you always visit human couches in our midst: you will be the first Roman maiden to lie with Jove.

[a] A sneeze was regarded as a good omen (cf. Catullus 45.9, etc.).

hac ego nunc mirer si flagrat nostra iuventus?
    pulchrius hac fuerat, Troia, perire tibi.
olim mirabar, quod tanti ad Pergama belli   35
    Europae atque Asiae causa puella fuit:
nunc, Pari, tu sapiens et tu, Menelae, fuisti,
    tu quia poscebas, tu quia lentus eras.
digna quidem facies, pro qua vel obiret Achilles;
    vel Priamo belli causa probanda fuit.   40
si quis vult fama tabulas anteire vetustas,
    hic dominam exemplo ponat in arte meam:
sive illam Hesperiis, sive illam ostendet Eois,
    uret et Eoos, uret et Hesperios.

IV

HIS saltem ut tenear iam finibus! ei mihi, si quis,
    acrius ut moriar, venerit alter amor!   3.46
ac veluti primo taurus detractat aratra,
    post venit assueto mollis ad arva iugo,
sic primo iuvenes trepidant in amore feroces,
    dehinc domiti post haec aequa et iniqua ferunt.
turpia perpessus vates est vincla Melampus,   51
    cognitus Iphicli surripuisse boves;
quem non lucra, magis Pero formosa coegit,
    mox Amythaonia nupta futura domo.

---

[33] flagrat ς: flagret Ω
[45-54] *ante* 4.1 *ed. Ald. 1502*
[45] ei *Lachmann* : aut Ω

---

[a] Cf. Ronsard, *Sonnets à Hélène: 'Menelas fut bien sage*

[33] Can I now wonder if all our youth is set on fire by her? Better, O Troy, had it been for her that you perished. Time was I used to marvel that a girl caused the mighty war at Pergamum between Europe and Asia: I see that you, Paris, were wise, and you, too, Menelaus; you for demanding, you for reluctance to comply.[a] Her beauty merited that even Achilles should die for it; even Priam had to approve the cause of the war.[b] If any desires to surpass the ancient painters in renown, let him take my mistress as a model for his art: whether he exhibits her to the lands of the West or the East, he will set on fire both East and West.

The miseries of love

WOULD that I be held at least within these bounds! God help me if another love come and I die in sharper agony! Even as at first the bull refuses the plough, but later, his yoke grown familiar, comes docile to the field, so in the first flush of love young men are excited and hot-headed, but then, broken in, put up thereafter with fair and foul alike. Melampus the seer endured dishonouring fetters when found guilty of stealing the cattle of Iphiclus; he was not prompted by gain, but by the beautiful Pero, who was soon to be his bride in the house of Amythaon.

et Paris, ce me semble, / L'un de la demander, l'autre de la garder.'   [b] Cf. Homer, Iliad 3.154–8.

129

PROPERTIUS

multa prius dominae delicta queraris oportet,   4.1
   saepe roges aliquid, saepe repulsus eas,
et saepe immeritos corrumpas dentibus ungues,
   et crepitum dubio suscitet ira pede!
nequiquam perfusa meis unguenta capillis,   5
   ibat et expenso planta morata gradu.

non hic herba valet, non hic nocturna Cytaeis,
   non Perimedaea gramina cocta manu;
15 nam cui non ego sum fallaci praemia vati?
16   quae mea non decies somnia versat anus?
non eget hic medicis, non lectis mollibus aeger,   11
   huic nullum caeli tempus et aura nocet;
ambulat—et subito mirantur funus amici!
   sic est incautum, quidquid habetur amor.
9 quippe ubi nec causas nec apertos cernimus ictus,
10   unde tamen veniant tot mala caeca viast.

hostis si quis erit nobis, amet ille puellas: 17
   gaudeat in puero, si quis amicus erit.
tranquillo tuta descendis flumine cumba:
   quid tibi tam parvi limitis unda nocet?   20
alter saepe uno mutat praecordia verbo,
   altera vix ipso sanguine mollis erit.

---

[8] Perimedaea . . . manu ς: -ae . . . -us Ω
[9,10] *cum* 15,16 *comm. Postgate*
[20] limitis *Palmer* : litoris Ω

---

[a] A unique comment on pederasty by Propertius, not

130

[1] Many transgressions must you first bewail in your mistress, oft must you ask a favour and oft depart disappointed; oft you must spoil a blameless nail with biting, and in your anger drum the ground with a perplexed foot. All for nothing was my hair drenched in perfumes, and my feet stepped slowly with measured tread.

[7] In such a case no herb avails, no night of Colchian sorcery, no drug distilled by the hand of a Perimede; for of what deceitful soothsayer am I not the prey? What witch does not a dozen times interpret my dreams? In such a case the sick man needs no doctor or soft bed; it is not the climate or weather that does him harm. He is out walking, and all of a sudden his friends are astonished at his demise! Such an intractable thing is love, whatever it is held to be. For dark is the path, whereon we discern neither cause nor drawn weapon, but yet along it come ills in profusion.

[17] If ever I have an enemy, let him love girls; let him delight in a boy, if ever I have a friend! Down a smooth stream in a safe skiff you glide: for how can the waves of a tiny channel hurt you? A boy's heart is often mollified by a single word, whereas a girl will scarce relent though your blood be shed.[a]

himself a lover of boys. Catullus (Lesbia/Juventius) and Tibullus (Delia/Marathus) continue the bisexuality commonly found in Greek pastoral and epigram.

PROPERTIUS

V

Hoc verumst, tota te ferri, Cynthia, Roma,
    et non ignota vivere nequitia?
haec merui sperare? dabis mihi, perfida, poenas;
    et nobis aliquo, Cynthia, ventus erit.
inveniam tamen e multis fallacibus unam,   5
    quae fieri nostro carmine nota velit,
nec mihi tam duris insultet moribus, et te
    vellicet: heu sero flebis amata diu.

nunc est ira recens, nunc est discedere tempus:
    si dolor afuerit, crede, redibit amor.   10
non ita Carpathiae variant Aquilonibus undae,
    nec dubio nubes vertitur atra Noto,
quam facile irati verbo mutantur amantes:
    dum licet, iniusto subtrahe colla iugo.
nec tu non aliquid, sed prima nocte, dolebis;   15
    omne in amore malum, si patiare, levest.

at tu per dominae Iunonis dulcia iura
    parce tuis animis, vita, nocere tibi.
non solum taurus ferit uncis cornibus hostem,
    verum etiam instanti laesa repugnat ovis.   20
nec tibi periuro scindam de corpore vestis,
    nec mea praeclusas fregerit ira fores,
nec tibi conexos iratus carpere crines,
    nec duris ausim laedere pollicibus:

Cynthia's wantonness

Is this right, Cynthia? Your name is a byword throughout Rome and you are flaunting a life of shame. Have I deserved to expect this? Faithless one, I shall punish you: a wind will waft me to some haven. Though many be false, I shall find one girl who will be happy to win fame in my verse, and will not trample on me with a harsh temper like yours, but will pluck you to pieces: oh, you will weep too late, you who have been loved too long.

[9] Now, while your anger is fresh, Propertius, is the time to part: once the pain has gone, believe me, love will return. Not so lightly do Carpathian waves change under a north wind or storm clouds veer before the shifting gale of the south as angry lovers relent at a word: while the chance is yours, withdraw your neck from an unfair yoke. To be sure, you will suffer considerable pain, but only for the first night; in love every ill is light, if you but put up with it.

[17] But, darling, by the sweet pledge of lady Juno, cease to harm yourself by your tantrums. It is not only the bull that strikes his foe with curved horns, but even the injured sheep turns upon an aggressor. I shall not tear the clothes from your perjured body, nor let my anger shatter your locked door, nor bring myself in my rage to pull at your plaited hair, nor hurt you with brutal thumbs. Let some boorish

rusticus haec aliquis tam turpia proelia quaerat,   25
    cuius non hederae circuiere caput.
scribam igitur, quod non umquam tua deleat aetas,
    'Cynthia, forma potens: Cynthia, verba levis.'
crede mihi, quamvis contemnas murmura famae,
    hic tibi pallori, Cynthia, versus erit.   30

VI

Non ita complebant Ephyraeae Laidos aedes,
    ad cuius iacuit Graecia tota fores;
turba Menandreae fuerat nec Thaidos olim
    tanta, in qua populus lusit Ericthonius;
nec, quae deletas potuit componere Thebas,   5
    Phryne tam multis facta beata viris.
quin etiam falsos fingis tibi saepe propinquos,
    oscula ne desint qui tibi iure ferant.

me iuvenum pictae facies, me nomina laedunt,
    me tener in cunis et sine voce puer;   10
me laedet, si multa tibi dabit oscula mater,
    me soror et quando dormit amica simul:
omnia me laedent: timidus sum (ignosce timori)
    et miser in tunica suspicor esse virum.

---

[8] ne desint *Salutati* : nec desunt Ω
[12] quan<do> *Alton* : [cum] qua Ω

---

[a] The inconcinnity spoils what the poet intended as a devastating line and raises a doubt about the accuracy of the manuscript tradition.

clown pick these vulgar quarrels, one whose head no ivy has ever circled.

[27] So I shall write what you can never live down or cancel: 'Cynthia, mighty beauty; Cynthia, fickle in speech.'[a] Believe me, however much you disregard the mutterings of gossip, this is a verse which will make you pale.

Jealousy and licentious art

NOT thus used they to throng the house of Lais at Corinth, and at her door all Greece lay suppliant; nor did so great a crowd ever gather about Menander's Thais, in whom the people of Athens took its pleasure; nor by so many men was Phryne enriched, she whose wealth could have rebuilt ruined Thebes.[b] But not content with that you often invent sham relatives, that there be no shortage of those who have a right to kiss you.

[9] The portraits of young men make me jealous, the mention of their names, even a baby boy in the cradle who cannot talk. I shall be jealous if your mother kisses you much, or your sister, or a girlfriend when she sleeps with you. Anything will make me jealous: I am anxious (pardon my anxiety) and torment myself with the suspicion that in a woman's dress there lurks a man.

[b] Phryne offered to rebuild Thebes, which had been destroyed by Alexander (cf. Athenaeus 13.59).

his olim, ut famast, vitiis ad proelia ventumst,   15
   his Troiana vides funera principiis;
3.18.29 hinc olim ignaros luctus populavit Achivos,
3.18.30   Atridae magno cum stetit alter amor;
aspera Centauros eadem dementia iussit   17
   frangere in adversum pocula Pirithoum.

cur exempla petam Graiûm? tu criminis auctor,
   nutritus duro, Romule, lacte lupae: 20
tu rapere intactas docuisti impune Sabinas:
   per te nunc Romae quidlibet audet Amor.

felix Admeti coniunx et lectus Ulixis,
   et quaecumque viri femina limen amat!
templa Pudicitiae quid opus statuisse puellis,   25
   si cuivis nuptae quidlibet esse licet?

quae manus obscenas depinxit prima tabellas
   et posuit casta turpia visa domo,
illa puellarum ingenuos corrupit ocellos
   nequitiaeque suae noluit esse rudis.   30
ah gemat in tenebris, ista qui protulit arte
   orgia sub tacita condita laetitia!

3.18.29,30 *post* 16 *Phillimore*
3.18.29 hinc *Phillimore* : hic Ω
31 tenebris *Fontein* : terris Ω (<tebris)
32 orgia *Ruhnken* : iurgia Ω

---

[a] Cf. Livy 10.23.6, Juvenal 6.308.
[b] This is not to be referred to the pornography illus-
trated in *Eros in Pompeii: The Secret Rooms of the*

[15] These vices of old, the story goes, led to wars, from these origins arose the slaughter at Troy; hence of old did mourning ravage the unwitting Achaeans, when Agamemnon's second love cost them dear; the same frenzy bade the Centaurs hurl embossed goblets against Pirithous and break them upon his head.

[19] Why seek I precedents from Greece? You, Romulus, nursed on the harsh milk of a she-wolf, were the instigator of the crime: you taught us to rape the Sabine virgins with impunity: through your fault Cupid dares any outrage at Rome.

[23] Happy the wife of Admetus, happy the partner of Ulysses' bed, and every woman such as respects her husband's threshold! What is the use of girls founding a temple of Chastity,[a] if any bride can behave exactly as she pleases?

[27] It was the artist who first painted lewd panels and set up indecent pictures in a virtuous house, who corrupted the innocent eyes of girls, refusing to leave them ignorant of his own depravity.[b] Oh, may he be stricken with blindness, whose art has revealed the mysteries that lay concealed behind

National Museum of Naples, Michael Grant and Antonia Mulas, New York 1975, but to the romantic depiction of adulteries such as *Mars and Venus,* Mus. Naz., Naples, wall-painting from the House of Mars and Venus, Pompeii. To the point Terence, *Eun.* 584f and Augustine, *Conf.* 1.16 (Jupiter and Danaë).

non istis olim variabant tecta figuris:
  tum paries nullo crimine pictus erat.

sed nunc immeritum velavit aranea fanum   35
  et mala desertos occupat herba deos.
quos igitur tibi custodes, quae limina ponam,
  quae numquam supra pes inimicus eat?
nam nihil invitae tristis custodia prodest:
  quam peccare pudet, Cynthia, tuta sat est.   40

VII

Nos uxor numquam, numquam seducet amica: 6.41
  semper amica mihi, semper et uxor eris.
gauisa's certe sublatam, Cynthia, legem,   7.1
  qua quondam edicta flêmus uterque diu,
ni nos divideret: quamvis diducere amantes
  non queat invitos Iuppiter ipse duos.
'at magnus Caesar.' sed magnus Caesar in armis: 5
  devictae gentes nil in amore valent.

nam citius paterer caput hoc discedere collo
  quam possem nuptae perdere more faces,

---

[35] nunc *Heinsius* immeritum *Luck*: non -o Ω
[41,42] *ante* 7.1 *Luck*
[1] es *Schrader*: est Ω   [3] ni *N* (= ne ς): qui(s) *A**

---

[a] Augustus boasted of restoring eighty-two such temples
(*Res Gestae* 4.17).

silent bliss. Not with those designs used the folk of old to adorn their homes: not then were walls painted with scenes of shame. But now spiderwebs curtain the undeserving temple and rank weeds encroach on our forsaken gods.[a]

37 What guards, then, what barred threshold shall I set for you, past which no enemy foot may tread? A stern guard set over an unwilling woman is a futile precaution: she who is ashamed to sin, Cynthia, is guarded well enough.

A threat removed

NEVER shall wife, never shall mistress part us: you shall ever be mistress, ever be wife to me. How you must have rejoiced, Cynthia, at the repeal of that law,[b] whose erstwhile issuance caused us to weep for many an hour in case it parted us! Still, not even Jove himself can part two lovers against their will. 'Yet Caesar is mighty.' True, but mighty in warfare: in love the defeat of nations counts for naught.

7 For sooner should I let my head be severed from my neck than I could quench the torch of love to

---

[b] The law, proclaimed shortly before Actium to bring in money Octavian desperately needed, would seem to have imposed on bachelors a substantial tax, which Propertius was in no position to pay; anxiety over his non-compliance was ended when the law was repealed in 28. It should not be confused with Augustus' later legislation on morals and marriage. See Ernst Badian, 'A Phantom Marriage Law,' *Philologus* 129 (1985) 82–98.

aut ego transirem tua limina clausa maritus,
    respiciens udis prodita luminibus.   10
ah mea tum qualis caneret tibi tibia somnos,
    tibia funesta tristior illa tuba!
unde mihi patriis natos praebere triumphis?
    nullus de nostro sanguine miles erit.

quod si vera meae comitarem castra puellae,   15
    non mihi sat magnus Castoris iret equus.
hinc etenim tantum meruit mea gloria nomen,
    gloria ad hibernos lata Borysthenidas.
tu mihi sola places: placeam tibi, Cynthia, solus:
    hic erit et patrio nomine pluris amor.   20

VIII

Eripitur nobis iam pridem cara puella:
    et tu me lacrimas fundere, amice, vetas?
nullae sunt inimicitiae nisi amoris acerbae:
    ipsum me iugula, lenior hostis ero.
possum ego in alterius positam spectare lacerto?   5
    nec mea dicetur, quae modo dicta meast?
omnia vertuntur: certe vertuntur amores:
    vinceris a victis, haec in amore rotast.

---

[8] a victis *Barber*: aut vincis Ω

---

[a] As Orpheus looked back at Eurydice.
[b] The presentation of the poem given here follows

humour a bride's whim, or as a married man pass by
your barred threshold, looking back with tearful
eyes at the house I had betrayed.[a] Ah, what dire
slumbers would my wedding-flute warble for you,
that flute more dismal than the trumpet of death!
How should I furnish sons for our country's tri-
umphs? No soldier shall ever be born of my blood.

[15] But if I were following the real camp, that of
my mistress, then Castor's charger would not be
grand enough for me. It is through service to her
that renown has so glorified my name, renown that
has travelled to the wintry northlands. You are my
only joy: be I your only joy, Cynthia: this love means
more to me than the name of father.

Propertius robbed of his sweetheart

I[b] am robbed of the sweetheart I have loved so long,
and you, my friend, bid me shed no tears? No enmi-
ties are savage compared with those of love: slay me
and I shall hate you less. Can I watch her couched
in another's arms? Is she not to be called mine, who
just now was? All things change, and loves not least
of all: you lose to those you vanquished—so turns
the wheel of Luck in love. Great generals and

Camps: the first and fifth stanzas are addressed to a
friend; the second and fourth to his sweetheart; the third
to himself.

141

magni saepe duces, magni cecidere tyranni,
    et Thebae steterunt altaque Troia fuit.   10
munera quanta dedi vel qualia carmina feci!
    illa tamen numquam ferrea dixit 'amo.'

ergo ego tam multos nimium temerarius annos,
    improba, qui tulerim teque tuamque domum?
ecquandone tibi liber sum visus? an usque   15
    in nostrum iacies verba superba caput?

sic igitur prima moriere aetate, Properti?
    sed morere; interitu gaudeat illa tuo!
exagitet nostros Manes, sectetur et umbras,
    insultetque rogis, calcet et ossa mea!   20
quid? non Antigonae tumulo Boeotius Haemon
    corruit ipse suo saucius ense latus,
et sua cum miserae permiscuit ossa puellae,
    qua sine Thebanam noluit ire domum?

sed non effugies: mecum moriaris oportet;   25
    hoc eodem ferro stillet uterque cruor.
quamvis ista mihi mors est inhonesta futura:
    mors inhonesta quidem, tu moriere tamen.

ille etiam abrepta desertus coniuge Achilles
    cessare in Teucris pertulit arma sua.   30

---

[10] steterunt *Scaliger*: steterant Ω
[13] ergo <ego> tam *Heinsius*: ergo iam Ω
[30] Teucris ς: tectis Ω

tyrants have oft taken a fall; Thebes is destroyed and lofty Ilion has ceased to be. What presents I gave, what poems I composed! But iron-hearted she never said 'I love you.'

¹³ So all these years I have been too bold, have I, wicked woman, I who supported you and your household? Did you ever treat me as a man with rights? Will you always be casting insulting language in my face?

¹⁷ Well, Propertius, is this then how you will die, so young? Die then; let her gloat over your demise. Let her harass my ghost and persecute my shade, let her outrage my pyre and trample on my bones! Say, did not Boeotian Haemon perish at Antigone's tomb, stabbed in the side by his own sword, and did he not mix his bones with the unhappy girl's, since without her he would not enter his Theban home?

²⁵ Still, you will not escape: you must die with me; let the blood of both drip from this same sword. Your death will be passing shameful for me: a shameful death indeed, but even so you will die.

²⁹ Even great Achilles was forlorn when his wife was stolen from him ᵃ and in the face of the Trojans stubbornly allowed his arms to lie idle. He had seen

---

ᵃ Cf. wall-painting from the House of the Tragic Poet, Pompeii, depicting the surrender of Briseis (Feder 92f).

viderat ille fuga stratos in litore Achivos,
    fervere et Hectorea Dorica castra face;
viderat informem multa Patroclon harena
    porrectum et sparsas caede iacere comas,
omnia formosam propter Briseida passus: 35
    tantus in erepto saevit amore dolor.
at postquam sera captivast reddita poena,
    fortem illum Haemoniis Hectora traxit equis.
inferior multo cum sim vel matre vel armis,
    mirum, si de me iure triumphat Amor?   40

IXA

ISTE quod est, ego saepe fui: sed fors et in hora
    hoc ipso eiecto carior alter erit.

Penelope poterat bis denos salva per annos
    vivere, tam multis femina digna procis;
coniugium falsa poterat differre Minerva,   5
    nocturno solvens texta diurna dolo;
visuram et quamvis numquam speraret Ulixem,
    illum exspectando facta remansit anus.
nec non exanimem amplectens Briseis Achillem
    candida vesana verberat ora manu;   10
et dominum lavit maerens captiva cruentum
    appositum flavis in Simoente vadis,

---

⁷ visuram ς: visura Ω
¹² appositum ς: propositum Ω

the Achaeans in flight cut down along the shore, and
the Greek camp ablaze with Hector's torch; he had
seen the unlovely corpse of Patroclus lying stretched
out on a heap of sand and his locks caked with blood,
enduring it all for the sake of lovely Briseis: such is
the grief which sears a man when he is robbed of his
sweetheart. But when with tardy redress his cap-
tive was restored, he dragged the valiant Hector
behind his Thessalian horses. Since I am far infe-
rior to him in mother and in arms, why wonder that
Love naturally triumphs over me?

Cynthia no Penelope

Wʜᴀᴛ that man is, I have often been: but perhaps he
will be discarded presently and another preferred.

³ Penelope was able to keep her honour intact for
twice ten years, a woman well meriting that multi-
tude of suitors; her crafty loom enabled her to put off
the hour of marriage, undoing the day's weaving in
nightly deceit; and although she never expected to
see Ulysses again, she stayed true and became an
old woman waiting for him. Briseis, too, holding the
lifeless Achilles beat her fair cheeks with frantic
hand: the mourning captive washing her bleeding
lord as he lay beside the sandy shoals of the Simois;

foedavitque comas, et tanti corpus Achilli
  maximaque in parva sustulit ossa manu;
cui tum nec Peleus aderat nec caerula mater, 15
  Scyria nec viduo Deidamia toro.
tunc igitur veris gaudebat Graecia nuptis,
  tunc etiam caedes inter et arma pudor.

at tu non una potuisti nocte vacare,
  impia, non unum sola manere diem! 20
29   quid si longinquos retinerer miles ad Indos,
30   aut mea si staret navis in Oceano?
quin etiam multo duxistis pocula risu:
  forsitan et de me verba fuere mala.
hic etiam petitur, qui te prius ipse reliquit:
  di faciant, isto capta fruare viro!
haec mihi vota tuam propter suscepta salutem, 25
  cum capite hoc Stygiae iam poterentur aquae,
et lectum flentes circum staremus amici?
  hic ubi tum, pro di, perfida, quisve fuit?

sed vobis facilest verba et componere fraudes: 31
  hoc unum didicit femina semper opus.
non sic incerto mutantur flamine Syrtes,
  nec folia hiberno tam tremefacta Noto,
quam cito feminea non constat foedus in ira, 35
  sive ea causa gravis sive ea causa levis.

[15] cui tum *Housman* : cum tibi Ω
[18] caedes *Giardina* : felix Ω
[29,30] *post* 20 *Housman*

146

she soiled her hair and in her little hand took up the body of the huge Achilles and his giant bones. He had not Peleus then to help him, nor his sea-born mother, nor Deidamia, who slept in a deserted bed on Scyros. Thus in those days Greece rejoiced in faithful brides, and in those days chastity existed even amid slaughter and strife.

[19] But you could not do without a man for a single night, impious one, could not remain alone for a single day! What would you do if active service kept me in distant India or my ship were held fast in a becalmed ocean? Moreover the pair of you prolonged your drinking with much merriment, and no doubt made nasty remarks about me. You are even courting the very man who once left you: God grant that you be tricked and have joy of him! Were these the vows I undertook for your recovery, when the waters of Styx had all but covered your head, and your friends stood in tears about your bed?[a] Where in heaven's name was this fellow then, faithless one, and what was he then?

[31] But it is easy for girls like you to contrive excuses and deceits: this is the one trade women have always learned. Not so quickly do the Syrtes shift in a veering wind or the leaves flutter in a wintry gale as a woman's promise is broken when she is angry, be the matter serious or be it slight.

[a] This seems to presuppose in the reader knowledge of 2.28.

nunc, quoniam ista tibi placuit sententia, cedam:
    tela, precor, pueri, promite acuta magis,
figite certantes atque hanc mihi solvite vitam!
    sanguis erit vobis maxima palma meus.   40
sidera sunt testes et matutina pruina
    et furtim misero ianua aperta mihi,
te nihil in vita nobis acceptius umquam:
    nunc quoque erit, quamvis sis inimica, nihil.
nec domina ulla meo ponet vestigia lecto: 45
    solus ero, quoniam non licet esse tuum.
atque utinam, si forte pios eduximus annos,
    ille vir in medio fiat amore lapis!

IXB

... non ob regna magis diris cecidere sub armis
    Thebani media non sine matre duces,   50
quam, mihi si media liceat pugnare puella,
    mortem ego non fugiam morte subire tua.

X

... sed tempus lustrare aliis Helicona choreis,
    et campum Haemonio iam dare tempus equo.
iam libet et fortis memorare ad proelia turmas
    et Romana mei dicere castra ducis.

---

[49] *secl. Wakker*   [1] *lac. Lachmann*

---

[a] Cf. Posidippus, *A.P.* 12.45.

[b] No literary parallels are found, but Pausanias (9.4.2;
5.11) tells us that she (Euryganeia in his version) was so
portrayed by the painter Onasias. Comments Boucher:

BOOK II.10

[37] Very well, since this is the course you are determined on, I will yield: bring forth, Cupids,[a] yet sharper weapons, compete in shooting them and cut short this life of mine! My blood will be your greatest triumph. The stars are my witness, and the morning rime, and the door that discreetly opened to my wretched self, that no one in all my life has ever been dearer to me than you: nor will anyone be so now, for all your unkindness to me. No other mistress will step into my bed: if I cannot be yours, I will lie alone. And how I would that, if I have given you years of loyalty, that fellow might turn to stone in the midst of love!

Fragment: fighting for Cynthia

... For lust of a throne the Theban princes perished in deadly combat while their mother strove to part them[b]: far less, if Cynthia strove to part us fighting, should I shrink from dying, provided you died too.

Time now to praise Augustus

... But now 'tis time to beat the bounds of Helicon with other dances, 'tis time to give the field to the Thessalian steed. Now am I minded to celebrate the squadrons valiant for battle and tell of the Roman camp of my leader. And should strength fail me, my

'When Propertius presents us with a version of a myth otherwise unknown, he may have derived it from painting, not literature' (p. 52, n. 2).

149

quod si deficiant vires, audacia certe   5
    laus erit: in magnis et voluisse sat est.

aetas prima canat Veneres, extrema tumultus:
    bella canam, quando scripta puella meast.
nunc volo subducto gravior procedere vultu,
    nunc aliam citharam me mea Musa docet.   10
surge, anime, ex humili; iam, carmina, sumite vires;
    Pierides, magni nunc erit oris opus.

iam negat Euphrates equitem post terga tueri
    Parthorum et Crassos se tenuisse dolet:
India quin, Auguste, tuo dat colla triumpho,   15
    et domus intactae te tremit Arabiae;
et si qua extremis tellus se subtrahit oris,
    sentiat illa tuas postmodo capta manus!

haec ego castra sequar; vates tua castra canendo
    magnus ero: servent hunc mihi fata diem!   20
ut, caput in magnis ubi non est tangere signis,
    ponitur his imos ante corona pedes,
sic nos nunc, inopes laudis conscendere currum,
    pauperibus sacris vilia tura damus.
nondum etiam Ascraeos norunt mea carmina fontes,
    sed modo Permessi flumine lavit Amor.   26

---

[11] anime *Heinsius*: anima Ω   [22] his *Scaliger*: hac Ω
[23] currum *Markland*: carmen Ω (<25 carmina)

---

[a] The campaign of Aelius Gallus in 25 proved a fiasco.

daring at least shall win me praise: in mighty projects even to have wished is enough.

[7] Let a poet's first years sing of love, his last of conflicts: henceforth I will sing of wars, since my girl's praises have been penned. Now will I step out in earnest and with serious mien; now my Muse teaches me a different harp. Rise, my soul, from the lowly; songs, now take on a greater strength; Muses, a loftier tone will now be needed.

[13] No longer does the Euphrates allow Parthian horsemen to glance behind their backs, and regrets keeping possession of the Crassi: even India presents its neck to your triumph, Augustus, and the house of virgin Araby trembles before you[a]; and may any land that retreats to the world's end hereafter be captured and feel your hand!

[19] This is the camp I shall follow; by singing of your camp I shall become a mighty poet: may destiny reserve this day for me! Just as, where it is not possible to reach the head of tall statues, a garland is placed below at their feet, so I now, unable to mount the chariot of praise, bring lowly incense in a poor man's sacrifice. Not as yet are my verses acquainted with the springs of Ascra; Love has dipped them only in Permessus' stream.[b]

[b] The passage alludes to Virgil, *Ecl.* 6.64ff, where Gallus receives the pipe of Hesiod (symbolizing admission to the ranks of epic poets); hitherto his verse had (like Propertius') been dipped only in Permessus' stream (i.e. granted the lesser status of love poetry).

XI

... scribant de te alii vel sis ignota licebit:
    laudet, qui sterili semina ponit humo.
omnia, crede mihi, tecum uno munera lecto
    auferet extremi funeris atra dies;
et tua transibit contemnens ossa viator,   5
    nec dicet 'cinis hic docta puella fuit.'

XII

Quicumque ille fuit, puerum qui pinxit Amorem,
    nonne putas miras hunc habuisse manus?
is primum vidit sine sensu vivere amantes,
    et levibus curis magna perire bona.
idem non frustra ventosas addidit alas,   5
    fecit et humano corde volare deum:
scilicet alterna quoniam iactamur in unda,
    nostraque non ullis permanet aura locis.
et merito hamatis manus est armata sagittis,
    et pharetra ex umero Cnosia utroque iacet: 10
ante ferit quoniam tuti quam cernimus hostem,
    nec quisquam ex illo vulnere sanus abit.

---

[a] A break with Cynthia has occurred, but these verses lack the focus necessary for an epigram and must be a fragment of a larger whole.

[b] Cf. *Carm.Cantabrig.* 'Iam dulcis amica venito' line 15, where *docta puella* may conceivably (so Dronke) echo Propertius.

BOOK II.12

Fragment: a break with Cynthia

... Others[a] may write about you or you may be unknown: let him praise who sows his seed in barren soil. Be sure of it, the black day of funeral at the end will consume all your endowments with you on the one bier; and the traveller will pass by your grave unheeding and never say: 'This dust was a learned maid.'[b]

The picture of Love

WHOEVER he was who painted Love as a boy,[c] think you not that he had wondrous skill? He was the first to see that lovers behave childishly[d] and that great blessings are lost through their petty passions. He too with good reason added fluttering wings, and made the god to fly in the human heart, since in truth we are tossed by the waves this way and that, and with us the wind never sits in the same quarter. And justly is his hand armed with barbed arrows, and a Cretan quiver is suspended from his shoulders, since he strikes while we feel safe and do not see the foe, and from that wound no one departs unscathed.

---

[c] Cf. Eubulus *ap.* Athen.13.562C, τίς ἦν ὁ γράψας πρῶτος ἀνθρώπων ἄρα / ἢ κηροπλαστήσας Ἔρωθ' ὑπόπτερον; / ... and Hunter in his edition of the Fragments, pp. 131ff.

[d] Cf. Shakespeare, *MND* 1.1.236–239.

in me tela manent, manet et puerilis imago:
  sed certe pennas perdidit ille suas;
evolat heu nostro quoniam de pectore nusquam,   15
  assiduusque meo sanguine bella gerit.
quid tibi iucundumst siccis habitare medullis?
  si pudor est, alio traice tela, puer!
intactos isto satius temptare veneno:
  non ego, sed tenuis vapulat umbra mea.   20
quam si perdideris, quis erit qui talia cantet,
  (haec mea Musa levis gloria magna tuast),
qui caput et digitos et lumina nigra puellae
  et canat ut soleant molliter ire pedes?

XIII

Non tot Achaemeniis armantur Susa sagittis,
  spicula quot nostro pectore fixit Amor.
hic me tam gracilis vetuit contemnere Musas,
  iussit et Ascraeum sic habitare nemus,
non ut Pieriae quercus mea verba sequantur,   5
  aut possim Ismaria ducere valle feras,
sed magis ut nostro stupefiat Cynthia versu:
  tunc ego sim Inachio notior arte Lino.

non ego sum formae tantum mirator honestae,
  nec si qua illustris femina iactat avos: 10

---

[18] tela puer ς: puella tuo Ω (*cf.* Ovid, *A.A.* 3.735*sq*)
[1] armantur Susa ς: armatur etrusca Ω

[13] With me still stay his darts, his boyish appearance stays: but he has certainly lost his wings, since nowhere from my breast does he fly away, but at the cost of my blood wages constant war.[a] What pleasure is it for you to lodge in my bloodless veins? For very shame, boy, shoot your arrows elsewhere! Better to attack those who have never felt the poison of your darts: it is not I, but a poor shadow of myself that you punish. If you destroy that, who will there be to sing such themes as these (for my slight Muse is your great renown), who will sing of my sweetheart's face, her hands, her dark eyes, and how daintily her footsteps fall?

Anticipations of death

NOT with so many Persian[b] shafts is Susa armed as the darts which Love has fixed in my heart. He suffered me not to scorn these delicate muses, but commanded me to dwell, as I do, in Ascra's grove; not that Pierian oaks should follow my words or I be able to draw wild beasts along in the valley of Ismarus, but rather that Cynthia be held spellbound by my verse: then would my skill bring me greater fame than Linus of Argos.

[9] I am not just an admirer of comely beauty or of any woman who boasts illustrious ancestors: be it

[a] Cf. Meleager, A.P. 5.212.
[b] Persian and Parthian are one to our poet.

me iuvet in gremio doctae legisse puellae,
    auribus et puris scripta probasse mea.
haec ubi contigerint, populi confusa valeto
    fabula: nam domina iudice tutus ero.
quae si forte bonas ad pacem verterit aures,   15
    possum inimicitias tunc ego ferre Iovis.

...   quandocumque igitur nostros mors claudet ocellos,
    accipe quae serves funeris acta mei.
nec mea tunc longa spatietur imagine pompa,
    nec tuba sit fati vana querela mei;   20
nec mihi tunc fulcro sternatur lectus eburno,
    nec sit in Attalico mors mea nixa toro.
desit odoriferis ordo mihi lancibus, adsint
    plebei parvae funeris exsequiae.

sat mea, sat magnast, si tres sint pompa libelli,   25
    quos ego Persephonae maxima dona feram.
tu vero nudum pectus lacerata sequeris,
    nec fueris nomen lassa vocare meum,
osculaque in gelidis pones suprema labellis,
    cum dabitur Syrio munere plenus onyx.   30

deinde, ubi suppositus cinerem me fecerit ardor,
    accipiat Manes parvula testa meos,

---

[17] *lac. Hemsterhuys*
[25] sat magna <est> ς: sit magna Ω

---

[a] The wax masks of the forefathers formed a regular
part of the funeral procession of those whose ancestors

my delight to recite my verses in the lap of a scholar girl and have them approved by the pure taste of her ear. When such a success falls to my lot, then goodbye to the confused babble of the people: for I shall be secure in the judgement of my sweetheart. If only she turns on me a kindly ear and grants a truce, then I can endure Jove's enmity . . .

[17] So, whenever death shall close my eyes, let me tell the arrangements you are to observe at my funeral. On that day let my cortege not march with a long line of masks,[a] no trumpet be the vain lament of my death; on that day let no bier be spread for me on ivory posts, nor my corpse rest on a couch of cloth-of-gold. Be absent a line of perfumed dishes; be present the humble humble rites of a common burial.

[25] Enough, yes grand enough,[b] will be my funeral train, did it amount to three[c] rolls of verse for me to present to Persephone as my most precious gift. But you must follow with your bare breast torn, and not tire of calling on my name and press the final kisses on my frozen lips when the casket filled with Syrian offerings is bestowed.

[31] Then, when the fire beneath has turned me into ash, let a little jar receive my ghost, and above,

had held a curule office.

[b] The anaphora must have appealed to Silius (6.122).

[c] This line must come from Propertius' third book of poems.

et sit in exiguo laurus super addita busto,
  quae tegat exstincti funeris umbra locum,
et duo sint versus, 'qui nunc iacet horrida pulvis, 35
  unius hic quondam servus amoris erat.'

nec minus haec nostri notescet fama sepulcri,
  quam fuerant Pthii busta cruenta viri.
tu quoque si quando venies ad fata, memento
  hoc iter: ad lapides cana veni memores. 40
interea cave sis nos aspernata sepultos:
  non nihil ad verum conscia terra sapit.

atque utinam primis animam me ponere cunis
  iussisset quaevis de Tribus una Soror!
nam quo tam dubiae servetur spiritus horae? 45
  Nestoris est visus post tria saecla cinis:
qui si longaevae minuisset fata senectae
  saucius Iliacis miles in aggeribus,
non aut Antilochi vidisset corpus humari,
  diceret aut 'o mors, cur mihi sera venis?' 50

tu tamen amisso non numquam flebis amico:
  fas est praeteritos semper amare viros.
testis, cui niveum quondam percussit Adonem
  venantem Idalio vertice durus aper;

---

[47] qui s<i> *Markland* : quis [tam] Ω
[48] saucius *Markland* : gallicus Ω
[50] <aut> *Mueller* : ille *A** : *om. N*

over a tiny tomb, let a laurel be planted to cast its shade over the site of the burned-out pyre, and add a line or so to say 'Who now is buried here as gruesome dust, once was the slave of a single love.'

[37] Nor will the fame of this my tomb be less widespread than was the blood-stained mound of Phthia's hero. And when the day you too come to your end, remember the way hither: come white-haired to the tombstone that remembers you. Meanwhile beware of slighting me when I am buried: man's dust has consciousness, and is not heedless of the truth.

[43] Ah, would that any one Sister of the Three had bidden me lay down my life in my infant cradle! For why should the breath of this precarious life be prolonged? Three generations passed before Nestor's ashes were seen: had he cut short his destiny of a venerable old-age, wounded in the fighting before the ramparts of Troy, he would not have witnessed the burial of Antilochus or complain 'Death, why do you come to me so late?'

[51] Yet you will sometimes weep the friend you have lost; it is a duty to love for ever a mate who is dead and gone. Be she my witness, whose snow-white Adonis, as he hunted upon Idalian peaks, was struck down by a cruel boar. In waters there is

illis formosum lavisse paludibus, illic   55
　　diceris effusa tu, Venus, isse coma.
sed frustra mutos revocabis, Cynthia, Manes:
　　nam mea quid poterunt ossa minuta loqui?

XIV

Non ita Dardanio gavisus, Atrida, triumpho's,
　　cum caderent magnae Laomedontis opes;
nec sic errore exacto laetatus Ulixes,
　　cum tetigit carae litora Dulichiae;
nec sic Electra, salvum cum aspexit Oresten,   5
　　cuius falsa tenens fleverat ossa soror;
nec sic, cum incolumem Minois Thesea vidit,
　　Daedalium lino cui duce rexit iter;
quanta ego praeterita collegi gaudia nocte:
　　immortalis ero, si altera talis erit.   10

13　nec mihi iam fastus opponere quaerit iniquos,
14　　　nec mihi ploranti lenta sedere potest;
at dum demissis supplex cervicibus ibam,   11
　　dicebar sicco vilior esse lacu.
atque utinam non tam sero mihi nota fuisset   15
　　condicio! cineri nunc medicina datur.

---

[55] lavisse ς: iacuisse Ω | illic ς: illuc Ω
[1] es *Volscus*: est Ω: *om. mss Charisii*
[7,8] sic <cum> ... cui *Housman*: sic ... cum Ω
[13,14] *post* 10 *Fontein*

Venus said to have laved her beauteous lover, there to have gone about with dishevelled hair. But in vain, Cynthia, will you call back my silent shade: for what answer shall my crumbled bones be able to make?

The poet's triumph

Nor thus did you rejoice, son of Atreus, in your triumph over Troy, when the mighty power of Laomedon collapsed in ruin; nor so jubilant was Ulysses when, his wanderings over, he reached the shore of his beloved Ithaca; nor so Electra, when she beheld Orestes safe, having wept a sister's grief as she held his supposed ashes; nor so Minos' daughter, when she saw Theseus unharmed, for whom, with thread for pilot, she had steered a course through Daedalus's maze: all their joys were as nothing to those I garnered this past night: come such another, and I shall be immortal.[a]

[13] No longer does she seek to answer me with wicked scorn or has the heart to sit unmoved at my tears; but while I walked as a suppliant with drooping neck, she said I was worth less than a trough run dry. Oh, would that the proper way had not become known to me so late! This is now giving

[a] Cf. Rufinus, *A.P.* 5.94.3f, elegantly translated by Paganelli: *'Heureux qui te voit; bienheureux qui t'entend; demi-dieu qui t'aime; immortel qui t'épouse.'*

161

PROPERTIUS

ante pedes caecis lucebat semita nobis:
    scilicet insano nemo in amore videt.
hoc sensi prodesse magis: contemnite, amantes!
    sic hodie veniet, si qua negavit heri.   20

pulsabant alii frustra dominamque vocabant:
    mecum habuit positum lenta puella caput.
haec mihi devictis potior victoria Parthis,
    haec spolia, haec reges, haec mihi currus erunt.
magna ego dona tua figam, Cytherea, columna,   25
    taleque sub nostro nomine carmen erit:
HAS PONO ANTE TUAM TIBI, DIVA, PROPERTIUS AEDEM
EXUVIAS, TOTA NOCTE RECEPTUS AMANS.

nunc a test, mea lux, veniatne ad litora navis
    servata, an in mediis sidat onusta vadis.   30
quod si forte aliqua nobis mutabere culpa,
    vestibulum iaceam mortuus ante tuum!

XV

O me felicem! nox o mihi candida! et o tu
    lectule deliciis facte beate meis!
quam multa apposita narrâmus verba lucerna,
    quantaque sublato lumine rixa fuit!

---

[27] tuam . . . aedem *Scaliger*: tuas . . . aedes Ω
[29] a te ς est *Luck*: ad te Ω | veniatne ad litora *Luck*:
veniet mea litore Ω
[1] nox o ς: o nox Ω

physic to a corpse. The path shone bright before my feet, but I was blind; of course no one uses his eyes when he is madly in love. This I have found to be the precept which works: show disdain, ye lovers! Do this, and she who said no yesterday will say yes today.

²¹ Others were knocking in vain and calling her their lady: but the girl unmoved had her head pillowed on me. This is a greater victory for me than the defeat of the Parthians: this shall be booty, captive kings, and chariot for me. I will nail a rich offering on the pillar of your temple, Venus, and this shall be the inscription beneath my name:

THESE GIFTS, GODDESS, PROPERTIUS SETS BEFORE YOUR SHRINE,
ADMITTED AS HIS MISTRESS' LOVER FOR A WHOLE NIGHT

²⁹ Now it depends on you, my darling, whether my ship[a] shall safely reach the shore or founder, overladen, amid the shoals. And if any offence shall alter you towards me, then may I fall down dead before your door!

The lover's ecstasy

O happy me! O night that shone for me! And O you darling bed made blessed by my delight! How many words we exchanged with the lamp beside us, and how much we wrestled when the light was put out!

[a] Cf. Meleager, *A.P.* 12.167.

nam modo nudatis mecumst luctata papillis,   5
   interdum tunica duxit operta moram.
illa meos somno lapsos patefecit ocellos
   ore suo et dixit 'sicine, lente, iaces?'
quam vario amplexu mutâmus bracchia! quantum
   oscula sunt labris nostra morata tuis!   10

non iuvat in caeco Venerem corrumpere motu:
   si nescis, oculi sunt in amore duces.
ipse Paris nuda fertur periisse Lacaena,
   cum Menelaeo surgeret e thalamo:
nudus et Endymion Phoebi cepisse sororem   15
   dicitur et nudus concubuisse deae.
quod si pertendens animo vestita cubaris,
   scissa veste meas experiere manus:
quin etiam, si me ulterius provexerit ira,
   ostendes matri bracchia laesa tuae.   20
necdum inclinatae prohibent te ludere mammae:
   viderit haec, si quam iam peperisse pudet.
dum nos fata sinunt, oculos satiemus amore:
   nox tibi longa venit, nec reditura dies.

atque utinam haerentis sic nos vincire catena   25
   velles, ut numquam solveret ulla dies!
exemplo iunctae tibi sint in amore columbae,
   masculus et totum femina coniugium.
errat, qui finem vesani quaerit amoris:
   verus amor nullum novit habere modum.   30

[16] nudus *Rossberg*: nudae Ω

For now she fought me with her breasts bared and sometimes she covered herself with her tunic and teased me with delay. With a kiss she opened my eyes which had drooped in sleep and said: 'So, lazy-bones, you dare to doze!' How we shifted our arms in a variety of embraces! How long my kisses lingered on your lips!

[11] There is no point in spoiling love by movements which cannot be seen: I'd have you know, the eyes are love's guides.[a] Paris himself is said to have burned at the sight of Helen naked, when she rose from the bed of Menelaus; and it was naked that Endymion enraptured Phoebus' sister and naked, they say, lay with the goddess. But if you persist in going to bed clothed, you will, with your gown ripped, experience the violence of my hands: indeed, if anger drives me on still farther, you will have bruised arms to show your mother. It's not as though sagging breasts bar you from fun and games: leave that worry to her who knows the shame of having given birth. While fate permits, let us feast our eyes with love: a long night is coming for you and day will not return.

[25] And would that you might so bind us with a chain as we embrace that no day might ever part us! Let doves yoked in love be your model, male and female, a perfect union. He errs who seeks to put a limit to the madness of love: true love knows no

[a] Cf. 1.2.8 note.

terra prius falso partu deludet arantis,
    et citius nigros Sol agitabit equos,
fluminaque ad caput incipient revocare liquores,
    aridus et sicco gurgite piscis erit,
quam possim nostros alio transferre dolores: 35
    huius ero vivus, mortuus huius ero.

quod mihi si interdum talis concedere noctes
    illa velit, vitae longus et annus erit.
si dabit et multas, fiam immortalis in illis:
    nocte una quivis vel deus esse potest.   40
qualem si cuncti cuperent decurrere vitam
    et pressi multo membra iacere mero,
non ferrum crudele neque esset bellica navis,
    nec nostra Actiacum verteret ossa mare,
nec totiens propriis circum oppugnata triumphis   45
    lassa foret crines solvere Roma suos.
haec certe merito poterunt laudare minores:
    laeserunt nullos proelia nostra deos.

tu modo, dum lucet, fructum ne desere vitae!
    omnia si dederis oscula, pauca dabis.   50
ac veluti folia arentis liquere corollas,
    quae passim calathis strata natare vides,
sic nobis, qui nunc magnum spiramus amantes,
    forsitan includet crastina fata dies.

---

[37] interdum *Housman*: tecum Ω
[39] et *Sh. Bailey*: haec Ω
[48] proelia *Fontein*: pocula Ω

bounds. Sooner shall the land mock ploughmen with the wrong crops, sooner the Sun drive a chariot of darkness, and rivers begin to recall their waters to their source, and the deep dry up and leave its fish athirst, than I be able to transfer my love-pangs elsewhere: hers will I be in life, hers will I be in death.

[37] But if she were willing now and again to allow me nights such as this, even a year would be long length of life. If she further gives me many, I will grow immortal in them: a single such night might make any man a god. If all men wished to spend a life like mine and lie with limbs weighed down with deep draughts of wine, there would be no cruel weapons or ships of war, nor would our bones be tossed on Actium's waves, or Rome, so oft beset on every hand by her own conquests, be weary of letting loose her hair in grief. One thing at least with justice shall posterity be able to praise in me: my battles never outraged any of the gods.

[49] Only, Cynthia, while there is light, do not disdain the rewards of life! If you give me all your kisses, you will yet give all too few.[a] And just as petals drop from a withered garland, petals you see strewn in profusion and floating in the cups, so for us, who now love with spirits raised high, perhaps tomorrow's day shall round our destinies.

---

[a] I.e. you cannot give me enough (cf. Catullus 7): no inadequacy on Cynthia's part is suggested.

PROPERTIUS

XVI

Praetor ab Illyricis venit modo, Cynthia, terris,
    maxima praeda tibi, maxima cura mihi.
non potuit saxo vitam posuisse Cerauno?
    a, Neptune, tibi qualia dona darem!
nunc sine me plena fiunt convivia mensa,   5
    nunc sine me tota ianua nocte patet.
quare, si sapis, oblatas ne desere messes
    et stolidum pleno vellere carpe pecus;
deinde, ubi consumpto restabit munere pauper,
    dic alias iterum naviget Illyrias!   10
Cynthia non sequitur fasces nec curat honores:
    semper amatorum ponderat una sinus;
17   semper in Oceanum mittit me quaerere gemmas,
18   et iubet ex ipsa tollere dona Tyro.

at tu nunc nostro, Venus, o succurre dolori,   13
    rumpat ut assiduis membra libidinibus!
ergo muneribus quivis mercatur amorem?   15
    Iuppiter, indigna merce puella perit.
atque utinam Romae nemo esset dives, et ipse
    straminea posset dux habitare casa!   20

17,18 *post* 12 *Housman*

BOOK II.16

The praetor back from Illyria

THE praetor[a] has just returned from Illyria, Cynthia, enormous prey for you, enormous worry for me. Could he not have lost his life on the Ceraunian rocks? Ah, Neptune, what gifts would I be giving you! Now—but I am not there—they are banqueting and the table is full; now—but I am not there— the door is open all night long. So, if you have any sense, neglect not the proffered harvest and pluck the foolish full-fleeced sheep; then, when his presents are used up and he is left penniless, tell him to sail again to some other Illyria. Cynthia does not court the rods of office or care for magistracies: she, as no other, always weighs her lovers' purses; she is always sending me to the ocean to look for pearls and ordering me to fetch gifts from Tyre itself.

[13] But do you, Venus, now bring aid to my distress, so that he rupture himself by his insatiate passions! So anyone can purchase love with presents? Jupiter, unworthy is the price for which my girl ruins herself! Oh, would that no man were rich at Rome and even our leader could live in a hut of straw![b] Never then would our girl-friends sell

[a] Presumably the rival of 1.8.

[b] An allusion to the *Casa Romuli,* preserved on the Palatine.

169

numquam venales essent ad munus amicae,
    atque una fieret cana puella domo;
numquam septenas noctes seiuncta cubares,
    candida tam foedo bracchia fusa viro;
non quia peccarim (testor te), sed quia vulgo   25
    formosis levitas semper amica fuit.

barbarus exutis agitat vestigia lumbis,
    et subito felix nunc mea regna tenet!
nullane sedabit nostros iniuria fletus?   31
    an dolor hic vitiis nescit abesse tuis?
tot iam abiere dies, cum me nec cura theatri
    nec tetigit Campi, nec mea mensa iuvat.
at pudeat! certe pudeat, nisi forte, quod aiunt,   35
    turpis amor surdis auribus esse solet.
cerne ducem, modo qui fremitu complevit inani
    Actia damnatis aequora militibus:
hunc infamis amor versis dare terga carinis
    iussit et extremo quaerere in orbe fugam.   40
Caesaris haec virtus et gloria Caesaris haec est:
    illa, qua vicit, condidit arma manu.

sed quascumque tibi vestes, quoscumque smaragdos,
    quasve dedit flavo lumine chrysolithos,
haec videam rapidas in vanum ferre procellas: 45
    quae tibi terra, velim, quae tibi fiat aqua.

[27] exutis *Sandbach* : exclusis Ω*
[29,30] *post* 46 *Carutti*
[44] quasve *Morgan** : quosve Ω

themselves for a gift, and a maiden would grow grey in a single house; never would you sleep apart for seven nights, with your white arms embracing so foul a man; and not because I have been untrue (that I swear), but because beautiful girls commonly love to be fickle.

²⁷ One moment a barbarian[a] with naked loins is skipping in the slave-market and the next he is a success and possesses my kingdom. Will no outrage of yours ever put an end to my tears? Or must this grief always attend on your betrayals? So many days have gone by since I felt any interest in the theatre or the Campus, and food has ceased to please. But I should feel shame! Indeed I should, unless, as the proverb has it, a shameful love is wont to have deaf ears. Look at the leader who lately, amid vain alarms, filled Actium's bay with his doomed soldiers: a base love made him turn his ships in flight and seek refuge at the ends of the world. Caesar's merit and Caesar's glory reside in this: the selfsame hand that conquered, sheathed the sword.

⁴³ But whatever gowns he has given you, whatever emeralds, whatever chrysolites of golden ray,[b] may I see them swept into empty space by swift storm-winds: may you find them turned to earth and

---

[a] Goethe as the *dives amator* from Germany calls himself *Der Barbare* at the end of *Röm. El.* 2.

[b] Cf. Gray's *Elegy*, 'Full many a gem of purest ray serene.'

29 aspice quid donis Eriphyla invenit amari,
30   arserit et quantis nupta Creusa malis.
    non semper placidus periuros ridet amantes
        Iuppiter et surda neglegit aure preces.
    vidisti toto sonitus percurrere caelo,
        fulminaque aetheria desiluisse domo: 50
    non haec Pleiades faciunt neque aquosus Orion,
        nec sic de nihilo fulminis ira cadit;
    periuras tunc ille solet punire puellas,
        deceptus quoniam flevit et ipse deus.

    quare ne tibi sit tanti Sidonia vestis,   55
        ut timeas, quotiens nubilus Auster erit.

XVII

Mentiri noctem, promissis ducere amantem,
    hoc erit infectas sanguine habere manus!
13 nunc iacere e duro corpus iuvat, impia, saxo,
14   sumere et in nostram trita venena necem.
    horum ego sum vates, quotiens desertus amaras   3
        explevi noctes, fractus utroque toro.

    vel tu Tantalea moveare ad flumina sorte,   5
        ut liquor arenti fallat ab ore sitim;
    vel tu Sisyphios licet admirere labores,
        difficile ut toto monte volutet onus;

---

[29] amari *Rossberg* : -is Ω   [49] vidisti ς : -is Ω

---

[a] I.e. nights without love, as 1.1.33.
[b] Evidently a double bed, cf. 4.3.56; Ovid, *Am.* 3.14.32; Martial 3.91.9; and Suetonius, *Jul.* 49.1.

turned to water. See what unhappiness Eriphyla
obtained from her gifts, and in what agony the bride
Creusa burned. Not always does Jupiter smile
serenely at forsworn lovers and turn a deaf ear to
prayer. You have seen thunder roll across the whole
sky and the bolt crash down from its heavenly home:
it is not the Pleiads who cause this, or watery Orion,
nor does the wrath of the thunderbolt fall thus for
no reason; on those occasions he is usually punish-
ing faithless girls, since he too, although a god, has
been deceived and wept.

55 Therefore count not a gown from Sidon worth
so much that you must fear every time the South
wind brings on clouds.

A pledged night denied

To deny a pledged night, to lead on a lover with
promises, this is as bad as having murder on one's
hands! Now, wicked girl, I want to throw myself
from a rugged cliff or imbibe a poison compounded
to bring about my death. Such is my prophecy as
often as I spend bitter nights[a] forlorn, bruising my
limbs on either side of the bed.[b]

5 Though you pity the fate of Tantalus at the
river, as the water, vanishing from his parched lips,
cheats his thirst, though you stand aghast at the
labours of Sisyphus, how his unmanageable load
rolls all down the hill: there is no one on earth that

PROPERTIUS

durius in terris nihil est quod vivat amante,
    nec, modo si sapias, quod minus esse velis.   10

quem modo felicem invidia maerente ferebant,
    nunc decimo admittor vix ego quoque die,
nec licet in triviis sicca requiescere luna,   15
    aut per rimosas mittere verba fores.
quod quamvis ita sit, dominam mutare cavebo:
    tum flebit, cum in me senserit esse fidem.

XVIIIA

... assiduae multis odium peperere querellae:
    frangitur in tacito femina saepe viro.
si quid vidisti, semper vidisse negato!
    aut si quid doluit forte, dolere nega!

XVIIIB

... quid mea si canis aetas candesceret annis,   5
    et faceret scissas languida ruga genas?

at non Tithoni spernens Aurora senectam
    desertum Eoa passa iacere domost:

13,14 *post* 2 *Housman*
14 nostram . . . necem *Camps* : nostras . . . manus Ω
17 maerente *Heinsius* : admirante Ω (<7)
5 *lac. coni. et sep. Rossberg*

174

lives a harder life than the lover, and no one that, if
you were wise, you would less wish to be.

[11] I, whom men called happy while Envy gnashed
her teeth, now scarce have entry every tenth day;
nor may I lie with her at the crossways beneath a
clear moon, or pass messages through a crack in her
door. Yet though these things be so, I shrink to
change my mistress: one day she will weep, when
she realizes there is constancy in me.[a]

Fragment: a hint to men

... Constant complaining has brought many into
disfavour: oft has a woman been won by a man's
silence. If you have seen aught, say always that you
have not! Or if aught perchance has hurt you, deny
that you are hurt![b]

Fragment: the young lover slighted

... What[c] if my youth were whitening with the
white of old age and drooping wrinkles furrowed my
cheeks?

[7] Aurora did not scorn Tithonus, old though he
was, or suffer him to lie deserted in the halls of the

---

[a] Cf. 2.18a and see note on 2.22.50.
[b] See note on 2.22.50.
[c] A manifestly headless poem.

13 illa deos currum conscendens dixit iniquos,
14   invitum et terris praestitit officium;
    illum saepe suis descendens fovit in ulnis,
      nec prius abiunctos sedula lavit equos;   10
    illum ad vicinos cum amplexa quiesceret Indos,
      maturos iterumst questa redire dies.
    cui maiora senis Tithoni gaudia vivi   15
      quam gravis amisso Memnone luctus erat.
    cum sene non puduit talem dormire puellam
      et canae totiens oscula ferre comae.

    at tu etiam iuvenem odisti me, perfida, cum sis
      ipsa anus haud longa curva futura die.   20

XVIIIC

... quin ego deminuo curam, quod saepe Cupido   21
      huic malus esse solet, cui bonus ante fuit.

XVIIID

    Nunc etiam infectos demens imitare Britannos,
      ludis et externo tincta nitore caput?
    ut natura dedit, sic omnis recta figurast: 25
      turpis Romano Belgicus ore color.

   [9] descendens *Markland* : decedens Ω
   [10] nec *Postgate* : quam Ω
   [13,14] *post 8 Burman*
   [21,22] *secl. Barber*
   [23] *sep. Kuinoel*

Dawn: she, as she mounted her car, called the gods unkind and performed unwilling service for the world; him, as she dismounted, she oft fondled in her arms and did not first busy herself with washing her unyoked steeds; him when she embraced, resting near the land of India, she lamented that the day returned again too soon. Deeper her joy that old Tithonus lives than heavy her grief when Memnon died. So attractive a girl was not ashamed to sleep with an old man and to heap kisses on his hoary hair.

¹⁹ But you, faithless girl, dislike me for all my youth, though at no distant time you yourself shall be a stooping crone.

Fragment: Cupid's contrariety

... Still, my anxiety lessens when I reflect that Cupid is oft unkind to whom he was kind before. [a]

Indignation at painted cheeks

Do you still in your madness imitate the painted Britons and play the wanton with foreign dyes upon your cheeks? All beauty is best as nature made it: Belgian rouge is shameful on a Roman face. If some

---

[a] The couplet cannot be connected with what precedes or follows.

31 an si caeruleo quaedam sua tempora fuco
32   tinxerit, idcirco caerula forma bonast?
    illi sub terris fiant mala multa puellae,   27
      quae mentita suas vertit inepta comas!

    desine! mi per te poteris formosa videri;
      mi formosa sat es, si modo saepe venis.   30
    cum tibi nec frater nec sit tibi filius ullus,   33
      frater ego et tibi sim filius unus ego.
    ipse tuus semper tibi sit custodia vultus,   35
      nec nimis ornata fronte sedere velis.
    credam ego narranti, noli committere, famae:
      et terram rumor transilit et maria.

XIX

ETSI me invito discedis, Cynthia, Roma,
  laetor quod sine me devia rura coles.
nullus erit castis iuvenis corruptor in agris,
  qui te blanditiis non sinat esse probam;
nulla neque ante tuas orietur rixa fenestras,   5
  nec tibi clamatae somnus amarus erit.

sola eris et solos spectabis, Cynthia, montes
  et pecus et fines pauperis agricolae.

---

[29] desine *Baehrens* : deme Ω | mi per te *Bosscha* : mihi
certe Ω
[31,32] *post* 26 *Lachmann*
[35] vultus *Goold** : lectus Ω

woman has stained her forehead with azure dye, is azure beauty on that account to be desired? In hell below may many an ill befall that girl who stupidly dyes her hair with a false colour!

[29] Stop it! To me you can appear beautiful as you are; to me you are beautiful enough if only you visit me often. Since you have no brother and no son, let me and no other be for you a brother and a son.[a] Let your own face unaided keep guard over you always, and do not display yourself with features too made up. I shall believe whatever gossip says, so sin not! Rumour leaps across both land and sea.

Cynthia in the country

THOUGH unhappy, Cynthia, that you are leaving Rome, I am relieved that when parted from me you will be living in rural seclusion. The pure fields there contain no young seducers whose blandishments will prevent your remaining virtuous. No brawl will occur outside your windows, nor will your slumbers be made bitter by voices clamouring your name.

[7] Lonely will you be, Cynthia, looking on lonely hills and flocks and poor farmers' fields. There no

---

[a] Echoing the famous words of Andromache, as at 1.11.23 (see note); *filius* in 35 strongly implies that the poet was younger than Cynthia.

illic te nulli poterunt corrumpere ludi,
    fanaque peccatis plurima causa tuis.   10
illic assidue tauros spectabis arantis,
    et vitem docta ponere falce comas;
atque ibi rara feres inculto tura sacello,
    haedus ubi agrestis corruet ante focos;
protinus et nuda choreas imitabere sura,   15
    omnia ab externo sint modo tuta viro.

ipse ego venabor: iam nunc me sacra Dianae
    suscipere et Veneris ponere vota iuvat.
incipiam captare feras et reddere pinu
    cornua et audacis ipse monere canes;   20
non tamen ut vastos ausim temptare leones
    aut celer agrestis comminus ire sues.
haec igitur mihi sit lepores audacia mollis
    excipere et structo fallere avem calamo,
qua formosa suo Clitumnus flumina luco   25
    integit, et niveos abluit unda boves.

tu quotiens aliquid conabere, vita, memento
    venturum paucis me tibi Luciferis.
hic me nec solae poterunt avertere silvae,
    nec vaga muscosis flumina fusa iugis,   30
quin ego in assidua metuam tua nomina lingua:
    absenti nemo non nocuisse velit.

[18] Veneris ς : veneri Ω
[24] fallere *Watt** : figere Ω
[29] hic *Passerat* : sic Ω
[31] metuam *Jacob* : mutem Ω (<muteam)

shows will be able to bring about your seduction, nor temples, the commonest birthplace of your sins. There you will regularly watch the oxen ploughing, and the vine laying aside her tresses at the sickle's deft touch; there you will offer a few grains of incense at some rude shrine, when a kid falls victim before the rustic altar; and then you will hitch up your dress to mimic the country dance, provided all be safe from an intruder's eyes.

[17] I myself shall go hunting: even now it is my pleasure to take up Diana's rites and lay aside the worship of Venus. I shall begin to hunt wild beasts, hang their horns as offering on pine-trees, and with my own voice urge on the eager hounds; not that I should venture to challenge mighty lions or hasten to confront at close quarters the wild boar. Let this then be daring enough for me: to catch a delicate hare or snare a bird with jointed fowling-rod, where the Clitumnus[a] cloaks its lovely stream with its glades, and its waters wash clean the snowy kine.

[27] Whenever you meditate some folly, sweetheart, remember that I shall come to you a few dawns hence. Here, the sight of lonely woods and vagabond streams issuing from mossy hills cannot relieve me of the fear that your name is ever on the lips of a persistent wooer: no one would be unwilling to take advantage of an absent lover.

[a] Cf. Pliny's encomium (Epist.8.8) and Byron, *Childe Harold's Pilgrimage* IV lxvi 'But thou, Clitumnus! In thy sweetest wave ...'

PROPERTIUS

XX

Quid fles abducta gravius Briseide? quid fles
    anxia captiva tristius Andromacha?
quidve mea de fraude deos, insana, fatigas?
    quid quereris nostram sic cecidisse fidem?
non tam nocturna volucris funesta querela   5
    Attica Cecropiis obstrepit in foliis,
nec tantum Niobe, bis sex ad busta superba,
    sollicito lacrimas depluit a Sipylo.

mi licet aeratis astringant bracchia nodis,
    sint tua vel Danaës condita membra domo,   10
in te ego et aeratas rumpam, mea vita, catenas,
    ferratam Danaës transiliamque domum.
de te quodcumque, ad surdas mihi dicitur aures:
    tu modo ne dubita de gravitate mea.
ossa tibi iuro per matris et ossa parentis   15
    (si fallo, cinis heu sit mihi uterque gravis!)
me tibi ad extremas mansurum, vita, tenebras:
    ambos una fides auferet, una dies.

quod si nec nomen nec me tua forma teneret,
    posset servitium mite tenere tuum.   20

---

[7] superba ς: superbe Ω
[8] lacrimas N: -ans A* | depluit *Scaliger*: defluit Ω

BOOK II.20

Faithful for ever

WHY do you weep more bitterly than the abducted
Briseis? Why in your anxiety do you weep more sor-
rowfully than captive Andromache? And why do
you frantically weary the gods with tales of my
infidelity? Why do you complain that my loyalty has
sunk so low? Not so shrilly does the mourning bird
of Attica utter her nightly dirge in Athenian trees;
not so does Niobe, whose pride caused twice six
deaths, pour down her tears from anguished
Sipylus.

⁹ Though my arms be bound with fetters of
bronze and your limbs be confined in Danaë's tower,
for you, sweetheart, I would break the bronze chains
and leap over the iron walls of Danaë's tower. My
ears are deaf to all men say about you: but you too
must not doubt my earnestness. By the bones of my
mother and my father I swear to you (if I lie, may
the ghosts of each come back to haunt me!) that I
will remain faithful to you, sweetheart, to my dying
hour: a single love, a single end shall take us both
away.[a]

¹⁹ If neither your renown nor your beauty kept
me true, yet the mildness of your bondage might do

[a] Cf. Gilbert, *Iolanthe*, 'None shall part us from each
other, / One in life and death are we: / All in all to one
another- / I to thee and thou to me!'

PROPERTIUS

septima iam plenae deducitur orbita lunae,
  cum de me et de te compita nulla tacent:
interea nobis non numquam ianua mollis,
  non numquam lecti copia facta tui.
nec mihi muneribus nox ullast empta beatis: 25
  quidquid eram, hoc animi gratia magna tui.
cum te tam multi peterent, tu me una petisti:
  possum ego nunc curae non meminisse tuae?

tum me vel tragicae vexetis Erinyes, et me
  inferno damnes, Aeace, iudicio,   30
atque inter Tityi volucres mea poena vagetur,
  tumque ego Sisyphio saxa labore geram!
ne tu supplicibus me sis venerata tabellis:
  ultima talis erit quae mea prima fides.
haec mihi perpetuo laus est, quod solus amator 35
  nec cito desisto nec temere incipio.

XXI

Ah quantum de me Panthi tibi pagina finxit,
  tantum illi Pantho ne sit amica Venus!
sed tibi iam videor Dodona verior augur?
  uxorem ille tuus pulcher amator habet!

[28] nunc curae *Suringar* : naturae Ω (<nccurae)
[33] ne *Camps* : nec Ω
[35] haec . . . laus *Housman* : hoc . . . ius Ω (<iaus)

184

so. Already the seventh full moon is drawing out its
course since every street corner started talking of
you and me; all this time your door has full often
shown favour to me, and full often have I gained
admittance to your bed. Nor have I purchased any
night with costly presents: whatever success I
enjoyed, I owe to the great kindness of your heart.
Whereas so many wanted you, you alone wanted
me: can I now forget your devotion?

²⁹ If I do, then may the very Furies of tragedy per-
secute me and may Aeacus convict me at the assize
in hell, and may one among Tityus' vultures range
to be my punishment, and then may I carry rocks,
enduring the toil borne by Sisyphus. Beseech me
not with letters of entreaty: at the last my devotion
shall be what it was at the first. This shall for ever
be my fame, that alone of lovers I neither abruptly
end nor lightly begin.

Panthus dupes Cynthia

AH, as greatly false as was Panthus'[a] report to you
about me, so greatly unkind may Venus prove to
that same Panthus! But don't you now consider me
a truer augur than Dodona? That pretty lover of

---

[a] From a nominative *Panthûs,* so Virgil, *Aeneid* 2.319,
being a transliteration of Πάνθους (Homeric Πάνθοος): the
Greek name is a pseudonym for a member of Propertius'
social set. As with *Demophoon* and *Lynceus* (*qq.v.*), the
poet confines the name to a single poem.

tot noctes periere: nihil pudet? aspice, cantat   5
   liber: tu, nimium credula, sola iaces.

et nunc inter eos tu sermo's, te ille superbus
   dicit se invito saepe fuisse domi.
dispeream, si quicquam aliud quam gloria de te
   quaeritur: has laudes ille maritus habet.   10
Colchida sic hospes quondam decepit Iason:
   eiectast (tenuit namque Creusa) domo.
sic a Dulichio iuvenest elusa Calypso:
   vidit amatorem pandere vela suum.

ah nimium faciles aurem praebere puellae,   15
   discite desertae non temere esse bonae!
huic quoque, qui restet, iam pridem quaeritur alter:
   experta in primo, stulta, cavere potes.
nos quocumque loco, nos omni tempore tecum
   sive aegra pariter sive valente sumus.   20

XXIIA

Scis here mi multas pariter placuisse puellas,
   scis mihi, Demophoon, multa venire mala.
nulla meis frustra lustrantur compita plantis;
   o nimis exitio nata theatra meo,
sive aliqua in molli diducit candida gestu   5
   bracchia, seu varios incinit ore modos!

---

[17] restet ς : restat Ω
[5] aliqua in *Markland* : aliquis Ω

yours has a bride! So many nights have gone for
nothing! Are you not ashamed? See, he is free and
crows, while you, who were too trusting, lie alone.

⁷ And now you are the talk between the pair; he
says scornfully that you were often at his house
when he would rather you had not been. I'll be
damned if anything other than a triumph over you
is his object: these are that husband's honours.
Thus once did Jason deceive his Colchian hostess:
she was expelled from her home because Creusa had
taken possession. Thus was Calypso cheated by the
Dulichian hero: she saw her lover unfurl his sails.

¹⁵ Ah, ye girls all too ready to lend an ear, learn
from being abandoned not to be rashly kind! My girl
too has now for days been looking for another lover
who will stay: duped by the first one, silly woman,
you had better watch out. As for me, at any time, in
any place, alike in sickness and in health, my heart
belongs to you.

One girl is not enough

You know that of late many girls all charmed me
equally; you know, Demophoon,ᵃ that thence for me
spring a host of woes. My feet pace no street in vain.
Alas, the theatre was created all too much for my
destruction, whether an actress spreads her white
arms in a melting gesture or pours from her lips a

ᵃ See note on 2.21.1.

interea nostri quaerunt sibi vulnus ocelli,
    candida non tecto pectore si qua sedet,
siue vagi crines puris in frontibus errant,
    Indica quos medio vertice gemma tenet.   10

quaeris, Demophoon, cur sim tam mollis in omnis? 13
    quod quaeris, 'quare' non habet ullus amor.
cur aliquis sacris laniat sua bracchia cultris   15
    et Phrygis insanos caeditur ad numeros?
uni cuique dedit vitium natura creato:
    mi fortuna aliquid semper amare dedit.
me licet et Thamyrae cantoris fata sequantur,
    numquam ad formosas, invide, caecus ero.   20

sed tibi si exilis videor tenuatus in artus,
    falleris: haud umquamst culta labore Venus.
percontere licet: saepest experta puella
    officium tota nocte valere meum;
11   quae si forte aliquid vultu mihi dura negarat,
12   frigida de tota fronte cadebat aqua.

Iuppiter Alcmenae geminas requieverat Arctos,   25
    et caelum noctu bis sine rege fuit;
nec tamen idcirco languens ad fulmina venit:
    nullus amor vires eripit ipse suas.

11,12 *post* 24 *Camps*

tuneful air; all the while my eyes are looking for
their own hurt, if some beauty sits with her bosom
uncovered or gadding locks wander over a smooth
forehead, clasped at the crown by a jewel of India.

¹³ Do you ask, Demophoon, why I am so suscepti-
ble to them all? Love knows not the meaning of your
question 'Why?' Why does a man gash his arms
with ritual blades and maim himself at the mad
rhythms of the Phrygian piper? To every one at
birth nature has allotted some fault: to me fortune
allotted the fault of ever having some object for my
love. Though the fate of Thamyras the singer befall
me, never, my envious friend, shall I be blind to a
pretty face.

²¹ But if you think my limbs are shrunk and thin,
you err: the worship of Venus has never been hard
work for me. You may put the question: often a girl
has discovered that I can do my duty all night
through, and if perchance with an unkind look she
called a halt, cold sweat would run all down my
brow.

²⁵ For Alcmena's sake Jupiter put the twin Bears
to rest, and for a doubled night did heaven lack a
king; yet he was not therefore faint when he turned
to wield the thunderbolt: never does the act of love
rob a lover of his strength. Say, when Achilles came

quid? cum e complexu Briseidos iret Achilles,
  num fugere minus Thessala tela Phryges?   30
quid? ferus Andromachae lecto cum surgeret Hector,
  bella Mycenaeae non timuere rates?
illi vel classes poterant vel perdere muros:
  hic ego Pelides, hic ferus Hector ego.

aspice uti caelo modo sol modo luna ministret: 35
  sic etiam nobis una puella parumst.
altera me cupidis teneat foveatque lacertis,
  altera si quando non sinit esse locum;
aut si forte ingrata meo sit facta cubili,
  at sciat esse aliam, quae velit esse mea.   40
nam melius duo defendunt retinacula navim,
  tutius et geminos anxia mater alit.

XXIIB

...   aut si's dura, nega: sive's non dura, venito!   43
  quid iuvat, heu, nullo pondere verba loqui?
hic unus dolor est ex omnibus acer amanti,   45
  speranti subito si qua venire negat.

  [33] illi vel *Baehrens*: ille vel hic Ω
  [39] ingrata ... cubili *Camps*: irata ... ministro (<35) Ω
  [40] at *Heinsius*: ut Ω
  [43] *sep.* ς | sive's *Heyworth**: sin es Ω
  [44] heu *Rothstein*: et Ω | pondere ... loqui *Beroaldus*:
ponere ... loco Ω

from Briseis' embrace, did the Trojans flee the less
from the Thessalian's shafts? And when fierce Hector
rose from Andromache's bed, did not Mycenae's fleet
tremble before his onset? They had the power to
destroy either ships or walls; in love I will be
Achilles, in love fierce Hector.

35 See how now the Sun and now the Moon serve
heaven: so too for me one girl is not enough. Let a
second girl hold and cherish me in passionate
embrace, whenever the first withholds her favour;
or if perchance she brings no pleasure to my bed, yet
let her be aware that there is another ready to be
mine. For a ship is better protected by two cables,
and an anxious mother has less to fear in raising
twins.

Fragment: the lover's bitterest agony

... Either[a] say no, if you are unkind: or, if not un-
kind, then come! Oh, what's the good of uttering
words that have no value? This is the bitterest of all
a lover's agonies, to be suddenly told at the peak of

[a] The verses conventionally numbered as poems 2.17;
2.18a; and 2.22b share in common the theme of a broken
assignation, and Richardson (*q.v.*, 275f) conjectures that
they form a single poem and re-orders them as 2.22b /
2.17/2.18a. Though the sequence is not completely satisfy-
ing (for further transposition seems necessary), he is very
likely on the right track.

quanta illum toto versant suspiria lecto,
    cum recipi, quasi non noverit, illa vetat!
et rursus puerum quaerendo audita fatigat,
    quem, quae scire timet, promere furta iubet.   50

XXIII

Cui fugienda fuit indocti semita vulgi,
    ipsa petita lacu nunc mihi dulcis aquast.

ingenuus quisquam alterius dat munera servo,
    ut commissa suae verba ferat dominae?
et quaerit totiens 'quaenam nunc porticus illam   5
    integit?' et 'campo quo movet illa pedes?'
deinde, ubi pertuleris, quos dicit fama labores
    Herculis, ut scribat 'muneris ecquid habes?',
cernere uti possis vultum custodis amari,
    captus et immunda saepe latere casa?   10
quam care semel in toto nox vertitur anno!
    ah pereant, si quos ianua clausa iuvat!

contra, reiecto quae libera vadit amictu,
    custodum et nullo saepta timore, placet.
cui saepe immundo Sacra conteritur Via socco,   15
    nec sinit esse moram, si quis adire velit;

---

48 cum ς: cur Ω | quasi *Markland*: quae Ω | illa ς: ille Ω
50 promere *Baehrens*: quaerere Ω | furta *Palmer*: fata Ω*

1 f.f.i. *Housman*: fuit indocti fugienda et Ω
4 commissa *Beroaldus*: promissa Ω

192

hope that she will not meet him. What deep sighs
keep him tossing all over the bed, when, as if he
were a stranger, she refuses him admittance!
And he exhausts the messenger by asking him
again and again questions that he has already
heard answered, commanding him to divulge the
infidelities he dreads to know.

The lover turned libertine

I who was bent on fleeing the path of the ignorant
mob now find tasteful even water taken from a pub-
lic trough.

[3] Does any free-born man give bribes to another's
slave to carry a message to his mistress, and ask
repeatedly 'What portico shades her now?' and 'In
what park does she wend her steps today?' And
then, when you have endured what rumour calls the
labours of Hercules, to have her write 'Have you any
present for me?' or to win the privilege of facing a
grim guardian and oft lying hidden, a prisoner in a
filthy hovel? How expensively does a night of joy
come round but once in the whole year! A plague on
those whom a closed door delights!

[13] Rather my fancy is taken by her who comes
forth free and unveiled, and is not inhibited by any
fear of guardians; who oft treads the Sacred Way in
shabby sandals; and brooks no delay, if anyone
wishes to date her; she will never put you off, nor

differet haec numquam, nec poscet garrula, quod te
    astrictus ploret saepe dedisse pater,
nec dicet 'timeo, propera iam surgere, quaeso:
    infelix, hodie vir mihi rure venit.'   20
et quas Euphrates et quas mihi misit Orontes,
    me iuerint: nolim furta pudica tori;
libertas quoniam nulli iam restat amanti,
    nullus liber erit, si quis amare volet.

'tu loqueris, cum sis iam noto fabula libro   24.1
    et tua sit toto Cynthia lecta foro?'
cui non his verbis aspergat tempora sudor?
    aut pudor ingenuis aut reticendus amor.
quod si iam facilis spiraret Cynthia nobis,   5
    non ego nequitiae dicerer esse caput,
nec sic per totam infamis traducerer urbem,
    ureret et quamvis, non mihi verba daret.
quare ne tibi sit mirum me quaerere vilis:
    parcius infamant: num tibi causa levis?   10

XXIVA

...   et modo pavonis caudae flabella superbae   11
    et manibus durae frigus habere pilae,

24.1–10 *cont. Scaliger*
4 ingenuis *Haupt*: -uus Ω
5 iam ς: tam Ω
8 non mihi *Palmer*: nomine Ω | daret *Barber*: -em (<7) Ω
11–16 *secl. Postgate*
12 durae ... pilae *Heinsius*: -a ... -a Ω

194

insistently demand what your frugal father will lament that you have often given her. Nor will she say: 'I am scared, please make haste to be off: unlucky boy, today my husband comes in from the country.' Be my delight the girls the Euphrates and the Orontes have sent: I want no respectable seductions. Since no lover any more stays free, the man who chooses to love must give up all thought of liberty.

24:1 'Do you talk thus, now that your famous book has made you a legend, and your "Cynthia"[a] is read all over the forum?' Whose brow would not break out in sweat at these words? Gentlemen either feel shame or have to keep their love a secret. But if indeed Cynthia were smiling indulgently upon me, I should not now be called the prince of debauchery; nor would my name be thus dragged in dishonour throughout Rome, and although she fired me with passion, at least she would not be hoodwinking me. Therefore wonder not if I seek common women: they defame less: surely that's reason enough!

Fragment: the plaything of a mistress

. . . and now she wants a fan from a proud peacock's tail and to hold in her hands the coolness of hard

---

[a] I.e. the First Book of Propertius.

et cupit interdum talos me poscere eburnos,
    quaeque nitent Sacra vilia dona Via.
ah peream, si me ista movent dispendia, sed me   15
    fallaci dominae iam pudet esse iocum!

XXIVB

Hoc erat in primis quod me gaudere iubebas?
    tam te formosam non pudet esse levem?
una aut altera nox nondumst in amore peracta,
    et dicor lecto iam gravis esse tuo.   20
me modo laudabas et carmina nostra legebas:
    ille tuus pennas tam cito vertit amor?
47 durast quae multis simulatum fingit amorem,
48   et se plus uni si qua parare potest.

contendat mecum ingenio, contendat et arte,
    in primis una discat amare domo:
si libitum tibi erit, Lernaeas pugnet ad hydras   25
    et tibi ab Hesperio mala dracone ferat,
taetra venena libens et naufragus ebibat undas,
    et numquam pro te deneget esse miser:
(quos utinam in nobis, vita, experiare labores!)
    iam tibi de timidis iste protervus erit,   30
qui nunc se in tumidum iactando venit honorem:
    discidium vobis proximus annus erit.
at me non aetas mutabit tota Sibyllae,
    non labor Alcidae, non niger ille dies.

[13] interdum *Phillimore*: iratum Ω
[17] *sep. Canter*

crystal; at times she is minded to ask me for ivory dice and glittering trumpery from the Sacred Way. I'm damned if the expense bothers me, but it humiliates me to be the plaything of a deceitful mistress.

A promise of infinite fidelity

Was it for this of all things that you bade me be happy? Are you not ashamed to be so beautiful and yet so fickle? We have hardly spent one or two nights in love, and already you say I am unwelcome in your bed. Just now you praised me and read my poems: has your love so quickly turned its wings elsewhere? Cruel is the woman who feigns false love for many, and she who has the gall to preen herself for more than one.

23 Let the man compete with me in wit and art, and of all things learn to confine his love to a single house: if you so wish, let him fight with Lernaean hydras and fetch you apples from the serpent of the Hesperides; let him cheerfully drink foul poisons and the waters of shipwreck, and never shirk misery for your sake (ah, darling, would you might test me in these ordeals!), and soon your dashing hero will become a coward, for all that his boasts have brought him such proud honour: next year will see you parted. But the whole lifetime of the Sibyl will not change me, nor the labours of Hercules, nor the black day of death.

tum me compones et dices 'ossa, Properti,   35
    haec tua sunt: eheu tu mihi certus eras,
certus eras eheu, quamvis nec sanguine avito
    nobilis et quamvis non ita dives eras.'
nil ego non patiar, numquam me iniuria mutat:
    ferre ego formosam nullum onus esse puto.   40
credo ego non paucos ista periisse figura,
    credo ego sed multos non habuisse fidem.
parvo dilexit spatio Minoida Theseus,
    Phyllida Demophoon, hospes uterque malus.
iam tibi Iasonia vectast Medea carina   45
    et modo servato sola relicta viro.

noli nobilibus, noli consuesse beatis: 49
    vix venit, extremo qui legat ossa die.   50
hi tibi nos erimus: sed tu potius precor ut me
    demissis plangas pectora nuda comis.

XXV

CYNTHIA nata meo, pulcherrima cura, dolori,
    excludi quoniam sors mea saepe vehit,

---

[35] tu\<m\> ς me *Porson* : tu mea Ω (cf. 2.1.71)
[45] vecta *Heinsius* : nota Ω
[47,48] *post* 22 *Rossberg*
[49] consuesse *Damsté* : conferre Ω
[1] Cynthia *Phillimore* : unica Ω
[2] excludi *Scaliger* : -it Ω | vehit *Lachmann* : venit N^1 : veni Ω

35 Then you will lay me to rest and say 'Here lie your bones, Propertius. Alas, you were faithful to me, faithful to me, alas, although sprung of ignoble ancestry and none too prosperous.' There is nothing I cannot endure for you; ill-treatment never changes my love: I count it no hardship to bear with one so beautiful. Many, I believe, have been smitten by such beauty, but many, I believe, have not remained true. For a short while Theseus loved the daughter of Minos and Demophoon loved Phyllis *a*—a wicked pair of guests. You see that Medea was one moment given passage in Jason's ship and the next abandoned by the husband she had saved.

49 Consort not with the high-born, consort not with the rich: scarce one comes to gather your bones when the end is come. I'll be that man for you, though I pray rather that with breast bare and locks dishevelled you will mourn for me.

The lover's frustrations

CYNTHIA, born to cause me pain (though comeliest of sorrows) since my lot oft brings exclusion, my books

---

a The story of Phyllis and Demophoon almost certainly derives from the lost Greek work which Ovid exploited for *Heroides* 2 (as he exploited *Odyssey* 1 for *Her.* 1 and *Aeneid* 4 for *Her.* 7 etc.), and this work is likewise Propertius' source too.

PROPERTIUS

ista meis fiet notissima forma libellis,
    Calve, tua venia, pace, Catulle, tua.
miles depositis annosus secubat armis,   5
    grandaevique negant ducere aratra boves,
putris et in vacua requiescit navis harena,
    et vetus in templo bellica parma vacat:
at me ab amore tuo deducet nulla senectus,
    sive ego Tithonus sive ego Nestor ero.   10

nonne fuit satius duro servire tyranno
    et gemere in tauro, saeve Perille, tuo?
Gorgonis et satius fuit obdurescere vultu,
    Caucasias etiam si pateremur aves.
sed tamen obsistam. teritur robigine mucro   15
    ferreus et parvo saepe liquore silex:
at nullo dominae teritur sub crimine amor, qui
    restat et immerita sustinet aure minas.
ultro contemptus rogat, et peccasse fatetur
    laesus, et invitis ipse redit pedibus.   20

tu quoque, qui pleno fastus assumis amore,
    credule, nulla diu femina pondus habet.
an quisquam in mediis persolvit vota procellis,
    cum saepe in portu fracta carina natet?
aut prius infecto deposcit praemia cursu,   25
    septima quam metam triverit axe rota?

17 crimine *Langermann* : limine Ω*
26 axe *Burman* : ante Ω

200

shall make your beauty renowned beyond all others, begging your pardon, Calvus, and by your leave, Catullus. The aged soldier puts away his arms and rests in retirement, the ox grown old refuses to draw the plough, the rotten ship lies idle on the deserted strand, and the warrior's ancient shield hangs at peace in the temple: but never shall old age stop me from loving you, whether I live to be a Tithonus or a Nestor.

[11] Would it not be better to serve a harsh tyrant and moan within the bull of cruel Perillus?[a] Better indeed to be petrified by the Gorgon's visage and even to suffer the vultures of the Caucasus. But I will not give in. The blade of iron is worn down by rust, and rock by frequent drops of water. Yet no abuse by a mistress can wear down that love which remains steadfast and listens with blameless ears to her threatening words, a love which pleads at once, when scorned; when injured, confesses itself in the wrong, and returns of its own accord with lagging feet.

[21] You, too, credulous one, who put on airs because your love is at the full, no woman can be relied on for long. Does any man fulfil his vows in mid-tempest, when many a ship floats shattered even in port? Does any man claim the prize with the race unfinished, before his chariot's axle has grazed the turning-post a seventh time? Fair winds

[a] Cf. the echo at 3.24.13.

mendaces ludunt flatus in amore secundi:
    si qua venit sero, magna ruina venit.

tu tamen interea, quamvis te diligat illa,
    in tacito cohibe gaudia clausa sinu.   30
namque in amore suo semper sua maxima cuique
    nescio quo pacto verba nocere solent.
quamvis te persaepe vocet, semel ire memento:
    invidiam quod habet, non solet esse diu.
at si saecla forent antiquis grata puellis,   35
    essem ego quod nunc tu: tempore vincor ego.
non tamen ista meos mutabunt saecula mores:
    unus quisque sua noverit ire via.

at, vos qui officia in multos revocatis amores,
    quantus sic cruciat lumina nostra dolor!   40
vidisti pleno teneram candore puellam,
    vidisti fuscam, ducit uterque color;
vidisti quandam Argiva prodire figura,
    vidisti nostras, utraque forma rapit;
illaque plebeio vel sit sandycis amictu: 45
    haec atque illa mali vulneris una viast.
cum satis una tuis insomnia portet ocellis,
    una sat est cuivis femina multa mala.

[41-44] vidisti *Camps* : vidistis Ω

in love deceive and mock us: the fall that comes late
is a mighty fall.

²⁹ Meanwhile, however much she love you, keep
none the less your bliss locked up in a silent breast.
For when a man has possession of his love, by some
strange law it is always his own boastful words that
do him harm. Although she calls you often, be sure
to go but once: what invites envy is not apt to last for
long. But if the times now were, which girls of old
liked well, I should now be in your shoes: I am
undone by the age. Still these bad times will not
alter my ways: let everybody know how to go his
own road.

³⁹ But those of you who direct men's attentions to
many loves, how sorely do you thus torment our
eyes! You have seen a pretty girl of fair complexion,
or again a swarthy beauty: either hue attracts you;
you have seen one of Grecian shape come forth, and
you have seen Italian girls: either form sends you
into raptures. Though she is clad in plebeian dress
or scarlet garb, both this and that are alike avenues
for a cruel wound. Since one woman is sufficient to
keep your eyes from sleep, one woman spells plenty
of trouble for any man.

PROPERTIUS

XXVIA

Vidi te in somnis fracta, mea vita, carina
  Ionio lassas ducere rore manus,
et quaecumque in me fueras mentita fateri,
  nec iam umore gravis tollere posse comas,
qualem purpureis agitatam fluctibus Hellen,   5
  aurea quam molli tergore vexit ovis.

quam timui, ne forte tuum mare nomen haberet,
  teque tua labens navita fleret aqua!
quae tum ego Neptuno, quae tum cum Castore fratri,
  quaeque tibi excepi, iam dea, Leucothoë!   10

at tu vix primas extollens gurgite palmas
  saepe meum nomen iam peritura vocas.
quod si forte tuos vidisset Glaucus ocellos,
  esses Ionii facta puella maris,
et tibi ob invidiam Nereides increpitarent,   15
  candida Nesaee, caerula Cymothoë.

---

[8] teque *Heinsius*: atque Ω

---

[a] André Chénier, confessedly drawing on Propertius,
handles the theme in *Chrysé* (*Idylles marines* III): . . .
  Dieux! je t'ai vue en songe. Et de terreur glacé,
  J'ai vu sur des écueils ton vaisseau fracassé,

BOOK II.26A

A dream of Cynthia

IN a dream,[a] my darling, I saw you shipwrecked and sweeping weary arms through the Ionian surge, confessing all your deceit towards me and no longer able to lift your tresses weighed down with water, like Helle tossed on the purple waves, whom the golden ram carried on his fleecy back.

[7] How I feared lest the sea perchance should take your name and mariners sailing your waters should weep for you. What vows did I then make to Neptune, to Castor and his brother, and to you, Leucothoë, a goddess now!

[11] But scarcely raising your fingertips above the swell, now on the point of death you call my name again and again.[b] If perchance Glaucus had seen your eyes, you would have become a mermaid of the Ionian Sea, and the Nereids for envy would be reproaching you, blond-haired Nesaee and cerulean Cymothoë.

> *Ton corps flottant sur l'onde, et tes bras avec peine*
> *Cherchant à repousser le vague ionienne. . . .*
> *Déjà tu n'élevais que des mains défaillantes;*
> *Tu me nommais déjà de tes lèvres mourantes,*
> *Quand, pour te secourir, j'ai vu fendre les flots*
> *Au dauphin qui sauva le chanteur de Lesbos.*

[b] Not for succour, but in remorse (cf. Virgil, *Aen.* 4.382ff).

sed tibi subsidio delphinum currere vidi,
    qui, puto, Arioniam vexerat ante lyram.
iamque ego conabar summo me mittere saxo,
    cum mihi discussit talia visa metus.   20

XXVIB

... nunc admirentur quod tam mihi pulchra puella   21
    serviat et tota dicar in urbe potens!
non, si iam Gygae redeant et munera Croesi,
    dicat 'de nostro surge, poeta, toro.'
nam mea cum recitat, dicit se odisse beatos: 25
    carmina tam sancte nulla puella colit.

multum in amore fides, multum constantia prodest:
    qui dare multa potest, multa et amare potest.

XXVIC

Heu, mare per longum mea cogitat ire puella,
    hanc sequar et fidos una aget aura duos.   30
unum litus erit sopitis unaque tecto
    arbor, et ex una saepe bibemus aqua;

---

[21] *sep. Burman*
[23] iam Gygae *Schrader*: cambysae Ω | munera *Camps*:
flumina Ω
[29] *nov. eleg. N* ... heu . . . cogitat *Guyet*: seu ... cogitet Ω

---

[a] And so he will be less likely to give to one girl the loyalty and constancy guaranteed by the poet.

[17] Instead I saw a dolphin racing to your aid, the same, I fancy, that once carried Arion and his lyre. And now I was making the effort to leap down from the cliff-top when my fear dispelled this wondrous vision.

Fragment: a man of consequence

... Now let men wonder that so beautiful a girl is my slave and let all Rome regard me as a man of consequence. Not though it should earn her the gifts of a Gyges or a Croesus, would she say 'Up, poet, out of my bed!' For when she recites my poems, she says she hates the rich: no other girl so devoutly worships poetry.

[27] Loyalty helps much in love, and much helps constancy: for he who can give many gifts, can also have many loves.[a]

Vision of a voyage

ALAS, my sweetheart meditates a long voyage over the sea! I will follow her, and a single breeze will escort a faithful pair. We shall share a single shore when we sleep,[b] a single tree for shelter, and oft shall we drink from a single spring; a single plank

[b] Cf. Rutilius Namatianus 1.345 for sleeping ashore during a long voyage.

et tabula una duos poterit componere amantes,
 prora cubile mihi seu mihi puppis erit.

omnia perpetiar: saevus licet urgeat Eurus,   35
 velaque in incertum frigidus Auster agat;
quicumque et venti miserum vexastis Ulixem,
 et Danaûm Euboico litore mille rates;
et qui movistis duo litora, cum rudis Argus
 dux erat ignoto missa columba mari.   40
illa meis tantum non umquam desit ocellis,
 incendat navem Iuppiter ipse licet.
certe isdem nudi pariter iactabimur oris:
 me licet unda ferat, te modo terra tegat.

sed non Neptunus tanto crudelis amori,   45
 Neptunus fratri par in amore Iovi:
testis Amymone, latices dum ferret, in arvis
 compressa, et Lernae pulsa tridente palus;
quam deus amplexus votum persolvit, at illi
 aurea divinas urna profudit aquas.   50

crudelem et Borean rapta Orithyia negavit:
 hic deus et terras et maria alta domat.

---

[39] rudis Argus ς: ratis Argo Ω
[49] quam *Sh. Bailey*: iam Ω | amplexus *Passerat*: amplexu Ω

will be able to accommodate us two lovers, whether my bed be in the prow or stern.

35 I will endure all things: though the savage East wind blow, though the wintry South drive our sails we know not where, and all ye winds that tormented luckless Ulysses and the thousand ships of the Greek armada upon Euboea's shore, and ye that set two coasts*a* in motion, when as a guide for the inexperienced Argo a dove was sent over the unknown sea. Only let her never be absent from my eyes, and Jupiter himself may set our ship on fire. At least our naked corpses will be cast up together on the selfsame shore: let the waves sweep me away, if only earth give you burial.

45 But Neptune is not unkind to such a love as ours, Neptune, who is equal to his brother Jupiter in love. Proof is Amymone, who yielded to him in the fields on condition she might have water, and Lerna's marsh struck by the trident; the god, embracing her, fulfilled his promise, and her golden urn poured forth a stream divine.

51 Orithyia when ravished denied that even Boreas was cruel: this god tames both the lands and

---

a Of the Symplegades (Clashing Rocks, Cyaneae, cf. Herodotus 4.85 and Apollonius 2.549ff), two islands outside the northern mouth of the Bosporus; they clashed together whenever anything attempted to pass between them.

crede mihi, nobis mitescet Scylla, nec umquam
    alternante vacans vasta Charybdis aqua;
ipsaque sidera erunt nullis obscura tenebris,   55
    purus et Orion, purus et Haedus erit.

quod mihi si ponenda tuo sit corpore vita,
    exitus hic nobis non inhonestus erit.

XXVII

AT vos incertam, mortales, funeris horam
    quaeritis, et qua sit mors aditura via;
quaeritis et caelo, Phoenicum inventa, sereno,
    quae sit stella homini commoda quaeque mala!

seu pedibus Parthos sequimur seu classe Britannos,
    et maris et terrae caeca pericla latent;   6
rursus et obiectum fles tu caput esse tumultu,
    cum Mavors dubias miscet utrimque manus;
praeterea domibus flammam metuisque ruinas,
    neu subeant labris pocula nigra tuis.   10

6 <la>tent *Smyth*: viae Ω
7 fles tu *Housman*: fletus *N*: flemus *A**
9 metuis *Mueller*: domibus Ω

the deep seas. Believe me, even Scylla will grow
kind towards us, and so will awful Charybdis, who
never ceases from her ebb and flow; the very stars
shall not be obscured by darkness, and clear shall
Orion be, and clear the Kid. [a]

[57] And if I had to lay down my life while in your
arms, such a death for me will not be a disgrace. [b]

The lover's return from the dead

YOU still seek, mortals, the uncertain hour of your
fate and wonder by what route death will come; and
in a cloud-free sky you seek the Phoenicians'
discoveries, what star is good for man, what star is
ill.

[5] Whether we advance on foot against the Parthi-
ans or by ship against the Britons, unseen perils
lurk on both land and sea. And again you lament
that your life is menaced by civil war, when Mars
brings battle-lines together with no sure victor on
either side; you further worry that your house may
burn or collapse, or that a poisonous draught may
touch your lips.

[a] The autumnal rising of Orion and Haedus was gen-
erally associated with stormy weather.

[b] Cf. Keats to Fanny Brawne: 'I have two luxuries to
brood over in my walks, your Loveliness and the hour of
my death. O that I could have possession of them both in
the same minute!' (Papanghelis).

solus amans novit, quando periturus et a qua
    morte, neque hic Boreae flabra neque arma timet.
iam licet et Stygia sedeat sub harundine remex,
    cernat et infernae tristia vela ratis:
si modo clamantis revocaverit aura puellae,   15
    concessum nulla lege redibit iter.

XXVIII

IUPPITER, affectae tandem miserere puellae:
    tam formosa tuum mortua crimen erit.
venit enim tempus, quo torridus aestuat aer,
    incipit et sicco fervere terra Cane.
sed non tam ardoris culpast neque crimina caeli,   5
    quam totiens sanctos non habuisse deos.
hoc perdit miseras, hoc perdidit ante puellas:
    quidquid iurarunt, ventus et unda rapit.

num sibi collatam doluit Venus? illa peraeque
    prae se formosis invidiosa deast.   10
an contempta tibi Iunonis planta Pelasgae?
    Palladis aut oculos ausa negare bonos?
semper, formosae, non nostis parcere verbis.
    hoc tibi lingua nocens, hoc tibi forma dedit.

---

[11] planta *Alton* : templa Ω

---

[a] Charon's.
[b] Cf. Philitas fr. 6 Powell, Catullus 3.11f.

[11] Only the lover knows when he will perish and by what death: he fears neither the North-wind's blasts nor the arms of war. Though he sit oar in hand beneath the reeds of the Styx and face the sombre sails of the infernal boat[a]: let but the echo of his mistress' cry recall him, and he will return on a journey no law permits.[b]

Cynthia gravely ill

JUPITER, have pity at last on my sweetheart gravely ill: you will be blamed for the death of one so fair.[c] For the season has come in which the air seethes with heat and the earth begins to glow under the scorching Dogstar. But it is not so much the fault of the heat or the malignity of heaven as her having so often failed to revere the gods. This proves, as it has proved before, the undoing of hapless girls: they may swear, but wind and water sweep all their oaths away.

[9] Was Venus annoyed that you were compared with her? She is a goddess jealous of all alike whose beauty outshines her own. Have you slighted the gait of Argive Juno, or ventured to deem the eyes of Pallas unlovely? You beautiful women never have the sense to moderate your words. This is what a hurtful tongue and what beauty have done for you.

[c] See note on 2.9.27.

sed tibi vexatae post multa pericula vitae 15
   extremo veniat mollior hora die.

Io versa caput primos mugiverat annos:
   nunc dea, quae Nili flumina vacca bibit.
Ino etiam prima terris aetate vagatast:
   hanc miser implorat navita Leucothoën. 20
Andromede monstris fuerat devota marinis:
   haec eadem Persei nobilis uxor erat.
Callisto Arcadios erraverat ursa per agros:
   haec nocturna suo sidere vela regit.

quod si forte tibi properarint fata quietem, 25
   ipsa, sepultura facta beata tua,
narrabis Semelae, quo sis formosa periclo,
   credet et illa, suo docta puella malo;
et tibi Maeonias omnis heroidas inter
   primus erit nulla non tribuente locus. 30
nunc, utcumque potes, fato gere saucia morem:
   et deus et durus vertitur ipse dies.

deficiunt magico torti sub carmine rhombi, 35
   et iacet exstincto laurus adusta foco;

---

[15] post *Pricaeus* : per Ω
[16] veniat ς : venit Ω
[26] illa sepulturae fata ... tuae Ω, *corr. Markland*
[27] sis ς : sit Ω
[33,34] *post* 46 *Heyworth**

But after the many perils of a troubled life may a happier hour come to you at the close of the day.

¹⁷ Io in her early years lowed, her head transformed: now she who as a cow drank the Nile's waters is a goddess. Ino also in early life wandered over the earth: now she is invoked as Leucothoë by sailors in distress. Andromeda was vowed as sacrifice to a monster of the deep: she, none other, became the famed wife of Perseus.[a] Callisto wandered as a bear through the fields of Arcady: with her constellation she now directs ships by night.

²⁵ So if destiny does hasten your last rest, you will in person, beatified through your burial, tell Semele at what peril one is beautiful, and she, the wiser for her misfortunes, will believe you; and among all the heroines of Homer first place will go to you with the consent of all. Now, as best you can, for all your pain, bear with your fate: both heaven and the very day of doom may change.

³⁵ The whirligig[b] spun to a magical chant has had no effect, and the laurel lies charred on a burned-out

---

[a] 'Andromeda was offered to a sea-serpent and respectably married to Perseus' (Ezra Pound).

[b] Evidently the ἴυγξ, *iynx,* a wheel (cf. 3.6.26) threaded with a string through two holes near the centre and spun to give off a hum while an incantation was recited. See A. S. F. Gow, *Theocritus* (Cambridge 1950) II, on 2.30 and his plate V.

et iam Luna negat totiens descendere caelo,
    nigraque funestum concinit omen avis.
una ratis fati nostros portabit amores
    caerula in inferno velificata lacu.   40
si non unius, quaeso, miserere duorum!
    vivam, si vivet; si cadet illa, cadam.

pro quibus optatis sacro me carmine damno:
    scribam ego 'per magnumst salva puella Iovem';
ante tuosque pedes illa ipsa operata sedebit,   45
    narrabitque sedens longa pericla sua.
33 hoc tibi vel poterit coniunx ignoscere Iuno:
34   frangitur et Iuno, si qua puella perit.
et tua, Persephone, maneat clementia, nec tu,   47
    Persephonae coniunx, saevior esse velis.

sunt apud infernos tot milia formosarum:
    pulchra sit in superis, si licet, una locis!   50
vobiscum Antiope, vobiscum candida Tyro,
    vobiscum Europe nec proba Pasiphaë,
et quot Creta tulit vetus et quot Achaia formas,
    et Thebae et Priami diruta regna senis:
et quaecumque erat in numero Romana puella,   55
    occidit: has omnis ignis avarus habet.

[40] <in> inferno . . . lacu *Palmer*: [ad] -os . . . -us Ω
[47] et *Heyworth**: haec *N*: nec A*
[51] Antiope ς: est iope Ω
[53] Creta *Rossberg*: troia Ω
[57,58] *post* 3.18.24 *Housman*

hearth; the Moon refuses to come down yet again from the sky, and the dark bird sings an omen of doom. One boat of death will carry our love, that boat whose sombre sails are hoisted upon the lake of hell. Have pity on both, if you cannot pity one! If she lives, I shall live; if she dies, so shall I.

43 For this blessing I pledge myself to a solemn poem. I shall write: Thanks to mighty Jupiter my girl is safe. She will sacrifice in person and before your feet she will sit herself and sitting will recount her long tale of peril. Even your wife Juno will be able to forgive your help: even Juno relents if a maiden dies. May your mercy continue, too, Persephone,[a] and may you, consort of Persephone, be not more harsh.

49 There are many thousands of the fair in the world below; on earth above let one pretty woman remain, if it may be.[b] You have Antiope, you have lovely Tyro, you have Europa, and the infamous Pasiphaë, and all the beauties that Crete and Achaea bore of old, and Thebes and the kingdom of old Priam, long destroyed; gone is every Roman girl of any account: all these the greedy pyre has taken.

[a] Compare Pound's first version of this passage (*Prayer for his Lady's Life*, 1911) with his second (*Homage*, IX 2).

[b] Tremenheere quotes 'Spare her, Immortals, spare / Till all our days are done: / Your heaven is full of angel forms, / Mine holds but one.'

tu quoniam's, mea lux, magno dimissa periclo,   59
   munera Dianae debita redde choros,   60
redde etiam excubias divae nunc, ante iuvencae;
   votivas noctes et mihi solve decem!

XXIXA

HESTERNA, mea lux, cum potus nocte vagarer,
   nec me servorum duceret ulla manus,
obvia, nescio quot pueri, mihi turba, minuti,
   venerat (hos vetuit me numerare timor);
quorum alii faculas, alii retinere sagittas,   5
   pars etiam visast vincla parare mihi.
sed nudi fuerant. quorum lascivior unus
   'arripite hunc,' inquit, 'nam bene nostis eum.
hic erat, hunc mulier nobis irata locavit.'
   dixit, et in collo iam mihi nodus erat.   10

hic alter iubet in medium propellere, at alter
   'intereat, qui nos non putat esse deos!
haec te non meritum totas exspectat in horas:
   at tu nescio quam quaeris, inepte, foris.

---

[3] minuti *Heinsius*: minuta Ω
[8] nam *A**: iam *N*
[14] quam *Paley*: quas Ω | foris *Dousa pater*: fores Ω

[59] My darling, since you have been released from mortal danger, perform the due service of a dance to Diana; perform also your vigil to her who, heifer once, is goddess now[a]; and pay the ten nights pledged to me!

The poet's reception: fantasy

LAST[b] night, my love, as I wandered steeped in wine with no band of slaves to guide me, a crowd of tiny boys accosted me, I know not how many, since fear prevented my counting them; some, I fancied, held torches, some arrows, and others were even getting fetters ready for me. But they were naked. One more impudent than the rest cried out: 'Arrest him, for you know him well enough. This was the man, this the one that the angry girl set us to deal with.' Hardly had he spoken when a noose was round my neck.

[11] Hereupon another bids them push me into their midst, and yet another 'Death to whoever does not believe us gods! This girl, though you deserve it not, has been awaiting you for hours, whilst you, stupid, were looking for a woman out of

[a] Isis, here as elsewhere (e.g. 17f) identified with Io.

[b] 2.29a and its sequel 2.29b, though two separate poems, are connected very much as are 1.8a and 1.8b; and they form a sophisticated variation on 1.3.

quae cum Sidoniae nocturna ligamina mitrae   15
    solverit atque oculos moverit illa gravis,
afflabunt tibi non Arabum de gramine odores,
    sed quos ipse suis fecit Amor manibus.
parcite iam, fratres, iam certos spondet amores;
    et iam ad mandatam venimus ecce domum.'   20

atque ita mi iniecto dixerunt rursus amictu:
    'i nunc et noctes disce manere domi.'

XXIXB

MANE erat, et volui, si sola quiesceret illa,
    visere: at in lecto Cynthia sola fuit.
obstipui: non illa mihi formosior umquam   25
    visa, neque ostrina cum fuit in tunica,
ibat et hinc castae narratum somnia Vestae,
    neu sibi neve mihi quae nocitura forent.
2.9   qualis et Ischomache Lapithae genus heroine,
2.10   Centauris medio grata rapina mero;
2.11   Mercurio aut qualis fertur Boebeidos undis
2.12   virgineum Brimo composuisse latus:
talis visa mihi somno dimissa recenti.
    heu quantum per se candida forma valet!   30

'quid tu matutinus,' ait, 'speculator amicae?
    me similem vestris moribus esse putas?
non ego tam facilis: sat erit mihi cognitus unus,
    vel tu vel si quis verior esse potest.

---

[23] *sep.* ς   [2.2.9–12] *post* 28 *Richardson**
[11] <aut> *Carutti* qualis *P* : satis Ω

doors. When she unties the strings of her Sidonian
nightcap and lifts her eyes heavy with sleep, no per-
fumes of Arabian spices will waft upon you but
those devised by Love with his very own hands.
Now spare him, brothers, now he pledges that his
love is true; and, see, now we have reached the
house to which we were to bring him.'

²¹ So they cast my mantle back on me and said:
'Go now and learn to stay at home of nights!'

The poet's reception: reality

Iᴛ was dawn, and I wished to see if she slept alone:
yes, Cynthia was alone in bed. I stood entranced:
never had she seemed to me more beautiful, even
when she wore her crimson tunic, and was off to tell
her dreams to chaste Vesta, in case they were
dreams to bring her harm or me. Like the heroine
Ischomache, the Lapith's daughter, welcome spoil of
the Centaurs amid their carousal, or like Brimo,
who as legend tells, by the waters of Boebeis laid her
virgin body at Mercury's side: so she seemed to me
when newly released from slumber. Oh, how great
is the power of a fair face unadorned!

³¹ 'What!' said she, 'do you come spying at dawn
on your sweetheart? Do you think I am like you
men in behaviour? I am not so fickle: enough for me
to know one man, yourself or somebody more

apparent non ulla toro vestigia presso,   35
    signa volutantis nec iacuisse duos.
aspice ut in toto nullus mihi corpore surgat
    spiritus admisso motus adulterio.'

dixit, et opposita propellens savia dextra
    prosilit in laxa nixa pedem solea.   40
sic ego tam sancti custos deludor amoris:
    ex illo felix nox mihi nulla fuit.

XXXA

19 Num tu, dure, paras Phrygias nunc ire per undas
20   et petere Hyrcani litora rauca maris,
21 spargere et alterna communis caede Penates
22   et ferre ad patrios praemia dira Lares?

quo fugis ah demens? nullast fuga: tu licet usque   1
    ad Tanain fugias, usque sequetur Amor.
non si Pegaseo vecteris in aere dorso,
    nec tibi si Persei moverit ala pedes;
vel si te sectae rapiant talaribus aurae,   5
    nil tibi Mercurii proderit alta via.

instat semper Amor supra caput, instat amanti,
    et gravis ipsa super libera colla sedet.

---

[38] motus *Marcilius*: notus Ω
[19] num *Scaliger*: non *N*: nunc *A** | tu dure paras ç: tu
(*om. F*) dura paras *A**: tamen immerito *N* (<3.19.27?)
[20] <ra>uca *Munro*: nota (<nta) Ω
[8] ipsa *Beroaldus*: -e Ω

222

faithful. No marks can be seen pressed into the bed, nor any indication that two have lain in love. See, no breath heaves in all my frame, stirred by adultery committed.'

39 She spoke and, repelling my kisses with a wave of her hand, tripped forth with loose sandals on her feet.[a] Thus am I foiled for spying on my virtuous mistress: since then there has been no happy night for me.

Fragment: Love the inescapable

HARD-HEARTED man, are you now planning to sail the Phrygian waves and seek the wild shores of the Caspian sea, to stain common house-gods with each other's blood and bring back dread trophies to ancestral hearths?

1 Whither do you flee, madman? There is no escape: though you flee to the Don, Love will follow you all the way. Not though you were to fly through the air on the back of Pegasus, or the pinions of Perseus were to move your feet; nor, if the cloven breezes were to sweep you along on winged sandals, would the lofty path of Mercury profit you at all.

7 Love ever looms above your head, looms above the lover, and sits, a heavy burden, even on a neck

---

[a] Unlike the girl in Ovid (*Am.* 3.7.82) who tripped forth barefoot.

excubat ille acer custos et tollere numquam
    te patietur humo lumina capta semel ...   10

et iam si pecces, deus exorabilis illest,
    si modo praesentis viderit esse preces.

XXXB

Ista senes licet accusent convivia duri: 13
    nos modo propositum, vita, teramus iter.
illorum antiquis onerentur legibus aures: 15
    hic locus est in quo, tibia docta, sones,
quae non iure vado Maeandri iacta natasti,
    turpia cum faceret Palladis ora tumor.

una contentum pudeat me vivere amica?   23
    hoc si crimen erit, crimen Amoris erit:
mi nemo obiciat. libeat tibi, Cynthia, mecum   25
    rorida muscosis antra tenere iugis.
illic aspicies scopulis haerere Sorores
    et canere antiqui dulcia furta Iovis,
ut Semelast combustus, ut est deperditus Io,
    denique ut ad Troiae tecta volarit avis.   30
quod si nemo exstat qui vicerit Alitis arma,
    communis culpae cur reus unus agor?

---

[10] *lac. Sh. Bailey*   [13] *sep. Heimreich*
[15] onerentur ς: onerantur Ω
[19-22] *ante* 1 *Carutti*

---

[a] This *non sequitur* is reminiscent of 2.18.21 f.
[b] Minerva invented the pipe but, catching sight of her
reflection in the Maeander as she played, perceived that

once free. He keeps vigil as a keen sentry and will never let you raise your eyes, once captured, from the ground . . .

[11] And now, should you offend, he is not a god deaf to prayers, if only he sees that they are prompt to follow.[a]

Be it your joy to live with me

LET stern old men denounce this revelling of ours; just let us continue, darling, on the path we have begun. Let their ears be burdened with old-fashioned morals: this is the place for you, skilled pipe, to play, you who, unjustly cast down, floated upon the Maeander, when swollen cheeks marred Pallas' face.[b]

[23] Am I to be ashamed to live content with a single mistress? If this is a crime, it is a crime of Love's. Let no one lay it to my door. Cynthia, be it your joy to live with me in a dewy grotto on the mossy hills. There you will see the Sisters sitting upon the rocks and singing of the sweet loves of Jove in legend, how he was inflamed by Semele and undone by Io and finally became a bird and flew to the homes of Troy. And if none has arisen to prevail over the weapons of the winged god, why am I alone accused of a universal fault?

her puffed out cheeks disfigured her beauty; revolted, she cast the pipe into the river.

PROPERTIUS

nec tu Virginibus reverentia moveris ora:
   hic quoque non nescit quid sit amare chorus,
si tamen Oeagri quaedam compressa figura   35
   Bistoniis olim rupibus accubuit.
hic ubi te prima statuent in parte choreae,
   et medius docta cuspide Bacchus erit,
tum capiti sacros patiar pendere corymbos:
   nam sine te nostrum non valet ingenium.   40

XXXI, XXXII

Quaeris, cur veniam tibi tardior? aurea Phoebi
   porticus a magno Caesare aperta fuit.
tota erat in spatium Poenis digesta columnis,
   inter quas Danai femina turba senis.
hic equidem Phoebus visus mihi pulchrior ipso   5
   marmoreus tacita carmen hiare lyra;
atque aram circum steterant armenta Myronis,
   quattuor artificis, vivida signa, boves.

---

[3] tota ç: tanta Ω | spatium *Heinsius*: speciem Ω
[5] Phoebus ç: phoebo Ω

[33] Nor need you address the maiden Muses with awestruck lips: their company also knows what it means to love, if after all it is true that one of them upon the rocks of Bistonia was once ravished by the semblance of Oeagrus. There, when they set you in the forefront of their dance, and Bacchus stands in the midst with his wand of song, then will I suffer the sacred ivy to be placed upon my brow: for without you my genius is naught.

Acceptance of Cynthia's infidelities

You ask why I come to you somewhat late? Apollo's golden portico has been opened by mighty Caesar.[a] The whole of it had been marked out for a promenade with Afric[b] columns, between which stood the many daughters of old Danaus. Here I thought that Phoebus' statue was fairer than Phoebus himself as he sang with silent lyre and parted lips of marble; and around the altar stood Myron's herd, four steers by the sculptor, statuary which seemed to be alive. Then in the middle rose

---

[a] The temple of Apollo on the Palatine, the most splendid of Augustus' buildings, was vowed in 36 after his defeat of Sextus Pompeius and dedicated in October 28 (commemorated by Horace, *Odes* 1.31). The whole complex was surrounded by a sumptuous portico. Cf. *Res Gestae* 19, Suetonius, *Aug.* 29.

[b] I.e. made of African marble, having a yellowish colour and known as *giallo antico*.

227

tum medium claro surgebat marmore templum,
    et patria Phoebo carius Ortygia: 10
in quo Solis erat supra fastigia currus,
    et valvae, Libyci nobile dentis opus;
altera deiectos Parnasi vertice Gallos,
    altera maerebat funera Tantalidos.
deinde inter matrem deus ipse interque sororem 15
    Pythius in longa carmina veste sonat.

hoc utinam spatiere loco, quodcumque vacabis, 32.7
    Cynthia! sed tibi me credere turba vetat,
cum videt accensis devotam currere taedis
    in nemus et Triviae lumina ferre deae.   10
qui videt, is peccat: qui te non viderit ergo   1
    non cupiet: facti lumina crimen habent.
nam quid Praenesti dubias, o Cynthia, sortes,
    quid petis Aeaei moenia Telegoni?
cur ita te Herculeum deportant esseda Tibur?   5
    Appia cur totiens te Via Lanuvium?
scilicet umbrosis sordet Pompeia columnis   11
    porticus, aulaeis nobilis Attalicis,
et platanis creber pariter surgentibus ordo,
    flumina sopito quaeque Marone cadunt,

[32.1] *cont.* Ω (*sep. Itali*)
[7–10] *ante* 1 *Hetzel*

[a] White marble from Luna (mod. Carrara), cf. Virgil, *Aen.* 8.720; Ovid, *Trist.* 3.1.60.

the temple, of dazzling marble,[a] dearer to Phoebus
even than his Ortygian home: upon the pediment of
this stood the chariot of the Sun, and doors which
were a famed piece of African ivory; one door
lamented the Gauls cast down from Parnassus'
peak, the other the deaths of Niobe and her chil-
dren. Then between his mother and his sister the
god of Pytho himself, wearing a long cloak, plays
and sings.

32.7 I wish you would promenade here in all your
leisure hours, Cynthia! But the world of men for-
bids me to trust you, when they see you hurrying
with kindled torches to worship at the Arician grove
and carrying lights for the goddess Trivia.[b] Who
sees you, sins: therefore who sees you not, will not
desire you: the eyes bear guilt for the deed. Why,
Cynthia, do you seek riddling oracles at Praeneste,
why seek the walls of Aeaean Telegonus? Why so
oft are you taken by your carriage to Herculean
Tibur, why so oft by the Appian Way to Lanuvium?
Pompey's portico,[c] I take it, is not good enough for
you, with its shady columns, resplendent with bro-
caded awnings, or the dense avenue of plane-trees
rising evenly, the streams which issue out of the

[b] Diana of Nemi, who was worshipped by processions of
women carrying torches. See especially J. G. Frazer, *The
Golden Bough* I 1–14.

[c] A rectangular court adjoining the theatre of Pompey in
the Campus Martius; a popular rendezvous (cf. 4.8.75).

et sonitus lymphis toto crepitantibus orbe,   15
    cum subito Triton ore refundit aquam.

falleris, ista tui furtum via monstrat amoris:
    non urbem, demens, lumina nostra fugis!
nil agis, insidias in me componis inanis,
    tendis iners docto retia nota mihi.   20
sed de me minus est: famae iactura pudicae
    tanta tibi miserae, quanta meretur, erit.
nuper enim de te nostras maledixit ad aures
    rumor, et in tota non bonus urbe fuit.

sed te non debes inimicae cedere linguae: 25
    semper formosis fabula poena fuit.
non tua deprenso damnatast fama veneno:
    testis eris puras, Phoebe, videre manus.
sin autem longo nox una aut altera lusu
    consumptast, non me crimina parva movent.   30
Tyndaris externo patriam mutavit amore,
    et sine decreto viva reducta domumst.
ipsa Venus, quamvis corrupta libidine Martis,
    nec minus in caelo semper honesta fuit,
quamvis Ida illam pastorem dicat amasse   35
    atque inter pecudes accubuisse deam;
hoc et Hamadryadum spectavit turba sororum
    Silenique senes et pater ipse chori,

---

[15] sonitus *Heyworth**: leviter Ω | lymphis ς: nymphis Ω
| toto ... orbe *Heinsius*: tota ... urbe Ω
[16] refundit *Heinsius*: recondit Ω
[23] maledixit *Schneidewin*: me laedit Ω (<me ladxt)
[25] cedere *Wakker*: credere Ω   [33] quamvis *A**: fertur *N*
[35] <illam> *Barber*: parim Ω (*a gloss*)

slumbering Maro, or the sound of the water which splashes all round the basin, when the Triton suddenly pours forth a fountain from his lips.

[17] You are mistaken, these journeys of yours indicate some furtive love affair: it is not Rome but my eyes that you flee, silly girl! You are wasting your time, the wiles you spin against me are futile, you are a novice laying familiar traps for me, who am an adept. But for me it matters less: the loss of your good name will cause you all the harm which is deserved. For lately rumour spoke ill of you to my ears, and all over the town there was nasty gossip.

[25] But you should not surrender to an unfriendly tongue: scandal has always been the penalty for beauty. Your good name has not been destroyed by a charge of poisoning: Phoebus, you will testify that her hands are pure. And if one or two nights have been spent in drawn out dalliance, I am not upset by peccadilloes. Tyndareus' daughter left her country for the love of a stranger, and was brought home unharmed and undivorced. Venus was never the worse thought of in heaven, though she herself yielded to her passion for Mars and though Ida tells that she loved a shepherd[a] and amid his flocks gave herself, a goddess, to him; their amour was witnessed by the band of sister Hamadryads as well as by the elderly satyrs and the father of the company

---

[a] Anchises (cf. Homer, *Il.* 5.313; *Hom. Hymn.* 3.53ff; Theocritus, 1.105f; Ovid, *Her.* 16.203f).

cum quibus Idaeo legisti poma sub antro,
    supposita excipiens, Nai, caduca manu.   40

an quisquam in tanto stuprorum examine quaerit
    'cur haec tam dives? quis dedit? unde dedit?'
o nimium nostro felicem tempore Romam,
    si contra mores una puella facit!
haec eadem ante illam iam impune et Lesbia fecit: 45
    quae sequitur, certest invidiosa minus.
qui quaerit Tatium veterem durosque Sabinos,
    hic posuit nostra nuper in urbe pedem.

tu prius et fluctus poteris siccare marinos,
    altaque mortali deligere astra manu,   50
quam facere, ut nostrae nolint peccare puellae:
    hic mos Saturno regna tenente fuit.
at cum Deucalionis aquae fluxere per orbem,
    et post antiquas Deucalionis aquas,
dic mihi, quis potuit lectum servare pudicum,   55
    quae dea cum solo vivere sola deo?
uxorem quondam magni Minois, ut aiunt,
    corrupit torvi candida forma bovis;
nec minus aerato Danaë circumdata muro
    non potuit magno casta negare Iovi.   60
quod si tu Graias, si tu's imitata Latinas,
    semper vive meo libera iudicio!

---

45 iam *add.* ç: om. Ω
47 Tatium veterem *Heyworth**: -ios -es Ω
61 <si> tu es *Heyworth** (seu tu es *Luck*): tu[que] es Ω

himself,[a] with whom were Naiads gathering apples in the vales of Ida, catching them as they fell into their waiting hands.

⁴¹ Does anyone ask in such a swarm of debauchery 'Why is she so rich? Who gave? Whence came his gifts?' Rome in our day is more than fortunate, if one girl acts contrary to prescribed behaviour! Lesbia has already done all this before her with impunity: Lesbia's follower is surely less to blame. Anyone who expects to find ancient Tatius and the stern Sabines has but lately set foot in our city.

⁴⁹ Sooner will you be able to dry the waves of the sea and pluck with mortal hand the stars set in high heaven than ensure that Roman girls are unwilling to sin: this was the fashion in the reign of Saturn. But when Deucalion's flood swept over the world and after Deucalion's legendary flood, tell me, who was able to keep his bed chaste, what goddess could live alone with one god only? Once was the wife of mighty Minos, so they say, seduced by the snow-white form of a glowering bull; and Danaë, although shut up within bronze walls, had not the virtue to resist mighty Jove. But if you choose to follow the example of Greek and of Roman women, then have my ruling to live for ever as you wish!

[a] Silenus.

PROPERTIUS

XXXIIIA

TRISTIA iam redeunt iterum sollemnia nobis:
　　Cynthia iam noctes est operata decem.
atque utinam pereant, Nilo quae sacra tepente
　　misit matronis Inachis Ausoniis!

quae dea tam cupidos totiens divisit amantes?　　5
　　quaecumque, illa suis semper amara fuit.
tu certe Iovis occultis in amoribus, Io,
　　sensisti multas quid sit inire vias.
cum te iussit habere puellam cornua Iuno
　　et pecoris duro perdere verba sono,　　10
ah quotiens quernis laesisti frondibus ora,
　　mandisti et stabulis arbuta pasta tuis!
an, quoniam agrestem detraxit ab ore figuram
　　Iuppiter, idcirco facta superba dea's?
an tibi non satis est fuscis Aegyptus alumnis?　　15
　　cur tibi tam longa Roma petita via?
quidve tibi prodest viduas dormire puellas?
　　sed tibi, crede mihi, cornua rursus erunt,
aut nos e nostra te, saeva, fugabimus urbe:
　　cum Tiberi Nilo gratia nulla fuit.　　20

at tu, quae nostro, nimium pia, causa dolori's,
　　noctibus his vacui, ter faciamus iter.

^{6} suis *Housman**: fuit Ω
^{8} vias. *et* ^{10} sono, *dist. Housman**
^{21} pia causa *Housman**: placa[ta] Ω (<pla c̄ā) | dolori
Scaliger: dolore Ω

234

Worship of Isis

ONCE again to my sorrow the dismal rites[a] have returned: now for ten[b] nights is Cynthia engaged in worship. Down with the rites which the daughter of Inachus has sent from the warm Nile to the matrons of Italy!

[5] The goddess that has so often sundered ardent lovers, whoever she was, was always harsh. In your secret love of Jove, Io, you certainly discovered what it means to travel on many paths. When Juno bade you, a human girl, put on horns and drown your speech in the hoarse lowing of a cow, ah, how often did you chafe your mouth with oak leaves and chew in your stall the arbute you had fed on! Is it because Jupiter has taken that wild shape from your features that you have become such a haughty goddess? Are the swarthy daughters of Egypt too few for your worship? Why did you take the long journey to Rome? What profit is it to you that girls should sleep alone? Take it from me, either you will have horns again or else, cruel creature, we will banish you from our city: the Nile has never found favour with the Tiber.

[21] But you, who through an excess of piety have caused my sufferings, when we are released from these nights, let us thrice make love's journey.

[a] See Index, *Isis*.   [b] Cf. 2.28.62.

XXXIIIB

Non audis et verba sinis mea ludere, cum iam
  flectant Icarii sidera tarda boves.
lenta bibis: mediae nequeunt te frangere noctes?   25
  an nondumst talos mittere lassa manus?

ah pereat, quicumque meracas repperit uvas
  corrupitque bonas nectare primus aquas!
Icare, Cecropiis merito iugulate colonis,
  pampineus nosti quam sit amarus odor!   30
tuque o Eurytion vino Centaure peristi,
  nec non Ismario tu, Polypheme, mero.
vino forma perit, vino corrumpitur aetas,
  vino saepe suum nescit amica virum.

me miserum, ut multo nihil est mutata Lyaeo!   35
  iam bibe: formosa's: nil tibi vina nocent,
cum tua praependent demissae in pocula sertae,
  et mea deducta carmina voce legis.
largius effuso madeat tibi mensa Falerno,
  spumet et aurato mollius in calice.   40

XXXIIIC

... semper in absentis felicior aestus amantes: 43
  elevat assiduos copia longa viros.

---

[23] *sep. Hertzberg*
[41-44] *sep. Heyworth**
[41,42] *post 44 Barber*

Cynthia holds her wine

You hear not my words and let them fall idly on the air, though already Icarus' oxen[a] are turning their slow-setting stars.[b] You drink unmoved: can midnight not wear you down? Is your hand not yet tired of throwing the dice?

27 Perish the man who discovered the heady grape and spoilt good water by mixing it with wine! The farmers of Athens had good cause to slay you, Icarus: you have learned how bitter is the scent of the vine. You, too, centaur Eurytion, were undone by wine and you, too, Polyphemus, by liquor of Ismarus. Wine ruins beauty, wine spoils youth, wine oft causes a mistress to mistake her man.

35 Mercy on us! She is not a bit affected by so much drinking! Well, drink on: you are beautiful: wine harms you not at all when garlands hang over your face and dip into your cups and you read my poems with dainty voice. Let the table swim even more liberally with floods of Falernian, let it bubble more lusciously in your golden goblet.

Fragment: absence increases fondness

... Woman's heart is ever fonder towards an absent lover: long possession lessens the appeal of the per-

---

[a] A misleading description of the constellation Bootes: only the Herdsman was catasterized, not his oxen.

[b] See note on 3.5.35.

41   nulla tamen lecto recipit se sola libenter:
42   est quiddam, quod vos quaerere cogat Amor.

XXXIV

Cur quisquam faciem dominae iam credat Amori?
    sic erepta mihi paene puella meast.
expertus dico, nemost in amore fidelis:
    formosam raro non sibi quisque petit.
polluit ille deus cognatos, solvit amicos,   5
    et bene concordis tristia ad arma vocat.
hospes in hospitium Menelao venit adulter;
    Colchis et ignotum nempe secuta virum.

Lynceu, tune meam potuisti, perfide, curam
    tangere? nonne tuae tum cecidere manus?   10
quid si non constans illa et tam certa fuisset,
    posset et in tanto vivere flagitio?

8 nempe *Housman**: nonne Ω (cf. Ovid, *Her.* 20.70)
11 quid si non *interpret. Pope* (cf. 1.9.15)
12 posset et *F*: posses et *LP*: posses *N*

sistent wooer. Yet no woman willingly retires to bed alone: there is something which Love compels you all to seek.

To Lynceus on Love Poetry

WHY should anyone henceforth entrust his sweetheart's beauty to Love? Thus was my sweetheart nearly stolen from me. I speak from experience: no man is faithful when it comes to love: rarely does any man, on seeing a beautiful woman, not want her for himself. That god pollutes kinsmen and separates friends, and provokes to bitter strife those linked in close harmony. The guest who came to Menelaus's hospitality proved an adulterer; and it was of course an unknown lover that Medea followed.

[9] Lynceus,[a] treacherous friend, had you the heart to touch the girl I love? Did not your hands then fall powerless? It would be different had she not been so staunch and devoted or could live in such shame!

---

[a] Boucher (*Revue des études anciennes* 60 [1958] 307–322) has plausibly argued that Lynceus is a pseudonym for Lucius Varius Rufus, who introduced Horace to Maecenas, was the posthumous editor of the *Aeneid,* and was (with his *Thyestes*) the leading dramatist of the age. See also Camps, Bk 2, page 235.

tu mihi vel ferro pectus vel perde veneno:
  a domina tantum te modo tolle mea.
te dominum vitae, te corporis esse licebit,   15
  te socium admitto rebus, amice, meis:
lecto te solum, lecto te deprecor uno:
  rivalem possum non ego ferre Iovem.
ipse meae solus, quod nil est, aemulor umbrae,
  stultus, quod nullo saepe timore tremo.   20

una tamen causast, qua crimina tanta remitto,
  errabant multo quod tua verba mero.
sed numquam vitae fallet me ruga severae:
  omnes iam norunt quam sit amare bonum.

Lynceus ipse meus seros insanit amores!   25
  serum te nostros laetor adire deos.
quid tua Socraticis tibi nunc sapientia libris
  proderit aut rerum dicere posse vias?
aut quid Cretaei tibi prosunt carmina plectri?
  nil iuvat in magno vester amore senex.   30
tu satius Musis leviorem imitere Philitan
  et non inflati somnia Callimachi.

---

15 dominum *Cornelissen* : socium Ω
16 socium *Cornelissen* : dominum Ω
19 meae ... umbrae *Heinsius* : meas ... umbras Ω
20 nullo *Heinsius* : stulto Ω (<stultus)
26 serum *Bergk* : solum Ω
29 Cretaei *edd. vett.* : crethei A* (erechti N) | plectri
Palmer : lecta Ω
31 leviorem *Santen* : memorem A* (memorem musis N)

[13] Take away my life with sword or poison: only remove yourself from my mistress. You may be lord over me, body and soul; I make you, friend, a partner in my wealth. Only from my bed, from my bed alone I beg you to abstain: not even Jupiter can I bear as a rival. When alone, I am even jealous of my shadow, a thing without substance, fool that I oft tremble with a baseless fear.

[21] Still there is one reason why I pardon such a crime: much wine had caused your words to stray. But the wrinkled brow of your ascetic life shall not deceive me: for by this time the whole world knows what a good thing is love.

[25] Even my friend Lynceus at this late hour is madly in love! I rejoice that even at this late hour you worship our gods. What will avail you now the wisdom you draw from Socratic books or the power to set forth the workings of the universe? Or what avail you the cantos of the Cretan's[a] lyre? Your ancient bard helps not in a passionate love. Better that you should imitate the slighter muse of Philitas and the dream of unpretentious Callimachus.

[a] Epimenides (see Index *s.v.* Cretaeus).

nam cursus licet Aetoli referas Acheloi,
    fluxerit ut magno fractus amore liquor,
atque etiam ut Phrygio fallax Maeandria campo   35
    errat et ipsa suas decipit unda vias,
qualis et Adrasti fuerit vocalis Arion,
    tristis ad Archemori funera victor equus:
num Amphiaraëae prosint tibi fata quadrigae
    aut Capanei magno grata ruina Iovi?   40
desine et Aeschyleo componere verba coturno,
    desine, et ad mollis membra resolve choros.

incipe iam angusto versus includere torno,
    inque tuos ignes, dure poeta, veni.
tu non Antimacho, non tutior ibis Homero: 45
    despicit et magnos recta puella deos.
harum nulla solet rationem quaerere mundi,   51
    nec cur fraternis Luna laboret equis,
nec si post Stygias aliquid restabimus undas,
    nec si consulto fulmina missa tonent.

---

[33] cursus ς: rursus Ω
[39] num *Unger*: non Ω | Amphiaraëae *Unger*: amphi-aree Ω*
[47-50] *post* 54 *Müller*
[53] restabimus <undas> *Wassenberg*: restabit *N*: resta-bit [erumnas] *A**

---

[a] When it warned Adrastus of the outcome of the fight (cf. Statius, *Theb.* 11.442).

[33] For though you should tell of the course of Aetolian Achelous, how its waters flowed shattered by the power of love, and also how the stream of the Meander wanders deceptively over the Phrygian plain and itself conceals the direction of its flow, and how Adrastus' Arion spoke aloud,[a] the horse which had gained victory[b] at the funeral games of ill-starred Archemorus: would the fate of Amphiaraus's chariot aught avail you or the destruction of Capaneus, which gave pleasure to mighty Jove? Cease to compose speeches for the buskin of Aeschylus and relax your limbs for gentle dances.

[43] Begin now to turn your verses on a narrow lathe[c] and come nearer, hard-hearted poet, to the fires you feel. You will not fare safer than Antimachus or Homer[d]: an attractive girl despises even the mighty gods. None of these girls is wont to inquire into the system of the universe, or why the Moon labours because of her brother's steeds, or if aught of us survives beyond the river Styx, or if the crashing thunderbolts are launched by a purposeful hand.

[b] Ridden by Polynices (*ib.* 6.316) and granted victory by favour of Neptune (*ib.* 6.529).

[c] Propertius seems to have originated the metaphor, which became popular (e.g. Horace, *A.P.* 441).

[d] Antimachus lost his heart to Lyde, Homer his (according to Hermesianax, *Coll. Alex.* p. 98f) to Penelope.

47 sed non ante gravi taurus succumbit aratro,
48   cornua quam validis haeserit in laqueis,
49 nec tu tam duros per te patieris amores:
50   trux tamen a nobis ante domandus eris.
    aspice me, cui parva domi fortuna relictast   55
        nullus et antiquo Marte triumphus avi,
    ut regnem mixtas inter conviva puellas
        hoc ego, quo tibi nunc elevor, ingenio!

    mi libet hesternis posito languere corollis,
        quem tetigit iactu certus ad ossa deus;   60
    Actia Vergilio custodis litora Phoebi,
        Caesaris et fortis dicere posse rates,
    qui nunc Aeneae Troiani suscitat arma
        iactaque Lavinis moenia litoribus.
    cedite, Romani scriptores, cedite, Grai!   65
        nescio quid maius nascitur Iliade.
77 tu canis Ascraei veteris praecepta poetae,
78   quo seges in campo, quo viret uva iugo.
79 tale facis carmen docta testudine quale
80   Cynthius impositis temperat articulis.

---

[59] mi lubet ... posito *Housman* : me iuvet ... positum Ω
[77-80] *post* 66 *Ribbeck*

---

[a] Clearly echoing the exordium of the *Aeneid:*
    Arma virumque cano, *Troiae* qui primus ab oris
    Italiam fato profugus *Lavina*que venit / *litora* ...

244

[47] But the stubborn bull does not yield to the yoke of the plough until his horns have been caught in the stout noose; nor will you by yourself be able to endure the stern hardships of love: though wild, you must first be subdued by me. Look at me, for whom was left a scanty fortune at home, and no ancestor ever won a triumph in battles of yore, and how I reign at the banquet among a crowd of girls thanks to the genius for which I am now disparaged by you.

[59] My pleasure is to loll amid the garlands of yesterday, for the god of unerring aim has pierced me to the bone: that of VIRGIL is to be able to sing the Actian shores o'er which Apollo watches, and the brave fleet of Caesar; even now he is stirring to life the arms of Trojan Aeneas and the walls he founded on Lavine shores.[a] Make way, ye Roman writers, make way, ye Greeks! Something greater than the Iliad is coming to birth.[b]

[77] You sing[c] the precepts of the old bard of Ascra, in what soil flourishes the corn, on what hill the grape. You make such music as Cynthian Apollo attunes with fingers placed upon his skilled lyre.

---

[b] 'Make way, ye Roman authors,
                 clear the street, O ye Greeks,
For a much larger Iliad is in the course of construction
                     (and to Imperial order)
Clear the streets, O ye Greeks!' (Ezra Pound).
  [c] Referring to the *Georgics,* which had as its literary ancestor Ascrean Hesiod's *Works and Days.*

tu canis umbrosi subter pineta Galaesi   67
    Thyrsin et attritis Daphnin harundinibus,
utque decem possint corrumpere mala puellas
    missus et impressis haedus ab uberibus.   70

felix, qui vilis pomis mercaris amores!
    huic licet ingratae Tityrus ipse canat.
felix intactum Corydon qui temptat Alexin
    agricolae domini carpere delicias!
quamvis ille sua lassus requiescat avena,   75
    laudatur facilis inter Hamadryadas.

non tamen haec ulli venient ingrata legenti,   81
    sive in amore rudis sive peritus erit.
nec minor hic animis, ut sit minor ore, canorus
    anseris indocto carmine cessit olor.

haec quoque perfecto ludebat Iasone VARRO,   85
    Varro Leucadiae maxima flamma suae;
haec quoque lascivi cantarunt scripta CATULLI,
    Lesbia quîs ipsa notior est Helena;

---

^a Referring to the *Eclogues,* which had as its literary
ancestor the *Idylls* of Theocritus (Thyrsis and Daphnis
point clearly to *Id.* 1).

You sing,[a] beneath the pinewoods of shady Galaesus,[b] of Thyrsis and Daphnis with his well-worn pipes, and how ten apples or the gift of a kid fresh from the udder of its dam may win the love of girls.

[71] Happy you, who can buy your love cheaply with apples! To her, unkind though she be, even Tityrus may sing. Happy is Corydon, who essays to steal Alexis yet unwon, the darling of his rustic master. Though the poet is weary and rests from his piping, he is praised by the compliant nymphs.

[81] But these songs of his will not fail to please any reader, be he a tiro in love or one accomplished. And the melodious swan, displaying no lesser genius in this lesser style, has not disgraced himself with the tuneless strain of a goose.[c]

[85] Such themes did VARRO also sport with, his tale of Jason ended, Varro, the brightest flame of his Leucadia; such themes the verse of wanton CATULLUS also sang, which made Lesbia better known than Helen herself; such passion also the

___

[b] Probably a fancy of our poet's: the river is not mentioned in the *Eclogues,* but at *Georg.* 4.125 Virgil testifies that he had visited the locality.

[c] Alluding to *Ecl.* 9.36, where Virgil makes a slighting pun on the name of Anser (cf. Ovid, *Trist.* 2.435), a contemporary erotic poet.

haec etiam docti confessast pagina CALVI,
    cum caneret miserae funera Quintiliae.   90
et modo formosa quam multa Lycoride GALLUS
    mortuus inferna vulnera lavit aqua!

Cynthia quin vivet versu laudata PROPERTI,
    hos inter si me ponere Fama volet.

[93] <viv>et *Barber* : et[iam] Ω

pages of learned CALVUS confessed, when he sang of
the death of hapless Quintilia. And in these recent
days how many wounds has GALLUS, dead for love of
fair Lycoris, laved in the waters of the world below!

93 Yea, Cynthia glorified in the pages of
PROPERTIUS shall live, if Fame consent to rank me
with bards like these.[a]

[a] Although this discursive poem has sharp divisions
after lines 24 and 58, the employment of a pseudonymous
addressee (see note on 2.21.1) establishes Propertius' con-
ception of it as a unity: (1–24) Lynceus has tried to steal
the poet's girl; (25–58) Lynceus should abandon highbrow
verse and turn to love poetry; (59–94) love poetry, not
spurned even by Virgil, is able to confer immortality.

BOOK THREE

Like the poet's first and last books, Book Three is readily recognizable as a unit. In the opening couplet Propertius formally announces that henceforth he is the Roman successor of Callimachus and Philitas and has freed himself from an exclusive commitment to personal love elegy, which nevertheless continues to be represented. The new poetry touches on a wide range of topics: the poet's status, the narration of myth (as in the story of Dirce), political comment (with reference to Cleopatra and the forthcoming Parthian campaigns), an encomium of Bacchus, another of Italy, and funeral elegies on Paetus and Marcellus. The last poem (the 24th, for 3.24 and 3.25, joined in A*, clearly cohere and form the recantation of 1.1) would seem to bid Cynthia a final farewell. But just as Conan Doyle was to discover with Sherlock Holmes, some fictional characters lie outside the power of their creators to dispose of, and we shall meet her again before the end.

LIBER TERTIUS

I

CALLIMACHI Manes et Coi sacra Philitae,
 in vestrum, quaeso, me sinite ire nemus.
primus ego ingredior puro de fonte sacerdos
 Itala per Graios orgia ferre choros.
dicite, quo pariter carmen tenuastis in antro   5
 quove pede ingressi? quamve bibistis aquam?

ah valeat, Phoebum quicumque moratur in armis!
 exactus tenui pumice versus eat,
quo me Fama levat terra sublimis, et a me
 nata coronatis Musa triumphat equis,   10
et mecum in curru parvi vectantur Amores,
 scriptorumque meas turba secuta rotas.
quid frustra immissis mecum certatis habenis?
 non datur ad Musas currere lata via.

multi, Roma, tuas laudes annalibus addent,   15
 qui finem imperii Bactra futura canent.

---

[13] immissis *Auratus* me<cum> *P* : missis in me Ω

---

[a] Right foot first was a superstition of the ancients: see
Mayor on Juvenal 10.5.

THE THIRD BOOK

The invocation

Shade of Callimachus and rites of Coan Philitas, suffer me, I pray, to come into your grove. I am the first to enter, priest from an unsullied spring, bringing Italy's mystic emblems in dances of Greece. Say, in what grotto did ye together spin the delicate thread of your song? With what foot[a] enter? What water drink?

[7] Begone the man who detains Phoebus with themes of war! Let my verse run smoothly, perfected with fine pumice, whereby soaring Fame uplifts me from the earth, and the Muse that is born of me triumphs with garlanded steeds; with me in the chariot ride little Loves,[b] and a throng of writers follows behind my wheels. Why do you loosen rein and vainly compete with me? No broad way is appointed for the race to the Muses.

[15] Many, O Rome, will add new praises to your annals, singing of Bactra as the future limit of

---

[b] Like the children of a triumphing general, who were often taken in the chariot with him.

sed, quod pace legas, opus hoc de monte Sororum
    detulit intacta pagina nostra via.
mollia, Pegasides, date vestro serta poetae:
    non faciet capiti dura corona meo.   20

at mihi quod vivo detraxerit invida turba,
    post obitum duplici faenore reddet Honos;
omnia post obitum fingit maiora vetustas:
    maius ab exsequiis nomen in ora venit.

nam quis equo pulsas abiegno nosceret arces,   25
    fluminaque Haemonio comminus isse viro,
Idaeum Simoenta Iovis cum prole Scamandro,
    Hectora per campos ter maculasse rotas?
Deiphobumque Helenumque et Pulydamantis in armi
    qualemcumque Parim vix sua nosset humus.   30
exiguo sermone fores nunc, Ilion, et tu
    Troia bis Oetaei numine capta dei.

nec non ille tui casus memorator Homerus
    posteritate suum crescere sensit opus;
meque inter seros laudabit Roma nepotes: 35
    illum post cineres auguror ipse diem.

---

[29] pulydamantis ς (*interpret. Postgate*): -es Ω

---

[a] Ezra Pound has 'I shall have, doubtless, a boom after
my funeral, / Seeing that long standing increases all things
regardless of quality.'

[b] I.e. the Trojan Horse, cf. Virgil, *Aen.* 2.16 sectaque
intexunt abiete costas.

empire. But this work for you to read in time of peace has my page brought down by an untrodden path from the Sisters' mount. Pegasid Muses, delicate be the garlands you bestow on your poet: an epic crown will not suit my brow.

21 But what the envious crowd disallows me in my lifetime, Fame will repay with double interest after my death. Time makes all things greater after death: after his funeral a man's name sounds greater on people's lips.[a]

25 Else who would know the fortress battered by the firwood horse,[b] the rivers that fought in combat with Thessaly's hero, Simois of Ida together with Jove's offspring Scamander, and the chariot that thrice befouled Hector's body on the plain? And Deiphobus and Helenus and Paris in Polydamas' armour, sorry figure though he cut,[c] their own country would scarcely know about. Ilion, you would now be little talked of, as you too, Troy, twice taken by the power of Oeta's god.

33 Homer also, the chronicler of your fate, has found his reputation grow with the passage of time. I, too, will be praised by late generations of Rome: I myself predict that after I am ashes such a day will

[c] No such incident is elsewhere reported, but the poet was probably thinking of Paris' inglorious combat with Menelaus (Homer, *Il.* 3.324ff) and misremembered that it was Lycaon's armour, not Polydamas', that he borrowed.

PROPERTIUS

ne mea contempto lapis indicet ossa sepulcro
    provisumst Lycio vota probante deo.

II

CARMINIS interea nostri redeamus in orbem,
    gaudeat ut solito tacta puella sono.

Orphea delenisse feras et concita dicunt
    flumina Threicia sustinuisse lyra;
saxa Cithaeronis Thebanam agitata per artem   5
    sponte sua in muri membra coisse ferunt;
quin etiam, Polypheme, fera Galatea sub Aetna
    ad tua rorantis carmina flexit equos:
miremur, nobis et Baccho et Apolline dextro,
    turba puellarum si mea verba colit?   10

quod non Taenariis domus est mihi fulta columnis,
    nec camera auratas inter eburna trabes,
nec mea Phaeacas aequant pomaria silvas,
    non operosa rigat Marcius antra liquor;
at Musae comites et carmina cara legenti,   15
    nec defessa choris Calliopea meis.
fortunata, meo si qua's celebrata libello!
    carmina erunt formae tot monumenta tuae.

nam neque pyramidum sumptus ad sidera ducti,
    nec Iovis Elei caelum imitata domus,   20

---

² ut ς: in Ω   ³ delenisse *Ayrmann*: detinuisse Ω
⁵ Theb<an>am *Heinsius*: thebas Ω
¹⁶ nec *Baehrens*: et *A**: *om. N*

256

come. Not neglected shall be the grave where the tombstone marks my bones: so decrees the Lycian god, who approves my prayer.

The power of song

LET me return meanwhile to my wonted round of song, so that my sweetheart is thrilled by the familiar strain.

³ They say that Orpheus tamed wild beasts and stayed rushing rivers with his Thracian lyre; the rocks of Cithaeron, they say, stirred by a Theban's art, joined together of their own accord to form a wall; nay, even Galatea beneath savage Etna turned her dripping horses at the sound of Polyphemus' serenade: what wonder then, if Bacchus and Apollo smile on me, that a throng of maidens should love my words?

¹¹ If my house rises not on pillars of Taenarian marble, and my ceiling is not vaulted with ivory between gilded beams, if I have no fruit-trees matching Phaeacia's orchards or man-made grottoes watered by the Marcian conduit; yet the Muses are my friends, my poems are dear to the reader, and Calliope never wearies of dancing to my rhythms. Happy woman, whoe'er you be, that are praised in a book of mine! Each poem will be a memorial of your beauty.

¹⁹ For neither the costly pyramids soaring to the skies, nor the temple of Jove at Elis that mimics

257

nec Mausolei dives fortuna sepulcri
    mortis ab extrema condicione vacant.
aut illis flamma aut imber subducet honores,
    annorum aut tacito pondere victa ruent.
at non ingenio quaesitum nomen ab aevo   25
    excidet: ingenio stat sine morte decus.

III

Vɪsᴜs eram molli recubans Heliconis in umbra,
    Bellerophontei qua fluit umor equi,
reges, Alba, tuos et regum facta tuorum,
    tantum operis, nervis hiscere posse meis;
parvaque iam magnis admoram fontibus ora   5
    (unde pater sitiens Ennius ante bibit,
et cecinit Curios fratres et Horatia pila,
    regiaque Aemilia vecta tropaea rate,
victricisque moras Fabii pugnamque sinistram
    Cannensem et versos ad pia vota deos,   10
Hannibalemque Lares Romana sede fugantis,
    anseris et tutum voce fuisse Iovem),

---

²⁴ <t>acito *Eldik* : ictu Ω   ⁵ iam *Guyet* : tam Ω

ᵃ For thought and expression cf. Shakespeare, *Sonnet*
55.1f, 'Nor marble, nor the gilded monuments / Of princes,
shall outlive this powerful rhyme ...' The temple of
Jupiter (Zeus) at Olympia mimics heaven not so much by
its height as by housing Phidias' statue of Zeus, one of the
seven wonders of the world.

heaven, nor the sumptuous magnificence of the
tomb of Mausolus are exempt from the ultimate
decree of death.[a] Either fire or rain will steal away
their glory, or they will collapse under the weight of
the silent years. But the fame my genius has won
shall not perish with time: genius claims a glory
that knows no death.

The poet's vision

I dreamed that lying in the soft shade of Helicon,
where flows the fountain of Bellerophon's horse, I
possessed the power to proclaim to my lyre's accom-
paniment Alba's kings and their deeds, a mighty
task. I had already put my puny lips to that potent
spring (whence father Ennius once thirstily drank
and sang[b] of the Curian brothers and the spears of
the Horatii, and Jupiter saved by the cackling of
geese; the victorious delays of Fabius, the calami-
tous battle of Cannae, gods that turned to answer
pious prayers, and Lares that drove off Hannibal
from their abode in Rome, and royal trophies tran-
sported on Aemilius' galleys), when Phoebus

[b] Of the Curiatii and the Horatii in *Annals* 1; of the Cap-
itol saved by the geese in *Annals* 4; of the events of the
Second Punic War in *Annals* 7–9; and of Aemilius Regillus'
victory at Myonnesus in *Annals* 14 (but Propertius seems
to have conflated this with the triumphal return of
L. Aemilius Paullus up the Tiber in 167, by which time
Ennius was dead).

259

cum me Castalia speculans ex arbore Phoebus
  sic ait aurata nixus ad antra lyra:

'quid tibi cum tali, demens, est flumine? quis te   15
  carminis heroi tangere iussit opus?
non hinc ulla tibi sperandast fama, Properti:
  mollia sunt parvis prata terenda rotis;
ut tuus in scamno iactetur saepe libellus,
  quem legat exspectans sola puella virum.   20
cur tua praescriptos evectast pagina gyros?
  non est ingenii cumba gravanda tui.
alter remus aquas alter tibi radat harenas,
  tutus eris: medio maxima turba marist.'
dixerat, et plectro sedem mihi monstrat eburno,   25
  quo nova muscoso semita facta solost.

hic erat affixis viridis spelunca lapillis,
  pendebantque cavis tympana pumicibus,
orgia Musarum et Sileni patris imago
  fictilis et calami, Pan Tegeaee, tui;   30
et Veneris dominae volucres, mea turba, columbae
  tingunt Gorgoneo punica rostra lacu;
diversaeque novem sortitae iura Puellae
  exercent teneras in sua dona manus:
haec hederas legit in thyrsos, haec carmina nervis
  aptat, at illa manu texit utraque rosam.   36

---

¹⁷ hinc *Volscus*: hic Ω

---

^a We are not to look at our atlases, for Castalia is on
Parnassus in Phocis, while the poet's dream takes place on
Helicon in Boeotia.

observed me from the Castalian*a* wood, and said, as
he leaned upon his golden lyre beside the cave:

¹⁵ 'Madman, what business have you at such a
stream? Who bade you touch the task of heroic
song? Not from here, Propertius, may you hope for
any fame: small wheels must run upon soft grass, so
that your book be oft paraded on the bench for a
lonely girl to read as she awaits her man. Why has
your page veered from the prescribed orbit? The lit-
tle bark of your genius*b* must not be burdened with
a heavy load. With one oar skimming the waters,
the other scraping the sand, you will be safe: out in
mid-sea occur the roughest storms.' So spoke he,
and with his ivory quill he directed me to a place
where a new path had been made along the mossy
floor.

²⁷ Here was a green grotto lined with mosaics and
from the hollow pumice timbrels hung, the mystic
instruments of the Muses, a clay image of father
Silenus, and the pipe of Arcadian Pan; and the birds
of my lady Venus, the doves that I love, dip their red
bills in the Gorgon's pool, while the nine Maidens,
each allotted her own realm, busy their tender
hands on their separate gifts: one gathers ivy for the
thyrsus-wand, one tunes her song to the strings of
the lyre, another with both hands plaits wreaths

b Cf. Dante, *Purg.* 1.2, 'the little bark of my genius' (*la
navicella del mio ingegno*).

261

e quarum numero me contigit una dearum
    (ut reor a facie, Calliopea fuit):

'contentus niveis semper vectabere cycnis,
    nec te fortis equi ducet ad arma sonus.   40
nil tibi sit rauco praeconia classica cornu
    flare, nec Aonium tingere Marte nemus;
aut quibus in campis Mariano proelia signo
    stent et Teutonicas Roma refringat opes,
barbarus aut Suebo perfusus sanguine Rhenus   45
    saucia maerenti corpora vectet aqua.
quippe coronatos alienum ad limen amantes
    nocturnaeque canes ebria signa morae,
ut per te clausas sciat excantare puellas,
    qui volet austeros arte ferire viros.'   50
talia Calliope, lymphisque a fonte petitis
    ora Philitea nostra rigavit aqua.

IV

ARMA deus Caesar dites meditatur ad Indos,
    et freta gemmiferi findere classe maris.
magna, Quiris, merces: parat ultima terra triumphos;
    Tigris et Euphrates sub tua iura fluent;
sera, sed Ausoniis veniet provincia virgis;   5
    assuescent Latio Partha tropaea Iovi.

[48] morae *Heyworth**: fugae Ω
[3] Quiris *Wistrand**: viri Ω

---

[a] Playing upon the etymology κάλλος 'beauty' + ὄψις 'face.'

of roses. Then from their number one of the goddesses laid her hand on me (by her looks I think it was Calliope[a]):

39 'You will always be happy to ride on snow-white swans; no galloping hooves of the war-horse will call you to arms. Be it no concern of yours to sound the martial summons on the blaring trumpet or stain with bloody warfare the groves of Helicon; care not in what fields the battle is arrayed beneath Marius' standards and Rome beats back Teutonic power, nor where the barbaric Rhine, steeped in Swabian blood, carries mangled bodies downstream in sorrowing waters. For you will sing of garlanded lovers at another's threshold and the tipsy tokens of midnight vigil, so that he who would artfully outwit stern husbands may learn from you how to charm forth a locked-up woman.' Thus Calliope, and taking water from the spring she moistened my lips with draughts that once Philitas drank.

War planned by Caesar

WAR is divine Caesar planning against rich India, and to cleave with his navy the waters of the pearl-bearing ocean. Great is the reward, O citizenry of Rome: the most distant of lands is preparing triumphs for you; Tigris and Euphrates will flow under your dominion; late though it be, it shall pass as a province beneath the rule of Italy, and Parthian trophies will grow accustomed to Latin Jupiter. Up

ite agite, expertae bello, date lintea, prorae,
    et solitum, armigeri, ducite munus, equi!
omina fausta cano. Crassos clademque piate!
    ite et Romanae consulite historiae!   10

Mars pater, et sacrae fatalia lumina Vestae,
    ante meos obitus sit precor illa dies,
qua videam spoliis oneratos Caesaris axes,
18   et subter captos arma sedere duces,
17 tela fugacis equi et bracati militis arcus,
    ad vulgi plausus saepe resistere equos,   14
inque sinu carae nixus spectare puellae   15
    incipiam et titulis oppida capta legam!
ipsa tuam serva prolem, Venus: hoc sit in aevum, 19
    cernis ab Aenea quod superesse caput.   20

praeda sit haec illis, quorum meruere labores:
    me sat erit Sacra plaudere posse Via.

V

PACIS Amor deus est, pacem veneramur amantes:
    sat mihi cum domina proelia dura mea.

18,17 *post* 13 *Butrica**
2 sat *Livineius*: stant Ω

---

a The manacled captives sat on floats below their
weapons, which were paraded as trophies on a higher

and away, ye prows well tried in war, unfurl your
sails! Ye warrior steeds, lead the way, your cus-
tomary task! Fair are the omens of my song. Make
expiation to the Crassi and their defeat! Away, and
serve Rome's history well!

[11] Father Mars, and fires of inviolate Vesta preg-
nant with destiny, let that day come before my
death, I pray, the day on which I see Caesar's
chariot laden with spoil and captured chieftains sit-
ting beneath their arms, shafts from cavalry in
retreat and bows of trousered soldiery,[a] the horses
oft halting at the people's cheers, and leaning on the
bosom of my sweetheart I begin to watch and read
on placards the names of captured cities! Venus,
preserve your offspring! May this being, in whom
you see the succession of Aeneas, endure forever!

[21] Theirs be the booty whose toil has earned it:
enough for me that I can cheer them on the Sacred
Way.

Love the god of peace

PEACE has Love for its god, we lovers worship peace:
enough for me is the stern war I wage with my

platform. The Romans regarded trousers, not an item of
their own dress, as exotic, but we hear of them worn by
Gauls (cf. 4.10.43), Scythians, and Persians, as well as
Parthians.

5 nec mihi mille iugis Campania pinguis aratur,
    nec bibit e gemma divite nostra sitis,
3 nec tamen inviso pectus mihi carpitur auro,
    nec mixta aera paro clade, Corinthe, tua.   6

o prima infelix fingenti terra Prometheo!
    ille parum caute pectoris egit opus.
corpora disponens mentem non vidit in arto:
    recta animi primum debuit esse via.   10
nunc maris in tantum vento iactamur, et hostem
    quaerimus, atque armis nectimus arma nova.

haud ullas portabis opes Acherontis ad undas:
    nudus in inferna, stulte, vehere rate.
victor cum victo pariter miscetur in umbris: 15
    consule cum Mario, capte Iugurtha, sedes.
Lydus Dulichio non distat Croesus ab Iro:
    optima mors, carpta quae venit ante die.

me iuvat in prima coluisse Helicona iuventa
    Musarumque choris implicuisse manus;   20
me iuvat et multo mentem vincire Lyaeo,
    et caput in verna semper habere rosa.

---

3 *cum* 5 *comm. Carutti*
6 mixta *Ruhnken* : miser Ω
9 arto *Housman* : arte Ω
14 <in> *Barber* inferna ... rate ς: [ad] inferna[s] ... rate[s] Ω
15 victo *Willis**: victis Ω | miscetur <in> *Housman* : miscebitur Ω
18 carpta *Baehrens* : parca Ω | ante *Helm* : acta Ω

mistress. I own no rich soil of Campania ploughed by a thousand yoke of oxen, nor do I refresh my thirst from jewelled goblets: yet my heart is not seized by greed for hateful gold, nor collect I fused bronzes from your destruction, Corinth.

⁷ O primal clay, so ill-starred for Prometheus' fashioning hand! The making of man's reason he performed with too little care. Arranging our bodies in so small a space he noticed not the wits: the mind ought first to have had its path made straight. And so we are blown by the wind far out to sea; we go in search of a foe, and link fresh wars to wars concluded.

¹³ You will take no wealth to the waters of Acheron: fool, you will be naked when you travel on the ferry of the world below.ᵃ Victor and vanquished meet as equals among the dead: beside consul Marius sits captive Jugurtha in the boat. Croesus of Lydia differs not from Irus of Dulichium: that death is best which comes when life has been first enjoyed.

¹⁹ 'Tis my delight to have worshipped Helicon in my early youth and joined hands in the Muses' dance; 'tis my delight also to tie up my mind with deep draughts of wine and ever to have my head garlanded with the roses of spring.

ᵃ Cf. Job 1:21, 'Naked came I out of my mother's womb, and naked shall I return thither.'

atque ubi iam Venerem gravis interceperit aetas,
    sparserit et nigras alba senecta comas,
tum mihi naturae libeat perdiscere mores,   25
    quis deus hanc mundi temperet arte domum,
qua venit exoriens, qua deficit, unde coactis
    cornibus in plenum menstrua luna redit,
unde salo superant venti, quid flamine captet
    Eurus, et in nubes unde perennis aqua;   30

sit ventura dies mundi quae subruat arces,
    purpureus pluvias cur bibit arcus aquas,
aut cur Perrhaebi tremuere cacumina Pindi,
    solis et atratis luxerit orbis equis,
cur serus versare boves et plaustra Bootes,   35
    Pleiadum spisso cur coit igne chorus,
curve suos fines altum non exeat aequor,
    plenus et in partes quattuor annus eat;

sub terris sint iura deûm et tormenta reorum,
42   num rota, num scopuli, num sitis inter aquas,
aut Alcmaeoniae furiae aut ieiunia Phinei,
40   Tisiphones atro si furit angue caput,

---

[39] reorum *Housman* : gigantum *A** : *om. N*
[40] *cum* 42 *comm. Housman*

---

[a] The rainbow was thought to drink up water to form
clouds (cf. Virgil, *Georg.* 1.380).

[b] The Herdsman (Bootes) is an elongated constellation:
it rises rapidly, then being in a horizontal position; but

[23] And when the weight of advancing years has cut off love, and white old age has speckled my black locks, then let my fancy turn to exploring the ways of nature, what god so skilfully controls this household that is the world, how comes the moon at her rising, how she wanes, how each month she draws her horns together and returns to fullness, how winds have mastery over the sea, what the East Wind chases with his blast, whence there is unfailing water to supply the clouds;

[31] whether a day will come to demolish the ramparts of the universe, why the coloured bow drinks up the rain-water,[a] or why the peaks of Thessalian Pindus have quaked and the sun's orb has mourned, his horses draped in black; why the Herdsman is so slow to turn his team and waggon,[b] why the band of Pleiads close together with thick-set fires, or why the deep sea exceeds not its bounds, and the whole year falls into four parts;

[39] whether in the world below exist assizes of gods and punishments of sinners, the wheel, the rolling rock, the thirst in the water's midst,[c] whether Alcmaeon is tormented with furies and Phineus with hunger, if Tisiphone's hair is a frenzy of black

when it sets, it does so vertically and takes hours to do so (cf. 2.33.24 and Catullus 66.67 *tardum ... Booten,* translating Callimachus).

[c] Alluding to Ixion, Sisyphus, and Tantalus.

num tribus infernum custodit faucibus antrum
    Cerberus, et Tityo iugera pauca novem,
an ficta in miseras descendit fabula gentes,   45
    et timor haud ultra quam rogus esse potest.

exitus hic vitae superet mihi: vos, quibus arma
    grata magis, Crassi signa referte domum.

VI

Dic mihi de nostra quae sensti vera puella:
    sic tibi sint dominae, Lygdame, dempta iuga.
omnis enim debet sine vano nuntius esse,   5
    maioremque metu servus habere fidem.
nunc mihi, si qua tenes, ab origine dicere prima
    incipe: suspensis auribus ista bibam.
3 num me laetitia tumefactum fallis inani,
4   haec referens, quae me credere velle putas?

sicin eram incomptis vidisti flere capillis?
    illius ex oculis multa cadebat aqua?   10
nec speculum in strato vidisti, Lygdame, lecto,
14   scriniaque ad lecti clausa iacere pedes,
ac maestam teneris vestem pendere lacertis?
12   ornabat niveas nullane gemma manus?

---

[47] superet ς: superest Ω   [1] sensti *Butrica**: sentis Ω
[3,4] *post 8 Housman*   [6] metu *Muretus*: timens Ω
[9] eram *Damsté*: eam Ω   [11] in *Heinsius, om.* Ω
[12] *cum* 14 *comm. Suringar*

snakes, whether Cerberus guards the cave of hell
with his three throats and nine acres are all too few
for Tityus; or whether it is a made-up tale that has
entered deep to trouble the minds of humans and
there can be no fear beyond the grave.

⁴⁷ Be this the close of life in store for me: do you,
who take more pleasure in warfare, bring Crassus'
standards home!

A plea to Lygdamus

TELL me exactly what you noticed about my sweet-
heart: then, Lygdamus, you may expect deliverance
from your mistress's yoke; for every messenger
should be devoid of falsehood, and a slave should out
of fear command greater credence. So now begin to
tell me all you can remember from the very begin-
ning: I will listen with ears alert. I hope you will not
deceive me, and fill me with baseless joy, reporting
what you think I wish to believe.

⁹ So you saw your mistress weeping and with hair
awry, a flood of tears streaming from her eyes? And
on the bedcover you saw no mirror, Lygdamus, and
at the foot of the bed her toilet-box lying locked? So
her dress hung forlornly from her delicate arms, and
no jewel adorned her snow-white hands? So the

tristis erat domus, et tristes sua pensa ministrae   15
    carpebant, medio nebat et ipsa loco,
umidaque impressa siccabat lumina lana,
    rettulit et querulo iurgia nostra sono?

'haec te teste mihi promissast, Lygdame, merces?
    est poena et servo rumpere teste fidem.   20
ille potest nullo miseram me linquere facto,
    et qualem nolo dicere habere domi?
gaudet me vacuo solam tabescere lecto?
    si placet, insultet, Lygdame, morte mea.
non me moribus illa, sed herbis improba vicit   25
    staminea rhombi ducitur ille rota.

illum turgentis sanie portenta rubetae
    et lecta exsuctis anguibus ossa trahunt,
et strigis inventae per busta iacentia plumae,
    cinctaque funesto lanea vitta toro.   30
si non vana canunt mea somnia, Lygdame, testor,
    poena erit ante meos sera sed ampla pedes;
putris et in vacuo texetur aranea lecto:
    noctibus illorum dormiet ipsa Venus.'

quae tibi si veris animis est questa puella,   35
    hac eadem rursus, Lygdame, curre via,

---

[20] poena et *Sh. Bailey* : poenae Ω
[27] sanie *Heinsius* : ranae Ω
[28] exsuctis *Burman* : exsectis Ω
[30] toro *Heinsius* : viro Ω

272

house was sad, and sad the maidservants as they
picked their wool, she spinning in their midst, and
she pressed the wool to her eyes to dry them as she
poured forth reproaches of me in plaintive tone?

¹⁹ 'Is this the reward he promised in your hear-
ing, Lygdamus? Even with a slave for witness there
is a penalty for perjury. Can he forsake me though I
have done nothing to deserve it, and keep at home a
creature I cannot bring myself to name? He rejoices,
does he, that I waste away, alone on an empty bed?
If he likes, let him jump for joy at my death, Lyg-
damus. That woman has triumphed not by winning
ways, but by magic herbs: he is drawn by the
whirligig's threaded wheel.ᵃ

²⁷ 'He is lured by the sorcery of the toad puffed
with venom and the bones she has gathered from
the dried bodies of snakes, a screech-owl's feathers
found among sunken tombs and a woollen fillet that
has decked a bier. If my dreams portend the truth,
Lygdamus, I swear that he shall pay a late but
ample penalty at my very feet; dusty cobwebs will be
woven over his empty bed and Venus herself will
sleep on their nights of love.'

³⁵ If my sweetheart so complained in all sincerity
to you then run back again, Lygdamus, by the same

ᵃ See note on 2.28.35.

PROPERTIUS

et mea cum multis lacrimis mandata reporta,
  iram, non fraudes esse in amore meo,
me quoque consimili impositum torquerier igni:
  iurabo bis sex integer esse dies.   40
quod mihi si e tanto felix concordia bello
  exstiterit, per me, Lygdame, liber eris.

VII

Ergo sollicitae tu causa, pecunia, vitae!
  per te immaturum mortis adimus iter;
tu vitiis hominum crudelia pabula praebes;
  semina curarum de capite orta tuo.
tu Paetum ad Pharios tendentem lintea portus   5
  obruis insano terque quaterque mari.
nam dum te sequitur, primo miser excidit aevo
  et nova longinquis piscibus esca natat.   8

quod si contentus patrio bove verteret agros,   43
  verbaque duxisset pondus habere mea,
viveret ante suos dulcis conviva Penates,   45
  pauper, at in terra nil nisi fleret opes.

Transpositions in 3.7. have been made as follows: 17,18
(*post* 66 *Scaliger*) *ante* 9 *Postgate;* 19–22 *post* 36 *Richard-
son;* 43–66 (*Baehrens*: 51 *cum* 53 *Fischer*) *post* 8 *Postgate;*
67–70 *post* 16 *Scaliger*: see Intro. p. 22.

---

[a] The theme of the elegy is briefly expressed in Julian,
Prefect of Egypt, *A.P.* 7.586.

[b] Like Athena from the head of Jupiter.

[c] Cf. Leonidas, *A.P.* 7.273 ἰχθύσι κύρμα.

route, and amid much weeping convey this message:
that there is anger but not betrayal in my love, that
I too am tortured on a fire like hers; I will swear to
having been continent these past twelve days.
Then, if a happy reconciliation emerges from so
great a conflict, so far as lies in my power, Lyg-
damus, you will be free.

Elegy for Paetus

So you then, Money, are the cause of our anguished
lives![a] Through you we travel an untimely road to
death; you furnish cruel nourishment for men's
faults; from your head have sprung the seeds of
woe.[b] It was you that thrice and again buffeted
Paetus in a raging sea as his sails were set for the
harbour of Pharos. For while pursuing you, the poor
boy was lost in the prime of life and floats as novel
food for distant fishes.[c]

[43] Yet, had he been content to plough his fields
with his father's ox and deemed my words to carry
weight, he would have lived[d] to dine happily before
his household gods, poor maybe, but on land he
would have naught but his poverty to lament.

[d] 'Car il ne voyait pas que bientôt sur sa tête
L'automne impétueux amassant la tempête
L'attendait au passage, et là, loin de tout bord,
Lui préparait bientôt le naufrage et la mort':
from a 37-line fragment (*Idyll. mar.* X) of André Chénier's,
partly based on this poem.

noluit hoc Paetus, stridorem audire procellae
 et duro teneras laedere fune manus,
sed thyio thalamo aut Oricia terebintho
 effultum pluma versicolore caput. 50

53 hunc parvo ferri vidit nox improba ligno,
  et miser invisam traxit hiatus aquam;
51 huic fluctus vivo radicitus abstulit ungues:
  Paetus ut occideret, tot coiere mala.
flens tamen extremis dedit haec mandata querelis
 cum moribunda niger clauderet ora liquor: 56

'di maris Aegaei quos sunt penes aequora, venti,
 et quaecumque meum degravat unda caput,
quo rapitis miseros primae lanuginis annos?
 attulimus longas in freta vestra comas. 60
ah miser alcyonum scopulis affligar acutis!
 in me caeruleo fuscina sumpta deost.
at saltem Italiae regionibus evehat aestus:
 hoc de me sat erit si modo matris erit.'

subtrahit haec fantem torta vertigine fluctus; 65
 ultima quae Paeto voxque diesque fuit. 66
17 Paete, quid aetatem numeras? quid cara natanti
18 mater in ore tibist? non habet unda deos.

---

[47] noluit *Skutsch* : non tulit Ω | hoc *F* : haec *N* : hunc *LP*
[50] effultum ς : et fultum Ω
[60] comas *Oudendorp* : manus Ω

Paetus desired not this, to hear the howling of the tempest and blister his dainty hands on the rough cordage, but rather in a bed of cedar or Orician terebinth[a] to pillow his head on iridescent feathers.

[53] The pitiless night beheld the poor boy adrift on a narrow spar, and his open mouth gulped in the dreaded water; whilst yet he lived, the waves tore out his nails by their roots: so many ills combined for Paetus' death. Yet with his last lament he tearfully gave this charge, as the black waters closed his lips in death:

[57] 'Ye gods of the Aegean, in whose power lies the sea, ye winds, and you every wave that press down my head, whither do ye snatch away the hapless years of my youth's bloom? I brought boyish locks into your waters. Alas, I shall be dashed against the jagged rocks where the seamew nests! The god of the azure deep has lifted his trident against me. But at least may the tide cast up my corpse on Italian shores: this that is left of me will suffice, if only it reach my mother.'

[65] As he spoke the waves sucked him down in a whirling eddy; these were the last words and moments of Paetus. Why, Paetus, do you reckon up your age? Why, as you drift, is your dear mother's name on your lips? The waves reck naught of gods,

---

[a] Cf. Virgil, *Aen.* 10.136, *inclusum buxo aut Oricia terebintho.*

et mater non iusta piae dare debita terrae 9
    nec pote cognatos inter humare rogos, 10
sed tua nunc volucres astant super ossa marinae,
    nunc tibi pro tumulo Carpathium omne marest.

infelix Aquilo, raptae timor Orithyiae,
    quae spolia ex illo tanta fuere tibi?
aut quidnam fracta gaudes, Neptune, carina? 15
    portabat sanctos alveus ille viros.

67 o centum aequoreae Nereo genitore puellae,
68   et tu, materno tacta dolore, Theti;
69 vos decuit lasso supponere bracchia mento:
70   non poterat vestras ille gravare manus.
reddite corpus, aquae! positast in gurgite vita; 25
    Paetum sponte tua, vilis harena, tegas;
et quotiens Paeti transibit nauta sepulcrum,
    dicat 'et audaci tu timor esse potes.'

ite, rates curvate et leti texite causas:
    ista per humanas mors venit acta manus. 30
terra parum fuerat fatis, adiecimus undas:
    fortunae miseras auximus arte vias.

[68] tacta ς: tracta Ω
[25] aquae *Damsté*: humo Ω
[29] curvate *Peskett*: curvae Ω

and your mother cannot perform the due rite of burial[a] or inter you among the ashes of your kin, but birds of the sea now hover above your bones, now the whole Carpathian sea is your tomb.[b]

[13] Hateful North Wind, bane of ravished Orithyia, what great booty did you get from him? And why, Neptune, do you gloat over the wrecking of his ship? That vessel was carrying innocent men.

[67] Ye hundred sea-nymphs sired by Nereus, and you, Thetis, that have felt a mother's grief, you should have placed your arms beneath his failing chin: he could not have weighed heavy on your hands. Give up the corpse, ye waters: his life was laid down in your flood; ye worthless sands, cover Paetus as ye will; and whenever a sailor passes by Paetus' tomb, let him say: 'You can cause fear even to the brave.'

[29] Go now, fashion curved ships and weave webs of destruction: his death was engineered by human hands. The land was not enough for doom, we have added the sea: our skill has extended the cruel avenues of fate.

---

[a] The Romans believed that the unburied were denied admittance to Hades and were doomed to wander endlessly; the minimum due was the casting of three handfuls of earth of earth upon a corpse (e.g. Horace, *Odes* 1.28.22ff).

[b] Cf. Glaucus, A.P.7.285, πᾶσα θάλασσα τάφος.

ancora te teneat, quem non tenuere penates?
    quid meritum dicas, cui sua terra parumst?
ventorumst, quodcumque paras: haud ulla carina 35
    consenuit, fallit portus et ipse fidem.
19 nam tibi nocturnis ad saxa ligata procellis
20   omnia detrito vincula fune cadunt.
21 sunt Agamemnonias testantia litora curas,
22   quae notat Argynni poena Athamantiadae.
23 [hoc iuvene amisso classem non solvit Atrides,
24   pro qua mactatast Iphigenia mora.]

natura insidians pontum substravit avaris:
    ut tibi succedat, vix semel esse potest.
saxa triumphalis fregere Capherea puppes,
    naufraga cum vasto Graecia tracta salost.   40
paulatim sociûm iacturam flevit Ulixes,
    in mare cui soliti non valuere doli.   42

at tu, saeve Aquilo, numquam mea vela videbis: 71
    ante fores dominae condar oportet iners.

VIII

DULCIS ad hesternas fuerat mihi rixa lucernas,
    vocis et insanae tot maledicta tuae.

22 Athamantiadae *Hertzberg*: minantis aquae Ω
23,24 *del. Jacob*

³³ Is an anchor to hold you, who were not held by
your home? Say, what does he deserve, whose coun-
try suffices him not? Whatever you build is at the
mercy of the winds: no ship has ever grown old, and
even the harbour betrays its trust. For though all
your cables are fastened to the rocks, in a night tem-
pest, with strands frayed, they break loose. There
are shores that testify to Agamemnon's woe, shores
branded by the fate of Athamantiad Argynnus. [On
the loss of this youth the son of Atreus did not weigh
anchor, a delay which brought about the sacrifice of
Iphigenia.]

³⁷ Nature has spread out the sea as a trap for the
covetous: it scarcely happens once that a man enjoys
success on it. The reefs of Caphereus shattered the
fleet of the conquerors, when Greece foundered in
shipwreck over the wild main. Ulysses wept at the
loss of his comrades one after another, his cus-
tomary cunning powerless against the sea.

⁷¹ But you, cruel North Wind, will never see my
sails: before my mistress's door must I, naught ven-
turing, be laid.

The lamplight brawl

I enjoyed the lamplight brawl we had last night and
all the abuse of your frenzied tongue. But I dare

tu vero nostros audax invade capillos   5
    et mea formosis unguibus ora nota,
tu minitare oculos subiecta exurere flamma,
    fac mea rescisso pectora nuda sinu!
3 cum furibunda mero mensam propellis et in me
4   proicis insana cymbia plena manu,
nimirum veri dantur mihi signa caloris:
    nam sine amore gravi femina nulla dolet.   10

quae mulier rabida iactat convicia lingua,
    haec Veneris magnae volvitur ante pedes.
custodum grege seu circa se stipat euntem,
    seu sequitur medias, maenas ut icta, vias,
seu timidam crebro dementia somnia terrent,   15
    seu miseram in tabula picta puella movet,
his ego tormentis animi sum verus haruspex,
    has didici certo saepe in amore notas.
non est certa fides, quam non in iurgia vertas:
    hostibus eveniat lenta puella meis.   20

in morso aequales videant mea vulnera collo:
    me doceat livor mecum habuisse meam.
aut in amore dolere volo aut audire dolentem,
    sive meas lacrimas sive videre tuas,
tecta superciliis si quando verba remittis,   25
    aut tua cum digitis scripta silenda notas.
odi ego quos numquam pungunt suspiria somnos:
    semper in irata pallidus esse velim.

^{3,4} *post* 8 *Heyworth** ^{13} grege seu *Heinsius*: gregibus Ω
^{27} quos ς: quae Ω

you: come, tear my hair and scratch my face with your pretty nails; threaten that you will light a flame and burn my eyes out, tear my tunic and strip my body bare. When, crazed with wine, you knock over the table and fling full cups at me with frenzied hand, you are without question giving me tokens of true ardour: for no woman smarts unless hers is a serious passion.

¹¹ She whose ranting tongue spits out insults is grovelling at the feet of mighty Venus. Whether, when going out, she surrounds herself with a throng of escorts, or rushes down the street like a possessed bacchante, whether nightmares frequently scare her out of her mind or the painted portrait of a girl brings her misery, of all these mental torments I am a true interpreter; I have learned that these are often the signs of a sure love. No love is sure that cannot be provoked to a quarrel: an unfeeling girl is what I wish my enemies.

²¹ Let rivals see the wounds I have sustained in neck-bites: let bruises on me show that I have had my girl with me. I want either to suffer in love or hear that you are suffering, I want to see my tears or else yours whenever you send a hidden message with a twitch of your eyebrows or trace with your fingers words that cannot be spoken. Anathema to me is a sleep which is never punctuated by sighs: I should always wish to be the wan lover of an angry mistress.

PROPERTIUS

dulcior ignis erat Paridi, cum Graia per arma
  Tynaridi poterat gaudia ferre suae: 30
dum vincunt Danai, dum restat barbarus Hector,
  ille Helenae in gremio maxima bella gerit.
aut tecum aut pro te mihi cum rivalibus arma
  semper erunt: in te pax mihi nulla placet.
gaude, quod nullast aeque formosa: doleres,   35
  si qua foret: nunc sis iure superba licet.

at tibi, qui nostro nexisti retia lecto,
  sit socer aeternum nec sine matre domus!
cui nunc si qua datast furandae copia noctis,
  offensa illa mihi, non tibi amica, dedit.   40

IX

MAECENAS, eques Etrusco de sanguine regum,
  intra fortunam qui cupis esse tuam,
quid me scribendi tam vastum mittis in aequor?
  non sunt apta meae grandia vela rati.
turpest, quod nequeas, capiti committere pondus   5
  et pressum inflexo mox dare terga genu.
omnia non pariter rerum sunt omnibus apta,
  palma nec ex aequo ducitur ulla iugo.

---

²⁹ graia ς: grata Ω

---

^a Like the snare which trapped Venus and Mars (cf.
Homer, *Od.* 8.266ff): see note on 1.9.16.

[29] Sweeter was love to Paris, when amid battle with the Greeks he could bring delight to his Tyndarid wife: while the Greeks were advancing and Hector savagely resisting, he was locked in the mightiest combat with Helen. I shall make endless war either with you or with rivals for you: with you I want no peace. Be glad that none has your beauty: you would be vexed if someone had: as it is, you may be justly proud.

[37] But as for you, sir, who have woven a snare about my bed,[a] may a father-in-law plague you all your life, and the house never lack a mother! If you have now been offered the chance of stealing a night, it is not because she loves you, but because she is vexed with me.

To Maecenas

MAECENAS,[b] knight sprung from the blood of Etruscan kings[c] and determined to remain within the bounds of your station, why do you launch me upon so vast an ocean of writing? Huge sails are not suited to my little boat. It is shameful to take on one's neck a burden one cannot carry, then collapse on one's knees and beat a retreat. All things in the world are not suited to all men alike, nor is any prize secured by a chariot no better than its rivals.

[b] A polite *recusatio* to Maecenas, and the only poem in the book to be addressed to him.
[c] Cf. Horace, *Odes* 1.1.1.

gloria Lysippost animosa effingere signa;
    exactis Calamis se mihi iactat equis;   10
in Veneris tabula summam sibi poscit Apelles;
    Parrhasius parva vindicat arte locum;
argumenta magis sunt Mentoris addita formae;
    at Myos exiguum flectit acanthus iter;
Phidiacus signo se Iuppiter ornat eburno;   15
    Praxitelen propria vendit ab urbe lapis.
est quibus Eleae concurrit palma quadrigae,
    est quibus in celeris gloria nata pedes;
hic satus ad pacem, hic castrensibus utilis armis:
    naturae sequitur semina quisque suae.   20

at tua, Maecenas, vitae praecepta recepi,
    cogor et exemplis te superare tuis.
cum tibi Romano dominas in honore secures
    et liceat medio ponere iura foro;
vel tibi Medorum pugnacis ire per hastas,   25
    atque onerare tuam fixa per arma domum;
et tibi ad effectum vires det Caesar, et omni
    tempore tam faciles insinuentur opes;
parcis et in tenuis humilem te colligis umbras:
    velorum plenos subtrahis ipse sinus.   30

---

[a] His *Aphrodite Anadyomene* was the most famous
painting of antiquity (see Pliny, *NH* 35.87 and 91). Unlike
Botticelli's masterpiece, it depicted Venus wringing

BOOK III.9

⁹ It is Lysippus' glory to mould statues breathing
life; Calamis wins my admiration by the perfection
of his horses; Apelles asserts his pre-eminence by
his painting of Venus[a]; Parrhasius claims his place
by his miniature art; scenes of story largely cover
the designs of Mentor, while with Mys it is the
acanthus which winds its slender path; the Jupiter
of Phidias plumes himself in an ivory statue; marble
from his native city commends the art of Praxiteles.
There are some whom the prize in the Olympic
chariot-race runs to meet, some for whose swiftness
of foot glory is destined; one is bred for peace,
another effective with the weapons of war: each man
follows the elements of his own nature.

²¹ But I have adopted your rule of life, Maecenas,
and am constrained to surpass you by your own
example. Though as a magistrate of Rome you
might establish your imperial axes and dispense
justice in the middle of the Forum; though you
might pass through the fierce Parthians' spears and
load your house with trophies nailed on the walls;
though Caesar gives you strength to achieve your
will, and at all times wealth comes so readily
flowing in: yet you hold back and humbly withdraw
to a modest background: of your own choice you furl
the full canvas of your sails. This wisdom of yours,

the water from her hair (cf. Ovid, *Trist.* 2.527, *Ex Pont.*
4.1.28).

crede mihi, magnos aequabunt ista Camillos
    iudicia, et venies tu quoque in ora virûm.

non ego velifera tumidum mare findo carina: 35
    tota sub exiguo flumine nostra morast.
non flebo in cineres arcem sedisse paternos
    Cadmi, nec semper proelia clade pari;
nec referam Scaeas et Pergama, Apollinis arces,
    et Danaûm decimo vere redisse rates,   40
moenia cum Graio Neptunia pressit aratro
    victor Palladiae ligneus artis equus.
inter Callimachi sat erit placuisse libellos
    et cecinisse modis, Coë poeta, tuis.
haec urant pueros, haec urant scripta puellas   45
    meque deum clament et mihi sacra ferant!

te duce vel Iovis arma canam caeloque minantem
    Coeum et Phlegraeis Eurymedonta iugis;
51 eductosque pares silvestri ex ubere reges,
    ordiar et caeso moenia firma Remo,   50
49 celsaque Romanis decerpta palatia tauris,
    crescet et ingenium sub tua iussa meum;

    33,34 *post* 2.1.38 *Housman*
    48 Eurymedonta *Huschke*: oromodonta Ω
    49 *cum* 51 *comm. Peiper*

---

  [a] Cf. Ennius' epitaph on himself (*Epigr.* II, p. 215V): *volito vivu' per ora virûm.*
  [b] Unlike the expedition of the Seven against Thebes, which proved equally disastrous to both sides, the attack

believe me, will match you with any great Camillus of old, and your name too will live on the lips of men.[a]

[35] Not in a ship with bellying sail do I cut through the the the swelling sea: I loiter all the time in the shelter of a creek. I shall not mourn the collapse of the Cadmean fortress upon the ashes of the defenders' fathers and the battle wherein the slaughter was no longer even-sided[b]; nor shall I tell of the Scaean Gates and Pergamum, fortresses of Apollo, and the return of the Danaan ships in the tenth spring, when the victorious wooden horse of Pallas' devising levelled with a Greek plough walls built by Neptune. It will satisfy me to have found favour with readers of Callimachus and sung, O Coan poet, in strains like yours. Let these verses of mine inflame boys and girls; let them acclaim me as a god and offer me worship.

[47] If you lead the way, I shall sing even of the arms of Jove, and Coeus and Eurymedon threatening heaven from the hills of Phlegra; I shall tell of the royal pair reared at a wild beast's teat, the walls that were established by the slaying of Remus, and the lofty Palatine grazed by the steers of Rome; my genius shall rise to the height of your command. I

by the Epigoni (sons of the Seven) was successful, and the city was razed to the ground. The story formed part of the Epic Cycle, and was a standard theme for epic poets.

prosequar et currus utroque ab litore ovantis,
  Parthorum astutae tela remissa fugae,
claustraque Pelusi Romano subruta ferro,   55
  Antonique gravis in sua fata manus.

mollia tu coeptae fautor cape lora iuventae,
  dexteraque immissis da mihi signa rotis.
hoc mihi, Maecenas, laudis concedis, et a test
  quod ferar in partis ipse fuisse tuas.   60

                        X

MIRABAR, quidnam visissent mane Camenae,
  ante meum stantes sole rubente torum.
natalis nostrae signum misere puellae
  et manibus faustos ter crepuere sonos.

transeat hic sine nube dies, stent aere venti,   5
  ponat et in sicco molliter unda minas.
aspiciam nullos hodierna luce dolentis,
  et Niobae lacrimas supprimat ipse lapis;
alcyonum positis requiescant ora querelis;
  increpet absumptum nec sua mater Ityn.   10

tuque, o cara mihi, felicibus edita pennis,
  surge et poscentis iusta precare deos.

<hr>

[55] claustra *Palmier*: castra Ω

shall celebrate the chariots that triumph from East
and from West, the shafts of the Parthian's crafty
flight now laid aside, the bastions of Pelusium
overthrown by Roman swords, and the heavy hand
of Antony fatal to himself.

⁵⁷ Take up the gentle reins, as patron of the
youthful work I have begun, and give an encourag-
ing signal to my speeding chariot! So much glory
you vouchsafe me, Maecenas, and it is your doing
that even I shall be reckoned one of those who
followed you.

Cynthia's birthday

I ᵃ wondered why the Muses had paid me a morning
visit when at the blush of sunrise they stood before
my bed. They signalled that it was my sweetheart's
birthday and thrice with propitious sound clapped
their hands.

⁵ May this day pass without a cloud, the winds be
stilled in heaven, and the wave calmly lay aside its
threats on the shore. May I see no one grieving on
this day's light, and even the rock that was Niobe
suppress its tears; let the halcyons give up their
complaints and their throats be at rest, and the
mother of Itys cease to lament his death.

¹¹ And you, my darling, born under happy
augury, arise and make supplication to the gods

ᵃ An elegiac version of the *genethliacon* or birthday
poem, but very different from those of Tibullus (1.7; 2.2).

at primum pura somnum tibi discute lympha,
    et nitidas presso pollice finge comas;
dein qua primum oculos cepisti veste Properti   15
    indue, nec vacuum flore relinque caput;
et pete, qua polles, ut sit tibi forma perennis,
    inque meum semper stent tua regna caput.

inde coronatas ubi ture piaveris aras,
    luxerit et tota flamma secunda domo,   20
sit mensae ratio, noxque inter pocula currat,
    et crocino nares murreus ungat onyx.
tibia continuis succumbat rauca choreis,
    et sint nequitiae libera verba tuae,
dulciaque ingratos adimant convivia somnos;   25
    publica vicinae perstrepat aura viae:
sit sors et nobis talorum interprete iactu,
    quem gravius pennis verberet ille puer.

cum fuerit multis exacta trientibus hora,
    noctis et instituet sacra ministra Venus,   30
annua solvamus thalamo sollemnia nostro,
    natalisque tui sic peragamus iter.

[13] at ς: ac Ω
[23] continuis *Housman* : nocturnis Ω
[26] perstrepat ς: perstrepet Ω
[28] gravius *Beroaldus* : gravibus Ω

that demand their due. But first with fresh water wash away your sleep and with the impress of your fingers bind up your shining hair: then put on the dress in which you first ensnared the eyes of Propertius, and let your head not lack a garland of flowers; and pray that the beauty which is your might may abide for ever and that your sovereignty may always hold dominion over me.

[19] Then, when you have hallowed the garlanded altar with incense, and an auspicious flame shines throughout the house, let our thoughts be of the table, let night speed on amid our drinking, and the jar of perfume anoint our nostrils with the scent of saffron. Let the hoarse-throated pipe become exhausted with all-night dancing, and the language of your naughtiness lack all restraint, and let sweet conviviality take away thankless slumbers; let the public air of the neighbouring street resound with noise: and let an oracle tell by cast of dice which of us two Cupid beats the harder with his wings.

[29] When the hours have been spent in many cups, and Venus prepares the sacred ceremonies of the night, let us perform the year's rites on our couch and so complete the course of your birthday.

XI

QUID mirare, meam si versat femina vitam
    et trahit addictum sub sua iura virum,
criminaque ignavi capitis mihi turpia fingis,
    quod nequeam fracto rumpere vincla iugo?
ventorum melius praesagit navita morem,   5
    vulneribus didicit miles habere metum.
ista ego praeterita iactavi verba iuventa:
    tu nunc exemplo disce timere meo.

Colchis flagrantis adamantina sub iuga tauros
    egit et armigera proelia sevit humo,   10
custodisque feros clausit serpentis hiatus,
    iret ut Aesonias aurea lana domos.
ausa ferox ab equo quondam oppugnare sagittis
    Maeotis Danaûm Penthesilea rates;
aurea cui postquam nudavit cassida frontem,   15
    vicit victorem candida forma virum.
Omphale in tantum formae processit honorem,
    Lydia Gygaeo tincta puella lacu,
ut, qui pacato statuisset in orbe columnas,
    tam dura traheret mollia pensa manu.   20

---

[5] ventorum *Postgate*: venturam Ω | morem *Barber*:
mor[t]em Ω

BOOK III.11

Female power

WHY wonder[a] that a woman governs my life, and
hauls off a man in bondage to her sway? Why do
you frame shameful charges of cowardice against
me because I cannot burst my bonds and break the
yoke? The sailor best predicts the temper of the
winds; the soldier has learned from his wounds to
feel fear. Words like yours I used to utter in my
bygone youth: learn now from my example to be
afraid.

[9] The witch of Colchis forced the fire-breathing
bulls under a yoke of adamant, sowed the seed of
battle for the soil to produce armed warriors, and
shut the fierce jaws of the guardian serpent, that
the golden fleece might go to Aeson's halls.
Penthesilea, the fierce maid of Maeotis, once dared
from horseback to attack the ships of the Greeks
with arrows, and when the golden helm was lifted to
reveal her face, her shining beauty conquered her
male conqueror. Omphale, the Lydian girl who
bathed in Gyges' lake, won such renown for her
beauty that he who had set up his pillars in the
world he had pacified plucked with his brute hands

[a] The Ludi Quinquennales were established in 28 to
mark the victory of Actium; and this poem may have been
written for the first anniversary celebration in 24
(Richardson).

PROPERTIUS

Persarum statuit Babylona Semiramis urbem,
    ut solidum cocto tolleret aggere opus,
et duo in adversum mitti per moenia currus
    nec possent tacto stringere ab axe latus;
duxit et Euphraten medium, quam condidit, arcis,
    iussit et imperio subdere Bactra caput.   26
nam quid ego heroas, quid raptem in crimina divos?
    Iuppiter infamat seque suamque domum.

quid, modo quae nostris opprobria nexerit armis,
    et, famulos inter femina trita suos,   30
coniugii obsceni pretium Romana poposcit
    moenia et addictos in sua regna Patres?
noxia Alexandria, dolis aptissima tellus,
    et totiens nostro Memphi cruenta malo,
tris ubi Pompeio detraxit harena triumphos   35
    tollet nulla dies hanc tibi, Roma, notam.
issent Phlegraeo melius tibi funera campo,
    vel tua si socero colla daturus eras.
scilicet incesti meretrix regina Canopi,
    una Philippeo sanguine adusta nota,   40
ausa Iovi nostro latrantem opponere Anubim,
    et Tiberim Nili cogere ferre minas,

---

[23] mitti *Tyrrell*: missi Ω
[29] nexerit *Sh. Bailey*: vexerit Ω

soft tasks of wool. Semiramis built Babylon, the Persians' capital, by rearing a solid edifice with wall of brick such that two chariots might be sent against each other along the ramparts and yet not scrape their sides with an axle's touch; and she channelled the Euphrates through the middle of the citadel she founded and commanded Bactra to bow its head to her sway. Enough, for why should I bring gods and heroes to trial on this account? Jupiter shames himself and his whole house.

²⁹ What of her who of late has fastened disgrace upon our arms, and, a woman who fornicated even with her slaves, demanded as the price of her shameful union^a the walls of Rome and the senate made over to her dominion? Guilty Alexandria, land ever ready for treason, and Memphis, so often blood-stained at our cost, where the sand robbed Pompey of his three triumphs no day shall ever wash you clean of this infamy, Rome. Better had your funeral processed over the Phlegrean fields, or had you been doomed to bow your neck to your father-in-law!^b To be sure, the harlot queen of licentious Canopus, the one disgrace branded on Philip's line, dared to pit barking Anubis against our Jupiter and to force the Tiber to endure the threats of the

^a With Antony, whose name Propertius studiously avoids.

^b Julius Caesar, whose daughter Julia he married.

Romanamque tubam crepitanti pellere sistro,
    baridos et contis rostra Liburna sequi,
foedaque Tarpeio conopia tendere saxo,   45
    iura dare et statuas inter et arma Mari!
quid nunc Tarquinii fractas iuvat esse secures,
    nomine quem simili vita superba notat,
si mulier patienda fuit? cane, Roma, triumphum
    et longum Augusto salva precare diem!   50
fugisti tamen in timidi vaga flumina Nili:
    accepere tuae Romula vincla manus.
bracchia spectasti sacris admorsa colubris,
    et trahere occultum membra soporis iter.
'Non hoc, Roma, fui tanto tibi cive verenda!'   55
    dixit et assiduo lingua sepulta mero.

septem urbs alta iugis, toto quae praesidet orbi,
    stat non humana deicienda manu.   58

[49] cane *Camps* : cape Ω
[53] spectasti *Markland* : spectavi Ω
[57] toti *Salutati* : toto Ω
[58] *om. N, suppl. e.g. Sandbach* : femineas timuit territa Marte minas *A** ('terrified by war feared a woman's threats'), *damn. Richmond*

Nile, to drive out the Roman trumpet with the rattling sistrum[a] and with the poles of her barge pursue the beaks of our galleys, to stretch effeminate mosquito-nets on the Tarpeian rock and give judgement amid the arms and statues of Marius. What profit now is it to have broken the axes of that Tarquin whose proud life gave him a title derived from it, had we been fated to bear a woman's yoke? Sing out your triumph, Rome, and, saved, pray long life for Augustus. Yet you fled to the wandering outlets of the craven Nile: your hands received Roman fetters. You endured the sight of your arms bitten by the sacred asps and your limbs channelling the stealthy route of the numbing poison. 'Having so great a citizen as this, O Rome, you need not have feared me'[b]: thus spoke even a tongue drenched in ceaseless toping.

[57] The city set high on seven hills which presides over the whole world *stands not to be destroyed by*

---

[a] 'The sistrum was an Egyptian instrument, a horseshoe-shaped frame across which ran loose, rattling rods of bronze, mounted on a handle. It was used in the worship of Isis by the priest and is often shown as an attribute on representations of the goddess. The verse suggests it was used like the sanctus bell to warn away those who were not initiates from the mysteries' (Richardson).

[b] Cf. Shakespeare, *Ant. and Cleop.* 3.10.16, 'Cleopatra does confess thy greatness.'

65 haec di condiderunt, haec di quoque moenia servant:
66 vix timeat salvo Caesare Roma Iovem.
67 nunc ubi Scipiadae classes, ubi signa Camilli,
68 aut modo Pompeia, Bospore, capta manu?
 Hannibalis spolia et victi monumenta Syphacis, 59
  et Pyrrhi ad nostros gloria fracta pedes?
 Curtius expletis statuit monumenta lacunis, 61
  admisso Decius proelia rupit equo,
 Coclitis abscissos testatur semita pontes,
  est cui cognomen corvus habere dedit:
 Leucadius versas acies memorabit Apollo: 69
  tanti operis bellum sustulit una dies. 70

at tu, sive petes portus seu, navita, linques,
 Caesaris in toto sis memor Ionio.

XII

Postume, plorantem potuisti linquere Gallam,
 miles et Augusti fortia signa sequi?
tantine ulla fuit spoliati gloria Parthi,
 ne faceres Galla multa rogante tua?
si fas est, omnes pariter pereatis avari, 5
 et quisquis fido praetulit arma toro!

tu tamen iniecta tectus, vesane, lacerna
 potabis galea fessus Araxis aquam.

[65-68] post 58 Housman [65] condiderunt ς: -erant Ω
[62] admisso Decius Scaliger: at D. misso Ω
[70] tanti ... bellum Housman: tantum ... belli Ω

300

human hand. These walls the gods have founded, and these the gods also protect: whilst Caesar lives Rome should hardly fear Jupiter. So what does Scipio's armada count for now, what Camillus' standards, or the recent capture of Bosporus by Pompey's might? What count the spoils won from Hannibal, the trophies of conquered Syphax, and Pyrrhus' glory shattered at our feet? Curtius by filling a chasm made himself a lasting memorial; spurring his horse Decius broke the enemy's line; the path of Cocles still tells of the cutting of the bridge, and there is the hero to whom a raven gave his name: Leucadian Apollo will tell of a host turned in flight: one day put an end to a war of such vast array.

[71] But do you, sailor, whether you enter or leave harbour, remember Caesar over all the Ionian sea.

Galla's fidelity

POSTUMUS, how could you leave Galla in tears and as a soldier follow the brave standards of Augustus? Was any glory from despoiling the Parthians worth so much, when your Galla was imploring you again and again not to go? Heaven pardon me, but perish all ye together that thirst for gain, and whoever prefers arms to a faithful wife!

[7] Yet you, madman, your cloak thrown over you as a hood, will drink from a helmet the water of

301

illa quidem interea fama tabescet inani,
    haec tua ne virtus fiat amara tibi,   10
neve tua Medae laetentur caede sagittae,
    ferreus armato neu cataphractus equo,
neve aliquid de te flendum referatur in urna:
    sic redeunt, illis qui cecidere locis.

ter quater in casta felix, o Postume, Galla!   15
    moribus his alia coniuge dignus eras.
quid faciet nullo munita puella timore,
    cum sit luxuriae Roma magistra suae?
sed securus eas: Gallam non munera vincent,
    duritiaeque tuae non erit illa memor.   20
nam quocumque die salvum te fata remittent,
    pendebit collo Galla pudica tuo.

Postumus alter erit miranda coniuge Ulixes:
    non illi longae tot nocuere morae,
castra decem annorum, et Ciconum mors, Ismara capta
    exustaeque tuae nox, Polypheme, genae,   26
et Circae fraudes, lotosque herbaeque tenaces,
    Scyllaque et alternas scissa Charybdis aquas,

---

¹² armato *Broekhuyzen*: aurato Ω
²⁵ mors ς: mons Ω | capta *Fontein*: calpe (talpe) Ω
²⁶ nox *Higt*: mox Ω

Araxes when you are exhausted, whereas she meanwhile will waste away from empty rumours, fearing that this valour of yours may prove fatal to you, that the Parthian archer may rejoice at your death, or the mailed warrior upon his armoured steed, or that a small part of you be brought home in an urn for her to mourn: thus they return who perish in those lands.[a]

[15] Thrice and four times blest, Postumus, are you in Galla's chastity! With ways like yours you deserved another wife. What will a girl do without fear for a safeguard, when there is Rome to teach its wanton ways? But you need not worry: no bribes will corrupt Galla, and she will not remember your cruelty. For, whenever Fate sends you safely home, chaste Galla will be clinging to your neck.

[23] Through his marvellous wife Postumus will be a second Ulysses: Ulysses suffered no hurt from so long an absence, from the campaign of ten years, and the capture of Ismara, which spelled death for the Cicones, the night of Polyphemus' blinding, the deceit of Circe, and the lotus[b] and the herbs that held men prisoner, and Scylla, and Charybdis who is torn between ebb and flow.

---

[a] Cf. Aeschylus, *Agamemnon* 433–6.
[b] In Homer the story of the Lotus-eaters comes between the capture of Ismara and the blinding of the Cyclops.

PROPERTIUS

Lampeties Ithacis veribus mugisse iuvencos
    (paverat hos Phoebo filia Lampetie),   30
et thalamum Aeaeae flentis fugisse puellae,
    totque hiemis noctes totque natasse dies,
nigrantisque domos animarum intrasse silentum,
    Sirenum surdo remige adisse lacus,
et veteres arcus leto renovasse procorum,   35
    errorisque sui sic statuisse modum.

nec frustra, quia casta domi persederat uxor.
    vincit Penelopes Aelia Galla fidem.

XIII

QUAERITIS, unde avidis nox sit pretiosa puellis,
    et Venere exhaustae damna querantur opes.
certa quidem tantis causa et manifesta ruinis:
    luxuriae nimium libera facta viast.
Inda cavis aurum mittit formica metallis,   5
    et venit e Rubro concha Erycina salo,
et Tyros ostrinos praebet Cadmea colores,
    cinnamon et multi pistor odoris Arabs.

haec etiam clausas expugnant arma pudicas
    quaeque gerunt fastus, Icarioti, tuos.   10

---

[8] pistor *Bury*: pastor Ω

[a] See Index, *Aeaeus*.

[31] It hurt him not that Lampetie's cattle had bellowed on Ithacan spits (Lampetie, the Sun's daughter, had pastured them for her father), and that he fled from the bed of Aeaea's[a] weeping queen, swam the seas for so many days and nights of storm, entered the dark halls of the silent dead, was rowed by deaf oarsmen to the pools of the Sirens, and brought his old bow to life with the killing of the suitors, so putting an end to his wanderings.

[37] And not for nothing, since his wife throughout remained true to him at home. Aelia Galla's fidelity surpasses Penelope's.

Noble savagery and corrupt civilization

YOU all ask why the greed of girls makes their nights so costly and why our coffers, drained by Love, complain of their losses. The cause of such ruin is certain and obvious: the path of high living has become too free. The Indian ant sends gold from the caves of her mines,[b] and from the Red Sea comes the shell of Venus; Cadmean Tyre purveys her crimson tints, and cinnamon, the Arab distiller of rich scents.

[9] These are the weapons that storm even the cloistered chaste and women who wear the disdain of Penelope. Matrons step forth arrayed in the for-

[b] Cf. Herodotus 3.102; Pliny, *NH* 11.111.

matrona incedit census induta nepotum
    et spolia opprobrii nostra per ora trahit.
nullast poscendi, nullast reverentia dandi,
    aut si quast, pretio tollitur ipsa mora.

felix Eois lex funeris una maritis,   15
    quos Aurora suis rubra colorat equis!
namque ubi mortifero iactast fax ultima lecto,
    uxorum fusis stat pia turba comis,
et certamen habent leti, quae viva sequatur
    coniugium: pudor est non licuisse mori.   20
ardent victrices et flammae pectora praebent,
    imponuntque suis ora perusta viris.
hoc genus infidum nuptarum, hic nulla puella
    nec fida Euadne nec pia Penelope.

felix agrestum quondam pacata iuventus,   25
    divitiae quorum messis et arbor erant!
illis munus erat decussa Cydonia ramo,
    et dare puniceis plena canistra rubis,
nunc violas tondere manu, nunc mixta referre
    lilia vimineos lucida per calathos,   30
et portare suis vestitas frondibus uvas
    aut variam plumae versicoloris avem.

his tum blanditiis furtiva per antra puellae
    oscula silvicolis empta dedere viris.

tunes of spendthrifts and flaunt the spoils of dishonour before our eyes. There is no shame in asking, no shame in giving in return, or if there be some reluctance, even that is got rid of for a price.

[15] Uniquely blessed is the law of funerals for Eastern husbands, whom the red Dawn darkens when rising with her steeds. For when the last torch is cast upon the dead man's bier, the devout band of his wives stands with streaming hair, and they compete for death, which shall follow her husband alive: shame it is not to be allowed to die. The victorious burn and offer their breasts to the flames and press their scorched lips upon their husbands. But ours is a faithless race of brides, no girl of ours will play faithful Evadne or loyal Penelope.

[25] Happy and in peace lived the youth of the country in those far off days, whose riches consisted of the harvest and the tree. For them it was a present to give quinces shaken from the bough, to bring panniers laden with crimson bramble-berries, now to pick a handful of violets, now to bring a mixed bouquet of lilies shining through their wicker baskets,[a] and to carry grapes clothed in their own leaves and some speckled bird of rainbow plumage.

[33] These were the blandishments that purchased the stealthy kisses that the girls of those days gave their sylvan gallants in the glens. A fawn's pelt

---

[a] Cf. *Copa* 16, *lilia vimineis attulit in calathis*, one of several echoes of Propertius in this delightful Julio-Claudian poem.

hinnulei pellis stratos operibat amantes,   35
    altaque nativo creverat herba toro,
pinus et incumbens laetas circumdabat umbras;
    nec fuerat nudas poena videre deas.

corniger Arcadii vacuam pastoris in aulam
    dux aries saturas ipse reduxit oves;   40
dique deaeque omnes, quibus est tutela per agros,
    praebebant vestri verba benigna foci:
'et leporem, quicumque venis, venaberis, hospes,
    et si forte meo tramite quaeris avem:
et me Pana tibi comitem de rupe vocato,   45
    sive petes calamo praemia, sive cane.'

at nunc desertis cessant sacraria lucis:
    aurum omnes victa iam pietate colunt.
auro pulsa fides, auro venalia iura,
    aurum lex sequitur, mox sine lege pudor.   50

torrida sacrilegum testantur limina Brennum,
    dum petit intonsi Pythia regna dei:
at mox laurigero concussus vertice diras
    Gallica Parnasus sparsit in arma nives.
te scelus accepto Thracis Polymestoris auro   55
    nutrit in hospitio non, Polydore, pio.
tu quoque ut auratos gereres, Eriphyla, lacertos,
    delapsis nusquamst Amphiaraüs equis.

---

35 stratos *Baehrens*: totos Ω
37 laetas *F*: lentas Ω*
39 Arcadii *Hertzberg*: atque dei Ω
53 mox *A**: mons *N*

would cover the reclining lovers, and the grass grew tall to make them a natural bed, and a pine leaning over curtained them with luxuriant shade; nor was it a sin to see a goddess naked.

[39] A hornèd marshal leading his full-fed ewes, the ram came home of his own accord to the Arcadian shepherd's empty fold. Ye gods and goddesses all, who have protection of the fields, your altars offered kindly words: 'Whoever you are who come as a guest, you will hunt the hare along my path or any bird you seek: and whether you pursue your prize with rod or hound, summon me, Pan, from the crag to be your companion.'[a]

[47] But now shrines suffer neglect in forsaken groves: gold commands the worship of all, with piety trampled underfoot. Gold has banished faith, for gold judgements can be bought, gold is courted by the law, and soon the conscience that requires no law goes the same way.

[51] Charred portals testify to the sacrilege of Brennus, when he attacked the Pythian realm of the unshorn god: and soon Parnassus shook its laurelled peak and scattered terrible snows upon the Gallic arms. Accepting a bribe of gold the villainous Polymestor of Thrace entertains Polydorus with murderous hospitality. That you, too, Eriphyla, might display golden bracelets on your arms, the horses of Amphiaraus sank into the earth and he is nowhere to be found.

[a] The quatrain translates Leonidas, *A.P.* 9.337.

proloquar (atque utinam patriae sim verus haruspex!
    frangitur ipsa suis Roma superba bonis.   60
certa loquor, sed nulla fides; neque vilia quondam
    verax Pergameis maenas habenda mali:
sola Parim Phrygiae fatum componere, sola
    fallacem Troiae serpere dixit equum.
ille furor patriae fuit utilis, ille parenti: 65
    expertast veros irrita lingua deos.

XIV

MULTA tuae, Sparte, miramur iura palaestrae,
    sed mage virginei tot bona gymnasii,
quod non infamis exercet corpore ludos
    inter luctantis nuda puella viros,
cum pila velocis fallit per bracchia iactus,   5
    increpat et versi clavis adunca trochi,
pulverulentaque ad extremas stat femina metas,
    et patitur duro vulnera pancratio:[a]

---

[61] vilia ς: enim ilia Ω (< ·n ·ilia)
[62] Pergameis *Willis** . . . mali *Luck* (*Housman**): -is . . . -is Ω
[64] Troiae *Sh. Bailey*: patriae Ω (<65)

---

[a] Evidently a game in which the players throw, catch, and return the ball at lightning speed.

[59] I shall speak out, and may my country accept me as a true seer! Proud Rome is being destroyed by its own prosperity. I speak the truth, but no credence is granted me; nor on a time spoke the bacchante worthless words whom they of Pergamum should have recognized as a predicter of calamity: for she alone said that Paris was sealing Phrygia's doom and that the horse creeping against Troy was laden with treachery. That frenzy carried profit for her country, for her father: that unavailing tongue proved that the gods speak true.

Admiration for Sparta

The many rules of your athletics, O Sparta, I admire, but even more the many merits of your training of virgins, for without disrepute a naked girl may engage in physical exercise in the presence of wrestling men, when the ball makes invisible its lightning flight from hand to hand,[a] and the hooked stick rings against the rolling hoop, and a dust-soiled woman stands at the end of the course and suffers hurt in the fight with no holds barred[b]:

[b] The translation slightly exaggerates: the pancratium combined boxing, wrestling, and karate, but biting and gouging were prohibited. Even so, it was not a joust for the genteel.

nunc ligat ad caestum gaudentia bracchia loris,
    missile nunc disci pondus in orbe rotat,   10
15 et modo Taygeti, crinis aspersa pruina,
16   sectatur patrios per iuga longa canes:
gyrum pulsat equis, niveum latus ense revincit,   11
    virgineumque cavo protegit aere caput,

qualis Amazonidum nudatis bellica mammis
    Thermodontiacis turba lavatur aquis;
qualis et Eurotae Pollux et Castor harenis,   17
    hic victor pugnis, ille futurus equis,
inter quos Helene nudis capere arma papillis
    fertur nec fratres erubuisse deos.   20

lex igitur Spartana vetat secedere amantes,
    et licet in triviis ad latus esse suae,
nec timor aut ullast clausae tutela puellae,
    nec gravis austeri poena cavenda viri.
nullo praemisso de rebus tute loquaris   25
    ipse tuis: longae nulla repulsa morae.
nec Tyriae vestes errantia lumina fallunt,
    est neque odoratae cura molesta comae.

at nostra ingenti vadit circumdata turba,
    nec digitum angustast inseruisse via;   30
nec quae sit facies nec quae sint verba rogandi
    invenias: caecum versat amator iter.

15,16 *post* 10 *Palmer*
31 sit *P* : sint Ω

[9] now she binds the glove to her arms that rejoice in its thongs, now whirls in a circle the flying weight of the discus, and now, hoarfrost sprinkling her hair, she follows her father's hounds over the long ridges of Taygetus: her horses' hooves thud round the ring, she girds the sword to her snowy hips, and shields her virgin head with hollowed bronze,

[13] like the warlike throng of Amazons with breasts exposed that bathe in the waters of the Thermodon; and like Castor and Pollux on the banks of the Eurotas, Pollux to be a champion at boxing, Castor in horsemanship, with whom Helen, her bosom bare, is said to have borne arms and not to have blushed with shame in front of her divine brothers.

[21] Thus Spartan custom forbids lovers to hold aloof, and one may keep to his sweetheart's side at the crossways; none need fear for her honour or keep her under lock and key, or dread the cruel revenge of a stern husband. You need no messenger: you may speak in person about your business and have not to endure the rebuff of a long delay. No Tyrian garments beguile the eyes into error, nor are you vexed by the care spent on scenting her hair.

[29] But when the Roman girl walks out of doors, she is surrounded by a vast crowd, so hemmed in that not even a finger could reach her, nor could one contrive the proper mien and phrases of entreaty: the lover has to grope his way in the dark. Ah,

313

quod si iura fores pugnasque imitata Laconum,
    carior hoc esses tu mihi, Roma, bono.

XV

Sɪc ego non ullos iam norim in amore tumultus
    nec veniat sine te nox vigilanda mihi,
45 fabula nulla tuas de nobis concitet aures;
46   te solam et lignis funeris ustus amem.
ut mihi praetexti pudor est relevatus amictus
    et data libertas noscere amoris iter,
illa rudis animos per noctes conscia primas   5
    imbuit, heu nullis capta Lycinna datis!

tertius (haud multo minus est) cum ducitur annus,
    vix memini nobis verba coisse decem.
cuncta tuus sepelivit amor, nec femina post te
    ulla dedit collo dulcia vincla meo.   10
43 at tu non meritam parcas vexare Lycinnam:
44   nescit vestra ruens ira referre pedem.

testis erit Dirce tam vano crimine saeva,
    Nycteos Antiopen accubuisse Lyco.
ah quotiens pulchros vulsit regina capillos,
    molliaque immitis fixit in ora manus!

---

³ <re>levatus *Fontein* : velatus Ω

Rome, had you but copied Spartan laws and combats, dearer for that blessing would you be to me.

The story of Dirce

As truly as I hope never again to know any storms in love and hope a night will never come when I lie awake without you, no gossip about me is to alarm your ears: even when consumed by the funeral pyre I can love only you. When the restraint of boyhood's garb was lifted from me and I was given freedom to learn the way of love, my accomplice on those first nights, who initiated my untried heart, was Lycinna, won, ah me, by never a gift of mine!

[7] Three years (not much less) have passed, and I can scarcely remember so much as a dozen words being exchanged between us. Your love has buried everything, nor since I met you has any woman cast sweet chains about my neck. But you must stop tormenting innocent Lycinna: the impetuous anger of you women knows no drawing back.

[11] Witness Dirce,[a] she who was mad with jealousy at the groundless charge that Antiope, daughter of Nycteus, had slept with her Lycus. Ah, how often did the queen wrench out her fair tresses and attack her tender face with pitiless hands! Ah,

---

[a] The story of Dirce is the subject of several extant wall- and vase-paintings; and was dramatized by Euripides in his *Antiope* (of which over 200 lines survive).

ah quotiens famulam pensis oneravit iniquis,　　15
　　et caput in dura ponere iussit humo!
saepe illam immundis passast habitare tenebris,
　　vilem ieiunae saepe negavit aquam.

Iuppiter, Antiopae nusquam succurris habenti
　　tot mala? corrumpit dura catena manus.　　20
si deus es, tibi turpe tuam servire puellam:
　　invocet Antiope quem nisi vincta Iovem?
sola tamen, quaecumque aderant in corpore vires,
　　regalis manicas rupit utraque manu.
inde Cithaeronis timido pede currit in arces.　　25
　　nox erat, et sparso triste cubile gelu.

saepe vago Asopi sonitu permota fluentis
　　credebat dominae pone venire pedes.
et durum Zethum et lacrimis Amphiona mollem
　　expertast stabulis mater abacta suis.　　30
ac veluti, magnos cum ponunt aequora motus,
　　Eurus et adversus desinit ire Noto,
litore sollicito sonitus rarescit harenae,
　　sic cadit inflexo lapsa puella genu.

sera, tamen pietas: natis est cognitus error.　　35
　　digne Iovis natos qui tueare senex,

---

[27] vago ς: vaga Ω
[32] et *Keil*: sub *N*: in *A** | adversus *Postgate*: -o *N*: -os
(... notos) *A**
[33] sollicito *Nairn*: sic tacito Ω

how often did she load the handmaid with unjust tasks and made her lay her head upon the stony ground! Oft she left her to dwell in foul darkness, oft she denied her water from the common well to quench her thirst.

¹⁹ Jupiter, do you give no aid to Antiope when she has such troubles? The hard chains chafe her arms. It is a reproach on you, if god you are, that she whom you loved should be a slave: to whom but Jupiter can the fettered Antiope appeal? Unaided though, summoning all the strength in her body, she burst the gyves the queen had put upon her hands. Then with trembling feet she runs to the heights of Cithaeron. It was night, and her couch was harsh with scattered frost.

²⁷ Oft, scared by the sound of Aesopus' restless current, she thought that the feet of her mistress were following behind. Her tears found Zethus unmoved, Amphion inclined to pity, when she, their mother, was driven from a steading that was of right her own. And just as, when the seas abate their mighty motions and the East Wind ceases to battle with the South, along the buffeted shore the howling of the sand dies down, so did the poor woman, sinking, bow her knee and fall.

³⁵ Late, but yet filial duty showed: the sons perceived their fault. You, old man, fit guardian of the sons of Jove, restore the mother to her boys; and the

tu reddis pueris matrem; puerique trahendam
    vinxerunt Dircen sub trucis ora bovis.
Antiope, cognosce Iovem: tibi gloria Dirce
    ducitur in multis mortem habitura locis.   40
prata cruentantur Zethi, victorque canebat
    paeana Amphion rupe, Aracynthe, tua.

XVI

Nox media, et dominae mihi venit epistula nostrae:
    Tibure me missa iussit adesse mora,
candida qua geminas ostendunt culmina turres,
    et cadit in patulos nympha Aniena lacus.
quid faciam? obductis committam mene tenebris 5
    ut timeam audacis in mea membra manus?
at si distulero haec nostro mandata timore,
    nocturno fletus saevior hoste mihi.
peccaram semel, et totum sum pulsus in annum:
    in me mansuetas non habet illa manus.   10

nec tamen est quisquam, sacros qui laedat amantes:
    Scironis medias his licet ire vias.
quisquis amator erit, Scythicis licet ambulet oris,
    nemo adeo ut feriat barbarus esse volet.

[43,44] *post* 10 *Vulpius*   [45,46] *post* 2 *Otto*
[12] medias his . . . vias *Heinsius*: -a sic . . . -a Ω
[14] feriat *CIL* 4.1950: noceat Ω

---

[a] Pliny, *NH* 36.34, refers to a sculpture by Apollonius
and Tauriscus of Tralles, carved from a single block of

boys bound Dirce to be dragged beneath the head of a fierce bull.[a] Antiope, recognize the hand of Jove: for your satisfaction Dirce is drawn along to find death in many a spot. The fields of Zethus are red with blood, and Amphion sang the paean of victory on your rocks, O Aracynthus.

Night journey to Tibur

MIDNIGHT, and a letter has come to me from my mistress commanding my presence at Tibur without delay, where the white hilltops display turrets on right and left and Anio's water cascades into spreading pools. What to do? Trust myself to the enveloping darkness and fear that ruffian hands be laid upon my person? But if out of fear for myself I put off this request, her tears will wound me worse than any nocturnal foe. I sinned once, and was rejected for a whole year: against me she does not wield merciful hands.

[11] Yet there is no one to hurt sacred lovers: these may boldly travel Sciron's road. Whoever is a lover, though he walk on Scythian shores, none will presume to be so barbarous as to attack him. For

stone, exhibiting Dirce being tied to the bull by Zethus and Amphion: of this the famous Farnese Bull in the Naples Museum is a copy. Cf. Pompeian wall-painting, from the House of the Vettii (Feder 100f).

19   sanguine tam parvo quis enim spargatur amantis
20   improbus, et cuius sit comes ipsa Venus?
    luna ministrat iter, demonstrant astra salebras,   15
      ipse Amor accensas praecutit ante faces,
    saeva canum rabies morsus avertit hiantis:
      huic generi quovis tempore tuta viast.

    quod si certa meos sequerentur funera cursus,   21
      tali mors pretio vel sit emenda mihi.
    afferet haec unguenta mihi sertisque sepulcrum
      ornabit custos ad mea busta sedens.
    di faciant, mea ne terra locet ossa frequenti   25
      qua facit assiduo tramite vulgus iter!
    post mortem tumuli sic infamantur amantum.
      me tegat arborea devia terra coma,
    aut humer ignotae cumulis vallatus harenae:
      non iuvat in media nomen habere via.   30

XVII

Nunc, o Bacche, tuis humiles advolvimur aris:
    da mihi pacato vela secunda, pater.
tu potes insanae Veneris compescere fastus,
    curarumque tuo fit medicina mero.

19,20 *post* 14 *Struchtmeyer*
20 et cuius sit (ς) *Palmer*: exclusis fit Ω
16 praecutit *Guyet*: percutit Ω
21 cursus *Markland*: casus Ω
22 tali ς: talis Ω

what villain would stain himself with the scanty blood of a lover or a man accompanied by Venus herself? The moon lights the way, the stars show the rough ground, Love himself waves a flaming torch in front of him, the fierce watchdog turns aside his gaping fangs: for such travellers the road is safe at any hour.

²¹ But if my journey were to result in certain funeral, death would even be worth procuring at such a price. She will bring me unguents and deck my grave with garlands, seated as guardian o'er my tomb. God forbid that she should bury my bones in a busy spot, where the crowd travels along an unsleeping thoroughfare! Thus are the tombs of lovers desecrated after their death. Let secluded ground cover me with leafy trees, or let me be buried where I am enclosed in an unmarked mound of sand: I like it not to have my name recorded on a highway.[a]

Homage to Bacchus

Now, Bacchus, I humbly prostrate myself at your altar: grant me, O Father, peace and prospering sails. You can quell the disdain of a furious mistress, and in your liquor a swain's sorrows find

---

[a] This poem derives much charm from its blithe air of utter unreality: we are not of course to take it seriously.

PROPERTIUS

per te iunguntur, per te solvuntur amantes: 5
    tu vitium ex animo dilue, Bacche, meo.

te quoque enim non esse rudem testatur in astris
    lyncibus ad caelum vecta Ariadna tuis.
hoc mihi, quod veteres custodit in ossibus ignes,
    funera sanabunt aut tua vina malum.   10
semper enim vacuos nox sobria torquet amantes;
    spesque timorque animos versat utroque modo.

quod si, Bacche, tuis per fervida tempora donis
    accersitus erit somnus in ossa mea,
ipse seram vites pangamque ex ordine colles,   15
    quos carpant nullae me vigilante ferae.
dum modo purpureo spument mihi dolia musto,
    et nova pressantis inquinet uva pedes,
quod superest vitae per te et tua cornua vivam,
    virtutisque tuae, Bacche, poeta ferar.   20

dicam ego maternos Aetnaeo fulmine partus,
    Indica Nysaeis arma fugata choris,
vesanumque nova nequiquam in vite Lycurgum,
    Pentheos in triplicis funera rapta greges,

---

[17] spument ç: numen Ω*
[24] <ra>pta *Scaliger*: grata Ω (<gta?>)

322

balm. With your aid lovers meet and lovers part: do you, Bacchus, wash the mischief from my soul.

⁷ For you too are not without experience: to that, carried by your lynx-drawn chariot to heaven, Ariadne bears witness among the stars.[a] This evil, which has long kept a lasting fire within my bones, only death or your wine will cure. For a sober night is always torment to lovers left desolate: hope and fear keep shifting their minds this way or that.

¹³ But if your gifts, Bacchus, make my temples glow and you bring sleep which puts my bones to rest, then I myself will sow vines and plant the hills in rows, staying awake to see that no wild beasts crop them. Only let my vats foam with the purple must and the fresh grape stain the feet that tread it, and I shall spend what life is left me honouring you and your horns, and shall be famed, Bacchus, as the poet of your power.

²¹ I shall tell how, stricken by a bolt from Etna, your mother gave you birth; how Indian warriors were routed by Nysa's dancers; how Lycurgus vainly raved over the new-found vine; how Pentheus' corpse was torn apart among three[b] Maenad bands;

[a] As the constellation Corona (Borealis).

[b] Cf. Euripides, *Bacch.* 680, ὁρῶ δὲ θιάσους τρεῖς γυναικείων χορῶν. In a Pompeian wall-painting (from the House of the Vettii) Pentheus is being assailed by three women (Feder 80f).

323

curvaque Tyrrhenos delphinum corpora nautas   25
    in vada pampinea desiluisse rate,
et tibi per mediam bene olentia flumina Diam,
    unde tuum potant Naxia turba merum.

candida laxatis onerato colla corymbis
    cinget Bassaricas Lydia mitra comas,   30
levis odorato cervix manabit olivo,
    et feries nudos veste fluente pedes.
mollia Dircaeae pulsabunt tympana Thebae,
    capripedes calamo Panes hiante canent,
vertice turrigero iuxta dea magna Cybebe   35
    tundet ad Idaeos cymbala rauca choros.

ante fores templi, cratere antistes et auro
    libatum fundens in tua sacra merum,
haec ego non humili referam memoranda coturno,
    qualis Pindarico spiritus ore tonat: 40
tu modo servitio vacuum me siste superbo,
    atque hoc sollicitum vince sopore caput.

XVIII

Clausus ab umbroso qua tundit pontus Averno
    fumida Baiarum stagna tepentis aquae,

---

[28] Diam *Palmer* : Naxon Ω (*a gloss*)
[37] cratere antistes et *Heinsius* : crater antistitis Ω
[1] tundit *Baehrens* : ludit Ω

how the Tuscan sailors, changed into the arched bodies of dolphins, leapt into the sea from a vine-clad ship; and how in the midst of Dia flow sweet-smelling streams in your honour, wherefrom the people of Naxos drink your wine.

[29] While your white shoulders bear trailing ivy-clusters, a Lydian turban will crown your hair, Bassareus; your smooth nape will stream with per-fumed oil, and your flowing robe will strike your bare feet. Dircean Thebes will beat the wanton tam-bourine, and goat-footed Pans will play on pipes of reed; nearby, wearing her turreted headdress, the great goddess Cybele will clash her hoarse cymbals to accompany the Idean dance.

[37] Before the temple doors, as priest pouring for your rites a libation of wine from a bowl of gold, I shall hymn these themes, meet for no humble strain, but with such voice as thundered forth from Pindar's lips: do you but set me free from imperious enslavement and overwhelm my troubled head with slumber.

Elegy for Marcellus

WHERE the sea, locked out from shadowy Avernus, beats against Baiae's steaming pools of warm water,

PROPERTIUS

qua iacet et Troiae tubicen Misenus harena,
  et sonat Herculeo structa labore via;
hic ubi, mortalis dexter cum quaereret urbes,   5
  cymbala Thebano concrepuere deo —
at nunc invisae magno cum crimine Baiae,
  quis deus in vestra constitit hostis aqua? —
Marcellus Stygias vultum demisit in undas,
  errat et inferno spiritus ille lacu.   10

quid genus aut virtus aut optima profuit illi
  mater, et amplexum Caesaris esse focos?
aut modo tam pleno fluitantia vela theatro,
  et per mirantis omina festa manus?
occidit, et misero steterat vicesimus annus: 15
  tot bona tam parvo clausit in orbe dies.
i nunc, tolle animos et tecum finge triumphos,
  stantiaque in plausum tota theatra iuvent;
Attalicas supera vestes, atque ostra smaragdis
  gemmea sint Indis: ignibus ista dabis.   20

---

[9] Marcellus *Phillimore* (>***pessus): his pressus Ω
[10] inferno *Housman* : in vestro Ω
[14] m.o. festa *Sh. Bailey*: maternas omnia gesta Ω
[19] ostra smaragdis *Housman* : omnia magnis Ω
[20] Indis *Housman* : ludis Ω

---

[a] Bacchus, but his visit is not recorded elsewhere.
[b] The death of the popular young Marcellus in 23 brought great grief to Rome; his adoption by Augustus (line 12), whose daughter he had married, unmistakeably marked him out for the succession. His funeral, described

where both the Trojan trumpeter Misenus lies
buried in the sand and the causeway built by the toil
of Hercules resounds; here, where cymbals clashed
to greet the god of Thebes[a] when on a kindly errand
he visited the cities of mankind—but, Baiae, now
detested for your heinous crime, what malign deity
has settled in your bay?—Marcellus[b] has lowered
his gaze to the waters of the Styx, and his noble
spirit wanders about the infernal lake.

[11] What availed him his lineage, his worth, the
best of mothers?[c] What availed him his union with
the house of Caesar, or the rippling awnings of the
theatre but now so thronged and the happy omens of
popular applause? He is dead, and the poor boy's
twentieth year was his fated term: within so brief a
span did time confine such excellence. You may
indulge your heart's desire and dream of triumphs;
imagine whole theatres rising to their feet to cheer;
outdo the golden cloth of Attalus and bejewel your
fine apparel with emeralds from Ind: you will
surrender all to the pyre.

---

by Servius on *Aeneid* 6.861, was one of passing splendour.
Propertius' elegy is sincere and dignified, but he has been
completely upstaged by Virgil, whose eloquent and
dramatic tribute (*loc. cit.*), when recited by him to the
imperial court, caused his mother to faint and all to weep.

[c] Octavia, the sister of Augustus.

PROPERTIUS

sed tamen huc omnes, huc primus et ultimus ordo:
    est mala, sed cunctis ista terenda viast.
exoranda canis tria sunt latrantia colla,
    scandendast torvi publica cumba senis.
2.28.57   nec forma aeternum aut cuiquamst fortuna perennis:
2.28.58   longius aut propius mors sua quemque manet.
ille licet ferro cautus se condat et aere,   25
    mors tamen inclusum protrahit inde caput.
Nirea non facies, non vis exemit Achillem,
    Croesum aut, Pactoli quas parit umor, opes.

at tibi nauta, pias hominum quo traicit umbras,   31
    huc animae portet corpus inane tuae:
qua Siculae victor telluris Claudius et qua
    Caesar, ab humana cessit in astra via.

XIX

Obicitur totiens a te mihi nostra libido:
    crede mihi, vobis imperat ista magis.
vos, ubi contempti rupistis frena pudoris,
    nescitis captae mentis habere modum.

2.28.57,58 *post* 24 *Housman*
29,30 *post* 2.6.16 *Phillimore*
31 quo *Jacob* : qui Ω | traicit *Paley* : traicis Ω
32 portet ς : portent Ω

328

²¹ Yet hither all shall come, hither the highest and the lowest class: evil it is, but it is a path that all must tread; all must assuage the three heads of the barking guard-dog and embark on the grisly greybeard's boat that no one misses. For none is beauty a lasting gift, for none lasts luck for ever: death sooner or later lies in store for all. Though yonder cautious man shut himself up behind walls of iron and bronze,ᵃ yet death will drag him forth from his hiding place. Beauty saved not Nireus, nor his might Achilles, nor Croesus the wealth produced by Pactolus' stream.

³¹ But as for you, may the ferryman convey to the place whither he gives passage to the shades of the righteous the body no longer tenanted by your soul: that soul, like Claudius, Sicily's conqueror, and like Caesar, has forsaken the paths of men and risen to the stars.

Women's lust

You are constantly reproaching me with men's lust: take it from me, lust commands women even more. When you scorn decency and have burst its bonds, you are unable to keep control of your mind that is possessed.

ᵃ As Acrisius shut up Danaë in a brazen tower.

flamma per incensas citius sedetur aristas,   5
    fluminaque ad fontis sint reditura caput,
et placidum Syrtes portum et bona litora nautis
    praebeat hospitio saeva Malea suo,
quam possit vestros quisquam reprehendere cursus
    et rabidae stimulos frangere nequitiae.   10

testis, Cretaei fastus quae passa iuvenci
    induit abiegnae cornua falsa bovis;
testis Thessalico flagrans Salmonis Enipeo,
    quae voluit liquido tota subire deo.
crimen et illa fuit, patria succensa senecta   15
    arboris in frondes condita Myrrha novae.

nam quid Medeae referam, quo tempore matris
    iram natorum caede piavit amor?
quidve Clytaemestrae, propter quam tota Mycenis
    infamis stupro stat Pelopea domus?   20
tuque, o, Minoa venumdata, Scylla, figura
    tondes purpurea regna paterna coma.

hanc igitur dotem virgo desponderat hosti!
    Nise, tuas portas fraude reclusit amor.
at vos, innuptae, felicius urite taedas: 25
    pendet Cretaea tracta puella rate.

---

[a] Fabricated by Daedalus to enable her to couple, cf.
4.7.57. This was a popular theme in wall-paintings, e.g.
that from the House of the Vettii, Pompeii (Feder 88f).

⁵ Sooner will flame die down when a cornfield has caught fire, sooner rivers run backwards to their fountain-head, and sooner the Syrtes provide safe anchorage and cruel Malea give the mariner kindly welcome on its shores than any man have power to check you in your career and put a stop to the mad wantonness that goads you on.

¹¹ Witness is she who suffered the disdain of a Cretan bull and put on the false horns of a timber cow*a*: witness is Salmoneus' daughter, who, afire for Thessalian Enipeus, was ready to yield totally to the watery god. Myrrha, too, was a reproach to women, who, lovestruck for her aged father, was hidden away in the foliage of a new-made tree.

¹⁷ Why need I tell of Medea's passion, when it appeased the mother's anger by the slaying of her children, or of Clytemnestra's, on whose account the whole house of Pelops at Mycenae stands disgraced for adultery? And you, O Scylla, shear away in the purple lock your father's realm, which you sold for Minos' beauty.

²³ This then was the dowry pledged by the maiden to the foe! Nisus, it was love that treacherously unlocked your door. But do you, unwed maidens, burn your torches with happier outcome: the girl is suspended from the Cretan ship and dragged through the sea. Yet not undeservedly

non tamen immerito Minos sedet arbiter Orci:
    victor erat quamvis, aequus in hoste fuit.[a]

XX

CREDIS eum iam posse tuae meminisse figurae,
    vidisti a lecto quem dare vela tuo?
durus, qui lucro potuit mutare puellam!
    tantine, ut lacrimes, Africa tota fuit?

at tu stulta adeo's? tu fingis inania verba: 5
    forsitan ille alio pectus amore terat.
est tibi forma potens, sunt castae Palladis artes,
    splendidaque a docto fama refulget avo,
fortunata domus, modo sit tibi fidus amicus.
    fidus ero: in nostros curre, puella, toros!   10

tu quoque, qui aestivos spatiosius exigis ignes,
    Phoebe, moraturae contrahe lucis iter.
nox mihi prima venit! primae da tempora nocti!
    longius in primo, Luna, morare toro.

---

⁵ adeo es *Rossberg*: deos Ω
¹⁴ da ... nocti *Palmer*: da[te] ... noctis Ω

---

^a I.e. he saw to it that his foe Nisus was avenged. The poet similarly emphasizes the justice of Tarpeia's execution, 4.4.92.

^b Perhaps Hostia. 'I think it plain, for many reasons, that this poem is not addressed to Cynthia, but to a per-

does Minos sit as the judge of the underworld: though he was victor, he was fair to his foe.[a]

Contract for a new love

Do you really believe that he can still remember your beauty,[b] that man whom you saw sail away from your bed? Cruel man, who could give up his sweetheart for profit! Was the whole of Africa worth making you weep?

[5] How can you be so silly? You are imagining promises that are worthless: no doubt he is warming his breast with another love. You have striking beauty, you have the skills of chaste Pallas, and your learned grandsire's glorious renown shines upon you. Blest is your house, had you only a faithful lover. I will be faithful: hasten, sweetheart, to my bed.

[11] You, too, Sun, who draw out to excess your summer fires, speed up the journey of your light that would linger—my first night of love is coming! Add time to my first night! Linger long, O Moon, over our first union!

son utterly different, and celebrates the marriage, or at least the "honourable addresses," of the narrator': A. W. Verrall, 'An Old Love Story' (a charming appreciation of Propertius ['the best poet of his time,' p. 29]), in *Collected Literary Essays*, Cambridge 1913, p. 47 n. 1.

19   quam multae ante meis cedent sermonibus horae
20   dulcia quam nobis concitet arma Venus!
   foedera sunt ponenda prius signandaque iura   15
     et scribenda mihi lex in amore novo.
   haec Amor ipse suo constringet pignora signo:
     testis sidereae torta corona deae.

   namque ubi non certo vincitur foedere lectus,   21
     non habet ultores nox vigilanda deos,
   et quibus imposuit, solvit mox vincla libido:
     contineant nobis omina prima fidem.

   ergo, qui tactis haec foedera ruperit aris,   25
     pollueritque novo sacra marita toro,
   illi sint quicumque solent in amore dolores,
     et caput argutae praebeat historiae,
   nec flenti dominae patefiant nocte fenestrae:
     semper amet, fructu semper amoris egens.   30

XXI

MAGNUM iter ad doctas proficisci cogor Athenas
   ut me longa gravi solvat amore via.
crescit enim assidue spectando cura puellae:
   ipse alimenta sibi maxima praebet amor.

19,20 *ante* 15 *Lachmann*
17 constringet *Beroaldus* : -it Ω
25 tactis haec . . . aris *Burman* : pactas in . . . aras Ω

[19] How many hours shall first give way to my wooing before Venus spurs us to her sweet warfare! First must the terms be made, the oath sealed, and the contract written for this new love of mine. Love himself with his own signet will ratify these pledges: the woven crown of Ariadne among the stars is witness.

[21] For when a union is not bound by fixed terms, the lover's sleepless nights have no gods to avenge them, and passion soon loosens the fetters of those whom it has bound: for us let the first omens guarantee lasting faith.

[25] Wherefore: whoever after touching the altar shall violate these terms and pollute the rites of marriage with another union, let him suffer all the pains love knows; let him expose himself to chattering gossip; let his mistress' window never open to him at night for all his weeping; let him ever be in love, and ever lack its enjoyment.

The only remedy

I am constrained to embark on distant travel to learned Athens, that the long journey may free me from oppressive love, for my passion for my sweetheart grows steadily with looking at her: love itself provides its chief source of sustenance.[a] I have tried

---

[a] Cf. Shakespeare, *Sonnet* 75.

omnia sunt temptata mihi, quacumque fugari   5
   posset: at exsomnis me premit ipse deus.
vix tamen aut semel admittit, cum saepe negarit:
   seu venit, extremo dormit amicta toro.

unum erit auxilium: mutatis Cynthia terris
   quantum oculis, animo tam procul ibit amor.   10
nunc agite, o socii, propellite in aequora navem,
   remorumque pares ducite sorte vices,
iungiteque extremo felicia lintea malo:
   iam liquidum nautis aura secundat iter.
Romanae turres et vos valeatis, amici,   15
   qualiscumque mihi tuque, puella, vale!

ergo ego nunc rudis Hadriaci vehar aequoris hospes,
   cogar et undisonos nunc prece adire deos.
deinde per Ionium vectus cum fessa Lechaeo
   sedarit placida vela phaselus aqua,   20
quod superest, sufferre, pedes, properate laborem,
   Isthmos qua terris arcet utrumque mare.
inde ubi Piraei capient me litora portus,
   scandam ego Theseae bracchia longa viae.

illic vel stadiis animum emendare Platonis   25
   incipiam aut hortis, docte Epicure, tuis;

---

[6] posset *Richards* : -it Ω | exs. *Barber* : ex omni Ω

---

[a] The long walls between the Piraeus and Athens.
[b] Recently owned by Gaius Memmius, to whom Cicero

all means by which it could be banished: yet the god
himself besets me unsleepingly. But she receives
me hardly ever or just once after many snubs: or if
she comes to me, she sleeps fully dressed on the edge
of the bed.

9 There is only one remedy: if I travel to another
land, love will be as far from my mind as Cynthia
from my eyes. Up now, my friends, and launch a
ship upon the sea, and draw lots in pairs for places
at the oars, and hoist to the mast-top the fair-
omened sails: already the breeze speeds the mariner
over his watery path. Farewell, ye towers of Rome,
and farewell, friends, and you, sweetheart, however
you have treated me, farewell!

17 So now I shall sail as a new guest of the Adri-
atic, and now be forced to approach with prayer the
gods of the roaring waves. Then when my yacht has
crossed the Ionian and rested its weary sails in the
calm waters at Lechaeum, for what remains of the
journey, hasten ye, my feet, to endure the toil,
where the Isthmus beats back either sea from the
land. Then when the shores of Piraeus' haven
receive me, I shall ascend the long arms[a] of
Theseus' Way.

25 There I will begin to improve my mind in
Plato's Academy or in the garden[b] of sage Epicurus;

appealed (*Ad Fam.* 13.1) for its preservation as the centre
of the Epicurean School.

persequar aut studium linguae, Demosthenis arma,
    libaboque tuos, culte Menandre, sales;
aut certe tabulae capient mea lumina pictae,
    sive ebore exactae, seu magis aere, manus.   30

et spatia annorum et longa intervalla profundi
    lenibunt tacito vulnera nostra sinu:
seu moriar, fato, non turpi fractus amore;
    atque erit illa mihi mortis honesta dies.

XXII

FRIGIDA tam multos placuit tibi Cyzicus annos,
    Tulle, Propontiaca qua fluit isthmos aqua,
Dindymis et sacra fabricata in vite Cybebe,
    raptorisque tulit quae via Ditis equos?

si te forte iuvant Helles Athamantidos urbes,   5
    nec desiderio, Tulle, movere meo,

^{28} libabo *Suringar*: librorum Ω | culte *Heinsius*: docte
Ω (<clte)
  ^{31} et ... et *Baehrens*: aut ... aut Ω
  ^{2} qua ς: quae Ω
  ^{4} quae ς: qua Ω
  ^{6} nec ς: et Ω

or I will pursue the study of language, the weapon of Demosthenes, and savour the wit of elegant Menander; or at least painted panels will ensnare my eyes, or works of art wrought in ivory or, better, in bronze.

[31] Both the passage of time and the sea's far-sundering will ease the wounds that linger in my silent breast: or if I die, it will be naturally and not laid low by a shameful love; and the day of my death will bring me no dishonour.[a]

In praise of Italy

Has[b] chilly Cyzicus found favour with you, Tullus, for all these years, where lies the isthmus which is washed by the waters of the Propontis, the statue of Dindymene Cybele wrought upon a sacred vine-stock, and the road which bore the horses of the ravisher Dis?[c]

[5] If perchance you like the cities of Athamantid Helle, and are not moved, Tullus, by any thought of

---

[a] He has changed his tune since 2.26.58 and 3.16.22.

[b] Another variation of the *propempticon*.

[c] Cyzicus is fixed by the author of the *Priapea* (75.12) as the scene of Proserpine's rape, though this honour is generally awarded to Henna in Sicily (Ovid, *Met.* 5.385ff, etc.).

15 si tibi olorigeri visendast ora Caystri,
16   et quae serpentis temperat unda vias;
tu licet aspicias caelum omne Atlanta gerentem,
    sectaque Persea Phorcidos ora manu,
Geryonis stabula et luctantum in pulvere signa
    Herculis Antaeique, Hesperidumque choros;   10
tuque tuo Colchum propellas remige Phasim,
    Peliacaeque trabis totum iter ipse legas,
qua rudis Argoa natat inter saxa columba
    in faciem prorae pinus adacta novae:
omnia Romanae cedent miracula terrae.   17
    natura hic posuit, quidquid ubique fuit.

armis apta magis tellus quam commoda noxae:
    Famam, Roma, tuae non pudet historiae.   20
nam quantum ferro tantum pietate potentes
    stamus: victricis temperat ira manus.

hic, Anio Tiburne, fluis, Clitumnus ab Umbro
    tramite, et aeternum Marcius umor opus,
Albanus lacus et foliis Nemorensis abundans,   25
    potaque Pollucis nympha salubris equo.

at non squamoso labuntur ventre cerastae,
    Itala portentis nec furit unda novis;

15,16 *post* 6 *Housman*
15 si tibi *Palmer*: et si quae Ω | <ol>orige<ri> ς: orige Ω
16 serpentes *Hubbard*: septenas Ω
25 foliis ... abundans *Housman*: socia ... ab unda Ω

340

me; if you must see the banks of the swan-famed Cayster and the river that restrains its serpentine course—though you behold Atlas supporting the whole of heaven and the Gorgon's head which the hand of Perseus severed, the stables of Geryon and the marks in the dust where Hercules and Antaeus wrestled, and the dancing-places of the Hesperides; and though you propel Colchian Phasis with your oars, and yourself repeat the whole journey of the Pelion-timbered ship, where on its maiden voyage the pine tree hewn into the shape of an unfamiliar prow sailed between the rocks thanks to the Argo's dove: all these marvels shall yield before the land of Rome. Whatever is best in all the world Nature has placed here.

[19] It is a land more fit for war than disposed to crime: Fame blushes not for your history, Rome. For we stand a strong nation as much through humanity as through the sword: our anger stays its hand in victory.

[23] Here you flow, Tiburn Anio, here flows Clitumnus from its path in Umbria, and the Marcian conduit, that everlasting monument; here is the Alban Lake, and Nemi's, thick with leaves, and the healing spring[a] whence drank the horse of Pollux.

[27] But here glide no horned asps on scaly bellies, nor do Italian waters swarm with strange monsters;

[a] The *lacus Iuturnae* in the Forum, where Castor and Pollux watered their horses after the battle of Regillus.

non hic Andromedae resonant pro matre catenae,
    nec tremis Ausonias, Phoebe fugate, dapes,   30
nec cuiquam absentes arserunt in caput ignes
    exitium nato matre movente suo;
Penthea non saevae venantur in arbore Bacchae,
    nec solvit Danaas subdita cerva rates;
cornua nec valuit curvare in paelice Iuno   35
    aut faciem turpi dedecorare bove; . . .
arboreasque cruces Sinis, et non hospita Grais
    saxa, et curtatas in fera fata trabes.

haec tibi, Tulle, parens, haec est pulcherrima sedes,
    hic tibi pro digna gente petendus honos,   40
hic tibi ad eloquium cives, hic ampla nepotum
    spes et venturae coniugis aptus amor.

[36] *lac. Livineius*
[38] curtatas *Pucci* : curvatas Ω

---

[a] Like that prepared by Atreus, who killed the sons of his brother Thyestes and served them up to him at table; the Sun in horror reversed his course.

not here do an Andromeda's chains rattle for her mother's crime, nor in Italy was ever a banquet[a] which made the Sun shudder and turn away; nor have distant fires burned for a victim's death as his mother works her own son's undoing[b]; no cruel Bacchants hunt Pentheus in a tree, no substitute[c] hind gives release to a Greek fleet, and Juno has not availed to fashion a crescent of horns on a rival's head or disfigure her beauty with the ugliness of a cow . . . (*not here will you see*) Sinis' trees of execution, the rocks that gave bitter welcome to the Greeks, and the planks shortened to inflict a cruel death.

[39] This, Tullus, is the land that gave you birth, this your fairest home; here you should seek the high office to match your noble birth. Here are citizens for your eloquence to sway, here rich hope of offspring, here awaits you perfect love from your bride to be.

---

[b] The Fates had told Meleager's mother Althaea that he would not die until a log on the fire was consumed; she took it off and preserved it; but later, when Meleager killed her brothers in a dispute over the spoils of the Calydonian boar, she burned the log in anger—and Meleager died.

[c] See Index, *Iphigenia*.

PROPERTIUS

XXIII

Ergo tam doctae nobis periere tabellae,
    scripta quibus pariter tot periere bona!
has quondam nostris manibus detriverat usus,
    qui non signatas iussit habere fidem.
illae iam sine me norant placare puellas,   5
    et quaedam sine me verba diserta loqui.
non illas fixum caras effecerat aurum:
    vulgari buxo sordida cera fuit.
qualescumque mihi semper mansere fideles,
    semper et effectus promeruere bonos.   10

forsitan haec illis fuerunt mandata tabellis:
    'irascor, quoniam's, lente, moratus heri.
an tibi nescio quae visast formosior? an tu
    non bona de nobis crimina ficta iacis?'
aut dixit: 'venies hodie, cessabimus una: 15
    hospitium tota nocte paravit Amor,'
et quaecumque volens reperit non stulta puella
    garrula, cum blandis dicitur hora dolis.

---

[11] fuerunt ς: fuerint *N*: fuerant *A**
[18] dicitur ς: ducitur Ω

BOOK III.23

The lost tablets

So my accomplished tablets are lost then,[a] and so much splendid writing lost with them! Long usage at my hands had worn them down and bade them, though unsealed, be credited as mine. They had by now learned how to mollify girls in my absence, and in my absence utter some persuasive phrases. No setting of gold had made them precious: they were just cheap wax on common boxwood. Even so they always remained faithful to me and always achieved good results.

[11] Perhaps this was the message entrusted to those tablets: 'I am angry because yesterday, you sluggard, you stayed away. Has some other girl seemed prettier to your fancy? Or are you spreading vile slanders about me?' Or perhaps she wrote this: 'Come today: we'll while away the time together. Love has prepared to put you up all night,' and all the witty things a talkative girl in a willing mood finds to say when an hour is being appointed for

---

[a] The theme of lost tablets was also handled by Catullus (42) and Ovid (*Am.* 1.12, where *ephemerides* in line 25 reveals his indebtedness to Propertius), and their poems suggest the circumstances of the loss.

345

me miserum, his aliquis rationem scribit avarus
    et ponit duras inter ephemeridas!   20

quas si quis mihi rettulerit, donabitur auro:
    quis pro divitiis ligna retenta velit?
i puer, et citus haec aliqua propone columna,
    et dominum Esquiliis scribe habitare tuum.

XXIV, XXV

FALSAST ista tuae, mulier, fiducia formae,
    olim oculis nimium facta superba meis.
noster amor talis tribuit tibi, Cynthia, laudes:
    versibus insignem te pudet esse meis.
mixtam te varia laudavi saepe figura,   5
    ut, quod non esses, esse putaret amor;
et color est totiens roseo collatus Eoo,
    cum tibi quaesitus candor in ore foret:

quod mihi non patrii poterant avertere amici,
    eluere aut vasto Thessala saga mari,   10
hoc ego non ferro, non igne coactus, at ipsa
    naufragus Aegaea (vera fatebor) aqua.

---

[11] hoc *Foster*: haec Ω | at ς: et Ω

---

[a] Like Virgil's (*Vit. Don.* 13), Propertius' house on the
Esquiline (cf. 4.8.1ff) was perhaps the gift of Maecenas.

amorous wiles. Oh dear! Now some profiteer is
writing his accounts on them and filing them with
his pitiless ledgers.

²¹ If anyone returns them to me, I shall reward
him with gold: who would care to keep wood when
he might have wealth? Go, slave, and quickly post
this notice on some pillar, and write that your mas-
ter lives on the Esquiline.[a]

Cynthia renounced

'TIS is a false confidence, woman, that you place in
your charms; 'twas my admiring eyes that long since
made you overproud.[b] 'Twas my love that bestowed
such honour on you; and I am ashamed that you are
renowned through my verse. Often I praised you as
combining all manner of charms, so that my love
fancied you to be what you were not; many a time I
have compared your complexion to the rosy dawn,
when the radiance on your face was all a sham.

⁹ The infatuation that neither family friends
could rid me of or witches of Thessaly wash away in
ocean, this I have effected myself, not brought
thereto by the knife or cautery, but (I will tell the
truth) after being shipwrecked in a very Aegean sea

---

[b] A designed repudiation of 1.1, which it echoes in
themes and structure, even to the number of lines.

correptus saevo Veneris torrebar aeno;
    vinctus eram versas in mea terga manus.
ecce coronatae portum tetigere carinae,   15
    traiectae Syrtes, ancora iacta mihist.

nunc demum vasto fessi resipiscimus aestu,
    vulneraque ad sanum nunc coiere mea.
Mens Bona, si qua dea's, tua me in sacraria dono!
    exciderunt surdo tot mea vota Iovi.   20
risus eram positis inter convivia mensis,   25.1
    et de me poterat quilibet esse loquax.
quinque tibi potui servire fideliter annos:
    ungue meam morso saepe querere fidem.

nil moveor lacrimis: ista sum captus ab arte;   5
    semper ab insidiis, Cynthia, flere soles.
flebo ego discedens, sed fletum iniuria vincit:
    tu bene conveniens non sinis ire iugum.
limina iam nostris valeant lacrimantia verbis,
    nec tamen irata ianua fracta manu.   10

at te celatis aetas gravis urgeat annis,
    et veniat formae ruga sinistra tuae!
vellere tum cupias albos a stirpe capillos,
    iam speculo rugas increpitante tibi,

---

[24] exciderunt ς: exciderant Ω
[25.1] *cont. A*, sep. N*
[14] iam *Sh. Bailey*: a Ω

of passion. Venus seized me and roasted me in her cruel cauldron[a]: I was a prisoner with hands bound behind my back. But, lo, my garlanded ship has reached harbour, the sandbanks are passed, my anchor dropped.

[17] Now at last, weary from the wild surge, I have recovered my sanity, and my wounds have now closed up and healed. Good Sense, if goddess indeed you are, I dedicate myself to your shrine! So many vows of mine have been lost on the deafness of Jove. I used to be a laughing-stock when the tables were set for the feast, and anyone could be witty at my expense. For five years I managed to serve you faithfully: now you will oft bite your nails and mourn the loss of my loyalty.

[25:5] Your tears move me not: it was that trick which ensnared me; always when you weep, Cynthia, you plan to deceive. I shall weep when I go, but wrongs outlast tears: it is you who do not allow a well-matched team to run. Farewell the threshold still tearful at my grievances, and farewell the door, never, in spite of all, shattered by my angry fists!

[11] May old age oppress you with the burden of the years you have dissembled, and may ugly wrinkles come upon your beauty. Then may you wish to tear out the white hairs by the roots now that the mirror chides you with your wrinkles. Shut out yourself in

[a] Like victims in the bull of Phalaris.

PROPERTIUS

exclusa inque vicem fastus patiare superbos,   15
  et quae fecisti facta queraris anus!
has tibi fatalis cecinit mea pagina diras:
  eventum formae disce timere tuae!

turn, may you suffer another's haughty scorn and, now a crone, complain that what you once did yourself is done to you. Such are the deadly curses my page prophesies for you: learn to dread the end that awaits your beauty.

BOOK FOUR

Propertius' last book consists of twelve poems. A programme of Roman elegies is announced, compromised at once by an astrologer's warning that the poet is fated to continue writing love-elegy. There follows an alternation of each kind, aetiological poems implementing 1A, love-elegies implementing 1B, save that instead of the intended order 8-9-7 the poet has juxtaposed the two Cynthia-poems, possibly to avoid ending with two funeral elegies, possibly to suggest that his love-affair with his sweetheart continues beyond the grave. The inclusion of national topics without mention of Maecenas feeds the suspicion that (as with the fourth book of Horace's Odes) Augustus himself had importuned the poet. Here and there Propertius softens the stark contrast between antiquarian and contemporary material by emphasizing the erotic in the one and the traditional in the other. If the results are mixed, yet he achieves notable successes with the legend of Tarpeia (4.4) and the speech of Cornelia (4.11), the latter not unworthily dubbed by Valckenaer 'The Queen of Elegies.'

LIBER QUARTUS

IA

Hoc quodcumque vides, hospes, qua maxima Romast,
   ante Phrygem Aenean collis et herba fuit;
atque ubi Navali stant sacra Palatia Phoebo,
   Euandri profugae procubuere boves.
fictilibus crevere deis haec aurea templa,   5
   nec fuit opprobrio facta sine arte casa;
Tarpeiusque Pater nuda de rupe tonabat,
   et Tiberis nostris advena murus erat.
qua gradibus domus ista, Remi se sustulit olim:
   unus erat fratrum maxima regna focus.   10
Curia, praetexto quae nunc nitet alta senatu,
   pellitos habuit, rustica corda, Patres.
bucina cogebat priscos ad verba Quirites:
   centum illi in prati saepe senatus erat.

---

⁴ procubuere ς: concubuere Ω
⁸ murus *Heyworth**: bubus Ω
⁹ qua ς (*dist. Watt**): quod *N*: quo *A**
¹⁴ prati *Heinsius*: prato Ω, *Lactantius*

---

a The poet acts as a guide to a stranger visiting Rome.

THE FOURTH BOOK

The poet plans to sing of Rome

ALL that you see here, stranger,[a] where mighty Rome now stands, was grass and hill before the coming of Phrygian Aeneas; and where stands the Palatine consecrated to Apollo of the Ships, the cattle of exiled Evander there lay down. These golden temples have grown up for gods of clay, who deemed it no shame that their huts were crudely built. Tarpeian Jupiter thundered from a bare rock, and the Tiber, though foreign, was our forbears' wall. Where upon a flight of steps yonder house[b] rears itself, once did that of Remus: a single hearth was the total realm of the brothers. The Curia, which now stands high and resplendent with its hemfrocked senate, then housed a rustic company of Fathers clad in skins. A horn summoned the oldtime citizens to parley: a hundred of them in an enclosure of the meadow formed the senate. Nor

---

[b] The *aedes Quirini* (temple of the deified Romulus) on the Quirinal, reconstructed and dedicated by Augustus in in 16 B.C., just before the poem was written; as at 2.1.23, *Remi* stands for the metrically impossible *Romuli*.

nec sinuosa cavo pendebant vela theatro,   15
    pulpita sollemnis non oluere crocos.

nulli cura fuit externos quaerere divos,
    cum tremeret patrio pendula turba sacro,
annuaque accenso celebrante Parilia faeno,
    qualia nunc curto lustra novantur equo.   20
Vesta coronatis pauper gaudebat asellis,
    ducebant macrae vilia sacra boves.
parva saginati lustrabant compita porci,
    pastor et ad calamos exta litabat ovis.
verbera pellitus saetosa movebat arator,   25
    unde licens Fabius sacra Lupercus habet.
nec rudis infestis miles radiabat in armis:
    miscebant usta proelia nuda sude.

prima galeritus posuit praetoria Lycmon,
    magnaque pars Tatio rerum erat inter oves.   30
hinc Tities Ramnesque viri Luceresque Soloni,
    quattuor hinc albos Romulus egit equos.

---

[19] celebrante *Housman* : celebrare Ω

  [a] The Parilia (April 21; but the docking of the horse took place on October 15).
  [b] The Vestalia (June 9–15).
  [c] The Compitalia (late December or early January).

did billowing drapes hang over the hollow theatre or
the stage reek of ceremonial saffron.

[17] No one then felt the need of foreign gods, when
the tense crowd thrilled at the ritual of their fathers
and bonfires of straw celebrated the annual festival
of Pales,[a] just as now purification is renewed with
the docking of a horse. Vesta was poor and rejoiced
in garlanded mules, and it was lean cattle that led
the procession for a paltry sacrifice.[b] Narrow were
the crossroads that fatted swine purified,[c] and to
the sound of the pipe the shepherd made acceptable
offering of a sheep's entrails. The skin-clad plough-
man waved his shaggy whip, whence derives the
wanton rite of Fabian Lupercus.[d] Nor gleamed
their rude soldiery with threatening weapons:
unprotected by armour they fought with stakes har-
dened by fire.

[29] The first captain's tent was pitched by Lycmon
wearing a wolf-skin helmet, and Tatius' wealth
lay largely in his flocks.[e] From such origins came
the Tities, the warrior Ramnes, the Luceres of
Solonium, from such came Romulus to drive his

[d] The Lupercalia (February 15), at which the Luperci
ran round the Palatine and struck with goat-skin thongs
any woman they encountered; the rite was believed to pro-
mote fertility.

[e] He is differently portrayed in 4.4.19ff.

PROPERTIUS

quippe suburbanae parva minus urbe Bovillae,
36   tunc ubi Fidenas longa erat isse via;
et stetit Alba potens, albae suis omine nata,   35
34   et, qui nunc nulli, maxima turba Gabî.
nil patrium nisi nomen habet Romanus alumnus:
      sanguinis altricem non putet esse lupam.

huc melius profugos misisti, Troia, Penates;
      heu quali vectast Dardana puppis ave,   40
47   arma resurgentis portans victricia Troiae!
48   felix terra tuos cepit, Iule, deos.
iam bene spondebant tunc omina, quod nihil illos
      laeserat abiegni venter apertus equi,
cum pater in nati trepidus cervice pependit,
      et veritast umeros urere flamma pios.
hinc animi venere Deci Brutique secures,   45
      vexit et ipsa sui Caesaris arma Venus,
si modo Avernalis tremulae cortina Sibyllae   49
      dixit Aventino rura pianda Remo,   50
aut si Pergameae sero rata carmina vatis
      longaevum ad Priami vera fuere caput:
87   'dicam: Troia, cades et Troica Roma resurges!
88   et maris et terrae regna superba cano.

---

[34] *cum* 36 *comm. Mueller*   [36] tunc *Ritschl*: hac Ω
[41] illos *Schrader*: -am Ω   [47,48] *post* 40 *Housman*
[88] regna superba *Housman*: longa sepulcra Ω (<renga sepubra?) | cano *Murgia**: canam Ω (<-am 87)

---

[a] Cf. Virgil, *Aen.* 8.42ff.   [b] Anchises.
[c] An allusion to the *Alexandra* of Lycophron, spoken by a slave who reports to Priam the prophecies of Alexandra

358

four white steeds. Bovillae, to be sure, was less of a
suburb when Rome was small, in days when it was a
long journey to Fidenae; and Alba stood and was
mighty, born of the omen of a white sow,[a] and Gabii,
which now is nothing, was then a vast multitude.
The Roman of today has nothing from his ancestor
but his name: he would not believe that a she-wolf
nurtured the blood from which he sprang.

[39] You did splendidly, O Troy, to send hither your
exiled gods. Ah, what blessed augury attended the
sailing of the Dardan ship which carried to victory
the arms of Troy reborn! Blessed indeed was the
land that received your gods, Iulus. Even then the
omens boded well, for the opened belly of the
Wooden Horse had done those gods no harm when
the trembling father[b] hung on his son's neck and
the flames feared to burn those dutiful shoulders.
Then came the heroism of Decius and the axes of
Brutus, and Venus herself bore her Caesar's arms, if
indeed the Avernian tripod of the quaking Sibyl told
that its fields were to be sanctified by the blood of
Remus of the Aventine, or if the predictions of
the Trojan prophetess, late fulfilled, were truly an-
nounced to the aged Priam[c]: 'This is my report:
"Troy, you will fall, and rise again as Trojan Rome; I
prophesy proud dominion over land and sea. Turn

(i.e. Cassandra): *dicam* translates λέξω, the first word of
the poem (Murgia); and the rest of the couplet, 1225ff;
Housman's bold conjecture is supported by 1229 γῆς καὶ
θαλάσσης σκῆπτρα καὶ μοναρχίαν.

359

vertite equum, Danai! male vincitis! Ilia tellus
    vivet, et huic cineri Iuppiter arma dabit.'

optima nutricum nostris, lupa Martia, rebus,   55
    qualia creverunt moenia lacte tuo!
moenia namque pio coner disponere versu:
    ei mihi, quod nostrost parvus in ore sonus!
sed tamen exiguo quodcumque e pectore rivi
    fluxerit, hoc patriae serviet omne meae.   60
Ennius hirsuta cingat sua dicta corona:
    mi folia ex hedera porrige, Bacche, tua,
ut nostris tumefacta superbiat Umbria libris,
    Umbria Romani patria Callimachi!
scandentis quisquis cernit de vallibus arces,   65
    ingenio muros aestimet ille meo!
Roma, fave, tibi surgit opus; date candida, cives,
    omina; et inceptis dextera cantet avis!
sacra deosque canam et cognomina prisca locorum:
    has meus ad metas sudet oportet equus.   70

IB

Quo ruis imprudens? fuge discere fata, Properti!
    non sunt a dextro condita fila colo.
accersis lacrimas: aversus cantat Apollo:
    poscis ab invita verba pigenda lyra.

---

[69] deosque *Sullivan**: diesque Ω   [71] *sep. Itali* |
\<f>uge *Livineius*: vage Ω | discere ç: dicere Ω
[73] aversus cantat *Sandbach*: cantas aversus Ω

back the horse, ye Greeks! Yours is a ruinous victory! The land of Ilium shall live, and to these ashes Jove will furnish arms."'

55 She-wolf of Mars, best of nurses for our fortunes, what walls have sprung up from your milk! For I would fain lay out those walls in duteous verse: ah me, that a voice so feeble sits upon my lips! But still, whatever the stream that gushes forth from my puny breast, the whole of it shall be given to the service of my country. Let Ennius crown his verse with a ragged garland: Bacchus, give me leaves of your ivy, that Umbria may swell with pride at my books, Umbria, the home of Rome's Callimachus! Let whosoever descries the citadels that climb up from the vale esteem those walls by my genius. Rome, smile on me; my work rises for you; citizens, give me a fair omen, and let a bird on the right augur success for my undertaking. I shall sing of rites and deities and ancient names of places: this is the goal to which my foaming steed must press.

The poet's horoscope

WHITHER do you hurry so thoughtlessly? Seek not to learn your fate, Propertius! From no auspicious distaff have its threads been spun. You are bringing sorrow on yourself: unfavourable is the response of Apollo. You are asking a reluctant lyre for words it is loth to grant.

certa feram certis auctoribus, aut ego vates   75
    nescius aerata signa movere pila,
83 felicisque Iovis stellas Martisque rapacis
84   et grave Saturni sidus in omne caput.
me creat Archytae suboles Babylonius Horops
    Horon, et a proavo ducta Conone domus.
di mihi sunt testes non degenerasse propinquos,
    inque meis libris nil prius esse fide.   80
nunc pretium fecere deos et fallimus auro
    (Iuppiter!) obliquae signa iterata rotae.

dixi ego, cum geminos produceret Arria natos   89
    (illa dabat natis arma vetante deo),   90
non posse ad patrios sua pila referre Penates:
    nempe meam firmant nunc duo busta fidem.
quippe Lupercus, equi dum saucia protegit ora,
    heu sibi prolapso non bene cavit equum;
Gallus at in castris, dum credita signa tuetur,   95
    concidit ante aquilae rostra cruenta suae:
fatales pueri, duo funera matris avarae!
    vera, sed invito, contigit ista fides.

[77] horops ς: orops Ω
[81] fallimus *Housman* : -itur Ω
[83,84] *post* 76 *Richmond*
[85,86] *post* 102 *Richmond*
[87,88] *post* 52 *Mueller*
[94] equum *Richmond* : equo Ω (<equom)

[75] Sure things I shall tell on sure authority, or I am a seer unskilled at moving the constellations on the sphere of bronze,[a] the planets of benign Jupiter and rapacious Mars, and the star of Saturn malign to one and all. Horops of Babylon, of the line of Archytas, begot me, Horos, and my house is derived from its ancestor Conon. The gods are my witness that I have not disgraced my kin and that in my books nothing comes before truth. Nowadays men have made profit of the gods and (heavens!) we even falsify for gold the revolving signs of the tilted zodiac.

[89] I said, when Arria was sending off her two sons (she was giving her sons arms against the advice of the god) that they would not bring back their weapons to the family hearth: and, sure enough, two graves now confirm my truthfulness. For Lupercus, in shielding the wounded face of his horse, slipped, alas, and failed to beware of the horse. And Gallus in camp, minding the standards entrusted to his charge, fell in front of his own eagle and stained its beak with his blood. Ill-starred lads, both brought to death by a mother's greed! That prophecy of mine found fulfilment, though I would it had not!

---

[a] A planetarium, like the orrery of Archimedes, described in Cicero, *De Rep.* 1.22.

idem ego, cum Cinarae traheret Lucina dolores,
    et facerent uteri pondera lenta moram,   100
'Iunonis facito votum impetrabile' dixi:
    illa parit: libris est data palma meis!
85   quid moneant Pisces animosaque signa Leonis,
86   lotus et Hesperia quid Capricornus aqua,
hoc neque harenosum Libyci Iovis explicat antrum,
    aut sibi commissos fibra locuta deos,
aut si quis motas cornicis senserit alas,   105
    umbrave quae magicis mortua prodit aquis:
aspicienda viast caeli verusque per astra
    trames, et ab zonis quinque petenda fides.

exemplum grave erit Calchas: namque Aulide solvit
    ille bene haerentis ad pia saxa rates;   110
idem Agamemnoniae ferrum cervice puellae
    tinxit, et Atrides vela cruenta dedit;
nec rediere tamen Danai: tu, diruta, fletum
    supprime et Euboicos respice, Troia, sinus!

---

85 moneant *L*: moveant Ω*
103 Libyci ς: libyae Ω

---

a Unlike Arria, Lupercus, and Gallus—all Roman
names—Cinara (κνάρα = artichoke) is Greek and typically
borne by *hetaerae,* the best known being the Horatian lady
(cf. *Odes* 4.1, 4.13; and *Epist.* 1.7, 1.14).

b The oracle of Jupiter Ammon.

c Haruspicy.

d The augur.

e The practice of hydromancy, in which ghosts appear

⁹⁹ So too when Lucina was prolonging Cinara's[a]
labour-pains and the burden of her womb was slow
and caused delay, I said: 'Let her make a vow that
shall prevail with Juno!' She gives birth: victory
was awarded to my almanacs! What portend the
Fishes and the Lion's fierce sign and Capricorn
bathed in the western ocean is not revealed by the
desert shrine of Libyan Jove,[b] or by the entrails
that communicate the godhead within them,[c] or by
him who understands the winged flight of the
crow,[d] or by the dead shade who comes forth from
magic waters[e]: you must observe the paths of
heaven and the road of truth that lies in the stars,
and seek trust from the five zones.[f]

¹⁰⁹ Calchas[g] will be a persuasive example: for he
released from Aulis the fleet that had been well tied
to merciful rocks; so doing he stained his knife with
the sacrifice of Agamemnon's daughter, and the son
of Atreus set forth with blood upon his sails; yet the
Greeks came not home: dry your eyes, ruined Troy,
and think of the bays of Euboea. Nauplius beckons

in a bowl of water to foretell the future.

[f] The road is the zodiac; but the five zones (cf. Virgil,
Georg. 1.233ff) play no part in astrology.

[g] A wall-painting from the House of the Tragic Poet in
Pompeii well depicts Calchas, sacrifical sword in hand, the
reluctant Ulysses and Achilles, and the grief-stricken
Agamemnon; in the background Artemis beckons to a
nymph bringing the substitute hind (Feder 90f).

Nauplius ultores sub noctem porrigit ignes,   115
   et natat exuviis Graecia pressa suis.
victor Oiliade, rape nunc et dilige vatem,
   quam vetat avelli veste Minerva sua!

hactenus historiae: nunc ad tua devehar astra;
   incipe tu lacrimis aequus adesse novis.   120
Umbria te notis antiqua Penatibus edit —
   mentior? an patriae tangitur ora tuae? —
qua nebulosa cavo rorat Mevania campo,
   et lacus aestivis non tepet Umber aquis,
scandentisque Asis consurgit vertice murus,   125
   murus ab ingenio notior ille tuo.
ossaque legisti non illa aetate legenda
   patris et in tenuis cogeris ipse lares:
nam tua cum multi versarent rura iuvenci,
   abstulit excultas pertica tristis opes.   130
mox ubi bulla rudi dimissast aurea collo,
   matris et ante deos libera sumpta toga,
tum tibi pauca suo de carmine dictat Apollo
   et vetat insano verba tonare foro.

at tu finge elegos, pellax opus (haec tua castra!), 135
   scribat ut exemplo cetera turba tuo.

[124] non tepet *Housman* : intepet Ω
[135] pellax *Heinsius* : fallax Ω

---

[a] Referring to the confiscation of lands for distribution among Octavian's soldiers.
   [b] The *bulla,* a charm worn by the sons of senators and

with his vengeful beacon at nightfall, and Greece is shipwrecked, sunk by its booty. Triumphant son of Oileus, now seize and make love to the prophetess whom, clinging to the goddess's robe, Minerva forbids to be wrenched away.

119 Enough of these stories: now I shall come down to your horoscope; compose yourself for fresh sorrows. Ancient Umbria bore you in an illustrious home—do I lie, or have I hit upon the borders of your native land?—where misty Mevania sheds its dews on the low-lying fields, and the waters of the Umbrian mere acquire no warmth in summer, where a wall rises on the peak of soaring Assisi, the wall made more famous by your genius. And you gathered, not to be gathered at that age, your father's bones, and were forced to move to a humble home: for whereas many a steer ploughed up your acres, the rod of the pitiless surveyor robbed you of well-tilled estates.[a] Next when the golden locket was removed from your innocent neck,[b] and you donned the toga of manhood before your mother's gods, then Apollo dictates a little of his song to you and forbids you to bawl forth speeches in the bedlam of the law-courts.

135 Now you must compose Elegy, an alluring task (here lies your camp), so that the rest of the

knights, was laid aside on the assumption of the *toga virilis*.

PROPERTIUS

militiam Veneris blandis patiere sub armis,
    et Veneris pueris utilis hostis eris.
nam tibi victricis quascumque labore parasti,
    eludet palmas una puella tuas: 140
143 illius arbitrio noctem lucemque videbis;
144   gutta quoque ex oculis non nisi iussa cadet.
et bene cum fixum mento decusseris uncum,
    nil erit hoc: rostro te premet ansa tuo.
nec mille excubiae nec te signata iuvabunt   145
    limina: persuasae fallere rima sat est.

nunc tua vel mediis puppis luctetur in undis,
    vel licet armatis hostis inermis eas,
vel tremefacta cavum tellus diducat hiatum:
    octipedis Cancri terga sinistra time!   150

II

QUI mirare meas tot in uno corpore formas,
    accipe Vertumni signa fatente deo.
Tuscus ego et Tuscis orior, nec paenitet inter
    proelis Volsinios deseruisse focos,

---

[140] eludet ς: eludit Ω
[141] decusseris *Broekhuyzen*: discusseris Ω
[142] tuo *N*: suo *A**
[143,144] *post* 140 *Housman*
[149] cavum ς: cavo Ω (<cavom)
[2] fatente deo *Sh. Bailey*: paterna (*N*: petenda *A**) dei Ω

throng will write after your example. You will suffer active service in the tender warfare of Venus, and you will be a profitable adversary for Venus' boys. For whatever victories you win by your toil, one girl will mock your triumphs. Darkness and daylight you will see at her dictation: not even a teardrop will fall from your eyes save at her command, and though you dislodge the hook that is well fixed in your chin, this will prove no gain: the gripper will secure you fast by your snout.[a] Nor shall a thousand watches help you, nor all the seals you place upon her doors: a chink is enough for a woman determined to deceive.

[147] Now though your ship be struggling in mid tempest, though you go an unarmed fighter against an armed host, though the earth should tremble and open up a gaping chasm: the sinister back of the eight-footed Crab is what you must fear.[b]

The tokens of Vertumnus

Do you who marvel that my one body has so many shapes learn from the lips of the god the tokens of Vertumnus. A Tuscan am I and from Tuscans sprung, nor feel remorse to have forsaken Volsinii's

[a] An obscure metaphor from fishing.

[b] Technically 'Beware when the Moon is in Cancer': but the injunction is simply a factitious piece of astrological hocus-pocus, for an explanation of which we shall look in vain.

PROPERTIUS

tempore quo sociis venit Lycomedius armis   51
    quoque Sabina feri contudit arma Tati.
vidi ego labentis acies et tela caduca,
    atque hostes turpi terga dedisse fugae.

49 et tu, Roma, meis tribuisti praemia Tuscis,
50   unde hodie Vicus nomina Tuscus habet.
sed facias, divûm Sator, ut Romana per aevum   55
    transeat ante meos turba togata pedes.   56
haec me turba iuvat, nec templo laetor eburno: 5
    Romanum satis est posse videre Forum.

hac quondam Tiberinus iter faciebat, et aiunt
    remorum auditos per vada pulsa sonos:
at postquam ille suis tantum concessit alumnis,
    Vertamnus verso dicor ab amne deus.   10
seu, quia vertentis fructum praecerpimus anni,
    Vertanni rursus creditur esse sacrum.
mendax fama, vaces: alius mihi nominis index: 19
    de se narranti tu modo crede deo.   20

---

[52] <quo>que *Morel* : [at]que Ω
[5] me *P* : mea *NFL* (cf. 2.1.71)
[10] Vertamnus *Paley* : vertumnus Ω
[11] praecerpimus *Fea* : praecepimus Ω
[12] Vertanni *Paley* : vertumni Ω | creditur ç : credidit Ω
[13–18] *post* 42 *Heyworth**
[19] vaces *DV* : voces *A** : noces *N*

370

hearths in the days of battle, at the time when
Etruscans[a] came with allied arms and crushed the
Sabine forces of fierce Tatius. I saw the wavering
ranks, arms thrown to the ground, and the enemy's
back turned in ignominious rout.

[49] And you, Rome, appointed a reward for my
Tuscan kin, whereby to this day the Tuscan Street
is so named. But grant, O Father of the gods, that
for all time the toga'd populace of Rome may pass
before my feet. I like this throng, and delight not in
an ivory temple: it is enough that I can see the
Roman Forum.

[7] Once the Tiber travelled this way,[b] and they
say that the sound of oars was heard over the smit-
ten shallows: but after he granted so much to his
foster-children, I am, from the diVERTing of AMNis,
the river, called VERTAMNus; and again, because I
receive the reVERTing ANNual first-fruits, people
believe this to be the offering due to VERTANNus. Be
quiet, lying rumour: there is another voucher for my
name: just listen to the god when he speaks about
himself.

---

[a] Etruscans (Lycomedians) from Volsinii (65 miles north
of Rome) came to help Romulus against the Sabines under
Tatius and brought the god Vertumnus with them.

[b] The area known as the Velabrum.

PROPERTIUS

opportuna meast cunctis natura figuris:
    in quamcumque voles verte, decorus ero.
indue me Cois, fiam non dura puella:
    meque virum sumpta quis neget esse toga?
da falcem et torto frontem mihi comprime faeno: 25
    iurabis nostra gramina secta manu.

arma tuli quondam et, memini, laudabar in illis:
    corbis in imposito pondere messor eram.
sobrius ad lites: at cumst imposta corona,
    clamabis capiti vina subisse meo.   30
cinge caput mitra, speciem furabor Iacchi;
    furabor Phoebi, si modo plectra dabis.
35 est etiam aurigae species cum verbere et eius
36   traicit alterno qui leve corpus equo.

cassibus impositis venor: sed harundine sumpta
    fautor plumoso sum deus aucupio.
sub petaso pisces calamo praedabor, et ibo   37
    mundus demissis institor in tunicis.
pastor me ad baculum possum curvare vel idem
    sirpiculis medio pulvere ferre rosam.   40

nam quid ego adiciam, de quo mihi maxima famast,
    hortorum in manibus dona probata meis?

35,36 *post* 32 *Goold**
35 cum verbere *Postgate*: vertumnus Ω
36 corpus *Schrader*: pondus Ω
37 sub petaso *Alton*: suppetat hoc Ω

22 My nature suits any role: turn me to which you please, and I shall fit it well. Clothe me in silks, and I will become a none too prudish girl: and who would deny that, wearing the toga, I am a man? Give me a scythe and bind my forehead with a wisp of hay: you will swear that my hand has cut grass.

27 I once bore arms and, as I recall, was praised therein: with a heavy basket on my back I was a reaper. Sober am I when dressed for court; but with a garland on my brows you will declare the wine has gone to my head. Bind my head with a turban, I will steal the semblance of Bacchus; and, given only his lyre, I will steal that of Phoebus. With a whip in my hand I also present the guise of a charioteer and of him who switches his nimble body from horse to horse.[a]

33 With nets on my shoulder I hunt: but carrying a fowler's reed I am the patron god of the hunt for feathered prey. Wearing a felt-hat I shall catch fish with a rod, and in trailing garb I will step abroad as a spruce pedlar. I can bend myself to the crook as a shepherd, and can as well carry roses in baskets amid the dust.

41 Need I add, wherein lies my chief renown, that my hands are filled with the garden's choicest fruit?

---

[a] Perhaps Fontein (followed by A. H. Griffiths) is right in deleting this couplet, which interrupts the hunting sequence. I have retained it transposed despite the emendation entailed, as there was no obvious reason for its interpolation.

prima mihi variat liventibus uva racemis,   13
    et coma lactenti spicea fruge tumet;
hic dulcis cerasos, hic autumnalia pruna   15
    cernis et aestivo mora rubere die;
insitor hic solvit pomosa vota corona,
    cum pirus invito stipite mala tulit.   18

caeruleus cucumis tumidoque cucurbita ventre
    me notat et iunco brassica vincta levi;
nec flos ullus hiat pratis, quin ille decenter   45
    impositus fronti langueat ante meae.
at mihi, quod formas unus vertebar in omnis,
    nomen ab eventu patria lingua dedit.

sex superant versus: te, qui ad vadimonia curris,   57
    non moror: haec spatiis ultima creta meis.
STIPES ACERNUS ERAM, PROPERANTI FALCE DOLATUS,
    ANTE NUMAM GRATA PAUPER IN URBE DEUS.   60
AT TIBI, MAMURRI, FORMAE CAELATOR AENAE,
    TELLUS ARTIFICIS NE TERAT OSCA MANUS,
QUI ME TOT DOCILEM POTUISTI FUNDERE IN USUS.
    UNUM OPUS EST, OPERI NON DATUR UNUS HONOS.

⁴⁹⁻⁵⁶ (49,50 *post* 54) *post* 4 *Housman*
⁶³ tot docilem *Hertzberg* : tam docilis Ω

It is for me that the first grape darkens on the purpling cluster, and the spiky corn-ear swells with milky grain; at my feet you see sweet cherries, at my feet autumn plums and the mulberry blushing in the summertime; here the grafter pays his vows with a garland of fruit, when the pear's reluctant stock has borne him apples.

43 The dark-green cucumber, the pot-bellied gourd, and the cabbage tied up with a frail rush mark me out; and not a flower opens in the meadows but will droop before my face in comely fashion when placed upon my brow. But because I could conVERT my Unity into oMNiformity, my native tongue[a] has named me VERTUMNus from the circumstance.

57 Six[b] verses remain: I will not detain you who hurry to answer your bail[c]: this is the finishing line[d] of my course.

ONCE I WAS A MAPLE STUMP, BY HURRIED SICKLE HEWN,

TILL NUMA'S TIME A POOR GOD IN A CITY I LOVE.

BUT MAY OSCAN SOIL NOT BRUISE THY EXPERT HANDS,

MAMURRIUS, WHO ENGRAVED MY FORM IN BRONZE

AND HAD THE SKILL TO CAST ME TO FILL SO MANY ROLES:

ONE IS MY STATUE, NOT ONE THE HONOUR IT RECEIVES.

[a] But the etymology is Latin, not Etruscan.

[b] The six verses are an imaginary inscription on the pedestal of Vertumnus' statue.

[c] The passer-by is conceived as hurrying to the forum, where, if not to lose his bail, he is obliged to appear.

[d] A chalk-line marked the finish of Roman races.

PROPERTIUS

III

HAEC Arethusa suo mittit mandata Lycotae,
  cum totiens absis, si potes esse meus.
si qua tamen tibi lecturo pars oblita derit,
  haec erit e lacrimis facta litura meis:
aut si qua incerto fallet te littera tractu,   5
  signa meae dextrae iam morientis erunt.
te modo viderunt intentos Bactra per arcus,
  te modo munito Persicus hostis equo,
hibernique Getae, pictoque Britannia curru,
  tunsus et Eoa decolor Indus aqua.   10

haecne marita fides et pacta haec praemia nuptae,
  cum rudis urgenti bracchia victa dedi?
quae mihi deductae fax omen praetulit, illa
  traxit ab everso lumina nigra rogo;
et Stygio sum sparsa lacu, nec recta capillis   15
  vitta datast: nupsi non comitante deo.

omnibus heu portis pendent mea noxia vota:
  texitur haec castris quarta lacerna tuis.

---

[7] intentos *Morgan** : iteratos Ω | arcus *Housman* : ortus
Ω

[8] Persicus *Dousa fil.* : hericus Ω

[10] tu\<n\>sus *Housman* : ustus Ω

[11] pacta haec *Bury* : parce *N* : pac(a)tae *A** | praemia
Housman : avia (*N* : mihi *A**) Ω (\<cmia?\>) | nuptae *Goold** :
noctes Ω

BOOK IV.3

To a husband at the wars

ARETHUSA to her Lycotas[a] sends this letter, if in spite of your frequent absences you can count as mine. But if when you read it any portion is smudged and missing, such a blot will have been caused by my tears; or if the unclear outline of any letter baffles you, this will be a sign that death was even now upon my hand. Now you were seen by Bactra amid drawn bows, now by the Persian foe mounted on his mailed charger, by the northern Getans, by Britain[b] with its painted chariots and the swarthy Indians pounded by orient waves.

11 Is this the husband's loyalty and are these the bridal gifts you pledged when all innocent I surrendered to your embraces? The torch which gave omen as it headed my wedding procession drew its murky light from a dying funeral pyre; I was sprinkled with water from the Styx, and the wreath was set awry on my hair: Hymen was absent when I wed.

17 On every gate hang my offerings that do naught, alas, but harm: this is now the fourth[c] cloak I am weaving for your warfare. Perish he who from

---

[a] The Greek names are romantic pseudonyms for a young Roman and his bride.

[b] Britain makes an odd appearance in this couplet, for Augustus' intended campaign never got beyond the Channel; but the text seems assured by 2.1.76.

[c] Suggesting four years of absence.

occidat, immerita qui carpsit ab arbore vallum
    et struxit querulas rauca per ossa tubas,   20
dignior obliquo funem qui torqueat Ocno,
    aeternusque tuam pascat, aselle, famem!

dic mihi, num teneros urit lorica lacertos?
    num gravis imbellis atterit hasta manus?
haec noceant potius, quam dentibus ulla puella   25
    det mihi plorandas per tua colla notas!
diceris et macie vultum tenuasse: sed opto
    e desiderio sit color iste meo.

at mihi cum noctes induxit vesper amaras,
    si qua relicta iacent, osculor arma tua;   30
tum queror in toto non sidere pallia lecto,
    lucis et auctores non dare carmen aves.
55 Craugidos et catulae vox est mihi grata querentis:
56   illa tui partem vindicat una toro.

noctibus hibernis castrensia pensa laboro
    et Tyria in chlamydas vellera secta suo;
et disco, qua parte fluat vincendus Araxes,   35
    quot sine aqua Parthus milia currat equus;
cogor et e tabula pictos ediscere mundos,
    qualis et haec docti sit positura dei,

[34] chlamydas *Barber* : gladios Ω | suo *Rossberg* : suos Ω

a guiltless tree plucked the soldier's stake and fashioned the trumpet to sound its mournful notes through screeching bone: he rather than Ocnus deserved to sit sideways twisting the rope and feed for ever the donkey's hunger!

23 Tell me, does not the breastplate blister your delicate shoulders, and the heavy spear chafe your unwarlike hands? Rather may this hurt you than that some girl should implant on your neck love-bites for me to lament. I hear too[a] that your face is thin and wan: but I hope that this pallor of yours comes from missing me.

29 As for me, when the evening star brings on the bitter nights, I kiss any arms of yours that lie left at home; then I complain that the blanket lies not smooth all over the bed, and that the dawn birds are slow to utter their song. Even the fretful whimper of my puppy Yapper is pleasant to my ears: she claims for herself your side in our bed.[b]

33 On winter nights I work at camp garb for you, and I sew together lengths of Tyrian wool to make a military cloak; I learn where flows the Araxes that you are to conquer, how many miles a Parthian horse can cover without water; and I am constrained to find out from a map the countries painted on it and the manner of this arrangement by the wise

---

[a] Perhaps indirectly from a fellow-soldier whose letters have reached home.
[b] See note on 2.17.4.

quae tellus sit lenta gelu, quae putris ab aestu,
   ventus in Italiam qui bene vela ferat.   40
assidet una soror, curis et pallida nutrix
   peierat hiberni temporis esse moras.

felix Hippolyte! nuda tulit arma papilla
   et texit galea barbara molle caput.
Romanis utinam patuissent castra puellis!   45
   essem militiae sarcina fida tuae,
nec me tardarent Scythiae iuga, cum Pater altas
   astrictam in glaciem frigore vertit aquas.

omnis amor magnus, sed adempto coniuge maior:
   hanc Venus, ut vivat, ventilat ipsa facem.   50
nam mihi quo Poenis nunc purpura fulgeat ostris
   crystallusque meas ornet aquosa manus?

omnia surda tacent, rarisque assueta kalendis
   vix aperit clausos una puella Lares.
flore sacella tego, verbenis compita velo,   57
   et crepat ad veteres herba Sabina focos.
sive in finitimo gemuit stans noctua tigno,
   seu voluit tangi parca lucerna mero,   60

---

[48] astrictam *Schippers*: africus Ω | vertit *Morgan**:
nectit Ω   [49] adempto *anon. Hoeufftii*: aperto in Ω
[51] nunc *Housman*: te *N*: tibi *A**
[55,56] *post 32 Housman*

---

[a] The alliteration suggests the fanning into flame.
[b] Perhaps the sister of line 41, since *puella* cannot denote a slave.
[c] A bad omen. Cf. Shakespeare, *Macbeth* 2.1.4.

creator, what lands are sluggish with frost, what crumbling with heat, what wind will bring sails safely back to Italy. Only my sister sits with me, and pale with anxiety my nurse swears falsely that your delay is due to the winter season.

43 Happy Hippolyta! Bare-breasted she took up arms and savage-hearted hid her soft locks beneath a helmet. Would that camps admitted Roman girls! Then should I be the trusty packload of your service. Nor should I be daunted by Scythian peaks, when the Sky Father turns with the cold even deep waters into solid ice.

49 Ever a mighty power, Love is mightier still when one is bereft of one's spouse: such a passion is fanned into flame by Venus herself.[a] For to what purpose now should I shine bright in crimson of Phoenician silks or rings of sparkling crystal adorn my hands?

53 The house is still and silent: at most, performing a familiar rite on occasional Kalends, a solitary girl[b] unlocks the shrine of the Household Gods. I deck chapels with flowers, I heap crossroad altars with vervain, and scented marjoram crackles on ancient hearths. If, perched on a neighbour's roof-beam, an owl has hooted,[c] or a sputtering lamp has signalled its need for some drops of wine,[d] that day

---

[d] When the lamp sputtered (which was considered a good omen), it was customary to sprinkle it with a few drops of wine (cf. Ovid, *Her.* 19.151).

PROPERTIUS

illa dies hornis caedem denuntiat agnis,
    succinctique calent ad nova lucra popae.

ne, precor, ascensis tanti sit gloria Bactris,
    raptave odorato carbasa lina duci,
plumbea cum tortae sparguntur pondera fundae,   65
    subdolus et versis increpat arcus equis!
sed (tua sic domitis Parthae telluris alumnis
    pura triumphantis hasta sequatur equos)
incorrupta mei conserva foedera lecti!
    hac ego te sola lege redisse velim: 70
armaque cum tulero portae votiva Capenae,
    subscribam SALVO GRATA PUELLA VIRO.

IV

TARPEIUM scelus et Tarpeiae turpe sepulcrum
    fabor et antiqui limina capta Iovis.

9   quid tum Roma fuit, tubicen vicina Curetis
10   cum quateret lento murmure saxa Iovis?

---

[1] scelus *Kraffert*: nemus Ω
[3-8] *ante* 15 *Sh. Bailey*

---

[a] Awarded for deeds of outstanding bravery.

passes sentence of death on this year's lambs, and aproned acolytes bustle to win fresh profits.

63 Let not the glory of scaling Bactra's walls, I pray, be worth too high a price, or the snatching of linen robes from some perfumed potentate, when leaden missiles are discharged from the whirling sling and the treacherous bow twangs from a horse that flees. Above all—so may the headless spear[a] follow your triumphal chariot when the sons of Parthia have been vanquished—keep inviolate the pledge of my marriage-bed! Only on this condition should I desire you to return; and when I offer up your arms at the Capene Gate, I shall write below: FROM A GRATEFUL GIRL ON HER MAN'S SAFE RETURN.

The crime of Tarpeia

THE crime of Tarpeia[b] and her shameful grave will be my tale, and how the dwelling of ancient Jove was captured.

9 What then was Rome when the trumpeter of Cures made quake with his lingering blast Jove's

[b] The topicality of the poem is suggested by denarii of 18 B.C. which depict the scene of her death. Whereas Livy (1.10) and other authorities relate that Tarpeia betrayed Rome for money, our poet represents her as motivated by love.

13 murus erant montes; ubi nunc est Curia saepta,
14   bellicus ex illo fonte bibebat equus,
11 atque ubi nunc terris dicuntur iura subactis,
12   stabant Romano pila Sabina Foro.

lucus erat felix hederoso conditus antro,
    multaque nativis obstrepit arbor aquis,
Silvani ramosa domus, quo dulcis ab aestu   5
    fistula poturas ire iubebat oves.
hunc Tatius contra vallo praecingit acerno
    fidaque suggesta castra coronat humo.

hinc Tarpeia deae laticem libavit: at illi   15
    urgebat medium fictilis urna caput.
vidit harenosis Tatium proludere campis   19
    pictaque per flavas arma levare iubas: 20
obstipuit regis facie et regalibus armis,
    interque oblitas excidit urna manus.

saepe illa immeritae causatast omina lunae,
    et sibi tingendas dixit in amne comas:
saepe tulit blandis argentea lilia Nymphis,   25
    Romula ne faciem laederet hasta Tati:
dumque subit primo Capitolia nubila fumo,
    rettulit hirsutis bracchia secta rubis,

---

[7] contra *Camps*: fontem Ω
[13,14] *post* 10 *Schippers*
[15] laticem *Barber*: fontem Ω (<14)
[17,18] *post* 92 *Broekhuyzen*

neighbouring cliffs? For a wall there were hills; where buildings now hedge in the Senate House, the war-horse drank from the spring there, and where justice is now dispensed to a subject world, Sabine javelins stood in the Roman forum.

³ A lush grove there was, ensconced in an ivy-mantled glen, and many a tree rustled in answer to the splash of natural rills, the leafy abode of Silvanus, whither in refuge from the heat melodious pipes directed the sheep to drink. Opposite this grove Tatius fences his camp with a stockade of maple and, for more assurance, rings it with a rampart of earth.

¹⁵ Here Tarpeia drew water for her goddess; and an urn of earthenware pressed squarely on her head. She saw Tatius manoeuvring on the sandy plain and uplifting his blazoned arms over his horse's golden mane: she was stupefied by the king's looks and his kingly armour, and the urn dropped from between her heedless hands.

²³ Often she feigned some untoward aspect of the blameless moon and declared that she must bathe her locks in running water; often she brought silvery lilies to the winsome nymphs that Romulus' spear not mar the looks of Tatius: and in climbing the Capitol misted with the first smoke of dusk, she brought home arms torn by the rough brambles and,

385

et Tarpeia sua residens ita flevit ab arce
   vulnera vicino non patienda Iovi: 30

'ignes castrorum et Tatiae praetoria turmae
   et formosa oculis arma Sabina meis,
o utinam ad vestros sedeam captiva Penates,
   dum captiva mei conspicer ora Tati!
Romani montes, et montibus addita Roma,   35
   et valeat probro Vesta pudenda meo!
ille equus, ille meos in castra reponet amores,
   cui Tatius dextras collocat ipse iubas!

quid mirum patrios Scyllam secuisse capillos,
   candidaque in saevos inguina versa canes?   40
prodita quid mirum fraterni cornua monstri,
   cum patuit lecto stamine torta via?
quantum ego sum Ausoniis crimen factura puellis,
   improba virgineo lecta ministra foco!
Pallados exstinctos si quis mirabitur ignes,   45
   ignoscat: lacrimis spargitur ara meis.

[29] Tarpeia sua *Palmer*: sua Tarpeia Ω
[34] ora *Gronovius*: esse Ω
[39] mirum ... secuisse ς (cf. 3.19.22): mirum [in] ...
saevisse Ω

---

[a] The poet means to distinguish the southern (where is
the temple of Jupiter Capitolinus) from the northern crest

sitting down, thus from her[a] citadel did Tarpeia
lament the love-pangs that were abhorrent to
nearby Jupiter:

[31] 'O ye campfires and command tent of Tatius'
squadron, and Sabine arms so handsome to my eyes,
would that I might sit as a captive before your
hearths, if as a captive I might only gaze on the face
of the Tatius I love! Farewell, ye hills of Rome, and
Rome that crowns those hills, and farewell, Vesta,
whom my sin must put to shame! That horse, whose
mane Tatius himself smoothes to the right, that
horse will carry back to camp with him my heart!

[39] 'Why marvel that Scylla sheared her father's
hair and had her white loins transformed into
savage dogs? Why marvel that the horns of a mon-
ster were betrayed by his sister,[b] when the twisted
path was revealed by the gathering of her thread?
What a reproach I shall bring upon the maidens of
Italy, a sinful girl chosen to be the servant of the vir-
gin hearth! Should any wonder that the fires of
Pallas[c] have gone out, let him pardon: her altar is
flooded with my tears.

of the hill (where is the Arx proper). It was commonly
called Tarpeia (cf. Dante, *Purg.* 9.137), but in this poem
the anachronism would be intolerable.

[b] Ariadne, half-sister of the Minotaur.

[c] The sacred fire belongs to Pallas as well as Vesta, since
her image was also brought from Troy and kept in the
temple.

cras, ut rumor ait, tota pigrabitur urbe:
    tum cape spinosi rorida terga iugi.
lubrica tota viast et perfida: quippe latentis
    fallaci celat limite caespes aquas.   50
o utinam magicae nossem cantamina Musae!
    haec quoque formoso lingua tulisset opem.
te toga picta decet, non quem sine matris honore
    nutrit inhumanae dura papilla lupae.

sic, hospes, spatiorne tua regina sub aula?   55
    dos tibi non humilis prodita Roma venit.
si minus, at raptae ne sint impune Sabinae,
    me rape et alterna lege repende vices!
commissas acies ego possum solvere nupta:
    vos medium palla foedus inite mea.   60
adde, Hymenaee, modos; tubicen, fera murmura conde:
    credite, vestra meus molliet arma torus.

et iam quarta canit venturam bucina lucem,
    ipsaque in Oceanum sidera lassa cadunt.
experiar somnum, de te mihi somnia quaeram: 65
    fac venias oculis umbra benigna meis.'

---

47 pigrabitur *Housman*: pugnabitur Ω
48 tum *Rossberg*: tu Ω (<tū)
49 latentis *Rossberg*: tacentis Ω
50 caespes *Palmer*: semper Ω
55 <s>patiorne *Heinsius*: pariāne *N*: patriāue(?)*A**
59 nupta *Lütjohann*: nuptae Ω
64 lassa ς: lapsa Ω

47 'Tomorrow, says rumour, the whole city will be off its guard: it is then you must climb the dewy ridge of this thorn-covered hill. The whole route is slippery and treacherous, for a deceptive track of grass covers up the waters hidden beneath. O that I were acquainted with the spells of magic incantations! This tongue of mine also would have aided my handsome hero. To you is suited the royal robe, not to that motherless waif[a] who was suckled by the hard teat of an inhuman she-wolf.

55 'Do I thus, Sir Stranger, parade as queen in your court? In my betrayal of Rome you have no mean dowry. If not that, then lest the Sabine rape go unavenged, rape me, and settle the score by the law of reprisal. As your bride I can part the armies locked in battle: make of my wedding-gown a treaty of reconciliation. Nuptial god, add your music! Trumpeter, silence your barbarous blasts! Trust me, warriors: my marriage-bed will put your strife to rest.

63 'And now the fourth bugle heralds the approach of dawn, and the stars, weary like me, sink below the horizon. I will venture sleep and look for dreams of you: be sure to appear to my eyes as a kindly vision.'

[a] Romulus.

dixit, et incerto permisit bracchia somno,
  nescia se furiis accubuisse novis.
nam Venus, Iliacae felix tutela favillae,
  culpam alit et plures condit in ossa faces: 70
illa furit, qualis celerem prope Thermodonta
  Strymonis abscisso pectus aperta sinu.

urbi festus erat (dixere Parilia patres),
  hic primus coepit moenibus esse dies,
annua pastorum convivia, lusus in urbe,   75
  cum pagana madent fercula divitiis,
cumque super raros faeni flammantis acervos
  traicit immundos ebria turba pedes.
Romulus excubias decrevit in otia solvi
  atque intermissa castra silere tuba.   80

hoc Tarpeia suum tempus rata convenit hostem:
  pacta ligat, pactis ipsa futura comes.
omnia praebebant somnos: sed Iuppiter unus   85
  decrevit poenis invigilare suis.
83 mons erat ascensus, dapibus festoque remissus:
84   nec mora, vocalis occupat ense canes.
prodiderat portaeque fidem patriamque iacentem,
  nubendique petit, quem velit ipse, diem.

[69] Venus *Kraffert* : vesta Ω   [71] furit *Baehrens* : ruit Ω
[83,84] *post* 86 *Barber*   [86] suis ς : tuis Ω
[83] ascensus dapibus *Jacob* : ascensu dubius Ω
[88] ipse ς : ipsa Ω

⁶⁷ With these words she surrendered her arms to fitful slumber, not knowing that she had bedded with new demons. For Venus, propitious guardian of the Trojan embers, feeds her sin and stores more firebrands in her bones. Tarpeia becomes delirious, like a Thracian bacchant on the bank of the swift Thermodon whose bare breast shows through her rent vesture.

⁷³ The city had a holiday (the Fathers named it the Feast of Pales[a]): it was the birthday of Rome's walls, the yearly banquet of the shepherds, a time of urban revelry, when village dishes flow rich with plenty and over the scattered heaps of burning hay the tipsy crowd kicks high its grimy feet. Romulus decreed that the sentries should relax at their ease and that the camp lie silent, with trumpet-calls suspended.

⁸¹ Tarpeia, judging this her moment, approaches the foe: she seals the bargain, herself to be part and parcel of the bargain. Everywhere was a spectacle of slumber: Jupiter alone resolved to be on watch that he might exact his penalty. Now had the hill been scaled, unguarded through feasting and revelry: in a moment she silences with a sword the watchdogs that might have given sound. Now she had betrayed the trusty gate and her defenceless country, and asks him to name the wedding-day of his choice.

[a] The Parilia.

at Tatius (neque enim sceleri dedit hostis honorem)
    'nube' ait 'et regni scande cubile mei!'   90
dixit, et ingestis comitum super obruit armis.
    haec, virgo, officiis dos erat apta tuis.
17 nec satis una malae potuit mors esse puellae,
18   quae voluit flammas fallere, Vesta, tuas.

a duce Tarpeium mons est cognomen adeptus:
    o vigil, iniustae praemia sortis habes.

V

TERRA tuum spinis obducat, lena, sepulcrum,
    et tua, quod non vis, sentiat umbra sitim;
nec sedeant cineri Manes, et Cerberus ultor
    turpia ieiuno terreat ossa sono!

docta vel Hippolytum Veneri mollire negantem,   5
    concordique toro pessima semper avis,
Penelopen quoque neglecto rumore mariti
    nubere lascivo cogeret Antinoo.
illa velit, poterit magnes non ducere ferrum,
    et volucris nidis esse noverca suis.   10

---

17 nec *Postgate* : et Ω   93 Tarpeium *Palmer* : -eio Ω

---

a A frieze (perhaps early Augustan) from the Basilica
Aemilia in the Roman Forum survives, depicting Tarpeia
being buried by the shields of the Sabines (Picard VII).

b More likely the Mons Tarpeius has an Etruscan origin
(cf. Tarquinius) which the story of Tarpeia has been

⁸⁹ But Tatius (for the foe allowed no honour to treachery) answered: 'Wed, and thus mount my royal bed.' So saying he crushed her beneath the massed shields of his company.^a This, maiden, was a meet dowry for your services. Nor could a single death suffice for the wicked girl who presumed to betray the sacred fire of Vesta.

⁹³ From the guide the hill took the name 'Tarpeian'^b: O watcher, you have your reward for this unjust fate.^c

The bawd Acanthis

MAY the earth cover your grave with thorns, bawd, and, what you abhor, may your shade feel thirst; may your spirit find no peace with your ashes, but may avenging Cerberus terrify your vile bones with hungry howl.

⁵ Skilled to win over even Hippolytus^d who said no to love, and ever the worst omen to a happy union, she could force Penelope herself to disregard the rumour of her husband's safety, and marry dissolute Antinous. Should she wish it, a magnet will refuse to draw iron and a bird will prove a step-

fabricated to account for.

^c The watcher is Jupiter (cf. 86), the unjust fate the naming of the hill after Tarpeia, and his reward her death.

^d Cf. The Archpoet's confession '*Si ponas Hippolytum hodie Paviae, | Non erit Hippolytus in sequenti die.*'

quippe et, Collinas ad fossam moverit herbas,
  stantia currenti diluerentur aqua:
audax cantatae leges imponere lunae
  et sua nocturno fallere terga lupo,
posset ut intentos astu caecare maritos,   15
  cornicum immeritas eruit ungue genas;
consuluitque striges nostro de sanguine, et in me
  hippomanes fetae semina legit equae.
exercebat opus tenebris, ceu blatta papyron
  suffossamque forat sedula talpa viam: 20

'chrysolithus si te Eoa iuvat aurea ripa,
  et quae sub Tyria concha superbit aqua,
Eurypylisve placet Coae textura Minervae,
  sectaque ab Attalicis putria signa toris,
seu quae palmiferae mittunt venalia Thebae,   25
  murreaque in Parthis pocula cocta focis:
sperne fidem, provolve deos, mendacia vincant,
  frange et damnosae iura pudicitiae!

---

¹⁹ exercebat *Housman*: exorabat Ω | tenebris *Goold**:
verbis Ω (<tebris) | blatta *Palmer*: blanda Ω | papyron
Havet: perure Ω

²⁰ suffossamque *Goold** forat *Rossberg*: saxosamque
ferat Ω | talpa ç: culpa Ω

²¹ chrysolithus s.t.E. *Reeve**, *Morgan**: s.t.e. dorozan-
tum (derorantum *A**) Ω

²³ Eurypylis *Heinsius*: eurypili Ω | -ve *Skutsch*: -que Ω

ᵃ Unchaste Vestals were buried alive in the Campus

mother to her brood. Indeed, if she has brought Colline herbs[a] to the magic trench, standing crops would dissolve into running water. She dared to put spells on the bewitched moon and to hide her shape under the form of a night-prowling wolf; she tore out with her nails the undeserving eyes of ravens so as to be able to blind watchful husbands by her arts; she consulted screech owls on how she might have my blood, and for my undoing gathered the charm that drips from the pregnant mare.[b] She would ply her trade in the darkness, like the bookworm which bores through papyrus and the untiring mole that drills its subterranean path.[c]

21 'If golden chrysolites from Orient shores take your fancy, and the shell that flaunts its purple in the Tyrian sea, or you like the Eurypylean weave of Coan silk and fragile figures cut from coverlets of gold, or the wares shipped from palm-bearing Thebes and glass cups baked in Parthian kilns, then tear up promises, cast down the gods, let lies prevail, and shatter all the laws of bankrupt chastity.

Sceleratus just outside the Colline Gate, and herbs gathered from this spot would, obviously, possess special efficacy in witchcraft.

[b] Hippomanes, ἱππομανές, a secretion discharged by a mare in heat or pregnancy, was used in concocting love-potions and aphrodisiacs.

[c] Before the next verse Guyet postulated the loss of a couplet to introduce the speech.

45 in mores te verte viri: si cantica iactat,
46   i comes et voces ebria iunge tuas.
si tibi forte comas vexaverit, utilis ira: 31
   post modo mercata pace premendus erit.
denique ubi amplexu Venerem promiseris empto,
   fac simules puros Isidos esse dies.
ingerat Apriles Hyale tibi, tundat Omichle   35
   natalem Maiis Idibus esse tuum.
supplex ille sedet: posita tu scribe cathedra
   quidlibet: has artes si pavet ille, tenes!
semper habe morsus circa tua colla recentis,
   dentibus alterius quos putet esse datos.   40

nec te Medeae delectent probra sequacis
   (nempe tulit fastus ausa rogare prior),
sed potius mundi Thais pretiosa Menandri,
   cum ferit astutos comica moecha Getas.
29 et simulare virum pretium facit: utere causis!
30   maior dilata nocte recurret amor.
ianitor ad dantis vigilet: si pulsat inanis,   47
   surdus in obductam somniet usque seram.

[29,30] cum 45,46 *comm. Goold**
[35] Hyale … Omichle *Palmer* : iole … omicle Ω (*nisi* am- *N*)
[40] dent- *Heinsius* : lit- Ω | alterius *A** : alternis *N*

---

[a] The month sacred to Venus, especially the Kalends, on which women worshipped Fortuna Virilis to secure happy relations with men.

[b] I.e., to an imaginary lover.

[45] 'Adapt yourself to the ways of the man: if he strikes up a song, accompany him and join your drunken voice to his. If he chance to have pulled your hair, let his anger bring you profit: he must be punished by purchasing peace later. Then when he has bought your embraces and you have promised him sex, make sure to feign that the days of Isis have arrived, commanding abstinence. Let Hyale impress on you that April[a] is coming, and Omichle harp on the fact that the Ides of May is your birthday. Should he sit in supplication before you, take your chair and write something[b]: if he trembles at these tricks, you have him! Ever have fresh bites about your neck which he may think have been given you by a rival's teeth.

[41] 'Let not the abuse of importunate Medea please you (naturally, she who presumed to ask first was repaid with rejection), but rather expensive Thais in urbane Menander's play,[c] where the stage harlot outsmarts the cunning slave. To feign a regular lover also raises your price: invent excuses! Postpone a night, and love will return with increased passion. Let your janitor be awake to those that give: if someone knocks empty-handed, let him be deaf and continue sleeping on the bar

---

[c] Menander's *Thais* is not extant, but a line of it (187K) was famous enough to be quoted by St. Paul (1 *Cor.* 15:33).

nec tibi displiceat miles non factus amori,
    nauta nec attrita si ferat aera manu,   50
aut quorum titulus per barbara colla pependit,
    cretati medio cum saluere foro.

aurum spectato, non quae manus afferat aurum!
    versibus auditis quid nisi verba feres?
qui versus, Coae dederit nec munera vestis,   57
    istius tibi sit surda sine aere lyra.
dum vernat sanguis, dum rugis integer annus,
    utere, ne quid cras libet ab ore dies!   60
vidi ego odorati victura rosaria Paesti
    sub matutino cocta iacere Noto.'
his animum nostrae dum versat Acanthis amicae,
    per tenuem ossa mihi sunt numerata cutem.

sed cape torquatae, Venus o regina, columbae   65
    ob meritum ante tuos guttura secta focos.
vidi ego rugoso tussim concrescere collo,
    sputaque per dentes ire cruenta cavos,
atque animam in tegetes putrem exspirare paternas:
    horruit algenti pergula curva foco.   70

[47] pulsat *CIL* 4.1894: pulset Ω
[55,56] = 1.2.1,2 *del. Itali*
[64] -em … -em *Jacob* : -es … -es Ω | mihi *Jacob: om.* Ω

---

[a] Imported slaves put on sale had their feet chalked and
were required to jump up and down to demonstrate

that bolts the door. Spurn not the soldier ill made
for love, or the seaman if his gnarled hand carries
coin, or yet one of those on whose barbarian neck a
label has hung and whose chalked feet have danced
in the marketplace.[a]

53 'Look at the gold, not the hand that brings it;
listen to their verses, and what will you gain save
empty words? Whoever brings verses and not gifts
of Coan silk, consider his penniless lyre to be
without a tune. While your blood is in its spring and
your years free of wrinkles, make the most of the
fact, lest the morrow take toll of your beauty. I have
seen rose-beds of fragrant Paestum that promised
enduring bloom lying withered by the scirocco's
morning blast.' With Acanthis thus working on my
sweetheart's mind, the bones could be counted
through my shrunken skin.[b]

65 But accept, Queen Venus, in return for your
favour a ringdove's throat cut before your altar. I
have lived to see the phlegm clotting in her wrinkled
throat, the bloody spittle that she coughed up
through her decayed teeth, and to see her breathe
out her last rank breath on heirloom rags: her sag-
ging shack shivered with its fire gone out. For her

their agility.
[b] Evidently Propertius had been eavesdropping on
Acanthis' harangue to the girl.

exsequiae fuerunt rari furtiva capilli
    vincula et immundo pallida mitra situ,
et canis, in nostros nimis experrecta dolores,
    cum fallenda meo pollice clatra forent.

sit tumulus lenae curto vetus amphora collo: 75
    urgeat hunc supra vis, caprifice, tua.
quisquis amas, scabris hoc bustum caedite saxis,
    mixtaque cum saxis addite verba mala!

VI

SACRA facit vates: sint ora faventia sacris,
    et cadat ante meos icta iuvenca focos.
serta Philiteis certet Romana corymbis,
    et Cyrenaeas urna ministret aquas.
costum molle date et blandi mihi turis honores,   5
    terque focum circa laneus orbis eat.
spargite me lymphis, carmenque recentibus aris
    tibia Mygdoniis libet eburna cadis.
ite procul fraudes, alio sint aere noxae:
    pura novum vati laurea mollit iter.   10

---

⁷¹ fuerunt *Passerat*: fuerant Ω
³ serta *Scaliger*: cera Ω

---

a Cf. Euripides, *Electra* 328, where Aegisthus pelts
Agamemnon's grave with stones.
b On the occasion of the Ludi Quinquennales held in 16
Propertius contributes an aetiological poem explaining the
temple of Palatine Apollo (dedicated in 28) as founded

BOOK IV.6

funeral she had the stolen bands that bound her scanty hair, a cap that had lost its colour through foul neglect, and the dog that to my chagrin was over-vigilant when my fingers needed to undo stealthily the latch of the door.

[75] Let the bawd's tomb be an old wine-jar with broken neck, and upon it, wild fig-tree, exert your might. All ye that love, pelt this grave with jagged stones,[a] and mingled with the stones cast curses!

Palatine Apollo and the victory at Actium

His rites the priest begins[b]: let tongues be hushed for the rites and let a calf fall smitten before my altar. Let the Roman garland rival the ivy crown of Philitas and let the pitcher pour out pure water of Callimachus. Give me soft unguents and offerings of appeasing incense, and thrice about the hearth let the woollen fillet be twined. Sprinkle me with water, and by the fresh turves of the altar let the ivory pipe pour forth libation of music from Phrygian jar. Deceit, far hence begone; let mischief dwell under another sky: a pure spray of laurel smoothes for the priest a path he has not trodden before.

for the god's aid at Actium. Like Callimachus in his *Hymn to the god* (2), the poet first appears as a priest making sacrifice; a description of the battle (15–68) forms the centrepiece; and the conclusion shows us himself with his fellow-poets celebrating the festival.

PROPERTIUS

Musa, Palatini referemus Apollinis aedem:
    res est, Calliope, digna favore tuo.
Caesaris in nomen ducuntur carmina: Caesar
    dum canitur, quaeso, Iuppiter, ipse vaces.

est Phoebi fugiens Athamana ad litora portus,   15
    qua sinus Ioniae murmura condit aquae,
Actia Iuleae Leucas monumenta carinae,
    nautarum votis non operosa via.
huc mundi coiere manus: stetit aequore moles
    pinea, nec remis aequa favebat avis.   20
altera classis erat Teucro damnata Quirino,
    pilaque femineae turpiter apta manu:
hinc Augusta ratis plenis Iovis omine velis,
    signaque iam patriae vincere docta suae.

tandem aciem geminos Nereus lunarat in arcus,   25
    armorum et radiis icta tremebat aqua,
cum Phoebus linquens stantem se vindice Delon
    (non tulit iratos mobilis ante Notos)
astitit Augusti puppim super, et nova flamma
    luxit in obliquam ter sinuata facem.   30

[17] Leucas *Markland* : pelagus Ω
[22] femineae *Markland* : feminea Ω
[26] icta *Dausqueius* : picta Ω
[28] non F^2: nam Ω | ante *Lipsius* : unda Ω

---

[a] Strictly, an anachronism (as also Virgil, *Aen.* 8.678),

¹¹ I shall tell, O Muse, of Apollo's temple on the Palatine: Calliope, the theme is worthy of your favour. My songs are sung for Caesar's glory: while Caesar is being sung, do even you pray attend, Jupiter!

¹⁵ There is a harbour of Phoebus which recedes to Athamanian shores, where a bay lulls the roar of the Ionian sea, Actian Leucas, the triumphal monument of Augustus' galleys, no difficult voyage for the seaman's prayers. Hither came to battle the forces of the world: motionless on the sea stood the huge mass of pine, but fortune smiled not equally on all their oars. On the one side stood a fleet doomed by Trojan Quirinus, and Roman javelins shamefully grasped in a woman's hand; on this the flagship of Augustus,[a] its sails swelling with Jove's auspicious breeze, and standards now skilled to conquer for their fatherland.

²⁵ The sea-god at last had curved the lines into two crescents, and the water quivered, reflecting the flashing of the weapons,[b] when Apollo, leaving Delos, which stands firm under his protection (once it was a moving island, powerless before the anger of the winds), stood over Augustus' ship, and a sudden flame thrice flashed forth, bent into the zigzag

for Octavian only received the title four years later.

[b] Cf. Byron, *Sennacherib,* 'The sheen of their spears was like stars on the sea.'

PROPERTIUS

non ille attulerat crines in colla solutos
    aut testudineae carmen inerme lyrae,
sed quali aspexit Pelopeum Agamemnona vultu,
    egessitque avidis Dorica castra rogis,
aut quali flexos solvit Pythona per orbes   35
    serpentem, imbelles quem timuere deae.

mox ait 'o Longa mundi servator ab Alba,
    Auguste, Hectoreis cognite maior avis,
vince mari: iam terra tuast: tibi militat arcus
    et favet ex umeris hoc onus omne meis.   40
solve metu patriam, quae nunc te vindice freta
    imposuit prorae publica vota tuae.
quam nisi defendes, murorum Romulus augur
    ire Palatinas non bene vidit aves.

en, nimium remis audent: pro, turpe Latinos   45
    principe te fluctus regia vela pati!
nec te, quod classis centenis remigat alis,
    terreat: invito labitur illa mari:
quotque vehunt prorae Centauros saxa minantis,
    tigna cava et pictos experiere metus.   50

[35] quali *Rossberg*: qualis Ω
[36] deae *ed. Eton.*: lyrae Ω (<32)
[45] en ς: et Ω | pro ς: prope Ω | Latinos *Markland*: latinis Ω
[49] quotque ς: quodque Ω | Centauro<s> *Guyet*: centaurica Ω

of lightning. He had not come with his locks
streaming over his shoulders or brought the unwar-
like melody of the tortoise lyre, but with aspect as
when he looked upon Pelopean Agamemnon[a] and
emptied the Greek camp upon the insatiable pyre,
or as when he put to rest throughout its winding
coils the serpent Python, the terror of the peaceful
Muses.

37 Anon he spoke: 'O saviour of the world who are
sprung from Alba Longa, Augustus, proved greater
than your ancestors who fought with Hector, now
conquer at sea: the land is already yours: my bow
battles for you, and all this load of arrows on my
shoulders is on your side. Free Rome from fear:
relying on you as her champion, she now has
freighted your ship with a nation's prayers. Unless
you defend her, it was in an evil hour that Romulus,
seeking omens for his walls, beheld the birds on the
Palatine.

45 'See, their oars dare a monstrous deed: ah,
shame that Latium's waves, while you are leader,
should bear the sails of a royal fleet! Nor let it
frighten you that their armada sweeps the waters
with many hundred oars: the sea o'er which it glides
likes it not. And all the Centaurs threatening to
throw rocks borne by their prows will prove to be
naught but hollow planks and painted scares. It is

---

[a] Who had wronged his priest Chrysis (cf. Homer, Il.
1.9ff).

frangit et attollit vires in milite causa;
    quae nisi iusta subest, excutit arma pudor.
tempus adest, committe ratis: ego temporis auctor
    ducam laurigera Iulia rostra manu.'

dixerat, et pharetrae pondus consumit in arcus: 55
    proxima post arcus Caesaris hasta fuit.
vincit Roma fide Phoebi: dat femina poenas:
    sceptra per Ionias fracta vehuntur aquas.
at pater Idalio miratur Caesar ab astro:
    'sum deus; est nostri sanguinis ista fides.'   60
prosequitur cantu Triton, omnesque marinae
    plauserunt circa libera signa deae.

illa petit Nilum cumba male nixa fugaci
    occultum, iusso non moritura die.
di melius! quantus mulier foret una triumphus,   65
    ductus erat per quas ante Iugurtha vias!
Actius hinc traxit Phoebus monumenta, quod eius
    una decem vicit missa sagitta rates.

bella satis cecini: citharam iam poscit Apollo
    victor et ad placidos exuit arma choros.   70
candida nunc molli subeant convivia luco;
    blanditiaeque fluant per mea colla rosae,
vinaque fundantur prelis elisa Falernis,
    perluat et nostras spica Cilissa comas.

[64] occultum *Rossberg*: hoc unum Ω
[74] perlu<at> et *Morgan**: per[que] lavet Ω

---

[a] Propertius avoids mentioning Cleopatra by name.

his cause that makes or breaks a soldier's strength;
unless his cause is just, shame dashes the weapons
from his hand. The hour has come, let the fleet
enter battle: I who have fixed the hour will with my
laurelled hand guide the beaks of the Julian fleet.'

⁵⁵ He spoke and emptied his quiverload in shoot-
ing from his bow: second only to his bow came
Caesar's spear. Phoebus keeps faith and Rome con-
quers: the woman[a] pays the penalty: her sceptre,
shattered, floats on the Ionian waves. But Father
Caesar from the star of Venus looks marvelling on:
'I am a god; this victory is proof that you are of my
blood.' Triton hails the outcome on his conch, and
about the standards of liberty all the goddesses of
the sea clapped their hands.

⁶³ She, with misplaced faith in her fugitive sloop,
makes for a hiding-place in the Nile, thereby avoid-
ing death at a bidden hour. Heaven be praised!
How paltry a triumph would one woman make in
streets through which Jugurtha once was led! For
this feat did Actian Apollo win his temple, that each
arrow he launched sank ten ships.

⁶⁹ I have sung enough of war: victorious Apollo
now demands his lyre, and doffs his armour for
dances of peace. Now let the white-clothed ban-
queters enter the leafy grove, and the charm of roses
stream around my neck; let wine crushed in Faler-
nian presses be poured, and let Cilician saffron
drench my locks.

ingenium potis irritat Musa poetis: 75
    Bacche, soles Phoebo fertilis esse tuo.
ille paludosos memoret servire Sygambros,
    Cepheam hic Meroën fuscaque regna canat,
hic referat sero confessum foedere Parthum:
    'reddat signa Remi, mox dabit ipse sua: 80
sive aliquid pharetris Augustus parcet Eois,
    differat in pueros ista tropaea suos.
gaude, Crasse, nigras si quid sapis inter harenas:
    ire per Euphraten ad tua busta licet.'

sic noctem patera, sic ducam carmine, donec 85
    iniciat radios in mea vina dies.

VII

SUNT aliquid Manes: letum non omnia finit,
    luridaque evictos effugit umbra rogos.
Cynthia namque meo visast incumbere fulcro,
    murmur ad extremae nuper humata tubae,
cum mihi somnus ab exsequiis penderet amoris, 5
    et quererer lecti frigida regna mei.
eosdem habuit secum quibus est elata capillos,
    eosdem oculos: lateri vestis adusta fuit,

---

⁷⁵ potis ς : positis Ω | irritat *Canter* : irritet Ω
⁴ tubae *Housman* : viae Ω
⁷ capillos *P* : capillis *NFL*

[75] When poets are in their cups, the Muse quickens their genius: Bacchus, you always inspire your brother Phoebus. Let one proclaim the subjection of the marsh-dwelling Sygambri, and another sing of the swarthy realms of Cephean Meroë; let another tell how by tardy terms the Parthian repented and say: 'He must return the Roman standards; presently he will surrender his own. Or if Augustus spare the archers of the Orient at all, let him defer those victories for his grandsons[a] to achieve. Rejoice, Crassus, if any consciousness be yours amid the grave's black sands: now we may cross the Euphrates to your tomb.'

[85] So will I spend the night with goblet and with song,[b] until the day sheds its rays upon my wine.

Cynthia's ghost

So ghosts do exist: death is not the end of all, and a pale shade vanquishes and escapes the pyre. For I dreamt that Cynthia, who had lately been buried to the drone of the funeral trumpet, was leaning over my bed when after my love's interment sleep hovered over me and I bemoaned the cold empire of my bed. Her hair, her eyes were the same as when she was borne to the grave: her dress was charred at

---

[a] Gaius and Lucius Caesar.

[b] Cf. Catullus, 64.23, *vos ego saepe mero, vos carmine compellabo.*

PROPERTIUS

et solitum digito beryllon adederat ignis,
   summaque Lethaeus triverat ora liquor.   10
spirantisque animos et vocem misit: at illi
   pollicibus fragiles increpuere manus:

'perfide nec cuiquam melior sperande puellae,
   in te iam vires somnus habere potest?
iamne tibi exciderunt vigilacis furta Suburae   15
   et mea nocturnis trita fenestra dolis?
per quam demisso quotiens tibi fune pependi,
   alterna veniens in tua colla manu!
saepe Venus trivio commissa, et pectore mixto
   fecerunt tepidas proelia nostra vias.   20
foederis heu pacti, cuius fallacia verba
   non audituri diripuere Noti!

'at mihi non oculos quisquam inclamavit euntis:
   unum impetrassem te revocante diem:
nec crepuit fissa me propter harundine custos,   25
   laesit et obiectum tegula curta caput.
denique quis nostro curvum te funere vidit,
   atram quis lacrimis incaluisse togam?
si piguit portas ultra procedere, at illuc
   iussisses lectum lentius ire meum.   30

¹⁵ exciderunt ς: exciderant Ω   ¹⁹ et *Guyet*: est Ω
²⁰ proelia *anon. ap. Lütjohann*: pallia *N*: pectora *A**
²¹ pacti *Palmer*: taciti Ω

ᵃ Cf. Homer, *Iliad* 23.69 εὕδεις, αὐτὰρ ἐμεῖο λελασμένος
ἔπλευ, Ἀχιλλεῦ;

the side, and the fire had gnawed at the familiar
beryl on her finger, and Lethe's water had withered
her lips. But it was a living voice and spirit that
emerged as her brittle fingers cracked with a snap of
her thumb:

13 'Treacherous one, from whom no girl can
expect better, can sleep so soon have power over
you?[a] Have you so soon forgotten our escapades in
the sleepless Subura and my window-sill worn away
by nightly guile? How oft by that window did I let
down a rope to you and dangle in mid-air, descend-
ing hand over hand to embrace you? Oft at the
crossways we made love, and breast on breast
warmed with our passion the road beneath. Alas for
the troth you plighted, whose deceitful words the
South Wind, unwilling to hear, has swept away!

23 'But no one cried out my name as my eyes
closed in death: I might, had you called me back,
have gained another day. No watchman[b] rattled
his cleft reed for my sake, and a jagged tile gashed
my unprotected head.[c] Besides, who saw you bowed
with grief at my funeral or your suit of mourning
warmed with tears? If it irked you to accompany the
cortege beyond the gates, still you might have bade
my bier move more slowly to that point. Why,

[b] He was usually appointed to guard the corpse await-
ing burial; the cleft reed was rattled to ward off evil spirits.
[c] Her head was propped up on the bier by a jagged tile.

cur ventos non ipse rogis, ingrate, petisti?
　　cur nardo flammae non oluere meae?
hoc etiam grave erat, nulla mercede hyacinthos
　　inicere et fracto busta piare cado?

'Lygdamus uratur, candescat lamina vernae:　35
　　sensi ego, cum insidiis pallida vina bibi.
ut Nomas arcanas tollat versuta salivas,
　　dicet damnatas ignea testa manus.
quae modo per vilis inspectast publica noctes,
　　haec nunc aurata cyclade signat humum;　40
47 te patiente meae conflavit imaginis aurum,
48 　　ardente e nostro dotem habitura rogo.
et graviora rependit iniquis pensa quasillis,
　　garrula de facie si qua locuta meast;
nostraque quod Petale tulit ad monumenta coronas,
　　codicis immundi vincula sentit anus;
caeditur et Lalage tortis suspensa capillis,　45
　　per nomen quoniamst ausa rogare meum.

'non tamen insector, quamvis merere, Properti:　49
　　longa mea in libris regna fuere tuis.　50

---

³⁷ ut ς: aut Ω
⁴⁷,⁴⁸ *post* 40 *Schrader*

---

a Cf. Robert Lowell (whose translation of the whole
poem is reprinted in Sullivan's *Ezra Pound*), 'Would it
have strained your purse / To scatter ten cheap roses on
my hearse?'

ungrateful man, did you not call the winds to fan my pyre? Why was my funeral fire not perfumed with spice? Was it then too much to cast hyacinths upon me, no costly gift,[a] and to hallow my grave with wine from a shattered jar?

35 'Let Lygdamus be tortured, let the branding-iron glow white for that slave: I knew it was his doing, when I drank the wine that foully struck me pale. Though artful Nomas get rid of her secret con-coctions, the red-hot brick will declare hers to be guilty hands.[b] She who lately offered herself in pub-lic for cheap nights of love now brushes the ground with the gilded hem of her cloak: you did nothing to stop her melting down a gold image of me and put-ting me to the flames so that she could have a dowry! And she unjustly assigns baskets with heavier loads of wool to any chattering servant who has referred to my beauty; because she placed a bouquet of flowers on my grave, aged Petale is shackled to a foul log of wood; and Lalage is hung by her twisted hair and flogged, because she dared to ask a favour in my name.

49 'But I chide you not, Propertius, though chid-ing you deserve: long did I reign supreme in your

---

[b] Slaves giving evidence were customarily tortured to ensure their telling the truth; but Cynthia's charges are not to be taken seriously.

iuro ego Fatorum nulli revolubile carmen,
  tergeminusque canis sic mihi molle sonet,
me servasse fidem. si fallo, vipera nostris
  sibilet in tumulis et super ossa cubet.

'nam geminast sedes turpem sortita per amnem,   55
  turbaque diversa remigat omnis aqua.
unda Clytaemestrae stuprum vehit altera, Cressam
  portans mentitam lignea monstra bovis.
ecce coronato pars altera rapta phaselo,
  mulcet ubi Elysias aura beata rosas,   60
qua numerosa fides, quaque aera rotunda Cybebes
  mitratisque sonant Lydia plectra choris.
Andromedeque et Hypermestre sine fraude marita
  narrant historias, pectora nota, suas:
haec sua maternis queritur livere catenis   65
  bracchia nec meritas frigida saxa manus;
narrat Hypermestre magnum ausas esse sorores,
  in scelus hoc animum non valuisse suum.
sic mortis lacrimis vitae sancimus amores:
  celo ego perfidiae crimina multa tuae.   70

'sed tibi nunc mandata damus, si forte moveris,
  si te non totum Chloridos herba tenet:

---

[57] unda *Hertzberg*: una Ω | Cressam / ... mentitam
Haupt: -ae ... -ae Ω
  [58] portans *Mueller*: portat Ω
  [63] marita *Heinsius*: maritae Ω
  [64] historias ... suas *Markland*: historiae ... suae Ω
  [69] sancimus *Rossberg*: sanamus Ω

works. I swear by the rune of the Fates that no man can unravel—as I speak true, so may the three-headed dog[a] bay gently for me—that I kept faith. If I lie, may a hissing viper nest in my grave and brood over my bones.

⁵⁵ 'For two abodes have been appointed along the foul river, and the whole host rows this way or that. One passage conveys the adulterous Clytemnestra, and carries the Cretan queen[b] whose guile contrived the wooden monstrosity of a cow. But see, the other group are hurried off in a garlanded vessel, where a happy breeze gently fans the roses of Elysium, where sound the strings of melody, Cybele's cymbals, and Lydian lyres struck in the turbaned dance. Andromeda and Hypermnestra, that bride unstained by treachery, tell, glorious heroines, their stories. The one complains that her arms are bruised by chains she suffered through a mother's pride, that her hands deserved not to be fettered to the cold rocks; Hypermnestra tells of the heinous deed dared by her sisters, and how her heart had not been hard enough for that crime. Thus by tears shed in Hades we confirm the love we gave on earth: I hide in silence your many sins of infidelity.

⁷¹ 'But now I give you instructions, if perchance you are moved, and Chloris' love potions have not

---

[a] Cerberus.
[b] Pasiphaë: see note on 3.19.11.

nutrix in tremulis ne quid desideret annis
    Parthenie: potuit, nec tibi avara fuit.
deliciaeque meae Latris, cui nomen ab usust,   75
    ne speculum dominae porrigat illa novae.
et quoscumque meo fecisti nomine versus,
    ure mihi: laudes desine habere meas.
pone hederam tumulo, mihi quae praegnante corymbo
    mollia contortis alliget ossa comis.   80
pomosis Anio qua spumifer incubat arvis,
    et numquam Herculeo numine pallet ebur,
hic carmen media dignum me scribe columna,
    sed breve, quod currens vector ab urbe legat:
HIC TIBURTINA IACET AUREA CYNTHIA TERRA: 85
ACCESSIT RIPAE LAUS, ANIENE, TUAE.

'nec tu sperne piis venientia somnia portis:
    cum pia venerunt somnia, pondus habent.
nocte vagae ferimur, nox clausas liberat umbras,
    errat et abiecta Cerberus ipse sera.   90
luce iubent leges Lethaea ad stagna reverti:
    nos vehimur, vectum nauta recenset onus.
nunc te possideant aliae: mox sola tenebo:
    mecum eris, et mixtis ossibus ossa teram.'

[79] pone *Sandbach* : pelle Ω | praegnante *Cornelissen* :
pugnante Ω (<p̄gnante)
[80] mollia ς : molli Ω | alliget *Sh. Bailey* : alligat Ω
[81] pom- ... spum- *Broekhuyzen* : ram- ... pom- Ω

---

[a] I.e., from λάτρις 'one who serves,' λατρεία 'service.'
[b] The air of Tibur, where Hercules was worshipped, was
thought to preserve the colour of ivory.

utterly bewitched you: let my nurse Parthenie lack
nothing in her feeble old age: though she might have
done, she showed no greed towards you; and let not
my darling Latris, named for her faithful service,[a]
hold up the mirror to another mistress. As for the
poems you composed in my honour, burn them, I
pray: cease to win praise through me. Plant ivy on
my grave, so that its swelling tendrils may bind my
delicate bones with intertwining leaves. Where
foaming Anio irrigates orchard fields and, by favour
of Hercules, ivory never yellows,[b] there on the mid-
dle of a pillar inscribe an epitaph worthy of me, but
brief, such as the traveller may read as he hastens
from Rome:

> HERE IN TIBUR'S SOIL LIES GOLDEN CYNTHIA:
> FRESH GLORY, ANIO, IS ADDED TO THY BANKS.

[87] 'Spurn not the dreams that come through the
Righteous Gate[c]: when righteous dreams come, they
have the weight of truth. By night we drift abroad,
night frees imprisoned shades, and even Cerberus
casts aside his chains, and strays. At dawn the law
compels us to return to Lethe's waters: we board,
the ferryman counts the cargo boarded. Other
women may possess you now: soon I alone shall hold
you: with me you will be, and my bones shall press
yours in close entwining.'

---

[c] Though echoing Homer, *Od.* 19.562ff, and Virgil, *Aen.*
6.894ff, Propertius signifies only that Cynthia abides with
the Righteous.

haec postquam querula mecum sub lite peregit,   95
    inter complexus excidit umbra meos.

VIII

Disce, quid Esquilias hac nocte fugarit aquosas,
    cum vicina novis turba cucurrit agris,
19 turpis in arcana sonuit cum rixa taberna,
20   si sine me, famae non sine labe meae.

Lanuvium annosi vetus est tutela draconis:
    hic tibi tam rarae non perit hora morae.
qua sacer abripitur caeco descensus hiatu,   5
    hac penetrat (virgo, tale iter omne cave!)
ieiuni serpentis honos, cum pabula poscit
    annua et ex ima sibila torquet humo.
ille sibi admotas a virgine corripit escas: 11
    virginis in palmis ipsa canistra tremunt.
9 talia demissae pallent ad sacra puellae,
10   cum temere anguino raditur ore manus.
si fuerunt castae, redeunt in colla parentum,
    clamantque agricolae 'fertilis annus erit.'

---

⁴ tibi ς: ubi Ω   ⁶ hac *Heinsius*: qua Ω
⁹,¹⁰ *post* 12 *Housman*   ¹³ fuerunt *F*: fuerint Ω*

ᵃ In spite of the different circumstances Goethe's
Euphrosyne, a moving elegy on a young Swiss actress,
shows unmistakeably the influence of Propertius' poem.

[95] When she had thus brought to an end her querulous indictment, the apparition vanished, baffling my embrace.[a]

Cynthia interrupts a party

LISTEN to an incident which last night put to flight the well-watered Esquiline and caused those living near the New Gardens[b] to take to their heels, when a shameful brawl could be heard in a backstreets tavern, if in my absence, yet not without a slur on my good name.

[3] Lanuvium has enjoyed from of old the protection of an ancient serpent (an hour spent here on so infrequent a visit is well worth while). Where the sacred slope is reft by a dark chasm, at that point the offering to the hungry serpent makes its way— maiden, beware of all such paths—when he demands his annual tribute and hurls hisses from the depths of the earth. He seizes the morsel held out to him by the virgin: the very basket trembles in the virgin's hands. Maidens sent down to such a rite turn pale when their hand is rudely brushed by the serpent's lips. If they have been chaste, they return to embrace their parents, and the farmers cry: 'It will be a fruitful year.'

[b] An old burial ground converted into a park by Maecenas.

419

huc mea detonsis avectast Cynthia mannis: 15
    causa fuit Iuno, sed mage causa Venus.
Appia, dic quaeso, quantum te teste triumphum
    egerit effusis per tua saxa rotis!
spectaclum ipsa sedens primo temone pependit,   21
    ausa per impuros frena movere iocos.
serica nam taceo vulsi carpenta nepotis
    atque armillatos colla Molossa canes,
qui dabit immundae venalia fata saginae,   25
    vincet ubi erasas barba pudenda genas.

cum fieret nostro totiens iniuria lecto,
    mutato volui castra movere toro.
Phyllis Aventinae quaedamst vicina Dianae,
    sobria grata parum: cum bibit, omne decet.   30
altera Tarpeios est inter Teia lucos,
    candida, sed potae non satis unus erit.
his ego constitui noctem lenire vocatis,
    et Venere ignota furta novare mea.

unus erat tribus in secreta lectulus herba.   35
    quaeris discubitus? inter utramque fui.

19,20 *post* 2 *Lütjohann*
22 iocos ς : locos Ω
36 discubitus *Palmer* : concubitus Ω

---

[a] Cf. James Elroy Flecker, 'And some to Meccah turn to pray, and I toward thy bed, Yasmin.'
[b] Of the bystanders (Luck).

¹⁵ Hither my Cynthia drove off in a chaise drawn
by close-clipped ponies: she pleaded the rites of
Juno, but they were rather those of Venus.ᵃ Tell,
please, O Appian Way, what triumphal progress you
saw her make as her wheels rattled over your pav-
ing stones. A sight she was to see, as she sat leaning
forward over the end of the pole, shamelessly plying
the reins amid ribald quips.ᵇ For I say nothing of
the smooth-skinned spendthrift's silk-hung trap and
his Molossian dogs with bracelets round their necks:
some day he will sell his life to eat the foul mash of a
gladiator, when to his shame a beard overruns his
shaven cheeks.

²⁷ Since she had so often wronged our bed, I
resolved to change my couch and pitch my camp
elsewhere. There is a girl named Phyllis, who
lodges near Diana of the Aventineᶜ: sober, she
pleases little; tipsy, she is all charm. There is
another, Teia, from the groves of Tarpeia, a pretty
thing, but when she is drunk, it takes more than one
man to satisfy her.ᵈ I decided to beguile the night
by inviting these, and add new experience to my
amorous ventures.

³⁵ A couch for three was set out in a garden
screened from view. You ask how we were placed? I
was between the two. Lygdamus was in charge of

ᶜ Diana's temple (cf. Livy 1.45.2ff).
ᵈ The two girls are referred to by Goethe, *Röm. El.* XIVa
19f.

Lygdamus ad cyathos, vitrique aestiva supellex
    et Methymnaei grata saliva meri.
Miletus tibicen erat, crotalistria Byblis
    (haec facilis spargi munda sine arte rosa),   40
Magnus et ipse suos breviter concretus in artus
    iactabat truncas ad cava buxa manus.

sed neque suppletis constabat flamma lucernis,
    reccidit inque suos mensa supina pedes.
me quoque per talos Venerem quaerente secundam
    semper damnosi subsiluere canes.   46
cantabant surdo, nudabant pectora caeco:
    Lanuvii ad portas, ei mihi, totus eram;
cum subito rauci sonuerunt cardine postes,
    nec levia ad primos murmura facta Lares.   50

nec mora, cum totas resupinat Cynthia valvas,
    non operosa comis, sed furibunda decens.
pocula mi digitos inter cecidere remissos,
    palluerunt ipso labra soluta mero.
fulminat illa oculis et quantum femina saevit,   55
    spectaclum capta nec minus urbe fuit.

---

38 grata ς: graeca Ω (<graia)
39 Miletus . . . Byblis *Palmer*: nile tuus . . . phillis Ω
40 haec *Baehrens*: et Ω
45 secundam *Palmer*: secundo Ω
48 totus *Kuypers*: solus Ω
50 nec ς: et Ω
54 palluerunt *Livineius*: palluerant Ω

the cups; there was a summer glassware service and
a Lesbian wine of choice vintage. Miletus was our
piper, Byblis played the castanets (she in her artless
elegance happy to be pelted with roses); and Lofty
himself, his limbs shrunken into his knotted frame,
clapped stunted hands in time to the boxwood flute.

43 But though the lamps were full, the flame kept
flickering, and the table-top fell upside down upon
its trestles. Further, at dice, when I kept hoping for
the lucky Venus-throw, the accursed Dogs came up
again and again.[a] I was deaf to their singing, blind
when they bared their breasts; ah me, all my
thoughts were at the gates of Lanuvium, when
without warning there was the strident sound of the
gate opening and a loud hubbub arose at the front of
the house.

51 Straightway Cynthia flings right back the
folding-doors, her hair disordered, yet attractive in
her fury. The cup fell from my slackened fingers,
and my lips, though steeped in wine, actually
turned pale. Her eyes flashed fire and she raged as
only a woman can: the scene was as terrible as the

---

[a] Four dice were used, Venus being the highest throw
(1, 3, 4, 6), the dog the lowest (1, 1, 1, 1). Originally the die
was a four-legged piece of metal: landing on its legs (the
commoner result) it was imagined to be a quadruped, on
its back a supine woman.

Phyllidos iratos in vultum conicit ungues:
    territa 'vicini,' Teia clamat, 'aquam!'
crimina sopitos turbant elata Quirites,
    omnis et insana semita voce sonat.   60
illas direptisque comis tunicisque solutis
    excipit obscurae prima taberna viae.

Cynthia gaudet in exuviis victrixque recurrit
    et mea perversa sauciat ora manu,
imponitque notam collo morsuque cruentat,   65
    praecipueque oculos, qui meruere, ferit.
atque ubi iam nostris lassavit bracchia plagis,
    Lygdamus, ad plutei fulcra sinistra latens,
eruitur geniumque meum prostratus adorat.
    Lygdame, nil potui: tecum ego captus eram.   70

supplicibus palmis tum demum ad foedera veni,
    cum vix tangendos praebuit illa pedes,
atque ait 'admissae si vis me ignoscere culpae,
    accipe, quae nostrae formula legis erit.
tu neque Pompeia spatiabere cultus in umbra,   75
    nec cum lascivum sternet harena Forum.
colla cave inflectas ad summum obliqua theatrum,
    aut lectica tuae se det aperta morae.

---

[58] vicini ... aquam *Palmer* : vicinas ... aquas Ω
[59] crimina *Goold** : lumina Ω
[60] voce *Fruter* : nocte Ω
[69] prostratus ς : protractus Ω
[78] se det *Gruter* : sudet Ω

sack of a city. Angrily she makes for Phyllis's face
with her fingernails; terrified, Teia cries out: 'Help,
neighbours! Fire!'[a] Screams of abuse awaken the
sleeping citizens, and the whole street resounds
with angry voices. With hair torn and clothes
ripped the girls take refuge in the first tavern[b] they
find in the dark.

[63] Cynthia rejoiced in her spoils and trium-
phantly hastens back to bruise my face with the
back of her hand, marks my neck, drawing blood
with toothbites, and especially pokes at my guilty
eyes. Then when she had exhausted her arms in
beating me, Lygdamus, who was hiding on the left
at the back of the couch, is dragged forth and, on his
knees, appeals to my guardian-spirit. (Lygdamus, I
was powerless, a captive like you!)

[71] Then at last, holding out my hands in supplica-
tion, I came to terms; and then she scarcely let me
touch her feet and said : 'If you wish me to pardon
the offence you have committed, listen to the condi-
tions of my settlement. You are not to dress up and
walk abroad in Pompey's colonnade,[c] or when the
sand is strewn for holiday in the Forum. Beware of
turning round in the theatre to look at the gallery or
allowing an open litter to offer itself to your gaze.

[a] Literally 'Water!' (the cry was a common alarm). Cf.
Aristophanes, *Thesm.* 241, ὕδωρ, ὕδωρ, ὦ γείτονες.

[b] Obviously that mentioned in line 19.

[c] A popular rendezvous (cf. 2.32.11).

Lygdamus in primis, omnis mihi causa querelae,
    veneat et pedibus vincula bina trahat.'   80

indixit legem: respondi ego 'legibus utar.'
    riserat imperio facta superba dato.
dein quemcumque locum externae tetigere puellae,
    suffiit, ac pura limina tergit aqua,
imperat et totas iterum mutare lucernas,   85
    terque meum tetigit sulpuris igne caput.
atque ita mutato per singula pallia lecto
    despondi, et noto solvimus arma toro.

IX

Amphitryoniades qua tempestate iuvencos
    egerat a stabulis, o Erythea, tuis,
venit ad invictos pecorosa Palatia montes,
    et statuit fessos fessus et ipse boves,
qua Velabra suo stagnabant flumine quaque   5
    nauta per urbanas velificabat aquas.
sed non infido manserunt hospite Caco
    incolumes: furto polluit ille Iovem.

---

[84] suffiit *Beroaldus* ac *Baehrens*: sufficat Ω (<suffitac)
[85] lucernas *N*: lacernas *A**
[88] despondi *Pucci*: respondi Ω | noto *Heinsius*: toto Ω
[5] quaque ç: quoque Ω

---

[a] The grandiose patronymic and generally solemn style
of the poem create a tone more elevated than that of love-
elegy and closer to that of epic; Virgil had given (*Aen.*

And Lygdamus in particular, the cause of all my
wrongs, shall have his feet shackled and be put up
for sale.'

[81] Such was the settlement she imposed: 'I shall
abide by the law,' said I. She laughed, exulting in
the dominion I had given her over me. Next she
fumigated every spot touched by the girls brought
in, and mopped the threshold with clean water; she
bade me change anew all the oil in the lamps, and
thrice with burning sulphur touched my head. Then
after every sheet on the bed had been changed, I
made my obeisance, and on the couch we knew so
well made peace.

The founding of the Ara Maxima

WHAT time Amphitryon's son[a] had driven his steers
from the stalls of Erythea, he came to that
unconquerable[b] hill, the sheep-grazed Palatine:
here the weary drover halted his weary cattle,
where the Velabrum made a lake of its river and the
mariner hoisted his sails over a city sea. But Cacus
proved a treacherous host, and the cattle were not
left unharmed: by his theft he violated the law of

8.185ff) a somewhat different version of the story, but Pro-
pertius follows Varro (*ap.* Macrobius, *Sat.* 1.12.27).

[b] Unconquerable as were Romulus and Augustus, who
had their homes on the Palatine.

incola Cacus erat, metuendo raptor ab antro,
    per tria partitos qui dabat ora sonos.   10

hic, ne certa forent manifestae signa rapinae,
    aversos cauda traxit in antra boves,
nec sine teste deo: furem sonuere iuvenci,
    furis et implacidas diruit ira fores.
Maenalio iacuit pulsus tria tempora ramo   15
    Cacus, et Alcides sic ait: 'ite boves,
Herculis ite boves, nostrae labor ultime clavae,
    bis mihi quaesiti, bis mea praeda, boves,
arvaque mugitu sancite Bovaria longo:
    nobile erit Romae pascua vestra Forum.'   20

dixerat, et sicco torquet sitis ora palato,
    terraque non ullas feta ministrat aquas.
sed procul inclusas audit ridere puellas,
    lucus ubi umbroso fecerat orbe nemus,
femineae loca clausa deae fontesque piandos,   25
    impune et nullis sacra retecta viris.
devia puniceae velabant limina vittae,
    putris odorato luxerat igne casa,
populus et glaucis ornabat frondibus aedem,
    multaque cantantis umbra tegebat aves.   30

huc ruit in siccam congesta pulvere barbam,
    et iacit ante fores verba minora deo:

---

[18] quaesiti *Heyworth**: -ae Ω
[29] glaucis *Housman* : longis Ω

428

Jupiter. Cacus was a dweller there, a robber making forays from his dreaded cave, whose utterance issued forth from three separate mouths.

[11] That there might be no sure sign of obvious theft, he dragged the cattle backwards by their tails to his cave, but not unwitnessed by the god: 'Thief' bellowed the steers; the thief's implacable[a] doors were battered down by rage. Cacus lay dead, smitten on his three foreheads by the Arcadian mace: and thus Alcides spoke: 'Go, cattle; go, cattle of Hercules, last labour of my club, cattle twice my quest and twice my booty, and hallow with long-drawn lowing the Fields of Cattle: your pasture will be Rome's famous Forum.'

[21] He spoke, and his palate was dry, his mouth tortured with thirst: the earth, though teeming with water, gives him none. Yet far off he hears the laughter of cloistered maidens, where a grove had created a covert of circled shade, the secret precinct of the Goddess of Women,[b] and a well for worship, and rites never with impunity observed by men. Crimson garlands screened its secluded portal; a mouldering hut glowed with incense fire; a poplar adorned the shrine with its grey foliage, and a wealth of shade concealed singing birds.

[31] Hither he rushes, the dust caking his parched beard, and before the threshold utters words

---

[a] Probably as being decorated with the bones of his victims.   [b] The Bona Dea.

PROPERTIUS

'vos precor, o luci sacro quae luditis antro,
    pandite defessis hospita fana viris.
fontis egens erro circum antra sonantia lymphis;   35
    et cava succepto flumine palma sat est.
audistisne aliquem, tergo qui sustulit orbem?
    ille ego sum: Alciden terra recepta vocat.
quis facta Herculeae non audit fortia clavae
    et numquam ad vastas irrita tela feras,   40
atque uni Stygias homini luxisse tenebras
    et gemere abstractum Dite vetante canem?   42

65 'angulus hic mundi nunc me mea fata trahentem
66   accipit: haec fesso vix mihi tecta patent.
quodsi Iunoni sacrum faceretis amarae,
    non clausisset aquas ipsa noverca suas.
sin aliquem vultusque meus saetaeque leonis   45
    terrent et Libyco sole perusta coma,
idem ego Sidonia feci servilia palla
    officia et Lydo pensa diurna colo,
mollis et hirsutum cepit mihi fascia pectus,
    et manibus duris apta puella fui.'   50

talibus Alcides; at talibus alma sacerdos,
    puniceo canas stamine vincta comas:

---

[35] circ<um antr>a *Burman* : circa[que] Ω
[42] *suppl. ex. grat. Phillimore* (attr-: abstr- *Skutsch*): 66
iterat Ω
[66] tecta patent *Weidgen* : terra patet Ω

430

unworthy of a god: 'I beseech ye, who sport in this grove's sacred bower, open your shrine as a hospice to a weary man. In need of a spring I wander about glens that echo with running water: all I ask is a drink cupped up in the hollow of my palm. Heard ye ever of him who carried the globe on his back? I am he: the world I shouldered calls me Alcides.[a] Who has not heard of the valiant deeds of Hercules' club and his arrows never shot in vain against monstrous beasts, and how only to one mortal has the Stygian darkness become light[b] *and Cerberus has howled to find himself dragged off against the will of Dis?*

65 'This corner of the world now finds me dragging out my life: though weary I am scarce welcomed by this abode. Even though you were consecrated to cruel Juno's worship, even she, my stepmother, would not have closed her waters to me. And if anyone is frightened by my aspect or my lion's mane or my locks burned by the African sun, I have also performed menial service[c] dressed in a Sidonian gown and completed my daily stint at the Lydian distaff; a soft breastband once confined my shaggy chest, and for all my rough hands I proved a likely girl.'

51 Alcides thus; but thus the gracious priestess, whose white locks were tied with a scarlet band:

---

[a] Here deriving the name from ἀλκή 'bodily strength.'

[b] Hercules was sent by Eurystheus to fetch Cerberus from Hades, his twelfth labour.

[c] To Omphale, queen of Lydia.

431

'parce oculis, hospes, lucoque abscede verendo;
    cede agedum et tuta limina linque fuga.
interdicta viris metuenda lege piatur   55
    quae se summota vindicat ara casa.
magno Tiresias aspexit Pallada vates,
    fortia dum posita Gorgone membra lavat.
di tibi dent alios fontes: haec lympha puellis
    avia secreti limitis unda fluit.'   60

sic anus: ille umeris postis concussit opacos,
    nec tulit iratam ianua clausa sitim.
at postquam exhausto iam flumine vicerat aestum,
    ponit vix siccis tristia iura labris:
'Maxima quae gregibus devotast Ara repertis,   67
    ara per has' inquit 'maxima facta manus,
haec nullis umquam pateat veneranda puellis,
    Herculis externi ne sit inulta sitis.'   70

hunc, quoniam manibus purgatum sanxerat orbem,
    sic Sancum Tatiae composuere Cures.   74
71 sancte pater, salve, cui iam favet aspera Iuno:
72   Sance, velis libro dexter inesse meo.

---

[60] unda *Housman* : una Ω
[65,66] *post* 42 *Jacob*
[70] externi *Heinsius* : exterminium Ω
[71,72] *post* 74 *Schneidewin*
[74] Sancum *Heinsius* : sanctum Ω
[72] Sance *Richmond* : sancte Ω

'Stranger, withhold your gaze, and depart from this
sacred grove. Depart, I say, and leave its portals
while 'tis safe to go. Forbidden to men and avenged
by a dread law is the altar that protects its sanctity
in this secluded hut. At great cost[a] did the seer
Tiresias set eyes on Pallas, when with her aegis laid
aside she bathed her valiant limbs. Heaven grant
you other springs: this water, a sequestered stream
of secret passage, flows only for maidens.'

[61] Thus the crone: but he pushed down the shady
entrance with his shoulders, nor could the closed
door withstand the wrath his thirst provoked. But
after he had slaked his parched throat and com-
pletely drained the stream, with lips hardly dry he
pronounces this stern decree: 'Let the Mightiest
Altar,' he said, 'dedicated on the recovery of my cat-
tle, made mightiest by my hands, never be open to
the worship of maidens, so that the thirst of the
stranger Hercules go not unavenged.'

[73] This hero, since with his hands he cleansed
and sanctified the world, Tatius' town of Cures thus
installed in his temple as Sanctifier.[b] Hail, sainted
Father, on whom even cruel Juno now smiles!
Sanctifier, be pleased to dwell propitiously in my
book!

---

[a] He was blinded for his indiscretion.

[b] Sancus, the actual cult-name, thus being derived from
sancio, sanxi, sanctum 'to sanctify.'

X

Nunc Iovis incipiam causas aperire Feretri
    armaque de ducibus trina recepta tribus.
magnum iter ascendo, sed dat mihi gloria vires:
    non iuvat e facili lecta corona iugo.

imbuis exemplum primae tu, Romule, palmae   5
    huius, et exuvio plenus ab hoste redis,
tempore quo portas Caeninum Acrona petentem
    victor in eversum cuspide fundis equum.
Acron Herculeus Caenina ductor ab arce,
    Roma, tuis quondam finibus horror erat.   10
hic spolia ex umeris ausus sperare Quirini
    ipse dedit, sed non sanguine sicca suo.
hunc videt ante cavas librantem spicula turres
    Romulus et votis occupat ante ratis:
'Iuppiter, haec hodie tibi victima corruet Acron.'   15
    voverat, et spolium corruit ille Iovi.
Urbis virtutisque parens sic vincere suevit,
    qui tulit a parco frigida castra lare.
idem eques et frenis, idem fuit aptus aratris,
    et galea hirsuta compta lupina iuba.   20

---

^a The Temple of Jupiter Feretrius, which had become
dilapidated by Augustus' time, was rebuilt by him (*Res
Gestae* 19); and the poem owes its existence to this event.
    ^b These spoils, *spolia opima,* were won when the
Roman commander-in-chief met and killed the enemy

The origins of Feretrian Jupiter

Now shall I begin to tell the origins of Feretrian Jupiter[a] and the three sets of arms he won from three chiefs.[b] I am scaling a great height, but hope of glory gives me strength: a crown plucked from an easy summit brings no pleasure.

5 You, Romulus, first set the example of such a prize,[c] returning from the foe laden with his spoils, when you vanquished Caeninian Acron as he attacked the gates of Rome, and with a spearcast felled him upon his fallen steed. Acron sprung of Hercules, chieftain from Caenina's citadel, once inspired terror in Roman territory. Daring to hope for spoils from Quirinus' shoulders he surrendered his own, and these he drenched in his own blood: him Romulus sees as he brandished his javelin before the hollow towers, and forestalls him with a vow that was fulfilled: 'Jupiter, today shall this victim, Acron, fall in your honour.' The vow was made, and Acron fell as the spoil of Jupiter. Thus the father of Rome and father of valour was wont to conquer, whose frugal home trained him to endure the rigours of the camp. He was a horseman skilled at handling alike the bridle, alike the plough, and his wolfskin helmet was decked with a shaggy

general in single combat, and stripped him of his arms.

c Cf. Livy 1.10.5f.

picta neque inducto fulgebat parma pyropo:
   praebebant caesi baltea lenta boves.

Cossus at insequitur Veientis caede Tolumni,
   vincere cum Veios posse laboris erat;
necdum ultra Tiberim belli sonus, ultima praeda   25
   Nomentum et captae iugera terna Corae.
heu Veii veteres! et vos tum regna fuistis,
   et vestro positast aurea sella foro:
nunc intra muros pastoris bucina lenti
   cantat, et in vestris ossibus arva metunt.   30
forte super portae dux Veiens astitit arcem
   colloquiumque astu fretus ab urbe dedit:
dumque aries murum cornu pulsabat aeno,
   vinea qua ductum longa tegebat opus,
Cossus ait 'forti melius concurrere campo.'   35
   nec mora fit, plano sistit uterque gradum.
di Latias iuvere manus, desecta Tolumni
   cervix Romanos sanguine lavit equos.

Claudius at Rheno traiectos arcuit hostes,
   Belgica cum vasti parma relata ducis,   40
Virdomari. genus hic Brenno iactabat ab ipso,
   mobilis e rectis fundere gaesa rotis.

[32] astu *Phillimore* : sua Ω
[39] at *Barber* : a Ω
[41] Brenno ς : rheno Ω
[42] e recti<s> *Canter* : erecti *N* : effecti *A**

436

plume. His was no gaudy shield shining with over-
lay of golden bronze; his tough belt was furnished by
hide of slaughtered kine.

²³ Next comes Cossus through his slaying of
Tolumnius of Veii,ᵃ when it took much effort to con-
quer Veii; not yet had the sound of war been heard
beyond Tiber's banks: Nomentum and the three
acres of captured Cora were Rome's farthest prey.
Alas, ancient Veii! You too were then a mighty
kingdom, and a throne of gold was set in your mark-
etplace: now within your walls sounds the horn of
the loitering shepherd, and men reap cornfields over
your graves. It chanced that Veii's chief stood on
the tower above the gate and trusting to guile gave
parley from the city. While the ram with its brazen
horn battered the wall, where the long mantlet
shielded the advance of siege-work, Cossus said:
'Better for the brave to fight in the open.' Without
more ado both stood on the level plain. The gods
aided the Latin's arm, and the slashed neck of
Tolumnius bathed Roman steeds with blood.

³⁹ Then Claudiusᵇ beat back the enemy that had
crossed the Rhine, when back to Rome was brought
the Belgic shield of the giant chief, Virdomarus.
Boasting descent from Brennus himself, he was
adept at hurling the Gallic spear from the chariot he

ᵃ Livy, 4.18–20, has a somewhat different account.
ᵇ Cf. Plutarch, *Marcellus* 8.

PROPERTIUS

illi virgatas maculanti sanguine bracas
   torquis ab incisa decidit unca gula.

nunc spolia in templo tria condita: causa Feretri, 45
   omine quod certo dux ferit ense ducem;
seu quia victa suis umeris haec arma ferebant,
   hinc Feretri dictast ara superba Iovis.

XI

Desine, Paulle, meum lacrimis urgere sepulcrum:
6   nempe tuas lacrimas litora surda bibent.
7 vota movent superos: ubi portitor aera recepit,
   non exorando stant adamante viae. 4
te licet orantem fuscae deus audiat aulae, 5
2   panditur ad nullas ianua nigra preces.
3 cum semel infernas intrarunt funera sedes,
   obserat eversos lurida porta rogos. 8
sic maestae cecinere tubae, cum subdita nostrum
   detraheret lecto fax inimica caput. 10

---

[43] virgatis iaculantis ab agmine bracis Ω, *corr. Schrader*
[2,3] *cum 6,7 comm. Goold**
[3] sedes *Heinsius*: leges Ω (<ledes)
[4] exorando *Fruter*: exorato Ω (<-ādo)
[8] eversos *Phillimore* (>ebersos?): herbosos Ω

---

[a] The name being derived from *ferire* 'to smite' . . .
[b] . . . or, alternatively, from *ferre* 'to bear.'
[c] By a dramatization typical of the poet the dead woman is represented as addressing her husband from

438

drove: as he stained his striped trousers with his own blood, the twisted necklace fell, a prize, from his severed throat.

[45] Now the three spoils are laid up in a temple: hence Feretrius' name, because with heaven's sure favour chief smote[a] chief with the sword: or perhaps the proud altar of Feretrian Jupiter is so called because victors bore[b] on their shoulders the armour of those they vanquished.

Cornelia from the grave

CEASE, Paullus,[c] to burden my grave with tears: doubt not that infernal shores will drink your tears unmoved. Prayers move the gods above: after the ferryman[d] has received his coin, the way stands fast in inexorable adamant.[e] Though the god of the hall of darkness hear your pleading, the black door opens to no prayers. When once the funeral procession has entered the world below, a wan portal closes on the collapsed funeral pyre. So sounded the mournful trumpets, when the cruel torch was placed beneath the bier and made away with my body.

the grave. But the poem is also envisaged as being engraved on a funeral stone, like the *Laudatio Turiae*.

[d] Charon.

[e] Cf. Alcaeus Mess., *A.P.* 7.412.8, εὖτε σιδηρείην οἶμον ἔβης Ἀιδέω.

quid mihi coniugium Paulli, quid currus avorum
    profuit aut famae pignora tanta meae?
non minus immitis habuit Cornelia Parcas:
    en sum, quod digitis quinque legatur, onus.
damnatae tenebris et vos, vada lenta, paludes,   15
    et quaecumque meos implicat ulva pedes,
immatura licet, tamen huc non noxia veni;
    nec precor huic umbrae mollia iura meae.

at si quis posita iudex sedet Aeacus urna,
    is mea sortita iudicet ossa pila: 20
assideant fratres, iuxta et Minoida sellam
    Eumenidum intento turba severa foro.
Sisyphe, mole vaces; taceant Ixionis orbes;
    fallax Tantaleo corripere ore liquor;
Cerberus et nullas hodie petat improbus umbras;   25
    et iaceat tacita laxa catena sera.
ipsa loquar pro me: si fallo, poena sororum
    infelix umeros urgeat urna meos.

---

¹⁴ en ς: et Ω
¹⁵ tenebris *Goold** : noctes Ω
¹⁶ ulva *Schrader* : unda Ω
¹⁸ nec precor *Peerlkamp* : det pater Ω* | huic *P* : hic Ω*
¹⁹ at *Nestor* : aut Ω*
²⁰ is *Heinsius* : in Ω*
²⁴ corripere ore *Auratus* : corripiare Ω*
²⁷ loquar ς : loquor Ω*

[11] What availed my marriage to Paullus, what the triumphs of my ancestors or such fine vouchers[a] for my good name? Cornelia has not found the Fates any less harsh for that? See, all I am now can be gathered with the fingers of one hand! O cursed with darkness, both ye, O waters, sluggish shallows, and whatever sedge entangles my feet, though here before my time, I come not as one guilty; nor do I seek indulgent treatment for this my shade.

[19] But if there is an Aeacus who sits as judge with the urn before him, let him judge my shade when my lot is drawn: let his brothers sit as assessors, and beside the chair of Minos the stern band of the Furies, while all the court is hushed to listen to my trial. Sisyphus, rest from your rock! Let Ixion's wheel be silent! Frustrating water, be caught on Tantalus's lips! Let fierce Cerberus rush at no shades today, but let his chain hang slack from a silent bolt. I shall speak in my own defence: if I speak falsely, let the luckless urn that is the Danaids' punishment weigh down my shoulders.

---

[a] Her children, cf. 73 below and *Proverbs* 31:28 'Her children arise up, and call her blessed.'

si cui fama fuit per avita tropaea decori,
    aera Numantinos nostra loquuntur avos: 30
altera maternos exaequat turba Libones,
    et domus est titulis utraque fulta suis.
mox, ubi iam facibus cessit praetexta maritis,
    vinxit et acceptas altera vitta comas,
iungor, Paulle, tuo sic discessura cubili,   35
    ut lapide hoc uni nupta fuisse legar.

testor maiorum cineres tibi, Roma, colendos,
    sub quorum titulis, Africa, tunsa iaces,
et, Persen proavi stimulat dum pectus Achilli,
    qui tumidas proavo fregit Achille domos,   40
me neque censurae legem mollisse neque ulla
    labe mea nostros erubuisse focos.
non fuit exuviis tantis Cornelia damnum:
    quin et erat magnae pars imitanda domus.

nec mea mutatast aetas; sine crimine totast: 45
    viximus insignes inter utramque facem.
mi natura dedit leges a sanguine ductas,
    nec possis melior iudicis esse metu.

---

30 <nos>tra *Palmer* : regna Ω* (<t[er]ra)
36 ut *Graevius* : in Ω*
39 stimulat *Plessis* dum *Goold** : stimulantem Ω* (<-andum)
40 qui tumidas *Heyne* : qui[que] tuas Ω*
42 nostros ς : vestros Ω*
48 nec ς : ne Ω*

²⁹ If any has ever derived ennobling fame from ancestral trophies, then our house has bronze spoils that tell of ancestors *ᵃ* who took Numantia: a second host claims equality for the Libones of my mother's line, and my family is sustained on either side by achievements of its own. Thereafter, when maiden's toga gave way to the nuptial torch, and a different headband caught up and bound my hair, I was wedded to your couch, Paullus, destined so to leave it that on this stone I shall be recorded as married to one man alone.

³⁷ I testify by the ashes of forebears *ᵇ* who command Rome's reverence, beneath whose triumphs Africa lies ground in the dust, and him, who, when Perses was spurred on by the spirit of his ancestor Achilles, crushed the house inflated by its ancestor Achilles, that I never caused the censor's law to be relaxed and that our hearth never blushed for any sin of mine. Upon the lustre of such grand trophies Cornelia brought no tarnish: rather was she an example to be followed in that noble house.

⁴⁵ Nor did my life change; it was spent wholly free from accusation: I lived with honour between torch of marriage and torch of death. Nature gave me rules of conduct drawn from my blood, nor could one attain greater virtue through fear of a judge.

ᵃ Scipio Africanus the Younger, who took Numantia (132).

ᵇ Principally the Elder Africanus, who defeated Hannibal at Zama (202).

quamlibet austeras de me ferat urna tabellas,
    turpior assessu non erit ulla meo,   50
vel tu, quae tardam movisti fune Cybeben,
    Claudia, turritae rara ministra deae,
vel cui, sacra suos cum Vesta reposceret ignes,
    exhibuit vivos carbasus alba focos.

nec te, dulce caput, mater Scribonia, laesi: 55
    in me mutatum quid nisi fata velis?
maternis laudor lacrimis urbisque querelis,
    defensa et gemitu Caesaris ossa mea.
ille sua nata dignam vixisse sororem
    increpat, et lacrimas vidimus ire deo.   60
65 vidimus et fratrem sellam geminasse curulem;
66   consul quo factus tempore, rapta soror.

et tamen emerui generosos vestis honores,
    nec mea de sterili facta rapina domo.
97 et bene habet: numquam mater lugubria sumpsi;
98   venit in exsequias tota caterva meas.
tu, Lepide, et tu, Paulle, meum post fata levamen,
    condita sunt vestro lumina nostra sinu.   64
filia, tu specimen censurae nata paternae,   67
    fac teneas unum nos imitata virum.

---

[49] quamlibet ç: quaelibet Ω*
[53] cui sacra [sr̄a] suos *Baehrens*: cuius rasos (iasos *N**)
Ω*
[63] tu . . . tu ç: te . . . te Ω*
[65,66] *post* 60 *Koppiers*

However exacting the scrutiny of me carried by the jurors' urn, no woman will be shamed by sitting at my side, whether you, Claudia, peerless servant of the tower-crowned goddess, who took hold of the cable and moved the grounded Cybele, or you[a] to whom, when Vesta inviolate claimed her fires, the white robe showed that the hearth was still alive.

[55] Nor, dear heart, have I injured you, mother Scribonia: what in me would you wish otherwise except this my death? I am praised by a mother's tears and a city's lamentations, and my bones are vindicated by Caesar's sighs. He grieves that in me died one worthy of being his daughter's sister,[b] and we saw a god's tears flow. We also saw my brother twice seated in the curule chair, and it was when he was appointed consul that his sister was snatched away.

[61] Yet I lived long enough to earn the matron's robe of honour,[c] nor was I snatched away from a childless house. So all is well: never as a mother did I put on mourning garb; all my children came to my funeral. You, Lepidus, and you, Paullus, my consolations after death, in your embrace were my eyelids closed. Daughter, born[d] to be the model of your father's censorship, do you, like me, hold fast to a

---

[a] Aemilia.   [b] Half-sister to Augustus' daughter Julia.

[c] Earned by women who had borne three children.

[d] Evidently in 22 B.C.

445

haec est feminei merces extrema triumphi,   71
   laudat ubi emeritum libera fama torum.

nunc tibi commendo communia pignora, Paulle:
   haec cura et cineri spirat inusta meo.
fungere maternis vicibus pater: illa meorum   75
   omnis erit collo turba ferenda tuo.
oscula cum dederis tua flentibus, adice matris:
   tota domus coepit nunc onus esse tuum.
et si quid doliturus eris, sine testibus illis!
   cum venient, siccis oscula falle genis!   80
sat tibi sint noctes, quas de me, Paulle, fatiges,
   somniaque in faciem credita saepe meam:
atque ubi secreto nostra ad simulacra loqueris,
   ut responsurae singula verba iace.

seu tamen adversum mutarit ianua lectum,   85
   sederit et nostro cauta noverca toro,
coniugium, pueri, laudate et ferte paternum:
   capta dabit vestris moribus illa manus;
nec matrem laudate nimis: collata priori
   vertet in offensas libera verba suas.   90

69,70 *post* 96 *Postgate*   71,72 *post* 68 *Baehrens*
72 torum *Koppiers* : rogum Ω*
73 Paulle *Butrica** : natos Ω* (*a gloss*)

---

  a Cf. Gray's *Elegy* 92, 'E'en in our ashes live their wonted fires.'
  b Cf. Euripides, *Alc.* 377 σὺ νῦν γενοῦ τοῖσδ᾽ ἀντ᾽ ἐμοῦ

single husband. This is the highest tribute in a woman's glory, when candid opinion praises the full course of her married life.

[73] Now, Paullus, I commend to you the common pledges of our love: branded upon my very ashes[a] this care lives on in me. You, their father, must play their mother's part[b]: all that little band of mine must now be borne upon your shoulders. When you kiss them as they weep, add too their mother's kisses: the whole house now begins to be your charge. And if you are about to grieve, do so when they cannot witness it; when they come, deceive their kisses with cheeks that are dry. Be the nights enough for you to wear out with thoughts of me, and the dreams which oft by faith assume my features[c]: and when in secret you speak to my image, utter every word as though I would reply.

[85] If, though, the house-door gets a new wedding-bed facing it,[d] and a wary stepmother sits on the couch that was mine, then, my children,[e] do you praise and accept your father's marriage: won over by your conduct she will surrender. Nor praise your mother overmuch: when compared to her predecessor she will turn your unguarded speech into slights

μήτηρ τέκνοις.

[c] Cf. Meleager, *A.P.* 5.166.5f.

[d] I.e., if Paullus re-marries: the bed of a married couple stood in the atrium facing the house-door.

[e] *Pueri* includes, as would *nati*, the daughter.

seu memor ille mea contentus manserit umbra
    et tanti cineres duxerit esse meos,
discite venturam iam nunc lenire senectam,
    caelibis ad curas nec vacet ulla via.
quod mihi detractumst, vestros accedat ad annos: 95
    prole mea Paullum sic iuvet esse senem.
69 et serie fulcite genus: mihi cumba volenti
70   solvitur aucturis tot mea fata meis.

causa peroratast. flentes me surgite, testes,   99
    dum pretium vitae grata rependit humus.   100
moribus et caelum patuit: sim digna merendo,
    cuius honoratis ossa vehantur avis.

93 lenire *Schrader* : sentire Ω
97,98 *post* 62 *Peerlkamp*

against herself. But if he remembers and rests content with my shade and thinks so highly of my ashes, learn even now to soften the old age destined to come upon him, and let no path be open for the sorrows of a widower. May the time that was taken from me be added to your years: thus, because of my offspring, may Paullus enjoy growing old. And support ye the house with a line of descendants: I am happy for the ferry to set forth with so many to prolong my destined span.

[99] My speech is ended. Arise, ye witnesses that weep my loss, while a grateful earth awards the verdict that my life has earned. To virtue heaven itself has opened its gates: may my merits secure my shade conveyance to its illustrious ancestors.

INDEX

ACADEMY, Plato's: 3.21.25

Acanthis ('Spiky'), a bawd and witch: 4.5.63

Achaemenius, adj. from Achaemenes, an ancient king of Persia, hence Persian: 2.13.1

Achaia, heroic Greece: 2.28.53

Achelous, a river in Aetolia, which fought Hercules over Deianira: 2.34.33

Acheron, a river of the underworld: 3.5.13

Achilles, son of Peleus: 2.1.37; 3.39; 8.29; 9.9, 13; 22.29: 3.18.27: 4.11.39, 40. *See also* Haemonius, Pthius

Achivi, the Greeks: 2.8.31; 3.18.29

Acron, Sabine king of Caenina: 4.10.7, 9, 15

Actiacus, adj. from Actium, a promonotory of the Ambracian gulf, the

scene of Octavian's decisive victory over Antony: 2.15.44

Actius = Actiacus: 2.1.34; 16.38; 34.61: 4.6.17, 67

Admetus, husband of Alcestis, who died to prolong his life: 2.6.23

Adonis, Cyprian youth beloved by Venus: 2.13.53

Adrastus, leader of the Seven against Thebes: 2.34.37

Adryades, nymphs of woods and springs: 1.20.12

adynata (impossibilities of nature adduced to prove the impossibility of something else): 1.15.29f: 2.3.5ff; 15.31ff: 3.19.5ff

Aeacus, son of Jupiter, a judge of the underworld (as were his brothers Minos [*q.v.*] and

451

INDEX

human speech: 2.34.37

Arionius, adj. from Arion,
the famous musician
who was saved by a
dolphin (cf. Herodotus
1.23f): 2.26.18

Armenius, adj., of Armenia:
1.9.19

Arria, a Roman matron,
mother of the twins
Gallus and Lupercus
(*qq.v.*): 4.1.89

Artacius, adj. from Artace,
a port on the Propontis:
1.8.25

artists, ancient: see Apelles,
Calamis, Mentor,
Myron, Mys,
Parrhasius, Phidia(cu)s,
Praxiteles

Ascanius, a river in Mysia:
1.20.4, 16

Ascraeus, adj., of Ascra in
Boeotia, the home of the
poet Hesiod: 2.10.25;
13.4; 34.77

Asia: Asia Minor 1.6.14:
the continent 2.3.36

Asis (*Mons*), mod. Assisi,
Propertius' birthplace:
4.1.125

Asopus, a river in Boeotia:
3.15.27

Athamantiades, Argynnus
(*q.v.*): 3.7.22

Athamantis, daughter of
Athamas son of Aeolus,
and brother of Phrixus,
Helle: 1.20.19: 3.22.5

Athamanus, adj. from
Athaman, one of a
people of southern
Epirus: 4.6.15

Athenae, Athens, famed for
its learning: 1.6.13:
3.21.1

Atlas, a Titan imagined to
bear the heavens on his
shoulders: 3.22.7

Atrides, son of Atreus,
Agamemnon: 2.14.1:
3.7.23; 18.30: 4.1.112

Attalicus, adj., of Attalus
III (c. 170–133), king of
Pergamum, said to have
invented cloth-of-gold:
2.13.22; 32.12: 3.18.19:
4.5.24

Atticus, adj., of Attica; of
the nightingale, into
which Philomela,
daughter of Pandion,
king of Attica, is said to
have been changed:
2.20.6

Augustus, Gaius Iulius
Caesar Octavianus
(63–A.D. 14)
  (*a*) 2.10.15: 3.11.50;
12.2: 4.6.29, 38, 81. *See*

INDEX

Capena, the gate through which the Via Appia entered Rome and the natural entry for one returning from campaigns in the east: 4.3.71

Caphereus, adj., of Caphereus, a promontory of Euboea, where Nauplius, to avenge his son Palamedes, put to death on a false charge by Ulysses, kindled misleading beacons and caused the wreck of the Greek fleet: 3.7.39 (cf. 4.1.115)

Capitolia (plural for metrical reasons), Capitol, one of the seven hills of Rome, on which stood the temple of Jupiter: 4.4.27

Capricornus, Capricorn, 10th sign of the zodiac: 4.1.86

Carpathius, adj., of Carpathus, an island between Crete and Rhodes: 2.5.11: 3.7.12

Carrhae (modern Haran, Turkey), scene of the Roman defeat by the Parthians in 53: *see* Crassus

Carthago, Carthage: 2.1.23

Cassandra, daughter of Priam: *maenas* 3.13.62: *Pergameae vatis* 4.1.51, *vatem* 117

Cassiope, a port on the northern coast of Corcyra: 1.17.3

Castalia (fons), a spring on Parnassus: 3.3.13 (*see note*)

Castor, twin son (with Pollux) of Jupiter and Leda: 1.2.15: 2.7.16 (C's horse, Cyllarus); 26.9: 3.14.17

catalogues: 1.2.9ff: 2.1.19ff; 2.7ff; 14.1ff; 20.1ff; 34.85ff: 3.3.6–12; 9.9ff, 37ff; 11.9–26, 57–70; 12.24–36; 19.11ff; 22.1–18, 23–38

Catullus, Gaius Valerius (84–54), the lyric poet from Verona who sang of his Lesbia; friend of Calvus: 2.25.4; 34.87

Caucasius, adj. from following: 2.1.69; 25.14

Caucasus, mountain range between the Black and Caspian Seas: 1.14.6

Cayster, a river of Asia

463

INDEX

conceived as the
monument he erected
after ridding the world
of monsters: 3.11.19

Conon, Alexandrian
astronomer, 3rd cent.:
4.1.78

Copa, echoes of Propertius
in:
1 ~ 4.2.31
4 ~ 4.8.42
16 ~ 3.13.30
22 ~ 4.2.43f
29 ~ 4.8.37f
34 ~ 2.33.27

Cora, an ancient own of the
Volsci in Latium:
4.10.26

Corinna, a famous
Boeotian poetess,
contemporary with
Pindar: 2.3.21. *See also*
Erinna

Corinthus, Corinth: famous
for its bronzeware, said
to be discovered by the
fusing of gold, silver,
and bronze in the
burning of the city by
Mummius (146): 3.5.6

Cornelia, daughter of
P. Cornelius Scipio (cos.
38) and Scribonia, and
wife of L.Aemilius
Paullus Lepidus (*q.v.*):

speaks her elegy
4.11.13, 43

Cornelius Gallus: *see*
Gallus (*d*) Cornelius
Scipio, P. (cos. 16),
brother of Cornelia:
fratrem 4.11.65

Corydon, a Virgilian
shepherd (cf. *Ecl.* 2 and
7): 2.34.73

cosmetics: 1.2: 2.18

Cossus, Aulus Cornelius
(cos. 428), who killed
Tolumnius, king of Veii:
4.10.23, 35

Cous, adj., of Cos, an island
not far from
Halicarnassus:
 (*a*) garments, silks:
1.2.2: 2.1.5, 6: 4.2.23;
5.23 (*Minerva* = craft,
silk), 57
 (*b*) the poet, i.e.
Philitas (*q.v.*): 3.1.1;
9.44

Crassus
 (*a*) Marcus Licinius,
the triumvir, killed at
Carrhae in 53: 3.5.48:
4.6.83
 (*b*) the former and
his younger son
Publius, also killed at
Carrhae: 2.10.14: 3.4.9

Craugis ('Yap' Camps), a

dog so called from
κραυγή 'barking': 4.3.55

Cressa, adj., Cretan:
perhaps the herb called
dictamnum (cf. Virgil,
Aen. 12.412ff) 2.1.61:
Pasiphaë (*q.v.*) 4.7.57

Creta, Crete: 2.28.53

Cretaeus, adj. from above,
Cretan: 2.34.29 (of
Epimenides, a
legendary sage and poet
of the 6th century,
credited by the ancients
with a collection of
oracles, a *Theogony,* and
an *Argonautica*):
3.19.11, 26

Creusa, daughter of Creon,
king of Corinth, whom
Jason married,
deserting Medea, who
took her revenge by
sending her a poisoned
robe which killed her
and Creon: 2.16.30;
21.12

Croesus, king of Lydia,
famed for his wealth:
2.26.23: 3.5.17; 18.28

Cumaeus, adj., of Cumae,
an ancient city of
Campania: *vates* = the
Sibyl 2.2.16. *See also*
Sibylla

Cupido, son of Venus:
2.18.21 (the plural
'Cupids' is used for a
fanciful conception of
beautiful young boys as
associates of Venus:
pueri 2.29.3)

Cures, ancient capital of
the Sabines: 4.9.74

Curetis, adj., of Cures:
4.4.9

Curia, the senate-house:
4.1.11; 4.13

Curii (a hypocoristic form),
the Curiātiī (which
would not scan) who
fought against the
Horatii (*q.v.* cf. Livy
1.24ff): 3.3.7

curses: 1.6.12; 11.30;
17.13f: 2.23.12; 29.12;
33.27f: 3.1.7; 8.37f;
12.5f; 25.11ff: 4.3.19ff;
5.1ff, 75ff

Curtius, Marcus, who
threw himself into a
chasm in the Forum,
which then
miraculously closed
(Livy 7.6): 3.11.61

Cybēbe, Cybĕle, the Great
Mother: 3.17.25; her
statue at Cyzicus carved
from a vine-stock 22.3:
4.7.61; 11.51. *See also*

INDEX

INDEX

INDEX

referring to the above:
3.13.54

Gallus (all different)

(*a*) an aristocratic
friend of Propertius:
1.5.31; 10.5; 13.2, 4, 16;
20.1, 14, 51

(*b*) a kinsman (cf.
1.22.7) of Propertius,
killed in the Perusine
War, 41 B.C.: 1.21.7

(*c*) a son of Arria
(*q.v.*) accidentally killed
by his own standard:
4.1.95

(*d*) C. Cornelius
Gallus (69–26), first of
the Augustan elegists
and first Prefect of
Egypt, who, incurring
Augustus' displeasure
through his arrogance,
committed suicide:
2.34.91

Geryones, a monster killed
by Hercules, who
carried off his oxen:
3.22.9

Geta

(*a*) a tribesman of
Scythia: 4.3.9

(*b*) a typical name
for the cunning slave in
New Comedy: 4.5.44

Giganteus, adj. of the

Giants: the Phlegrean
plain immediately north
of Naples 1.20.9

gladiators: 4.8.25f

Glaucus, a sea-god: 2.26.13

Golden Age: 3.13.25ff

Gorgo, a Gorgon: Medusa
2.25.13: the Gorgon's
head set in the aegis of
Pallas Athena: 2.2.8:
4.9.58

Gorgoneus, adj., of the
Gorgon Medusa, from
whose blood the winged
horse Pegasus sprang; a
blow from his hoof
brought forth
Hippocrene, the
Gorgon's fount: 3.3.32

Graecia, Greece: 2.6.2;
9.17: 3.7.40: 4.1.116

Graius, adj., Greek: 2.6.19;
32.61; 34.65: 3.1.4; 8.29;
9.41; 22.37

Gygaeus, adj. from the
following: a Lydian lake
near Sardis: 3.11.18

Gyges, king of Lydia: as an
example of wealth
2.26.23

HADRIA, the Adriatic sea:
1.6.1

Hadriacus, adj., of Hadria:
3.21.17

476

INDEX

INDEX

Ilius, adj., Trojan: 4.1.53

Illyria (only in Propertius), Illyricum: 1.8.2: 2.16.10

Illyricus, adj., Illyrian: 2.16.1

Inachis, daughter of Inachus, Io (*q.v.*): 1.3.20; also identified with Isis: 2.33.4

Inachius, adj., of Inachus, king of Argos, hence Argive, Greek: heroines 1.13.31: Linus (*q.v.*) 2.13.8

India: 2.10.15

Indicus, adj., of India: 2.22.10: 3.17.22

Indus
(*a*) an inhabitant of India: 2.9.29; 18.11: 3.4.1: 4.3.10
(*b*) adj., of India: 1.8.39: 3.13.5; 18.20

Ino, daughter of Cadmus and wife of Athamas, smitten with madness by Juno; she threw herself into the sea and became a sea-goddess Leucothea (called by Propertius Leucothoë, *q.v.*): 2.28.19

Io, daughter of Inachus, loved by Jupiter; turned through Juno's jealousy into a cow, sometimes (e.g. 2.28.18, 62; 33.14) identified with Isis: 2.28.17; 30.29; 33.7. *See also* 3.22.35 (*in paelice*), Inachis

Iolciacus, adj. from Iolcos (modern Volos), a city of Thessaly on the Pagasean gulf, the home of Jason: 2.1.54

Ionia, the western coast of Asia Minor: 1.6.31

Ionium, sc. mare, the Ionian Sea, i.e. the sea south of the Adriatic: 3.11.72; 21.19

Ionius, adj., of the above: 4.6.16, 58

Iphiclus, son of Phylacus: 2.3.52 *See* Melampus

Iphigenia, daughter of Agamemnon, sacrificed at Aulis: 3.7.24. A later version had Diana substitute a hind for her at the last moment, Iph. being translated to the Taurians to become her priestess: 3.22.34. *See also* Agamemnonius

Irus, a beggar at Ulysses' palace in Ithaca (cf. Homer, *Od.* 18.1ff): 3.5.17

INDEX

him 71

Iuppiter, Jupiter, king of
the gods:
  (*a*) god: 1.13.29,32:
2.1.39; 2.4, 6; 3.30; 7.4;
13.16; 16.16, 48; 22.25;
26.42, 46; 28.1, 44;
30.28; 32.60; 33.7, 14;
34.18, 40: 3.1.17; 2.20;
3.12 (his temple on the
Capitoline); 4.6; 9.15,
47; 11.28, 41, 66; 15.19,
22, 36, 39; 24.20: 4.1.54,
82, 103 (Ammon); 4.2,
10, 30, 85; 6.14, 23; 9.8;
10.1, 15, 16, 48
  (*b*) planet: 4.1.83.
See also Sator divûm,
Tarpeius, vigil

Ixion, king of the Lapiths,
who for attempting to
seduce Juno was bound
to a perpetually
revolving wheel in the
underworld: 4.11.23.
See also 3.5.42 *rota*

Ixionides, Pirithous (*q.v.*),
son of Ixion: 2.1.38

KALENDAE, the first day of
the month: 4.3.53. *See
also* Aprilis

LABYRINTH, the maze
which was the

Minotaur's lair;
Theseus was enabled to
escape from it by a
magic ball of thread
given him by Ariadne:
see 2.14.7: 4.4.42

Lacaena, she of Sparta,
Helen: 2.15.13. *See also*
Helena, Tyndaris

Lacon, an inhabitant of
Laconia, hence a
Spartan: 3.14.33

Lais, a courtesan of
Corinth, the most
beautiful woman of her
age: 2.6.1

Lalage, a slave of Cynthia:
4.7.45

Lampetie, daughter of the
Sun and guardian of his
cattle: 3.12.29f

Lanuvium, a small town 20
miles southeast of Rome
on the Appian Way,
famed for its shrine of
Juno Sospita: 2.32.6:
4.8.3, 48

Laodamia, wife of
Protesilaus
(Phylacides): 1.19.7
iucundae conjugis

Laomedon, father of Priam:
2.14.2

Lapitha, one of a mythical
people inhabiting the

483

mountains of Thessaly;
the father of
Ischomache (*q.v.*): 2.2.9

Lar

(*a*) usually plural
Lares, the spirits of
dead ancestors who
watched over a
household: 2.30.22:
3.3.11: 4.3.54; 8.50
(*b*) simply as a
synonym for house,
home: 4.1.128; 10.18

Latinus, subst., a Latin,
Roman: Cynthia
2.32.61: Romans 4.6.45

Latius, adj., poetical for the
above: of Capitoline
Jupiter 3.4.6: of Cossus
4.10.37

Latris, a favourite slave of
Cynthia: 4.7.75 (*see note*)

Lavinus, (hypocoristic) adj.,
of Lavinium, a city of
Latium founded by
Aeneas: litora (cf. Virgil,
Aen. 1.2f) 2.34.64

Lechaeum, the western
port of Corinth: 3.21.19

Leda, mother of Castor,
Pollux, and Helen by
Jupiter: 1.13.29f

Leo, the Lion, 5th sign of
the zodiac: 4.1.85

Lepida, daughter of
Cornelia: *filia* 4.11.67

Lepidus: *see* Aemilius
Lepidus

Lerna, the name of the fen
where dwelt the hydra,
the slaying of which
formed the 2nd labour
of Hercules: 2.26.48

Lernaeus, adj. from above:
2.24.25

Lesbia, the mistress of
Catullus (the notorious
Clodia): 2.32.45; 34.88

Lesbius, adj., of Lesbos,
famed for its wines:
1.14.2

Lethaeus, adj., of Lethe
('forgetfulness'), river of
the underworld: 4.7.10,
91

Leucadia, the mistress of
Varro of Atax (*q.v.*):
2.34.86

Leucadius, adj. from
Leucas, a promontory
overlooking the Bay of
Actium, on which was
built a temple of Apollo:
3.11.69

Leucippis, daughter of
Leucippus: 1.2.15. *See*
Hilaïra

Leucothoë, a sea-goddess
(more usually

INDEX

INDEX

Mausolus (d.353), king of Caria, whose wife Artemisia erected a splendid tomb to his memory, which became numbered among the seven wonders of the world: 3.2.21

Mavors, Mars (*a: q.v.*): 2.27.8

Maxima: *see* Ara Maxima

Medea, wife of Jason: 2.24.45; 3.19.17; 4.5.41. *See also* Colchis, Cytaeis

Medus, Median, but used synonymously as Parthian: 3.9.25; 12.11

Melampus, son of Amythaon, undertook to rustle the herd of Iphiclus for Neleus, that Bias, his brother, might marry Neleus' daughter Pero; he was captured and imprisoned, but escaped and eventually succeeded in his task (Propertius makes Melampus himself the suitor of Pero): 2.3.51

Meleager: see note on 3.22.32

Memnon, son of Aurora and Tithonus, king of Ethiopia, killed by Achilles at Troy: 2.18.16

Memnonius, adj., of Memnon, hence Ethiopian: 1.6.4

Memphis, a town of Egypt: 3.11.34

Menandreus, adj. from the following: 2.6.3. *See* Thais

Menandrus, Menander (c. 344–292), the greatest poet of New Comedy: 3.21.28; 4.5.43. *See also* Thais

Menelaëus, adj. from the following: 2.15.14

Menelaus, king of Sparta, husband of Helen: 2.3.37; 34.7

Menoetiades, Patroclus (*q.v.*), son of Menoetius: 2.1.38

Mens Bona, the goddess of Good Sense, to whom a temple was dedicated on the Capitol in 217: 3.24.19

Mentor, a famous Greek silversmith of about 350: 3.9.13

Mentoreus, adj. from the above: 1.14.2

Mercurius, the god Mercury (Greek

INDEX

of Telephus, king of
Mysia, who was
wounded by by the
spear of Achilles and
later healed by its rust:
2.1.63

NAIS, Naiad, a water-
nymph: as a collective:
2.32.40

Nauplius, king of Euboea,
father of Palamedes:
4.1.115. *See* Caphereus

Navalis, adj., Actian: of
Apollo, referring to his
temple on the Palatine:
4.1.3

Naxius, adj., of Naxos (also
Dia, *q.v.*), a large island
in the Cyclades and
sacred to Bacchus,
where was said to flow a
spring of wine: 3.17.28

Nemean Games: see
Archemorus

Nemorensis, adj., of Nemi,
a lake in the Alban hills:
3.22.25. *See also on*
2.32.10

Neptunius, adj., of
Neptune: 3.9.41

Neptunus, Neptune, the
god of the sea: 2.16.4;
26.9, 45, 46: 3.7.15. *See
also* 3.7.62 and

Taenarius

Nereides, daughters of
Nereus (*q.v.*), the sea-
nymphs: 2.26.15 (cf.
4.6.61f)

Nereus, a god of the sea,
father of of the sea-
nymphs: 3.7.67: 4.6.25

Nesaee, a sea-nymph:
2.26.16

Nestor, king of Pylos who
lived through three
generations of men (cf.
Homer, *Il.* 1.250ff):
2.13.46; 25.10

Nilus, the river Nile:
2.1.31; 28.18; 33.3, 20:
3.11.42, 51: 4.6.63; 8.39

Niobe, daughter of
Tantalus, boasted that
her children were fairer
than Apollo and
Artemis; the latter slew
them, and she was
turned to stone: 2.20.7:
3.10.8. *See also*
Tantalis

Nireus, the handsomest
man (after Achilles) in
the Greek army at Troy
(Homer, *Il.* 2.673f):
3.18.27

Nisus, king of Megara,
whose life depended on
his purple lock of hair;

491

INDEX

INDEX

Phorcis, the Gorgon
  Medusa, daughter of
  Phorcys: 3.22.8
Phrygia, a country south of
  Bithynia in Asia Minor
  often, like its
  inhabitants, equated
  with Troy, Trojans:
  3.13.63
Phrygius, adj., of Phrygia:
  Pelops 1.2.19: Trojan
  2.1.42; waves =
  Hellespont 30.19; plain
  (watered by Meander)
  34.35
Phryne, a famous
  courtesan of Thespiae
  (4th cent.): 2.6.6
Phryx, a Phrygian: piper of
  Cybele 2.22.16, Trojans
  30: Aeneas 4.1.2
Phylacides, Protesilaus,
  son of Phylacus,
  husband of Laodamia;
  went to Troy
  immediately on his
  marriage and was the
  first to be slain;
  permitted to leave
  Hades to visit his wife:
  1.19.7
Phyllis
  (a) daughter of
  Sithon, king of Thrace,
  beloved by Demophoon

(q.v.): 2.24.44
  (b) a courtesan:
  4.8.29, 57
Pierides, Muses, so called
  from Pierus, a mountain
  in Thessaly sacred to
  them: 2.10.12
Pierius, adj., of the Muses
  (cf. Pierides): 2.13.5
Pindaricus, adj., of Pindar
  (518–438), the greatest
  lyric poet of Greece:
  3.17.40
Pindus, a mountain range
  separating Epirus from
  Thessaly: 3.5.33
Piraeus, the port of Athens:
  3.21.23
Pirithous, king of the
  Lapiths; at his wedding
  Ischomache was carried
  off by centaurs: 2.6.18
  See also Ixionides
Pisces, the Fishes, 12th
  sign of the zodiac: 4.1.85
Plato, of Athens, the great
  philosopher
  (c. 429–347): 3.21.25
Pleiades, daughters of
  Atlas, metamorphosed
  into a compact group of
  stars whose setting in
  October marked a
  stormy season: 2.16.51:
  3.5.36. See also

INDEX

a boy, cf. Cicero, *De Div.*
2.86): 2.32.3

Praxiteles, famous
Athenian sculptor (fl.
mid-4th cent.), creator
of the Venus of Cnidos,
which is here alluded to:
3.9.16

priamel (*<praeambulum>*
preamble), rhetorical
figure listing
illustrations of the main
theme, which comes at
the end: 1.3.1ff; 4.5–7;
14.1–6: 2.1.17ff, 43ff;
27.1ff; 34.33–8: 3.11.5ff.
See also: catalogues

Priamus, Priam, king of
Troy: 2.3.40; 28.54:
4.1.52

Prometheus
  (*a*) son of Iapetus, a
  Titan: 2.1.69: 3.5.7
  (*b*) adj., of
  Prometheus: (hills =
  Caucasus) 1.12.10

propempticon: 1.6 (*see
note*), 8A: 2.19: 3.22

Propertius: 2.18.17; 14.27;
24.35; 34.93: 3.3.17;
10.15: 4.1.71; 7.49

Propontiacus, adj. from
Propontis, the sea
which serves as an
entrance to the Black

Sea: 3.22.2

Protesilaus: see Phylacides

Pthius, adj., of Pthia (*Eng.*
Phthia), a town in
Thessaly, home of
Achilles, hence Achilles:
2.13.38

Ptolemaeus, adj. from
Ptolemaeus (Soter
367–283), the general of
Alexander who obtained
the kingship of Egypt
after A's death, hence
Egyptian: 2.1.30

Pudicitia, goddess of
chastity: 1.16.2: temple
of 2.6.25

Puellae novem, Muses:
3.3.33. *See also* Musa(e)

Pulydamas, son of
Panthous, friend of
Hector: 3.1.29

Pyrrhus (319–272), king of
Epirus, invaded Italy
and defeated by Rome
only with the greatest
difficulty 3.11.60

Pythius, adj. from Pytho,
the ancient name for
Delphi, hence of Delphi:
Apollo 2.31.16: 3.13.52.
See also Apollo

Python, a gigantic snake
slain by Apollo at
Delphi: 4.6.35

INDEX

INDEX

4.2.52; 4.32: herba (*Juniperus Sabina* = savin) 4.3.58: pila 4.4.12

Sacra Via, the Sacred Way, by which the triumphal procession passed to the Capitol: 2.1.34; 23.15 (the haunt of courtesans); 24.14 (where lovers buy trinkets for their mistresses): 3.4.22

Salmonis, = Tyro (*q.v.*), daughter of Salmoneus, raped by Neptune disguised as the river-god Enipeus: 1.13.21: 3.19.13

Sancus, a Sabine god, Semo Sancus Dius Fidius, identified with Hercules: 4.9.71, 72, 74 (*see note*)

Sator divûm, Father of the gods, = Jupiter, form of address used by the god Vertumnus: 4.2.55

Saturnus
    (*a*) god, king of the Golden Age: 2.32.52
    (*b*) planet: 4.1.84

Scaeae, adj., sc. portae, the western gate of Homer's Troy: 3.9.39

Scamander (or Xanthus),

said by Homer (*Il.* 21.1) to be the son of Jupiter, a river in the Trojan plain which, with the Simois (*q.v.*), battled with Achilles: 3.1.27

Scipiades (a Grecism to avoid the unmetrical Scīpīō), P. Cornelius S. Africanus, who in his consulship (205) built a fleet to invade Africa and so transfer the war to enemy soil: 3.11.67

Sciron, a robber who infested the cliff-road from Corinth to Megara and Athens, casting his victims into the sea until finally destroyed by Theseus: 3.16.12

Scribonia, mother of Cornelia (by P. Cornelius Scipio) and Julia (by Augustus): 4.11.55

Scylla
    (*a*) daughter of Nisus, king of Megara, whom she betrayed to Minos by cutting off the purple lock of hair on which his life depended: 3.19.21: 4.4.39 (here also identified with [*b*]

503

INDEX

INDEX

INDEX

INDEX